DOCTORED TRUFFLES

A MYSTERY NOVEL

SUZANNE GRANT

Published in the United States

Author: Suzanne Grant

ISBN-13: 978-0-984015467

suzannegrant.com

For my seaside-loving sisters and brothers-in-law—Sandy, Anne, Rick, and Steve—who have embraced life on the Oregon coast and shared it with me. Thank you.

When I first heard of Nancy Boggs' floating brothel, I was intrigued by the resourceful madam who managed to evade paying taxes for more than a decade by conducting her business on a floating vessel in the middle of the Willamette River. Yes, she had her challenges, but she used the river and the fact that, at that time, Portland was actually three separate cities, with different police forces and different governments, to solve them. I hope you enjoy learning about Portland's seedy early days and Nancy's floating brothel as much as I did.

Cover photo of the beach at Lincoln City, Oregon courtesy of Ian and Mackenzie Lewallen

CHAPTER 1

Stan looked dead, mouth hanging open like a dying fish, hand dangling lifelessly. My insides leaped, then wilted. Birthday wishes didn't come true.

Besides, I really hadn't meant it, had I? It was only a vengeful blip, a gut reaction to his unceasing thoughtlessness. Only lately those wicked flickers were more a raging blaze.

"Well, you deserve it, you jerk," I muttered, eyeing the sheen reflecting from the empty beer bottles dumped beside his cedar recliner. No doubt, come morning they'd still be there for me to haul to the recycling tub.

"*Grrr,*" I snarled as my eyes searched the shadowed deck. Something had jerked me from my late night napping. Certainly not Stan.

Pools of hazy light floated around the solar lights nestled in clay pots overflowing with summer foliage—petunias and geraniums, sweet alyssum and daisies. Beyond the deck, the golf course, a rippling sea of dark hues, reached out to the sprinkling of lights beyond.

Not enough lights; it was later than I'd thought. Evidently, my few minutes of rest had turned into several hours of sleep. And Stan had taken advantage of it. I pictured him tip-toeing to his sanctuary, six-pack in hand, careful not to awaken me and have to face his latest transgression. Jerk! Well, he could just snooze there until morning.

A shadow shifted on the darkened course not far from the deck. I squinted hard, a sharp prickle running up my spine, and watched an ashen blob flit toward me, then dart to the right and disappear from view.

I sighed. Probably some *über* fitness fanatic running the golf course trails while the pro shop patrol wasn't around to nail him.

Maybe he'd twisted his ankle or tripped over a raccoon or something equally as painful. All else was deep-into-the-night still.

But who knew what lowlifes and pesky animals lurked in the shadows? Plus, if Stan ended up sick from lying in the cool night air in his shorts and precious Guns N Roses tee-shirt, I'd have to nurse him back to health. My stomach tightened at the thought.

"You don't have to, Polly," I protested. But I knew I would. I'd chosen this path and now I was stuck, like one of those old paint-chipped windup toys, plodding the same worn, rutty surface over and over until there were times I had to clamp my hand over my mouth to keep from shrieking.

This was one of those times. With my free hand, I rubbed at a gritty eye, a futile attempt to wipe the fog from my brain, then grasped the doorknob and pushed the French door open. Heavy dampness saturated my face and hair. I breathed deeply of the salt-tinged air, and the cloying fragrance of ripe blossoms tickled my nostrils. Steeling myself, I stepped toward my sleeping husband.

Tinglings of unrest crept across my shoulders. Actually, he did look dead, splayed on the cushioned lounge as if a giant seagull had dropped him there, legs spread-eagle, both arms hanging awkwardly, a thin strip of pudgy belly exposed. A pillow from our bed lay on the deck—glaringly out of place—not far from him, as if it had been thrown there.

I rubbed my fluttering stomach. Except for the faint whisper of ocean waves, all was quiet. Too quiet. Stan snored like a struggling chainsaw, especially when he was drunk. Where were those snores now?

I stood rooted, unable to move. A sick, panicky feeling throttled me and tingled in my limbs. There had to be an explanation—Stan was sleeping so soundly that he didn't require much air. Or his body temperature had dipped so low that he was barely breathing. Or his body had finally acclimated to an inebriated snooze.

Or he was dead.

Get a grip, Polly. You're overreacting again—please, God, I prayed as I inched forward to stare down at the man whom I had to have once loved.

Soft rays from the solar lights created dark crevices and contours across his slackened features. His dark hair was tousled, his eyes closed. I stood as still as the iron cranes guarding the deck from errant golfers, fearing, yet willing, those eyes to pop open. In the dim light, I noticed that his chest didn't rise and fall. Leaning down, I placed a trembling hand on it. No movement. No heartbeat. Nothing.

A strangled whimper seeped through my lips, and I sank to my knees and leaned forward to place an ear next to his open mouth. Nothing.

"No. No. No," I pleaded as I grabbed his wrist to feel for a pulse, his hand like lead in mine. When I thought about death, which wasn't often, I'd imagined that it would feel like this—cold and clammy and firm, like beeswax. Stan wasn't just dead; he was *really* dead.

But why? He didn't have any fatal health issues, none that I was aware of anyway. He was relatively young, still a couple of months from his forties.

My eyes flitted over his body, searching. No bullet holes. No knife wounds. No face frozen in terror. No blood. Nothing.

Then they landed on the rumpled pillow. When had Stan ever brought a pillow on the deck? Never, that's when. So how had it gotten here?

Ever so slowly, my gaze traveled to the open door and beyond to the puddle of amber light enfolding the bed we still shared in sleep, if nothing else. When he'd come home, I'd been asleep on that bed, still wearing the pricey dress I'd purchased for our evening of celebration, the one he'd blown off. With that memory, anger jabbed aside some of the fear that had my insides tangled into tight knots.

Yes, I'd been furious . . . and hurt. Surely not furious enough to wish him dead though?

But I had, hadn't I?

I pictured myself staring at that truffle with the one lonely candle—it should've been a luscious, three-layer cake covered with forty blazing candles—and replayed the fleeting death wish in my mind. Then I'd blown out that candle and eaten every bite of sinfully rich, liqueur-laced chocolate. But something, maybe the alcohol or maybe the burning ache inside me, hadn't sat well in my empty stomach. I'd dragged myself to my bed, where I'd curled into a ball, tears tickling my cheeks.

And that's all I remembered until something awakened me hours later, and I'd spied Stan sleeping on the deck.

"Only he isn't sleeping, is he?" I murmured, an effort to affirm the reality of this nightmare. "He's dead. And you need to call for help." But whom? Phil and Javier from next door or Laura from across the street? An ambulance? The police?

Dragging my neighbors into this mess in the middle of the night seemed selfish. And since Stan was already dead, he certainly didn't need an ambulance. Which left the cops.

But what if he was murdered, and they think I did it? my mind screamed.

My eyes flicked to the pillow. Had I done it, some out-of-mind experience of which I now had no knowledge? It happened. I'd seen it on television and in movies, read about it in books. Had hurt and anger consumed me to the point that some vengeful inner demon took control over my body to seek retribution?

I stared at Stan's dead hand, panic churning inside me, then placed it across his exposed midriff. Had I seen him sleeping off his six-pack and snuck out here, his pillow clutched in my hands, my intention to press it over his lying mouth until it could lie no more?

It didn't feel right. If I were to kill someone—a huge "if"—it wouldn't be like that. Too personal. Too up close. No. I'd need to be far away from my victim when it happened. The idea of murdering someone with my own two hands, of witnessing a death, was downright terrifying. Deep down, I knew I hadn't murdered Stan. Didn't I?

But the police didn't know me, didn't know what I was incapable of doing. I covered my eyes with my hands and rubbed hard, searching my muddled brain for a way out of this mess, then studied the darkened golf course. In a few short hours, it would be daylight, and someone golfing past the house would surely notice Stan sprawled on his recliner. Then they'd yell at him and figure out something was amiss.

It was hopeless. Unless I dragged his cold body across the darkened golf course and buried him in the sand trap or pushed him into the irrigation pond, I had to deal with Stan's death now. There was no way out of it. I needed to get my butt into that house and call for help.

I closed my eyes and breathed evenly, then pushed myself up onto my trembling feet and plodded to the door. "Just tell the truth, and everything will be fine," I assured myself. More than likely, Stan's caustic lifestyle choices had simply taken their toll.

Still, before I entered the house, I turned back and grabbed Stan's pillow off the deck. Inside, I tucked it neatly into place on the bed, stacking throw pillows haphazardly around it. The comforter was disheveled where I'd slept on it; I didn't touch that.

My cell phone lay on the kitchen counter next to a gold-foil-lined box that held the five remaining truffles—someone had remembered my birthday. My empty stomach churned. Chocolate might settle it until I ate some decent food. Grabbing my phone with one shaky hand, I selected a glossy mound with the other and bit into it. Rich, sweet decadence enhanced with a kick of alcohol melted across my tongue, but I barely tasted it, my mind futilely scrambling for words that made sense.

Stan was really dead. How could that be? Some deep down part of me wanted to curl up and cry over my loss, mostly over the loss of hope that things would again be as they once were. Or maybe it was only as I thought they once were. Whatever the case, an aching emptiness wallowed inside me. Now there was no hope.

My body felt too heavy; my limbs too weak. I swiped at the prickle of a tear on my cheek and bit a chunk from the lump of chocolate, then shuffled into the living area to settle into an overstuffed chair. My thumb flicked the phone. Lights flashed, but they were blurred, other worldly. Squinting at the shifting colors, I stuffed the rest of the chocolate into my mouth and touched the screen.

But my eyelids closed and refused to open. Giving in to the overpowering urge, I swallowed the lump of sweetness in my mouth and relaxed into the chair's comfort.

〜 ✧ 〜

Stan's incessant snoring was so irritating. Every time I drifted off, the gravely drone of his breathing or a loud snort disturbed me. I reached out a hand to shake him—anything to get the raucous racket to stop.

But Stan wasn't there. And I wasn't in my bed. Tugging my mind from the drowsy shadows, I lifted my eyelids. Stan wasn't there, but the annoying noise was. And I lolled in a chair in my living room, not in my bed.

Murky light sifted in through the wall of windows that faced the golf course. It was early, very early, and a hazy layer of beach fog hovered beyond the glass, obscuring my view. Some poor soul was preparing the course for today's herds of tourists, the sonorous buzz of his lawnmower a crime at this early hour. So if Stan wasn't here beside me sawing logs, where was he?

Like a havoc-wreaking sneaker wave, it hit me: Stan was on the deck—dead.

A bomb landed in my stomach and burst, burning in my throat until I thought I'd choke on it. I grabbed my gut and touched soft fluff.

"What the heck," I breathed as my eyes dropped to the furry mound stirring in my lap. Bright eyes stared up at me.

The kitten—the scruffy, shrieking stray I'd found on the deck several days ago. The one that was supposed to be hidden away behind closed doors in my office. It stretched its mini legs and rose onto its tiny white paws, arching its back.

My heart hammered in my chest. Kitty claws stung my thighs. If Stan saw the kitten, its life would be a short one. Stan hated cats.

"Stan's dead," I reminded myself.

Air seeped from my lungs. I tugged the claws from my legs, then rose unsteadily to my feet. Something hit the floor, and my eyes dropped—my cell phone. That's right; I'd planned to call 9-1-1. Only I hadn't, had I? The shock must've been too much for me to handle because, instead, I'd drifted into a deep sleep.

What was happening to me? Was I going crazy? It could happen. I'd read about it happening to others. When stress in your life becomes more than you can handle, your mind does all kinds of bizarre things. But surely it wouldn't make you murder your husband, even if he is lazy and self-centered, and he lies to you, and he forgets your fortieth birthday and. . . .

I shook my head to rid myself of useless thoughts. After all, I could reminisce forever about Stan's shortcomings. It wouldn't help me now. Or him.

But maybe my mind *had* played a trick on me. Maybe it had all been a bad dream. Maybe Stan wasn't even out on that deck, his body now bloated and frigid, legs and arms rigid.

I stiffened my spine and set my back teeth. Then I tucked the kitten close to my chest, stroking its softness, and stepped resolutely to the windows to gaze into the misty morning. Fog muted everything—the gray decking, the lime green umbrella, the vibrant blossoms, and the body sprawled in the cedar recliner.

Tears stung my eyes. I closed them to swallow at the fire in my throat. I wouldn't cry for him, not now. He'd made my life intolerable at times. And I'd stuck with him, determined that things would improve, that if I worked at it hard enough, everything would get better. Well, it hadn't gotten better. And now it was even worse; he'd left me with this mess.

The sight of his body stretched out in the cold mist made me feel like ocean waves were churning and swelling inside me. I turned from it and retrieved my phone from the oak floor, then set the kitten down and sank into the overstuffed chair. Punching numbers, I said a silent prayer that there was a rational explanation for Stan's abrupt demise, one that had nothing to do with me.

༄ ✿ ༄

Twenty minutes later I was again cocooned in the comforting folds of that overstuffed chair, numb and shaky, my insides roiling, clutching the poor kitty like it was my only link to sanity. Brewing coffee fumes pestered my queasy stomach.

The county sheriff had arrived. I'd gathered what remained of my fortitude to trek to the door and face the man who might soon incarcerate me.

After minimal introductions, I'd pointed toward the deck, then plopped back into the chair. No way was I going back out there until Stan's body was gone. An image of him lying there, mouth gaping, was imbedded in my mind. Every time I closed my eyes it tormented me.

Three chimed notes chased the vision away. I glanced down. Another message from my best friend Laura who lived across the street. Clearly, Laura had noticed the official-looking vehicle outside my house, and her rabid nosiness had her speed texting. I'd thumbed a brief note to assure her I was okay, but I couldn't reply to her other messages yet. Not until I knew what was going on.

It was odd that I hadn't received a barrage of texts from Phil and Javier next door, too. I pictured them sitting at the wrought iron table Phil had artfully welded, sipping on their flavored lattes and perusing the newspaper while they tried to inconspicuously peer through the fog, as if they lounged on their deck in the mist every morning. If they figured out it was Stan's body that sheriff was examining, they'd be cheering and dancing a saucy salsa. They'd probably even throw a party to celebrate the neighborhood's loss. Phil and Javier detested Stan.

But not George and Denise, my next-door neighbors to the left. No, George would be in his garage buffing his boat. And Denise, she'd plaster her surgery-enhanced nose against the kitchen window and secretly watch the goings-on on my deck, hoping to catch a glimpse of Stan—a living, breathing Stan. I was pretty sure Denise had a thing going on for Stan. I was even more certain that Stan wouldn't jeopardize a lifetime of free fishing trips with George to fulfill Denise's latest fantasy.

The melodic chime of the doorbell jolted me. I clutched the kitten to my heart to still it and pushed myself out of the chair, then paused. Was it Laura, her curiosity running amuck? Give her two minutes on my deck, and she'd be joining the latte celebration next door. Laura would claim that Stan had given me the perfect birthday gift.

I sighed in resignation, then stepped to the door and opened it.

Two men in dark blue uniforms greeted me. My eyes dropped to the gurney they carried, and my stomach heaved. Reality washed through me, zapping my remaining strength. They would take Stan away. Forever. I couldn't talk through the painful lump in my throat, so I just pointed.

After they disappeared through the French doors, I eyed the chair's comforting arms. "No," I whispered. The sheriff would want to talk with me. I had to pull myself together, to think clearly.

My eyes dropped to the red dress I'd been so proud of, now wrinkled and, under the circumstances, garish. I was a denim and cotton woman, but I'd wanted to surprise Stan, to show him that I was still attractive, so I'd paid way too much for a dress I'd never wear again.

How many times in the past few months had I mentioned that all I wanted for my fortieth birthday was a romantic evening on the town with him there to help me get over that steep peak? Too many to count, that's how many. As so many times in the past, I'd convinced myself that this time he would come through. That our forties would be the start of our new life together.

Laura had even seemed convinced, enough to help me prepare for my special night out. She'd treated me to a day at Saunia's Spassage—massages, facials, manis and pedis, makeup and hair. I'd felt like a princess sipping champagne and nibbling on chocolate-coated strawberries while being oiled and rubbed, buffed and polished. And for what? So I could sit at home all evening by myself, hope gradually turning to a deep, aching throb in my gut that had become way too familiar.

The click of a doorknob drew my eyes toward the deck. My breath hitched. My pulse skyrocketed. I fought to blink back tears while I searched my memory for the sheriff's name. Dickson or

Johnson or Bronson—that was it—Sheriff Bronson, like Charles Bronson. Only he was as far from Charles Bronson as a man could get with his roly-poly body and short, toothpick legs that were now marching toward me. Large horn-rimmed glasses perched on his pudgy cheeks, their lenses so thick that his eyes appeared miniscule as he studied me.

He sniffed the air, his nostrils flaring. "Coffee?" he asked.

I nodded. "Help yourself. The mugs are in the cabinet above the pot." If he doctored it with cream or sugar, let him search for it. I needed to get off my trembling legs before I fell off of them.

Plopping down into my cushy haven, I set the squirming kitten on the floor and forced myself to breathe slowly and evenly. *Just tell the truth . . . well, except about the pillow,* I told myself. Maybe Stan had died from a stroke or a heart attack or some weird disease he'd picked up from wild game. It happened all of the time; I'd seen it on TV reality shows and read about it on *facebook*.

After all, Stan's main nutrient sources were Doritos and queso dip, Twinkies, chili dogs, and Tillamook's latest ice cream flavor. If Sheriff Bronson "pooh-poohed" that, I'd walk him out to the garage and show him Stan's stockpile of Twinkies. Now that they were being produced again, they'd probably end up in a landfill. Or maybe I could butter up Sheriff Bronson with a crate or two. He was still in the kitchen rooting for something—coffee additives or maybe breakfast.

"You got any sugar?" he demanded.

I struggled out of the chair and trudged to the kitchen, then pulled a plastic container from a cabinet and set it on the granite countertop next to a mug filled with what looked to be more cream than coffee. When I opened a drawer to get a teaspoon, my eyes landed on the box of truffles. One chocolaty mound nestled in the beautiful box. I'd only eaten two, which meant that someone else had eaten three. Surely, not the sheriff? As I handed him the spoon, I searched his mouth for telltale brown smudges, then sniffed for chocolate whiffs in the air. There were none.

So who had indulged in my birthday truffles? For sure, it wasn't Stan. He detested everything about chocolate—the look, the taste, the smell. Once a chocolate chip had accidently strayed into Stan's pancake, and he'd ranted and raved for days about it, as if I'd tried to poison him, which is something I was quite truthfully contemplating by the time he finally let it go.

"Thanks," Sheriff Bronson muttered as he stirred his coffee, his bespectacled eyes drifting toward the deck, then back to me. He dropped the spoon on the counter. "We need to talk."

My insides clenched. Would I soon be flaunting my new dress and hairdo in my mug shot?

I considered a cup of black coffee for myself—maybe my last taste of gourmet roast—to help me think more clearly, but my gurgling stomach shrieked *no*.

"Let's sit in the living room," I mumbled.

There was something reassuring about my safe chair, its comforting arms enfolding me. Sheriff Bronson sat facing me in Stan's leather Barcalounger. He took a healthy swig of coffee, then shuffled a bit, struggling to perch his ample midsection with it's arsenal of gadgets onto the edge of the mammoth chair. His boot-clad toes barely touched the floor. With his free hand, he pushed aside a couple of Stan's remotes on the side table and set his mug in the bared spot.

After a few final squirms, he removed his cap and set it on top of Stan's stash of outdoor magazines, revealing an unruly mop of grayish hair. Finally, he pulled a small notebook and pen from his jacket pocket. Then his chunky lenses landed on me. "So what happened here?" he asked.

Where to start—three years back when I'd ignored the barrage of glaring warnings and, instead, had ridden a white-knuckled shotgun in Stan's dent-riddled red Firebird to my seedy wedding in Reno? Would he understand that I was going through a rough spell, that after watching my father pass on and my daughter head off to Oregon State, I'd panicked at the thought of being alone?

Would he believe me when I assured him that, though Stan had a few faults—well, actually, more than a few—I really did love him? Or maybe it was more that I'd loved him at one time. Or had I only convinced myself that I loved him? I honestly didn't know. Whatever the case, I'd willingly become Mrs. Stan Morton, and I was determined to make my marriage work.

Probably, it would be best not to burden Sheriff Bronson with the minutiae of my less than perfect marriage. The many sordid details would be unveiled later, during my trial.

I fought to distance myself, then shoved my protesting memory back to the previous night. My insides clenched. My pulse pounded. "Well, I saw Stan sleeping out there on the deck. When I went outside to wake him up, I noticed he was dead. So I called the police."

"That was this morning?"

Why not? my mind screamed. But what if someone had seen me holding Stan's lifeless hand—someone like nosy Denise from next door? "Well, actually it was more in the middle of the night," I admitted.

Like two furry creatures, his bushy eyebrows crawled up from behind the thick black rims on his glasses. "I thought you made the 9-1-1 call this morning?"

"I did. Only, I really meant to make the call earlier. I was trying to punch in the numbers, but I . . . fell asleep." Even to my ears it sounded lame.

He nodded. "You'd been drinking."

Why not? I swallowed the urge. "No, not at all. The only thing I had last night were a couple of chocolate truffles."

"The ones on the kitchen counter?"

"Yes. Someone left them at my front door yesterday. It was my birthday."

"And your husband ate the other three?"

"Oh, no. Stan doesn't eat chocolate." Evidently, Sheriff Bronson didn't snack on those truffles either. So who did?

"Someone else was here then?" He dropped his notepad and grabbed his coffee to take a healthy swig.

"No, I was home alone, well, except for Stan. He must've come home after I fell asleep."

I paused, my mind swirling. Was I a sleepwalker, eating and murdering during the nighttime hours? Was that why I could no longer squeeze into my skinny jeans? "I don't know what happened to those truffles," I quickly added.

He gulped coffee, studying me with his tiny eyes. "You have somewhere special to be today?" he finally probed.

"Somewhere special?" What was he getting at? The funeral arrangements? Jail? I shook my head. "No."

His brows levitated again, and his gaze slid from my gel-set auburn bed hair down to my flashy red toenails.

Mine did the same. "Oh, you mean my dress. I . . . we'd planned to go out for dinner, to celebrate my birthday. But Stan must've been held up. Finally, I went to bed."

"In your dress?"

"I lay down on my bed for a few minutes, and I fell asleep." It happened—all of the time, actually.

"Last night?"

"Yes. Then I woke up several hours later." Like a speeding slideshow, disturbing images flashed in my mind. "Like I said, I glanced out on the deck, and there was Stan . . . dead."

"What made you think he was dead?"

I didn't want to think about it, let alone talk about it. When I did, my voice was shaky. "He wasn't breathing. His chest didn't move at all. No heartbeat. And he felt like he'd been that way a while, cold and kind of . . . rubbery. Dead." The moment felt right to sneak in a little inside information. "I thought he'd had a heart attack or something—he had a thing for junk food, and he spent a lot of time in that chair watching TV.

"Anyway, I rushed inside to get my cell phone, but I fell asleep as soon as I sat down. I made the call when I woke up this morning."

He rubbed the rim of the mug against his lips, then sipped. "And no alcohol? Maybe a glass of wine . . . or two? Medication?" His voice dripped skepticism. And why wasn't he writing any of this down?

"No. None," I affirmed. "The only thing I can think of is maybe my brain couldn't handle the shock, so it shut down."

Yeah, right, his look said. "Did you go out and check on him this morning?"

"No." Another mark against me. "I looked out there. He was still there, and he was still dead."

He huffed, then eyeballed his mug and set it on the table. "So you're all gussied up, ready to celebrate your birthday, and he doesn't come home. That make you angry?"

It'd make any woman furious, I silently avowed. "I was a little upset," I admitted.

"Did he call?"

I shook my head. Did he ever?

"He do that very often?"

My insides clenched, the hurt too raw. "You know men . . . sometimes," I murmured.

"Did it make you mad enough to wish he was dead? Mad enough to do something about it?"

"No! I was angry and hurt, but I would *never* do something like that." But I *had* wished he were dead, right before I'd blown out that candle. "It's like I said: I finally got tired of waiting and fell asleep, maybe around ten o'clock. Stan must've come home after that. The security alarm wasn't set, so it didn't beep. I didn't hear him come into the house."

I eyed the streak of black clawing its way up my drapes. "But I know he did, because my kitten was behind closed doors in my office. When I woke up this morning, it was in my lap."

Of course, that didn't make sense either. If Stan had seen that kitten, it wouldn't be shredding my window décor now.

"He drink a lot?"

Blinking my focus back to the sheriff, I contemplated his question. "Sometimes." It was really more like *always*. "When it's warm enough, he sits on the deck before he comes to bed. It's not unusual that he was out there drinking beer late at night. The unusual part is that for no apparent reason, my husband is dead."

Sheriff Bronson worked his lips and shook his head. "No, the unusual part is you claiming he's dead."

I stared at him, trying to make sense of his words, then muttered, "Why's that unusual? If someone's dead, they're dead."

He leaned forward, hands on his thighs. "Mrs. Morton, your husband is *not* dead."

CHAPTER 2

I knew my mouth gaped. I couldn't help it. Sheriff Bronson had just tossed a grenade, one that left me shell-shocked.

Stan was alive—living and breathing and surely plotting payback for my rash decision to drag the county sheriff into this nightmare. Then he'd rant about how callous it was of me to leave him out on that cold, damp deck all night. Forget about my trashed birthday celebration and all of the other dreams I'd discarded due to Stan's callousness. No, I was going to hear about this for a *long* time.

Why can't you be dead? The words flitted through my mind. I eyed the sheriff, hoping he hadn't heard them or seen the guilt I felt over that one renegade thought.

After all, the possibility of growing old in prison no longer loomed before me, and I was being given a second chance to salvage my marriage. I'd work harder. I'd be more understanding, not so sensitive. Maybe I was too self-centered. I could work on that, too.

No! Stan was dead—or at least he was last night. No doubt about it, he'd been dead. Had he come back to life—some miracle? I'd heard people on television talk shows claim it had happened to them. But Stan? Would God think Stan deserved a second chance at life?

"Alive?" I wheezed. I hefted myself out of the chair and shuffled shakily to the French doors, my heart pounding so hard I pressed on my chest to contain it.

Angelic rays of sunlight pierced the filmy haze, revealing blue sky in splotchy patches. It promised to be a glorious July day on the Oregon coast for golfers and tourists and beach junkies. But not for me.

Stan's eyes settled on me, remote and listless. I braced for the venomous glare that didn't materialize. Something was off. Why didn't he leap off that gurney and storm across the deck to yell at me? And why was he lying on it, cocooned in layers of blankets?

Sensing Sheriff Bronson's approach, I murmured, "Is something wrong with him?"

"Not sure. Acts like he's on drugs. That a possibility?"

Drugs? Is that why he'd passed for dead? "I don't think so. I've never known Stan to mess with illegal drugs," I reasoned. But what if he had? On top of everything else, I'd have that to deal with, too.

The gurney moved toward us, the two uniformed men wheeling it along. I stepped back to open the door. Stan's eyes drifted shut.

I studied him as he passed by. He didn't look right—shorter hair, leaner features, faded tan, and no scruffy beard stubble.

Of course, it's Stan, I told myself. But was it? Had it been so long since I'd looked at Stan—*really* scrutinized him—that I didn't recognize my own husband?

Sheriff Bronson's prying gaze burned in my cheeks, but I refused to meet it. He was probably wondering why I didn't throw myself on Stan and weep with joy over his resurrection. Well, I couldn't. At the moment, my feelings were up in the air, but joy was one thing I was certain I didn't feel.

"We're taking him to the hospital in Lincoln City, just to check him out," the older of the two men told me.

"Okay. I'll be a few minutes behind you," I muttered.

Then Stan was gone, and the air felt lighter, the room less confining. I exhaled the pent-up air I'd been holding since I'd awakened that morning. Chimed notes screamed into the silence. I twitched, then eyed the kitchen counter where I'd dropped my cell phone.

"I need to change my clothes and get to the hospital," I told the sheriff.

He eyeballed me through those thick lenses, an odd look on his face. "They're gonna run some tests on your husband, see if they can figure out what's going on. You stay close. We might need to chat again."

What was he implying, that my botched murder attempt wouldn't get by him? I might as well have looked into the sheriff's eyes through several inches of filmy water; they were unreadable. So I just nodded and walked him and his bulging leather case to the door.

Sheriff Bronson could believe whatever he wanted. I knew I hadn't done anything to harm Stan. I hoped I was right.

≋ ☼ ≋

My eyes drifted around the waiting room, then paused on the TV, where images of uniformed men hacking at bushy plants flashed from the screen—another marijuana farm busted. According to recent media hype, the backwoods slopes of the Coast Range teemed with hemp growers. If Sheriff Bronson had any sense, he'd focus on illegal pot, not on me.

I sighed and returned my focus to Laura's shrill voice. "I'm fine," I assured my best friend. "I'll be home as soon as they discharge Stan. We can talk then, and I'll tell you all about it."

"I'd rather drive up there. You need someone with you when that asshole you call your husband is released. What if he *is* a druggie, and now he's in trouble with the law? You're gonna wish *you* were dead, Pol."

Laura's concern wasn't helping. Thoughts of being alone with Stan after this fiasco had my insides swirling. If my stomach had even a morsel of food in it, I'd be in the restroom hugging a germ-infested toilet instead of on the phone trying to convince Laura to stay put until I sorted out this mess.

"If he's anything like he was when they brought him here, he'll be lucky to crawl to my car," I argued. "I swear he didn't even know who I was—just gave me this vacant stare." I didn't add that I'd done a double take when I'd glanced in the restroom mirror with my ratty hair, runny makeup, and eyes that resembled a couple of sinkholes.

"Maybe he blew his brain on some bad acid or something. That might not be a bad thing you know, especially if it shuts him up."

I rubbed at the pain behind my frown. "As you pointed out, this is my husband you're trashing?" A husband who now shuffled a bit unsteadily toward me on feet encased in baby blue hospital booties.

"Gotta go. Stan's here," I blurted before I thumbed off the phone.

My innards turned somersaults as I took a deep breath and stepped toward Stan in his crab-emblazoned tee-shirt. One of his hands gripped the waistband of his sagging cargo shorts; the other clasped a handful of folded papers. A hefty older woman in a nurse ensemble and sensible shoes marched beside him. It was her alert eyes that locked on me.

"Mrs. Morton, your husband can go home now," she announced

to every ear within a hundred yards. "Why don't you bring your car to the emergency room door. He's still a bit shaky." She huffed and threw him an annoyed look. "He insisted on walking."

My eyes flicked to Stan. He looked gaunt and pasty, his eyes dull, as if something out on that deck really had sucked the life out of him. In truth, he still looked dead. Except he wasn't.

"What's wrong with him?" I asked.

"Triazolam. It's a sedative. Most of it's out of his system now, but he's still dealing with the aftereffects. He needs to take it easy for a day or so. Then he should be back to normal."

Sensing that all eyes in the waiting room had turned from the drug-harvesting cops to my drug-guzzling husband, I inched forward and lowered my voice. "So it's a drug. Is it legal?"

"Oh, yeah. It's prescribed for people who have difficulty sleeping at night, and for that, it works well. But you need to take the correct dosage. Your husband was way over that."

I eyed Stan. "You took too many pills . . . on purpose?" I murmured. *And you washed them down with a six pack of beer*, my mind screamed. And why in the world did Stan even have sleeping pills? I'd always been awed by his sleeping prowess. Once, he'd fallen asleep on the beach at the mouth of Siletz Bay in his canvas butterfly chair and nearly been washed out to sea. I'd found him, fishing pole tucked beneath his butt, waves licking his calves.

As I studied him now, something inside me wondered if he'd intentionally taken those pills, if we were both living our misery in silence. He looked lost—there was no other way to describe it—like he'd time-traveled to an unfamiliar time and place.

"I didn't take any pills," he finally muttered, his voice husky.

Nurse loud mouth shrugged noncommittally. "They're running tests. In the meantime, you might want to keep a close eye on the medicine cabinet."

Stan flashed her a nasty look, which actually calmed me down some. Evidently, old Stan was still in there somewhere.

"Where can I pick up his clothes?" I asked the nurse.

Her pencil-thin eyebrows shot up, and she eyeballed me as if it were what she'd expect from the loony man's wife. "He's wearing them," she informed me.

My gaze perused Stan. He still had a death grip on his waistband. If he let go, his shorts would pool around his booties. There was no way a miraculous weight loss like that had slipped by me, not with him consuming a couple of bags of chips a day. And I swore his Guns N Roses tee-shirt had swathed his ample midriff the night before. If I lost that tee-shirt, tracking down an exact match would be easier than confessing to it.

"These aren't the clothes he was wearing when he left home," I argued. But did I really know that for sure? I hadn't taken a close look at Stan that morning. Maybe he'd risen from his deathbed in the wee hours to change his shirt. The crabby tee looked vaguely familiar, but I couldn't be certain. Stan's dresser drawers were stuffed with motif-emblazoned tee-shirts.

Stan's eyes flicked mine, then settled behind me. "I'm wearing my clothes," he muttered. "Why don't you get the car, so we can get out of here?"

Was he, like me, wondering if this whole encounter would be soaring through YouTube by the end of the day, something titled *Druggie Couple Wacked Out in E.R.*? Well, it was his precious tee-shirt, not mine. "I'll meet you at the front door," I told him before I turned to slink past the eavesdroppers and hightail it to the parking lot.

By the time Stan had settled into the passenger seat of my Sonata and the hospital had faded in my rearview mirror, I was craving a sugar blast from that last truffle. It'd been more than twenty-four hours since I'd taken a healthy bite, and my body was running on fumes. All I could think about was getting home to eat my way through the kitchen. Then I'd crawl into bed. With luck, I'd forget I'd ever had a fortieth birthday.

Even Stan's nurse thought he'd downed the pills himself, so I was surely off the hook with Sheriff Bronson. If Stan stayed in this subdued state for the rest of the day, things were definitely looking up.

"You suppose we could get something to eat?" he murmured from beside me.

I glanced his way and felt a tiny, errant piece of my heart reach out to him. He really did look bad—ghostly pale, lids droopy, holding his stomach. If he felt even half as bad as I, he deserved sustenance.

"How does clam chowder sound?" I asked.

"Thank you," he whispered, his eyes drifting shut.

Thank you? I was so shocked that I nearly slammed into the car in front of me. When my heart finally calmed, I swiped side glances at Stan. Sure, he looked kind of different, but that could be due to all he'd been through in the past few hours. And yes, I had to admit that Stan had become a fixture in my life, one that I didn't examine closely.

But "thank you"? I couldn't remember the last time I'd heard him utter those two words.

We were headed south on the Coast Highway, perfect from my standpoint, since we'd pass by my chowder Mecca—Mo's. I knew things were looking up when I pulled into the crowded parking lot just as someone backed out. Stan lifted a lazy lid to stare at the beachy mural on the gray building, took a deep breath, and seemed to gather himself.

"You need some help?" I asked.

He shook his head as if shaking off a pesky fly. "I've got it," he muttered before he climbed out into the brilliant afternoon sunshine and began a lengthy shuffle to the entrance. Evidently, droopy britches and paper shoes weren't a concern. I trailed, arms flexed, prepared to catch him should his wobbly legs give out. Seagulls squealed shrilly, revving my edginess.

As usual, the wait for a table wound through a plethora of seaside tourist souvenirs, everything from tee-shirts and hats to shell-plastered boxes and starfish wind chimes. Stan seemed content to lean against a shelf and stare into space, so I pretended to peruse the merchandise while I plotted our lunch conversation.

The chances of Stan disclosing what had transpired the previous night were close to nil. Still, I had to know. Where was he before he plopped himself into that deck chair? And why did he look so dead if he wasn't? Even more important, why did he overdose on sleeping pills? Something even worse than our marriage must be eating away at him to resort to that.

Or maybe it was a stupid mistake. I pictured the scenario: Stan guzzles beer in an effort to numb his conscience to the fact that he forgot my birthday—I wanted to think it was a slip of his memory. But he still feels like the louse that he is and can't sleep, so he swallows a couple of sleeping pills, then a couple more, then. . . .

I peeked at him from the corner of my eye. That vacant, kicked-in-the-gut look still lurked on his face. I couldn't help but wonder how my life would change if he stayed like this, and I knew; Laura was right.

No more snide, hurtful comments. No more stormy, foul-mouthed tirades. No more whining and sulking. And no more tip-toeing around on pins and needles, always fearful that I'd do or say something to set him off. Yes, I'd pick zombie Stan over real Stan any day.

You have to escape from this life, some part of me screamed.

My eyes darted to him to confirm that he hadn't heard. My stomach heaved. I rubbed it, telling myself hunger caused the agitation. After all, things could change. Maybe now it would be better between Stan and me. We'd talk—share our feelings—and work together to make our life what I'd once envisioned it would be.

"How many in your group?"

The voice wrenched me from my fantasizing. I blinked hard and stared into a pair of eyes as blue as the sky behind them. "Two," I told the young lady in the black tee-shirt and skin-hugging jeans.

She grabbed a couple of menus and led us through the jam-packed dining area to a long plank table. I slid onto the far end of the bench to gaze out at Siletz Bay. If Stan remained mum, I'd watch the sprinklings of people fishing from the dock that stretched out over the rippling water.

With a bit of fumbling, Stan managed to drop onto the bench across from me. Our eyes met and held for several brief moments. This time his were dark, intense and probing, as if he were inside my head poking around, searching for secrets.

"Would you like something to drink?"

My gaze flicked to the waitress. "Iced tea, please," I told her.

"Water's fine," Stan mumbled.

"And I'll have a bowl of Slumgullion," I quickly added.

Stan's eyes dropped to his plastic-coated menu. He appeared to study it. Why? He'd eaten here hundreds of times, maybe thousands. I glanced at the waitress. A tight smile settled onto her lips as she scanned the surrounding diners.

Finally, Stan looked up. "Oyster stew," he murmured.

She grabbed the menus and scurried off.

While the waitress seemed satisfied with Stan's choice, I wasn't. "Since when do you eat oysters?" I challenged.

He stared at me long and hard. "I figured they would stay in my stomach."

So would what you always have—clam chowder, I wanted to remind him. And that is exactly what he always ordered, along with something deep-fried, a healthy portion of garlic cheese bread, a calorie-laden dessert, and a couple of beers. I let it go. For all I knew, death changed one's taste buds.

And I truly was turning to death as an explanation for Stan's uncharacteristic behaviors. Unless it had been a dream, one that felt very real, Stan had been as dead as a bloated toad when I'd touched him the previous night. Had he somehow returned from his grave a changed man?

"Polly Morton?" a deep male voice queried.

I glanced up at a vaguely familiar face—strong jaw line, cold eyes, and expensively styled salt-and-pepper hair. "Yes," I admitted hesitantly, my mind scurrying to place his features.

A phony smile curved his lips. "Brad Ellis. You're writing my dad's life story."

I stood so he wouldn't have to look down and nearly collided with the waitress when she set our drinks on the table. "Oh, of course. I just didn't expect to see you here in Lincoln City," I explained. And I couldn't help but wonder why he was here. Brad had his dad's multi-million dollar lumber business to run. Surely, he didn't get much playtime.

"We have property here. My son manages it. I was visiting him down in Depoe Bay. I'm on my way back to Portland and was in the mood for some good chowder. Can't beat Mo's for that."

At least, he and I agreed on that point. From hints his father had dropped, I'd ascertained that Brad wasn't thrilled with my writing endeavors—primarily, the one that involved his father. Evidently, Brad's idea of a quality family history and mine didn't jibe. He'd insisted that I keep my nose out of the nooks and crannies in the Ellis family annals. I knew the tidbits secreted in those nooks and crannies would transform a mundane retelling into a spicy adventure. No way was I going to keep my nose clean. Frank Ellis had hired me to record his whole life story, as well as that of his ancestors, and I planned to do just that.

So why did Brad Ellis have that bogus "glad to see you" smile on his face? I was about to speak when Stan struggled to his feet, and Brad's gaze darted to him.

Stan reached out the hand that didn't have a death grip on his shorts. "Stan Morton," he murmured, "Polly's husband."

Shock flashed on Brad's features. Frown lines creased his forehead. He reached out to shake Stan's hand. "Husband?" he queried, turning to me. "I . . . uh . . . . Yeah, it's nice to meet you, too," he murmured to Stan.

"Yes, Stan and I have been married for almost three years now," I informed him. Only three years? There were times when I'd swear we'd been together for decades—long, grueling, endless decades.

Brad's voice drew me back. "When do you plan to meet with

Dad again?"

Was that why he'd stopped for a visit, so he could be present to oversee what transpired between his father and me? Well, I could play this game, too.

"I'm not sure," I informed him. "I have a box of family records to go through and some leads to follow up on. Then I'll need to talk with him again."

His sterling jaw line tightened, and fire flickered in his amber eyes. That stunning smile vanished. He pulled a card from his pocket and held it out to me. "Please give me a call when you do," he instructed.

Though I knew I wouldn't make the call, I took the card. This tussle was between him and his father, not the two of us. Let them hash it out. I had every confidence that his father would be the victor. From what I'd observed, Frank Ellis pulled his own strings.

At that moment, our food arrived, steaming, melting pats of butter floating on rich milk. It looked so good that I nearly lapped it up with my tongue when it passed by me. "Thank you for stopping to visit," I murmured to Brad, sinking onto the bench.

"I'll be waiting for your call," he informed me. Before he headed toward the cash register, he gave Stan a lengthy perusal.

When I glanced at Stan, his troubled eyes were glued to Brad. "Who is that guy?" he asked, his voice so husky it seemed as alien as the rest of him.

"The lumber baron's son—the one I'm writing the biography on."

"He have a problem with you?"

Chowder aromas wafted around me, enticing. My stomach gurgled. "According to his father, Brad tried to talk him out of hiring me. He thinks I'm too snoopy."

"Does he have something he wants to stay hidden?"

I shrugged. "Not that I know of. I've interviewed his father several times, and I have a box of old family mementos to examine— letters and journals, receipts and news clippings, stuff like that. So far, I haven't come across anything even remotely scandalous or incriminating. The papers you picked up at the museum in Newport were from that box."

When his gaze slid from Brad to me, his frown said he had no idea what I was talking about. "On Monday. Remember? You asked me about them—what they were and where they came from. They're so fragile that I was afraid they'd tear. I had copies made, so I don't have to handle them. Bev's with the historical society. She knows how to deal with old documents, so I hired her to copy them. You said you'd pick them up."

He nodded, but it didn't fool me. He hadn't a clue what I was talking about. No doubt, I'd have to make the twenty-five-mile trek to Newport to pick them up though he passed right by the museum driving to and from work.

"I guess I forgot," he muttered, eyeing his oyster stew.

Another upshot of death? I wanted to ask. At the moment, I was too hungry to push the issue.

We both spooned soup into our mouths. Buttery warmth melted my insides. I chewed on potatoes, clams, and fresh shrimp and watched to see what Stan would do when he bit into an oyster. To my surprise, he swallowed, then scooped another spoonful.

"You don't want crackers in that?" I probed.

His eyes met mine. "You seem to have a problem with what I'm eating?"

Whoa! That old look was in his eyes. "You usually load your soup with crackers. I wondered if you wanted some." *And you hate oysters,* I silently added.

He glanced at the basket of packaged saltines. "My stomach's still queasy, so I thought I'd better keep it light."

The chime of my cell phone drew my attention. I pulled it from my purse and checked the number—Laura. I needed to run this weirdness by her. But not now. Not while Stan could listen in. I took a deep breath and sweetened my tea with a packet of chemicals, then turned back to appeasing my empty stomach.

In the noise-filled room, silence screamed between us. It felt like tiny lightning bugs scurried along my nerves. I flicked glances at Stan, but he appeared unfazed, totally immersed in his stew slurping. If I didn't act soon, my opportunity might be lost.

I set my spoon down and stiffened my backbone. "Can we talk about last night?" I probed in a shaky voice.

His hand dropped, and he studied me. "What about it?"

"Where were you?"

He hesitated, and I swore I heard the cogs turning as he concocted a feasible excuse. "It's all kind of hazy, but it seems like something came up. Why?"

Which wasn't unusual. With Stan, something always came up. I never questioned what it was. Mostly, I didn't want to know. "Well . . . it was my birthday," I reminded him. "I thought we were going out."

He frowned, and his face glowed rosily. "I must've forgot."

I really wanted to believe he'd forgotten, that it wasn't that something came up that he'd rather do.

"I'm sorry. How about if we celebrate another night," he offered.

I know my jaw dropped like one of those diggers on a monster steam shovel. I felt it dangling while I tried to make sense of what was going on with Stan. Finally, I managed to murmur, "It's okay. You don't have to do that."

"I want to."

Like hell you do, I almost snapped. But I let it go. At the moment, it was best to move on to solving our problems, not creating more. I sucked air and pressed forward. "Why did you take those pills?"

Sparks flickered in his dark eyes. "I told you; I didn't take any pills," he uttered, his voice steely.

"Then how did they get inside your body?"

He shook his head, frowning, clearly as baffled as I. "Maybe they were in something I ate or drank."

"Like that six-pack of beer?"

His frown lines turned to furrows. "I don't know. I just know I didn't take any pills. All I remember is that cop shaking me awake this morning."

"What time was it when you fell asleep out there?"

"I'm not sure."

I hesitated, unsure of whether to press on or end it here. He claimed he hadn't taken the pills. And he was alive . . . now. Still, I had unanswered questions that would, no doubt, gnaw at me in the weeks to come.

"Well, I woke up in the middle of the night," I pressed. "I'm not sure what time it was. And when I went outside to wake you up, you were . . . well . . . you sure looked like you were . . . dead."

Shock flashed on his face, but he recovered quickly, narrowing his steely eyes. "Dead! You thought I was dead?"

"Well, no. Actually, I *know* you were."

A smile touched his lips. "Do I look dead?"

In fact, he looked like he'd joined the living . . . now. A hint of color had returned to his face, and his eyes were no longer two empty orbs. His whole demeanor whispered of life. "No, not now. But you did."

"So you think I was dead and came back to life?"

"I'm not sure what happened," I hedged. "I just know that at that moment, you were dead. And now you're alive. And you're different."

"Different, in what way?" he challenged.

Where to start? "Well, for one thing, you hate oysters. And you never say 'thank you' or apologize for anything. And you didn't yell at me for calling the cops. And look at you; you have to hold onto your shorts to keep them up. And you don't seem to give a rip that you've lost your precious Guns N Roses tee-shirt," I rattled off, picking up speed with each accusation. I paused to take a breath. "But what really scares me is that you're sitting here having a normal conversation with me. You *never* do that."

His eyes blinked like a stuck turn signal. After a couple of dead beats, he spoke. "Well, I don't know what to tell you. Maybe it's the Triazolam. But I can assure you that I'm alive."

Perhaps he was right. People take drugs to calm their nerves and annihilate depression. They take them so they don't act so crazy. Perhaps Triazolam was Stan's miracle drug. If that were the case, come Monday morning, I'd be at the front of the pharmacy line, prescription in hand.

And his death? Was Triazolam responsible for that, too? And his rebirth?

Susan Boyle's voice singing "Cry Me a River" blasted from my cell. I bounced and glanced at the screen. *Lincoln County Sheriff's Office* screamed at me in dark letters. My heart rate screamed, too. "I better take this call," I muttered.

I gazed out the window at a young boy and his shaggy mutt while they sprinted on the wet sand and splashed in the sparkling water, braced myself, and clicked on the phone. "This is Polly Morton."

"Yes, Mrs. Morton. Sheriff Bronson here." He cleared his throat, then continued. "That box of chocolates on your counter, you said someone left it at your front door, right?"

Why in the world would Sheriff Bronson call me to discuss truffles? "Yes," I murmured.

"You know who it was?"

"The card just said *Happy Birthday*. I assume it's a surprise gift from one of my neighbors."

"And you ate a couple of the chocolates, right?"

"Yes."

"And how'd you feel after you ate them?"

As lousy as I felt before I ate them thanks to my shoddy husband, I wanted to say. But I doubted that was what the sheriff wanted to hear. "Okay, I guess. My stomach was a little queasy, but I hadn't eaten since lunch. I fell asleep, but it was nighttime."

"And there were three more missing when you woke up this morning. You know what happened to them?"

"No." Was that why the sheriff had called, to confess that he'd devoured my birthday candy in a chocolate-craving frenzy? "Why?"

He cleared his throat again. "Well, I just got the report on the contents of your husband's stomach. Appears he's the one who ate those chocolates."

My eyes snapped to Stan. He was shoving a slimy oyster into his mouth. And now the sheriff claimed he'd eaten chocolate, too—before or after the Triazolam and his death episode?

"There must be a mistake. Stan doesn't eat chocolate. Not ever," I argued, my heart racing.

Stan's sharp gaze latched onto mine. His eyes narrowed. His pallor returned.

"Well, he definitely did last night," Sheriff Bronson assured me. "And they were loaded with expensive brandy and Triazolam."

CHAPTER 3

Stan lay stretched out in his coffee Barcalounger, lids closed, mouth open. I studied him from my kitchen. It was actually a relief that his Triazolam experience hadn't nabbed his snoring, too—more familiar. Too bad I couldn't say the same about the black kitten curled up on his lap.

"No label on the box anywhere," Sheriff Bronson informed me. "Could be they're homemade."

Homemade! I turned back to watch him stuff the foil-lined box with the remaining truffle into a plastic bag. He added the miniature card and sealed the contents.

His bushy brows furled up over the tops of his horn rims like a pair of fuzzy, gray caterpillars. "Maybe we'll pick up a print. You have any ideas on who might've left them at your front door?"

I shook my head. "Not a clue. I assumed they were a birthday gift from a friend, but I guess not. All of my friends know how much I love chocolate and how much Stan detests the stuff."

He tugged the plastic gloves off his hands and shoved them into a pants pocket. "So you think they were meant for you?"

My insides squeezed. "I guess. But why would someone give me something laced with sedatives?" Surely, not one of my friends.

"You have any enemies?"

"No. I don't think so." But does one ever know for sure?

His obscure gaze intensified. "You and your husband been getting along?"

"Pretty much," I lied. After all, we'd gotten along okay today. "Why?"

"Could be he wanted you out of the picture for several hours."

I knew Stan hadn't left that beautifully prepared box—it was way out of his league. Still, some part of me refused to badmouth him. "But he ate the truffles, too. Too many of them. And he hates chocolate," I argued.

"If he hates it so much, why'd he eat it?"

That question had pestered me since I'd received Sheriff Bronson's phone call. "The only thing I can figure out is he drank too much. Maybe he didn't realize what he was eating." *Or maybe his whole chocolate revulsion was a scam fabricated to annoy me,* I wanted to offer. "But if he knew what was in those truffles, even drunk, I don't think he would've eaten them."

Sheriff Bronson studied Stan's dozing. "What'd he say about it?"

"Nothing. He doesn't remember anything about last night. Just you waking him up this morning."

To keep from spouting off about the plethora of red flags waving around me, including Stan's timely memory loss, I patted my lips and swallowed words. Until I figured out what was going on, I wouldn't be spilling my guts to the law.

And mark my word, I would find out. With my chocolate addiction and the emotional state I'd been in the previous night, it was a wonder I hadn't devoured every one of those alcohol and sedative packed truffles.

I shuddered with prickly chills. "He seems to have forgotten a lot of things," I murmured. The sheriff looked skeptical. *Yeah, you and I both,* I mentally confessed.

The minute the sheriff left, I planned to meet with Laura and run this whole mind-boggling mess by her. She was practical and grounded; not much got by her. Surely, she would come up with a logical explanation for the mysterious truffles *and* Stan's metamorphosis.

Sheriff Bronson rubbed his pudgy chin and eyeballed Stan again.

"Do you want me to wake him up?" I asked.

He shrugged. "Nah. Let him sleep it off. You're both okay. I guess that's what matters. If I need to talk with him, I'll contact him later." With that, he grabbed his bulging baggy and his leather bag and headed for the front door. I trailed and watched him toddle to his county SUV from the open door, my inner tension deflating a bit with each step he took.

Across the street, Laura sat on her porch in a lilac rocker, her eyes peeking over the top of the magazine in her hands. Thank goodness the houses on both sides of hers were vacation homes.

Rarely, did anyone cross their thresholds, which meant less nosy neighbors.

I squinted at the bright sun hovering above Laura's roofline. Frothy cloud wisps trailed across the azure sky. Soon that sky and the ocean waters would be washed in magnificent shades of orange and gold. On any other evening, I'd be a part of that sunset, my toes curled in the warm sand or running down closer to the water. Not today.

I sighed and looked away. Next door George scrubbed a tire on his boat trailer while Denise mutilated a helpless rhododendron with a pair of kitchen shears. Her puffy, red-rimmed eyes met mine. She opened her mouth to speak, but I turned away. Either Denise was battling allergies, or she was seriously upset about something. Again. Whatever the case, I had my own crisis and was in no mood to hear about hers.

Instead, my eyes shifted south one-hundred-eighty degrees. No Phil or Javier? I hadn't heard a peep from them—another conundrum.

Rubbing at the unrest agitating in my gut, I stared at Sheriff Bronson's taillights and ignored all of the other eyes scrutinizing the goings-on at my house. When they turned the corner, I motioned Laura over. She dropped the magazine and power-walked across the pavement in her orange Crocs, blonde curls and ample curves bouncing. Floral shorts hugged her thighs, and a spandex tangerine tank contained her midriff—perfect. For the first time that day, a smile touched my lips. Laura embraced her curvaceous body. That was one of the many things I loved about her.

"OMG, Pol. You need a huge girlfriend hug," she chirped. "But inside, away from prying eyes."

I didn't point out that she'd been snooping, too. Instead, I stepped back, so she could pass by. Inside, she stood on tiptoes to wrap her arms around me.

A stinging in my eyes told me it better not be too huge or I'd be sobbing so loud the neighbors would know I was having a meltdown. Cocooned in her soft embrace, I felt like everything just might turn out okay, but when her arms loosened, my angst crept right back.

"Did he take that last truffle?" she asked, her face scrunched into worry.

I nodded. I'd texted Laura earlier to tell her the source of Stan's affliction, so her question didn't surprise me.

"We can talk in my office," I murmured. "But first will you take a look at Stan, and see if you think there's anything odd about him? He's asleep in the living room."

"Stan *is* odd, Pol. I've been telling you that since you met the bum."

"Please, just look at him and see if he looks different. Something's off. It is Stan. But it's not him."

Laura's eyes pinched into a puzzled frown, but she shrugged and tiptoed into the living room with me at her heels. Though Stan's snores reverberated, the kitten slept through the ruckus. We stood over the Barcalounger and examined Stan as if we were at his funeral viewing.

Late afternoon had dimmed the lighting, but his features were still clearly visible—high cheekbones, chiseled jaws and chin, and classy nose. He was a handsome man. At least I'd thought so when I'd married him.

But my memory had those features more muddled, less angles and more rounded lines—scruffy. I'd never seen him with hair this short before . . . or dark. Was Stan dyeing his hair?

Then Stan's eyes popped open. His whole body jerked, and he stared up at me, black irises stark against the whites. His brows slashed into a frown before his puzzled gaze flicked from me to Laura. A hand reached out to settle the restless kitten.

My pulse accelerated. Fear blazed in my gut. How would Stan respond to our scrutiny?

Locking eyes with mine, he lowered the chair and pushed himself up onto his feet, then held the kitten out and dropped it into my arms. "Excuse me," he uttered in his throaty voice before he shuffled off, cargo shorts inching down his narrow hips. The click of a doorknob told me he was in the bathroom.

When I turned to Laura, her eyeballs had popped, too, like a startled puffer fish. "*Brrr*," she shivered, her whole body shaking. "FYI—downright creepy."

"So I'm not crazy?"

She was rattled, enough that she chewed on a freshly polished thumbnail. "No. It's definitely Stan—a better Stan. You know, like he did a month-long makeover at some rehab spa or something. I wouldn't complain, Pol. He looks hot."

"Yeah, he does, doesn't he," I admitted.   "Only he's acting strange, too."

"Uh-huh, I got that. He didn't even take one jab at me. In fact, I'd swear he didn't know who I was." Her gaze focused on the fluff ball climbing up my chest. "And what's with the kitten? I thought you were keeping it hidden."

"I tried," I told her, tugging the tiny ball of fur loose to set it on the floor. "It was running around this morning, which makes me think Stan was in my office last night. What's with that? He never goes in there. And we all know how much he hates cats."

She shook her head and shrugged. "Doesn't usually use the hall bath either, does he?"

Another oddity to add to my list. "No. He seems to have a memory loss—or so he claims. He probably *didn't* recognize you. In fact, I'm not sure he knows who I am. It's so eerie. I feel like I'm starring in one of those old episodes of the 'Twilight Zone.'" None of this makes sense."

A doorknob's snap warned us Stan was returning. Laura and I watched him mosey into the kitchen, one hand fisted around his droopy shorts. He returned to the living room with a Diet Pepsi clutched in his hand, eyeballing us like we were his pesky kid sisters.

His eyes looked more alive, his complexion more vivid—more like the old Stan. But he walked more erect than before, and his shoulders had gained several inches in the last twenty-four hours.

"Mind if I watch some TV?" he muttered.

We both shook our heads and watched him plop back down into his recliner. He set the pop on the side table and studied his remotes as if he hadn't a clue which one turned on the tube. Finally, he selected the wrong one. Inhaling a huge breath, he set his jaw and eyeballed me. "Did you want something?"

Yes, I'd like to know when you stopped drinking sugar in your pop, I almost blurted. "The sheriff was here," I informed him.

"And?"

I watched the kitten climb up a hairy leg, settle into his lap, and lick a tiny white paw. Then I watched Stan's fingers stroke its baby fur, my insides twisting into painful knots. "He took the box and the last truffle. He wanted to know if I had any idea who might've left them. I don't. Do you?"

"No. Since I don't usually eat chocolate, they were obviously left for you."

"Maybe one of your friends doesn't like me."

He shrugged halfheartedly. "Like who?"

"I don't know. Maybe one of the guys you work with, a fishing or golfing buddy, or someone at that bar you hang out at. I can't see George doing something like that." Denise, on the other hand. . . .

I turned to Laura for support, but she just arched her penciled brows and shook her head. What was going on with her? She usually went out of her way to needle Stan. Today she seemed content to scrutinize him.

"Sheriff Bronson thinks someone wanted me out of the way for a few hours," I informed him, "which made me think that someone might've wanted me to sleep through my birthday celebration. The only person I can think of is you. It would certainly get you off the hook."

"Right," he sniggered. "And then I ate three of the deadly things to throw you off my track."

"Yeah, I know. That part doesn't make sense. But why did you eat them. You hate chocolate."

"Like I told you, last night is one big blur."

"Even earlier in the evening, before you came home?"

"Everything," he claimed, enunciating each syllable. He paused to take a deep breath. "All I remember is waking up this morning feeling like a semi rolled through and flattened me."

Which just seems too convenient, I almost refuted. But the sparks in his eyes told me it might be one push too many. After all, real Stan was still somewhere inside that enhanced body. I wanted him to stay there.

"Maybe your memory will return once the drugs are out of your system," I offered.

"If it does, you'll be the first to know." He rubbed his forehead, a pained look settling on his features. "Right now, grilling me isn't helping my headache, so if you don't mind. . . ."

"We'll be in my office," I informed him, nodding Laura toward the front of the house and my writing room. We hustled inside, and I closed the doors behind us.

"OMG, Pol," Laura gasped, plopping into a tangerine armchair. "I'm speechless. Honestly, I don't know what to say. And what's with his voice?"

I shrugged and dropped down into my cushy desk chair. "Maybe they rammed something down his throat at the hospital."

"He's like a brand new Stan, one who's not mean and hateful." She took a deep breath, shook her head resignedly, and added, "And I'm thinking that it's so creepy—supernatural almost. But I'm also thinking how it would be so great if he stays this way. You know what I mean?"

"Yeah," I confessed, little prickles of shame poking me with my admission. "And I feel kind of guilty about it, like I'm deserting my marriage."

She rolled her eyes and gave me her "poor Polly" look. "Well, he's still Stan, so you're not leaving him or cheating on him."

"I suppose," I murmured as I eyed my laptop and remembered that I hadn't checked my email that day. "I do want to find out what's going on, but at the same time, I'd kind of like things to stay like they are right now. I'm afraid to push him too much, afraid he'll suddenly morph into old Stan. Still, someone did leave me a box of doctored candy."

"And you really don't have any idea who it was?"

"No. You?" I lifted the computer lid and pushed the *on* button. Lights flashed as it hummed to life.

Laura shook her head. "Maybe Denise. We both know she has the hots for Stan—lord knows why. Maybe she wanted to get you out of the way for a few hours, so she could have a shot at him."

"Yeah, that thought crossed my mind, too," I confessed. Poor Denise; if George golfed and fished less often and spent more time at home, she might not be sharing her surgically enhanced wares elsewhere. "But the sheriff thinks those truffles were homemade. You and I both know what Denise can do to a boxed cake mix. Those truffles were amazing and beautifully boxed. There's no way she made them." My sign-in page lit up the screen, and I reached out to type in my password.

"Hmmm . . . sounds more like Javier, huh?"

"Javier?" I gasped, my focus flashing to Laura. She looked serious. Sure, Javier was an amazing cook. He could prepare anything as well as a five star chef. He was also a dear friend and a treasured next-door-neighbor. "He'd never do something like that, not to me, anyway."

Her brows lifted. "Unless he knew Stan was going to flake out on you again. He might've been worried that you'd sit here by yourself, feeling more and more angry and hurt."

"Then he'd just flit over here to calm me down and console me," I argued, turning back to my computer screen.

"He and Phil left for Ashland yesterday morning. Phil welded a sculpture for some guy down there, and they delivered it. They're coming home tonight."

"Oh, right. I forgot about that." I paused to consider Laura's speculation. "Well, he wouldn't have given me six of those things. Maybe one or two, so I'd sleep off my anger. Not six."

"And he knows Stan doesn't eat chocolate?"

I nodded and typed in my password. I knew Javier worried about me. "You need to ditch that dirt bag," he'd say. "Someday he's going to physically abuse you, or you're going to reach your breaking point and hurt yourself. I worry you'll do something you'll later regret." I could picture Javier giving Stan a pint of laxative-laced homemade Gelato, a knowing smile on his face. Not chocolates, and certainly not sedatives.

While images flashed onto the screen, I thought back to the previous day. "You were with me all day, so you weren't around to notice anything strange going on outside my house," I reminded her. "How about in the early morning?"

She shook her head. "Was Stan at home yesterday?"

"No. He left before I did. He's working on a restaurant south of Newport. That is, when George doesn't drag him off to golf or fish. By any chance did you see him come home last night?"

She shook her head again. "I honestly thought Stan would come through for you this time. I mean, it was your fortieth birthday, for God's sake. Guess I underestimated his sliminess. Anyway, I was exfoliated and polished from our day at Saunia's. Couldn't let that go to waste. You know how Benny and I loved to dance. Well, since his passing, whenever I thought about getting out there again, I'd end up physically ill. Last night I forced myself to go for it. Glad I did, too. It was after midnight when I got home."

My heart warmed with Laura's words. It'd been a couple of years since her husband's death, difficult years for Laura. She and Benny had been soul mates since our high school days. Their marriage was what I dreamed mine would be. But Stan was not a Benny—light-years from it, in fact.

"I'm so proud of you," I told her. "And thrilled that you enjoyed yourself."

"Thank you," she murmured, her voice husky, tears shining in her eyes.

"It's what Benny would want you to do."

She brushed at a renegade tear. "I know. It's just so hard."

"I know," I whispered, my own throat burning. I'd lost a husband, too—a Benny-perfect husband—so long ago that it now seemed more a dream than reality. A freak accident, they'd said—two veteran skiers tearing down the slopes and colliding at the wrong time and place. The other skier had streaked away on his skis. My David died before he reached the bottom of the run, strapped to a sled. Being eight months pregnant, I'd stayed in the lodge that day. But Benny and Laura had been on the ski slopes with David. They'd delivered the news to me.

"Stan's truck was here."

"What?" I asked, blinking my way back to present day Laura.

"When I got home. Stan's truck was in your driveway."

"I wish I knew where he was before that and what happened after he finally did come home. I'd swear he was stone cold dead, Laura. I mean, really, really dead." I almost told her about the misplaced pillow, then decided it best to keep that tidbit to myself for now. "I know he had a different tee-shirt on this morning. I've looked everywhere I can think of, and I can't find the one he had on last night. And you saw his shorts. They're at least a couple of sizes too large."

"So he got up off his deathbed, changed his clothes and hid them, and ate three chocolate truffles, even though he detests chocolate. Then he returned to the deck to sleep through the night."

"And sometime last night he came into my office." I glanced around the room. "I wonder why?"

Being borderline anal with my things—I constantly assured myself that I hadn't crossed that border—my office was usually immaculate, everything neatly in its place. Two bookcases filled with reference books and treasured mystery novels of varying colors and sizes rested against one wall, spines lined in a row an inch from the edge of each shelf. A library table covered with stacks of papers stood at the back of the room. I pushed myself to my feet and stepped to the table to scrutinize the sorted piles. Something seemed off.

When I worked on a project with a client, I'd make copious notes and organize those notes into piles on this table, based on content in prospective chapters. Frank Ellis had insisted that his life story was only a reflection of what his ancestors had accomplished in Oregon's early days. He wanted a large portion of his biography to be devoted to their stories. I'd planned to start the book with his great-grandfather and move forward from there.

As I studied my handiwork, it suddenly hit me: the chapters weren't in the correct order. In fact, they were completely mixed up. Had Stan knocked them on the floor and then just randomly stacked them back onto the table? No. If he'd sent papers flying, he'd have left them where they landed.

I thumbed through a couple of stacks. The pages appeared to be in the right stacks.

"Is something wrong?" Laura asked from behind me.

"He messed with my paperwork."

"Stan?"

"Who else?" I muttered. My eyes flicked over the litter pan and bowls of food and water I'd left for the kitten. "I thought maybe he'd heard the kitten's cries and opened the door to check out the noise. It makes no sense that he'd look through these notes."

My gaze traveled on around the room, past a cabinet covered with tech equipment, cassette tapes, printer paper, and notebooks, and on to my desk. I stepped to the desk and stared at the photos flashing on the screen.

My daughter Sara's image smiled at me for several seconds. She stood in the OSU Quad in faded jeans and a Beaver tee-shirt, cherry trees blooming pink cotton candy-like puffs around her. I rubbed my forehead, frustrated with the knowledge that she didn't yet have a clue what was going on here. And maybe she didn't need to. Rather than spend another tension-filled summer vacation in this house with Stan, she'd opted for an internship on the college campus. The only way we'd be meeting face-to-face is if I drove east for a visit.

"It's going to be okay, Pol. There's probably some simple explanation we're just not seeing right now," Laura assured me.

"I hope so," I murmured, examining the pile of papers beside my computer. They were disheveled just enough to be noticeable. I eyed the printer on the file drawer, then pulled open a couple of drawers to glance inside at the files. Sure enough, Stan had pawed through them, too."

"He looked through my files," I muttered, "and these papers on my desk."

"This is getting weirder and weirder."

"Tell me about it. Why in the world would Stan suddenly show an interest in my work?"

Laura chewed on a thumbnail, her face scrunched up in thought. "Maybe it wasn't Stan," she finally offered.

"Not Stan? Then who?" It didn't make sense. No more sense than thinking Stan was the culprit.

"Maybe someone wanted you out of the way, so they could sneak in here last night and search for something."

"There's nothing of interest to anyone but me here." I pointed to the library table. "Those are notes on that lumber family I'm writing about—snooze material so far. Unless I uncover something titillating soon, I can't imagine anyone but family members purchasing a copy of the book, so it's fortunate I'm being paid by the hour."

"What's in the files?"

"Just my bookkeeping and records of work I've done in the past, notes on information sources, technical blurbs—all business related."

"Well I don't know, Pol. It's just plain spooky. I keep thinking that there were six truffles in that box. Why six? What if you'd eaten more than just those two? I mean, you said Stan looked dead after eating three. If you'd eaten four, would it have killed you?"

"My gut twisted painfully as an image of my naked body laid out behind a steel door in the county morgue flashed before me—thanks to Saunia's, there was no unsightly stubble. Though I didn't want to consider it, someone might want me dead. If so, I needed to find him, or her, before he got me.

Prickly shivers rushed through me with the knowledge that I might be good at uncovering juicy tidbits for my writing endeavors, but I had no idea how to track down a murderer.

〰 ✿ 〰

"Your chips are in the pantry," I reminded Stan as I traipsed past the kitchen.

His gaze met mine, then dropped to the litter pan in my hands before returning to the refrigerator's interior. I set the pan on the laundry room floor and headed back to my office for the kitty's water and food dishes. Sure enough, Stan's head was still in the open fridge.

"Ice cream's in the freezer," I prompted as I passed by him.

On my return trip, the pantry door was open. Hopefully, he'd emerge with a box of Twinkies or bag of cheese puffs, something familiar to alleviate this gut-wrenching zaniness.

With the kitten's supplies now firmly rooted in the laundry room, I went in search of the little monster. Stan had returned to fridge browsing. Black athletic shorts now covered his thighs, their elastic band holding them in place. His white feet were bare.

I postponed my search to offer some help. "How about if I make you a chili dog or some nachos?"

He shut the stainless steel door and frowned at me as if I'd offered him a spinach salad with nonfat dressing. "Maybe something healthier?"

"Healthier?" I blurted, too stunned to stifle my reaction. "Since when are you worried about your health?"

"Since I woke up this morning feeling like shit," he muttered. "And the fact that I did wake up seems to have your panties in a bind. You want me dead?"

His words were a punch in my gut. I grabbed my middle and blinked hard, determined to come off sane. "No. You're just so different. And you're acting strange," I argued. "It's like you're not Stan anymore." *And you were so dead last night,* I silently added.

"I'm acting strange? You're the one who examined me like I was some form of deadly bacteria resting in a Petri dish."

My cheeks burned. "Well, you look different, too. I wanted to get a closer look, to see if it's my imagination. It's not. Where's your tan. And how long have you been dyeing your hair?"

The glint in his eyes shifted from irritated to wary. "You don't think a man can change?"

"Of course, I do. But not as much as you have in the last eighteen hours. It's downright spooky."

"Could be you haven't been paying attention. How long's it been since you took a really good look at me?"

The heat in my cheeks kicked up a notch. He had a point, and the twitch of his upper lip told me he knew it. "That might be. But it doesn't explain the drastic changes in your eating habits. I know. I've been buying your junk food."

His spunk seemed to fizzle. "Well, I don't know what to tell you. Maybe the Triazolam did something to my brain. Everything's foggy—out of focus. Nothing seems familiar. It's like. . . ."

The doorbell's chime halted his words and was probably my saving grace since I was about to bring up the possibility of his death and rebirth. He didn't make a move, so I huffed and headed toward the front of the house. I honestly expected to see Laura's face, or perhaps Javier's, when I opened the door so was totally unprepared for Denise's red-rimmed eyes and splotchy cheeks. My eyes dropped to the casserole she clutched between two black potholders.

"I thought some yummy smoked salmon enchiladas might hit the spot tonight, so I whipped some up for you," she said. Her voice sounded forced and shaky. Tears sparkled in her eyes.

"That's so thoughtful of you," I murmured. And I meant it. It was also out of character for her to do something so thoughtful. *Just add it to the "Weird Goings-on" list,* I told myself as I stepped back to let her enter the house.

She sashayed into the kitchen and dropped the casserole onto the granite countertop with so much force that the dish should've shattered. Stan jerked and turned from his fridge rooting to stare at Denise, eyes as round as the tomato in his hand, mouth gaping.

I didn't blame him. Denise had done herself proud this evening. An orange midriff-and-cleavage-baring halter top clung to her ample breasts. Long, slender legs stretched from faded barely-there cutoffs down to a pair of ridiculously high platform sandals. To top it off, her bright orange mane shimmered lustrously, framing her pasty, splotched face and puffy eyes, eyes that now glared at Stan like he was soon to be chopped up and added to a certain casserole.

"Denise brought us enchiladas," I informed Stan, hoping to burst the tension and wondering what in the heck was going on. "Wasn't that thoughtful of her?"

Stan's gaze flicked to me, then back to Denise. He nodded warily. "Very thoughtful," he murmured. "You must've read my mind. I was searching for something to eat."

"Well you've got it now," she barked. "So eat it and enjoy every delicious bite of it. And when you're done with it, just dump it. You're good at that." Her voice cracked, and she blinked several times and stared at me with desperate eyes.

"Are you okay?" I asked. When it came to drama, Denise could be a bit out there, but this performance was well beyond that.

She shook her flaming tresses and breathed deeply, then whispered, "I will be." With that, her focus returned to Stan. "Cat got your tongue?"

"No," Stan uttered, looking even more desperate than Denise.

"I don't think Stan knows who you are," I informed Denise.

"Like hell he doesn't!" she barked, fire in her eyes. Then she narrowed that searing glare at Stan and really studied him.

Stan slowly shook his head. Either he was a very good actor—which took more patience and mind control than he'd ever before exhibited—or he was telling the truth.

I let myself lean toward the latter and felt weights lifting from my shoulders, coils in my stomach unwinding. After all, such things did happen, at least on the TV screen they did.

"He woke up this morning . . . not feeling well—thus, the

ambulance ride—and *poof*, for some strange reason, his memory is gone," I assured Denise.

"And you believe that?" Clearly, she didn't.

"I don't think he even recognizes me."

Stan lifted his very fine brows and seemed to mull over his response. "I know you're my wife," he mumbled. "The minutia of our relationship is just . . . vague."

Minutia? I nearly screamed. Real Stan wouldn't even know that word existed. Instead, I fixed my eyes on Denise and switched topics. "Did you see anyone in our yard yesterday?"

Her splotches became rosier, her eyes twitchy. "No. Why?"

"Just wondering. Someone left something at my front door, and I wanted to thank them. The card wasn't signed. I thought you might've seen them drop it off."

She visibly relaxed. "I took advantage of the sunshine and spent most of the day at the pool. George played thirty-six holes yesterday, so he wasn't around either." Brushing me aside, she eyeballed Stan intently.

I had to hand it to him; he met her stare and didn't concede, his look as bland as boiled cabbage. I swore Denise growled before she finally ended the standoff. "Well I gotta go. I'm meeting some friends for drinks and dinner, maybe a little dancing," she informed Stan in a taut voice.

"Is George going with you?" I probed, hoping for a peek at what was going on next door without opening the floodgates.

Her lethal eyes met mine. "He's getting up early to go crabbing. You know George; he has to be the first one to launch his boat or the weekenders will get the best crab, or something else equally as devastating," she barked, though her eyes had turned sad.

Breathing deeply, she blinked hard, then gazed at Stan intently for several unsettling moments before she wiggled toward the front door on her platforms.

"Thank you for the enchiladas," I yelled at her barely covered back as I followed her.

She jerked the door open. "Enjoy them," she commanded before she slammed it shut in my face.

I reached down to snap the deadbolt into place while I considered the impetus behind Denise's uncharacteristic neighborly visit. Was it her rabid nosiness? Or was it a ploy to check on Stan?

Though she'd examined him closely, she hadn't seemed to

question his appearance. She was definitely ticked off at him, or maybe it was men in general. Or just George. And maybe Stan, being right there in front of her, got the brunt of her anger, a stand-in for her husband.

Whatever the case, I had enough to decipher in my own life without getting involved in my neighbors'. Assuring myself that Denise was just being Denise, I traipsed back into the kitchen.

Stan, fork in hand, was peeling the aluminum foil from the enchiladas.

"You don't want to go there," I warned him.

He gave me a look that said I was more of a lunatic than Denise.

I glanced at her casserole and had to admit that it looked good—yellow melted cheese oozing over corn tortillas topped with some kind of red sauce. Then I studied Stan. If he took a bite of Denise's cooking, I knew he was totally out of touch with his old self.

"It's your stomach," I murmured.

His fork tines slid into the gooey mess. "It can't be that bad."

Smoked salmon fumes filled the room, which wouldn't have been a bad thing if it hadn't been battling whatever else Denise had dumped into her concoction. I grabbed my stomach to still it.

Stan eyed his fork and stuffed its contents into his mouth. He chewed a couple of times, then gagged. His face paled, and his cheeks puffed out like a hoarding chipmunk before he marched to the sink and spit his mouthful into it.

I filled a glass with water from the fridge and handed it to him, then watched him swish and spit until his sickly pallor faded.

"If you *really* have lost your memory, you might want to listen to my advice," I told him. "Stay away from Denise's cooking. But even more important, stay away from Denise. Her husband, George, has a boat, and you like to fish, so he's your buddy."

"I *do* like to fish," he mumbled.

"Yes, you do, so if you don't want to seriously tick off your other self, should your memory return, avoid Denise."

He narrowed his dark eyes, frowning. "What's her problem?"

How to answer: toxic Botox? Bad implants? Prescription meds? Alcohol? All of the above? "I don't know. I didn't ask because I really don't want to know," was my honest answer. Then my thoughts turned to George, and my gut twisted. Denise and I did have one thing in common—negligent husbands.

"Denise can be a drama queen, no doubt about that. But she

was red-eyed earlier today, so she and George probably had a tiff," I informed him.

He shrugged and drank the rest of the water in his glass.

I was ready to move on, too. "Why don't you track down the kitten and show it where its litter box is. I'll make us something to eat—something healthy," I offered.

"Sure. But first I'm going to get rid of this," he said grabbing the enchiladas from the countertop. "I doubt I could down a bowl of ice cream with that smell in the room." Casserole in hand, he headed toward the garage.

"So you still like ice cream," I murmured, feeling some comfort with those words.

Before I foraged for healthy grub, I rubbed at the pressure between my brows and pondered my transformed marriage. It actually felt kind of nice—better, at least. It felt like it was what it should've been all along.

I honestly liked new Stan. I could picture us living together contentedly, maybe not blissfully, the rest of our lives.

So why did I feel like I had a time bomb strapped to my back, one that would explode at any moment, annihilating this glimpse I'd been given of a rather pleasant life?

CHAPTER 4

I shot up out of a deep sleep, my heart hammering like an over-zealous woodpecker. Stilling it with the palm of my hand, I gazed around, confused. It was early morning—very early. Gray light filtered into the bedroom through the wall of windows that faced the golf course, hinting that the sun had not yet risen. I rubbed at the sleep in my eyes, and my gaze dropped to Stan. He was curled into fetal position near the edge of his side of the bed, facing away from me with the kitten snuggled against his back, his deep breaths barely discernible. Real Stan would be sprawled spread-eagle, hogging my space and his and snoring like each breath was his last. Which I had to admit, they might have been.

The doorbell's chime echoed through the room. I twitched, then slid from my bed and pulled my robe on over my flannel pajamas as I strode to the front door. With luck, I'd stop the racket before it roused Stan.

George stood on my front porch in camo—cap, jacket, and sweatpants—peppery brows slashed in a perturbed line, stubble-riddled jaw set. "Is Stan ready?" he muttered gruffly.

"Ready for what?" I asked, still fighting a drowsy brain.

"Crabbing. When I talked with him on Friday, he said he'd go with me."

"What time Friday?" I asked, suddenly wide awake.

"Afternoon. We played eighteen holes."

"Stan didn't work on Friday?"

"Guess not."

Which meant he was still old Stan Friday afternoon. "What time did you finish golfing?" I probed.

George huffed and stretched his husky neck to gaze past me. "Around six. Then we had a couple of beers."

"Where did he go after that?"

"I'm not his babysitter." He paused to glare at me. "But what's that got to do with crabbing? Where is he?"

"He's asleep. I don't think he'll be going out with you this morning."

"Shi-it," he hissed. "I can't drive the boat and pull traps, too. Wake his lazy ass up, and tell him to shake a leg, or we're gonna miss high tide."

"I'm serious, George. He's not going crabbing with you."

"Why the hell not?" he barked.

I was surprised Denise hadn't already filled George in on Stan's affliction since she had a mouth on her like a stressed out Chihuahua. Of course, she and George might not be conversing at the moment. "Stan's not feeling well," I informed George. "He woke up early yesterday morning . . . sick. Somehow, he's lost his memory. He won't know who you are. Probably won't even know what a crab is."

In the bright rays from the porch light, I watched his jaw drop and his face turn a pasty hue. "Are you shittin' me?" he finally groused.

I shook my head, puzzled by George's reaction; it seemed extreme being that George only cared about George. He didn't give a rip about Stan's wellbeing.

"His memory you say? So he doesn't remember *anything*?" He wheezed the words, like he was dying and had something to say before he headed to the great beyond.

"Apparently."

His eyes blinked; his head twitched. "So why were the cops here?"

"Stan was so ill that I called 9-1-1. The sheriff showed up." I knew I'd stretched the truth but was confident I hadn't lied.

"That the only reason?"

"Pretty much." And it was. There was just that one other little issue—the doctored truffles. For now, I thought it best to keep that information in house, except for Laura, of course.

"I gotta talk to Stan. It's important," George demanded. "I've been tryin' to call him. He lost his phone?"

My mind slid back to the previous day, fast-forwarding through it. I didn't remember seeing or hearing Stan's phone at all during the day. "I don't know," I told him. "Stan was still feeling pretty lousy when I went to bed last night, so I'm not going to wake him up."

He shook his head, irritated. "Well damn. Unless I can drag

Denise out of bed, crabbing's a bust. Guess I'll check back later."

"Have a good one," I mumbled.

He raised his eyebrows and pursed his lips, then turned and stomped away.

I watched until he disappeared into the early morning mist, then shrugged off the odd conversation by chocking it up to George's self-absorption and bad manners. He and Denise really did deserve to put up with each other. It was just too bad they were doing it next door to me.

Sighing, I shut and locked the door, then tiptoed into the living room. I was wide awake now, so I might as well take advantage of the solitude and get some work done. First, I had something else to take care of.

Sharing a bed with a complete stranger, who was also my husband, had been unsettling. Not sure how to handle the situation the night before, I'd gone to bed early and left the particulars up to him. Evidently, he had no qualms about sleeping with strange women, because he'd crawled into our king-size bed sometime during the night.

Still, me stepping from the shower while he's using the toilet. Brushing our teeth side-by-side at his-and-her sinks, me in my not-so-hot cotton underwear, his loins wrapped in a bath towel. Him shaving while I'm slathering on makeup. Those were not places I wanted to go with a man I didn't know. I shivered at the visions and tiptoed toward the bedroom. If I was really quiet, I'd be dressed and out of there before he stirred.

Thirty minutes later, clad in jeans and a lightweight sweater, my hair in a damp ponytail, I stood in the kitchen and contemplated the dusting of coffee flecks in the canister, then opened the refrigerator and perused the meager pickings. I definitely needed to hit the grocery store. Not today though. It was Sunday, and weekend shopping on the Oregon coast was a marathon.

The omelet I'd whipped together the previous evening had taken all of the eggs and cheese, and there was no bread for toast. Or yogurt. I was not a cereal eater. And after the previous day's paltry meals, I was starved and craving a cup of coffee.

Given the choice of digging into Stan's stash of junk food or going out for breakfast, I chose the latter. Besides, it would give new Stan time to himself, to check out the house and snoop a bit. I'd lock my office door to keep him out of there.

I grabbed my cell phone off the kitchen desk, then froze. George had asked about Stan's phone. He said he'd been calling, so if it was in our bedroom, it would've been screeching some acid rock tune in the mega decibels.

My eyes slid over the kitchen counters. No phone. I strode to Stan's pile of remotes and pawed through them, then checked the Barcalounger cushions. Not there. Finally, I grabbed my keys and traipsed outside to check his truck.

A misty haze had settled in during the night, muting the sun's rays and enveloping me in dampness. From not far away, the ever-present, soothing rhythm of ocean waves rolled on.

A seagull's screech broke the serenity, and prickles zapped across my shoulders and neck. It wasn't just the seagull. Someone was watching me. I felt it deep inside with a certainty that refused to listen to reason. *Since you can't see more than a few feet, neither can a snoop*, I insisted.

Telling myself it was because of all of the weirdness going on, I took a deep breath, stiffened my spine, and opened the passenger door of Stan's blue Ford truck. Junk was piled on the seat, spilling onto the trashed floor—empty fast-food cartons and cans, discarded clothing and tools. And paper; lots of paper. No phone that I could see. I flicked my phone on and pressed his name. Nothing.

Then I noticed the boxes nearly hidden by the garbage in the back seat. I opened the rear door and wrestled one closer to peek inside. The paperwork looked familiar. So Stan *had* picked up my research materials in Newport after all. Score one brownie point for him.

I pulled the box from the truck and carried it into my office, then returned for the second. I wouldn't have time to examine all of the information before my meeting with Frank Ellis the following day but decided it might help me formulate ideas for our prospective conversation if I listened to the tape from our previous visit. Before I locked the office up tight, I grabbed my Sony recorder and an earphone. A quick tiptoe into my bedroom to grab my purse assured me that Stan still slept soundly. I'd probably be back home before he knew I was gone. I stuffed the recorder into my purse and headed for my car in the garage.

But what if I needed to get hold of Stan? Or he, me? I didn't want to awaken him, but a quick call from outside the bedroom might be okay. Standing in the middle of the living room, I flicked my phone on and pressed his name again, listening intently for the familiar racket.

Muffled noise trickled in from the deck. "Bingo," I whispered as I turned my phone off and made my way outside to search the area around Stan's cedar recliner. My eyes glided over the lime green and navy cushion and the gray decking. No phone. I lifted the cushion and searched the seat. Still no phone.

Huffing irritably, I flicked my phone on and pressed his name, yet again. Electric guitars shrieked from beyond the deck. I followed the noise and finally dug Stan's phone from hydrangea foliage bordering the steps. He must have dropped it there. But why? It didn't make sense.

"Why should it," I mumbled to myself. "Nothing else does."

A blinking green light indicated that he had unanswered texts or calls. I turned it on, and an image of Stan clutching a mammoth salmon appeared on the screen—real Stan, with bleary eyes and lots of scruffy stubble. Though covered with moisture, the phone appeared to be working okay.

Obviously, the only way to know for certain was to check it out. At least, I told myself that was the reason I pressed the *text* button. With nerves jumping and my heart racing, I peeked toward the bedroom door, then turned my back to it and perused the list of people who'd texted Stan—George, several guys whose names didn't ring any bells, a woman named Amber and, of course, me in my birthday texting frenzy. Since George had seemed anxious to speak with Stan, I thought it prudent to check his messages in case Stan might have something of his that needed to be returned. At least, that's how I rationalized my decision.

I tapped George's name, and a long list of unread messages popped up. I read the first: *we're on for Monday. Traps are set. Bring bait.* Just crabbing plans. Nothing that should have George in such a lather. It had been posted Friday evening at eight thirty-six, which seemed odd since George had planned to see Stan today. Why not just tell him in person?

The barrage of texts began at seven forty-three Saturday morning, not long after Sheriff Bronson had appeared at my front door. They were all one sentence probes: *what's going on over there? I'm counting on you, dude. We gotta talk. Hold it together.* The texts went on in the same vein, but George seemed to grow more and more anxious with each new message.

Why in the world was George so worked up over what was going on with Stan? It didn't make sense. I'd never seen anything to indicate they had a close relationship. Sure, the two men fished and golfed together, but that was only because Stan towed the line and didn't cross George. If Stan were out of the picture, George would shrug his shoulders and replace him with another minion.

I flicked back to the list of people who'd texted and studied Amber's name. My heart rate kicked up a notch. Did I dare? Not only that, but did I really want to know?

Suddenly, the phone screeched, blasting gnarly notes into the early morning stillness. My whole body twitched. Revved up by the adrenaline punch, I punched off the volume.

My eyes slid to my bedroom windows and then on around the deck. Sunlight battled through the haze, creating a diffused golden glow. The not-too-far-off growl of a diesel truck on the Coast Highway melded with the lull of ocean waves. No grass groomers this morning, not yet anyway.

I studied Stan's cedar recliner and thought of all that had transpired during the past thirty-six hours and the emotional squall I'd weathered so far. Was it over or was this just the calm before the real storm hit?

Whatever the case, when it came to Stan's infidelity, I knew I didn't have the fortitude to deal with the truth right now. I wasn't even sure that it mattered anymore. Something told me I had much bigger fish to fry.

I flicked his phone off and strode back into the house. There, I set it on the kitchen counter. It was Stan's; let him deal with it.

〰☼〰

Surrounded by breakfast smells—greasy bacon and hash browns, pancakes with maple syrup, and freshly baked cinnamon rolls—I nestled into my corner booth in The Galley, my favorite breakfast joint, my back to the sprinkle of diners. Fortunately, I'd beat the Sunday morning crowd. In another hour, the restaurant would be packed and overflowing onto the front porch.

Outside the smudged window, vehicles plodded by on Highway 101. The day had barely begun, and traffic was already heavy. Morning haze had retreated, though it still shrouded the ocean with a filmy layer of vapor. Sunrays warmed the sandy beaches, which would soon be crawling with beach buffs. Maybe after I finished breakfast, I'd head down there and join them. A brisk walk might help me make sense of the conundrum my life had become in the past twenty-four hours.

"Coffee?" someone inquired.

"Yes, please. Black," I murmured, turning my focus to an attractive woman who looked to be in her early thirties. Her strawberry blonde hair was pulled back into a tight ponytail, highlighting her perfect features. Distress oozed from her green eyes. "And I'll have a waffle and bacon, please. The bacon crisp."

She didn't move, just stood there like a foraging heron, chewing her lower lip. I turned my coffee mug over, hoping it would spur her on. She reached out a trembling hand and filled the mug, sloshing several drops onto the table. "I'm sorry," she gasped.

"It's fine," I assured her, wiping up the mess with a napkin I slid from under my silverware.

"Is someone joining you?"

"No, just me," I said, glancing up at her.

And still she stood.

"That's all," I prodded, pasting a smile on my face. "Just the waffle and bacon."

She swallowed hard, blinked and seemed to pull herself together. "Oh . . . uh . . . I'll tell Ginger. She's your waitress. I'm just pouring coffee." With that, she scurried off.

Maybe she was in training. That would explain her nervousness. Except that she looked familiar. Both Stan and I ate here often, and the more I thought about it, the more certain I became that she'd waited tables here for, at least, several weeks.

"Just more nuttiness," I whispered to myself before I sipped steaming coffee. It had to end soon, didn't it?

Rustling sounds and male voices piqued my interest. I glanced around the side of the booth to see three men in shorts and polos slide into the booth behind me—most likely, golfers. Two were middle-aged and one a little older. With my luck, they'd probably visit so loudly that I wouldn't be able to focus on the interview I'd taped with Frank Ellis.

I sighed and retrieved my voice recorder and earphone from my purse and set it near the edge of the table, safe from any more spillage. I'd made an attempt at going digital but had given it up when several important recordings had vanished into thin air due to my hi-tech ineptitude. It might not look professional, but for now, I was doing it the old fashioned way—with cassettes.

After turning it on to check the batteries, I plugged in the earphone and secured the other end in my ear. With the push of a button, Frank's gravelly voice filled my head: "It was my great-grandfather, Jesse Ellis, who came to Oregon. Left Missouri in the spring of 1848 and arrived here in late September with almost nothing left to claim as his own. Settled where downtown Portland is today.

"Course, back then most people called it Stump Town 'cause they'd cut down all the trees but left the stumps. You know, they had to whitewash those stumps, so people could see them at night. Otherwise they'd run right into them. There were that many.

"Course, Jesse downed his share of trees, too. He's the one who got the family started in the lumber industry. Good thing he did, too. At that time, he was one of the wealthiest men in Portland. Through the years, the business has continued to be profitable. Even helped us survive the rough times—fires and floods, a couple of world wars, even The Depression.

"Jesse and his family lived right down there in Portland. Course, most people did back then. Just put up with the flooding and unsanitary conditions and all that mud. The family didn't move up here until the early 1920s. That's when the business really took off.

"Everyone was moving to the outlying areas and building houses, and we were shipping a lot of lumber overseas. We even had our own dock down on Front Street for several years. It was all docks down there at that time, of course, not like it is now. Dangerous, too. A lot of bad things went on down near the waterfront back in the early days. Shanghaiing—they called it 'crimping'—was an everyday occurrence. A man would have a few drinks and wake up the next morning on some ship headed out to sea. But we'll talk about that later.

"Like I said, Jesse. . . ."

Frank droned on while I sipped coffee and pondered where our conversation might head the next day. Finally, a plate of food materialized in front of me, and I pushed the *pause* button to focus on my breakfast. A familiar waitress, most likely Ginger, filled my empty mug. I smiled at her and murmured, "Thank you," while I stuffed the earphone into my purse.

"Will there be anything else?"

"No, this looks delicious," I assured her. And it did. The bacon looked crisp, not burnt, the waffle golden brown and crispy and served with a small pitcher of warm syrup. It smelled good, too. My stomach growled in anticipation.

She set my bill on the table. "Enjoy," she chirped before she strode away.

I snapped off a bite of bacon and crunched on it while I prepared the waffle. Sweet saltiness filled my mouth. Perfect.

From the booth behind me, the deep drone of male voices reached my ears, one man's louder than the other two. It sounded like they were discussing some big construction project that was going in up north near Pacific City, but I couldn't be sure since I only heard tidbits of the conversation. Seeing as it dealt with the building industry, I eavesdropped while I ate, in hopes of hearing a company name. If Stan kept missing work, he'd soon be looking for a new job. Again.

Halfway through my waffle, I heard the rustling sounds of the men sliding from their booth and doing whatever it is men do when they're pulling themselves together. I forked a bite of waffle, but my hand stopped before it reached my mouth. Just like earlier that morning, chills spread across my shoulders. Someone was watching me.

I glanced up, and sure enough, the older man stood there glaring down at me. Warmth blossomed in my cheeks. My insides clenched. First the waitress, and now him. Did I smear my lipstick or have mascara running down my face? Maybe stress had caused ugly red welts to sprout.

I dropped the fork and forced a smile. "Do I know you?" I probed.

He flashed me a nasty look, harrumphed dismissively, and disappeared.

Brushing my fingers over my face, I peeked around the booth and watched him complete his transactions at the cash register near the front door. I knew I'd never seen that guy before, or the other two men, for that matter. So what was his problem?

Maybe he'd had grapefruit and a boiled egg for breakfast and begrudged me my waffles and bacon. Or maybe I reminded him of a girlfriend who'd dumped his butt—for good reason. Or maybe he was just ticked off at the world, and I was a handy punching bag.

But deep down, I fretted that somehow it had something to do with Stan.

I turned back to my table and fished a compact out of my purse, then opened it to examine my face. Dark brown eyes stared back at me. They slid over my features—petite nose, prominent cheeks, full lips, and rather pointed chin. Dark smudges beneath my eyes testified to my anxiety level. No unruly lipstick or mascara and no welts.

"Well, that's a relief," I murmured as I stuffed the compact back into my purse and searched for my earphone, figuring I might as well get some work done while I finished my breakfast.

Fifteen minutes later I gulped the chilled dregs from my coffee mug and dropped the earphone back into my purse, along with the voice recorder, while I played Frank's words over in my mind. During the session, he'd focused on his great-grandfather, Jesse Ellis—his life in Portland's early years, his marriage to a beautiful woman, whom he adored, and the rocky start to a family business that soon burgeoned into one of Oregon's leading lumber companies. With money that was soon rolling in, Jesse had purchased land cheap, lots of it, land that was covered with prime forest. Soon the family holdings stretched from Portland west and into the Coast Range.

Evidently, the family still owned a good deal of forested land. Brad Ellis had said that his son managed acreage here on the coast. Of course, unlike the early days, the federal government now had its hand in there, overseeing the use of that family land.

I sighed. Frank had a good deal to say on that topic, and it didn't flatter those in the political arena. I'd listened to him rant, biting my tongue so hard it hurt afterward. It seemed to me that, government interference or not, Frank Ellis Lumber thrived. Frank was a millionaire many times over. Unfortunately, I'd never had personal experience with being in that predicament. Still, I wondered how a man could be wealthy beyond belief and be ticked off because laws prevented him from making even more money.

But my opinion was irrelevant. It was Frank's story, not mine, and he paid me big bucks to put his words down on paper, not to make judgments. However, if his mind wanderings didn't get juicier soon, I might have to do some serious truth-stretching to move the tome from downright boring to bearable.

Thoughts of a humdrum life brought to mind my own, since that's exactly what it had been until now. If I discussed Stan's death, rebirth, and transformation, or all of the other crazy things going on right now, with anyone but Laura, people would point at me and gossip about me behind my back. And not in a good way.

I really didn't want to drag Laura into this zaniness any more than I had to. So it looked like, if I wanted answers, I'd have to track them down myself. Or not.

Did I really need those answers? Even peppered with wackiness, I had to admit that my life now was an improvement over what it had been two days ago. *So quit all of this complaining and worrying and enjoy what you've got,* I told myself.

After all, I had no problem with new Stan replacing old Stan. In truth, it was my dream come true.

The realization took root and blossomed within me, a warm glow that spoke of hope. I'd been given a gift. This was my chance to have a marriage like Benny and Laura's. I'd start by ordering breakfast to take home to my husband.

Pounds lighter, I gazed around the side of the booth, searching for Ginger. She bustled midst the packed tables along with the strawberry-blonde and an older waitress. A crowd near the front door eyeballed the dining room hungrily, waiting for their turn at breakfast. Caught up in my ruminations, I hadn't noticed that the chatter level had kicked up several notches. The place was hopping, and like the Ellis clan, I possessed prime acreage.

I snatched my purse and the bill and worked my way toward the cash register where a tall, gray-haired man stood smiling. "How was your breakfast, Polly?" he asked pleasantly.

"Perfect, as always," I informed him. "But I'd like to order something to take home to Stan."

He grabbed a pad and pen. "What would you like?"

"Well, he loves your cinnamon rolls." Or did he? New Stan might prefer a healthier alternative. "Scratch that. Make it ham and eggs with whole wheat toast—eggs scrambled—and a large coffee."

"You have him on a diet? Good luck with that."

I smiled. "No, he's just trying to watch what he eats. It probably won't last long."

My stomach clenched. *Please, let it last,* I silently prayed. I pulled my debit card from my wallet and handed it and the bill to him. "I'll wait outside," I informed him once the transaction was completed.

"It'll be about ten minutes. We'll bring it out."

Fortunately, the masses parted, so I could make my exit. Outside, a young couple murmured together, arms locked around each other, and a set of what must be grandparents corralled two squirmy boys. I separated myself from them at the end of the building and gazed across the highway to where the ocean waves peeked between a couple of storefronts.

The sky was a clear blue, sprinkled with wispy clouds and several colorful kites. A light breeze blew from the north and made me glad I'd worn a sweater. After several gorgeous days, it looked like we might be heading into a cooling trend. Our typical western Oregon weather—drizzle.

A car pulled into the parking lot, drawing my attention. I watched three young women climb out of an orange Jeep Wrangler, clothed in college gear and flip-flops, hair in ponytails. My mind shot to my daughter Sara, and my heart twisted. No matter what she claimed, I knew she'd taken the Oregon State job to avoid another summer of Stan's antagonism and tirades. The two of them were like a couple of feral cats, constantly lashing out at each other, claws extended and fangs gnashing. With my attempts to maintain some semblance of peace, I was constantly trapped between them.

Yes, I'd spent too many summer evenings on Laura's back porch guzzling margaritas, trying to drown the pain from watching the two people I cared most about battle each other. Though I hated to admit it, I'd been relieved when Sara had told me she wouldn't be home this summer. But I missed her, and I missed what we'd once shared—a close friendship that I'd thought was indestructible.

Tears stung my eyes. A fireball burned in my throat. Maybe new Stan would be my ticket to getting my daughter back. "Please, let it happen," I whispered as the chattering girls passed by me and disappeared inside the restaurant.

Suddenly, chilly shivers rushed through me. For the third time that morning, I experienced that same creepy feeling—someone was watching me. My pulse skyrocketed. I rubbed my arms and squinted across the street to scan in front of the hodgepodge of businesses that bordered the highway. No pair of eyes appeared to be staring at me. My eyes flicked left to study the restaurant entrance. The three girls had joined the other two groups awaiting their tables, all of them too caught up in each other to notice me. A glance to my rear assured me no one was peering out at me through a window.

That left the parking lot. I turned to it and scrutinized the medley of automobiles facing me. Of course, the orange Jeep was empty as was the silver sedan next to it. My Sonata was next, followed by a mammoth canopied truck—empty. I couldn't see beyond it. My gaze slid over to the vehicles on the other side of the lot and froze on a sporty-looking black car. The driver had backed it into the space. He sat behind the steering wheel, his eyes hidden behind sunglasses.

Get a grip, Polly. That doesn't mean he's watching you, I told myself. Like me, he was probably avoiding the noisy dining room while he waited for a takeout order. I just happened to be in his line-of-sight to the front door.

"Here's your order."

I jumped about a foot and twirled around to meet the strawberry-blonde's troubled eyes. "Oh, thank you," I murmured, grasping the bag and cup of coffee.

She stood there staring at me in that odd way again. "For your husband?" she asked.

"Uh . . . yes. You know him?"

"I've seen you in The Galley with him. It's nice you're taking him breakfast." And still she stood.

Maybe she was having husband problems and envied me because of something I didn't actually have—a happy marriage. I checked her left hand. No wedding ring. Well maybe boyfriend troubles then.

"I better get this home to him before it gets cold," I muttered before I turned and carted Stan's breakfast to my car.

When I slid into the driver's seat, I glanced back. She was still planted there, her fretful eyes fastened on me.

"What a weird morning," I uttered through clenched teeth, determined to slough off the bad vibes coursing through me. I closed my eyes, breathed deeply, and assured myself it was only coincidence and my overactive imagination—too many Lifetime movies, too many true crime TV shows, and too many mystery novels.

Still, as I drove out of the parking lot, I glanced right and swore a pair of sunglass-shrouded eyes zeroed in on me.

෴ ✿ ෴

What if old Stan is back? The question hounded me as I crawled down the Coast Highway with a zillion other vehicles. It had me tied into tight knots by the time I pulled into my garage.

"Then you're back where you started, that's all," I murmured, trying to convince myself I really could return to that bleak, volatile existence. I rubbed my forehead, an attempt to relieve the building pressure, then shook my head resignedly. "Oh, Polly, who are you kidding? You know you can't go back to old Stan."

I knew it, but still I fabricated excuses—Stan would learn from his mistakes. I needed to be more patient and understanding. Some serious couple's counseling would help. As always, the list went on and on *ad nauseam*. To stop it, I finally growled, exasperated with myself for being such a flake.

"Well, the only way to find out is to get your butt into that house," I snapped.

After a fortifying breath, I grabbed my purse and Stan's breakfast and stepped cautiously into the kitchen. No Stan.

I set the bag and coffee on the counter and my purse on the desk next to a check. "What the heck?" I muttered as I picked the check up to examine it closely. It was signed by Phil, and it was made out to Stan. I actually felt my eyes pop and my stomach punch my throat when I read the amount—twenty-five thousand dollars!

Why in the world would Phil give Stan a check in the first place, let alone one for that kind of money? Phil detested Stan, and Stan, Phil. The two men weren't even civil to each other.

Woman on a mission, I went in search of Stan and eventually found him lounging on the deck, nose in a magazine with a giant fish on the cover, which was so old Stan that it kicked my heart rate to the top of the charts. He glanced up when I opened the door, but the look on his face spoke only of mild curiosity.

I braced myself for whatever. "Where did this check come from?" I asked, my voice so strained it squeaked.

His eyes narrowed, studying me. "A guy next door brought it over."

"Phil?" I probed, searching the empty deck to my right.

"In his forties. Six feet or so. Looks like he lives at the gym. Maybe Latino."

Relief swept through me so quickly it left me wobbling. Old Stan used numerous words to describe Phil. Never *Latino*. "Did he say why?"

Stan shrugged and lifted his brows. "No. I figured you'd know."

Deep in my gut, I knew old Stan would know the answer to my question. But he wasn't here now. "Well what did he say?"

"Nothing. I noticed a couple of men over there earlier," he said, nodding his head at the deck next door. "They pretended to water those flowers, but a plant can only consume so much water. So I waved to them. The red-haired guy. . . ."

"Javier."

His dark eyebrows arched higher. "Javier?"

"Yes. When Javier moved in with Phil, he decided to get in touch with his Latino heritage. Turns out it was only a tiny twig back eons ago, but he embraced it and changed his name from Connor to Javier. Then he took Phil's last name."

Stan glanced next door, paused, then turned back. I braced for old Stan's hateful rant about Phil and Javier's relationship.

Instead, he appeared to shake off something, then continued with his story. "Well, Javier raised a fist at me and looked like he was going to shoulder his oozie and finish what those chocolates didn't. They both disappeared into the house, and a few minutes later Phil marched over here and threw that check at me."

"And he didn't say anything?" Like maybe something about your transformation?

Stan shook his head. "Nope. And the way he looked at me, I didn't push it. Afraid he'd pull out his Bowie knife and gut me." He flashed me an appealing smile and added, "I didn't want you to come home to that."

"This isn't funny," I warned him. "I'm having one of the weirdest mornings of my life, and you're making jokes?" Though I had to admit that it didn't come close to the previous morning's nuttiness.

His eyes turned to stone. "What happened?"

He kept throwing me off balance with his responses, which were so unlike those of his former self. It was unsettling, and it messed with my brain.

"First, George rang the doorbell before the sun was up," I told him. "He claims you played golf with him Friday afternoon—and by the way, why weren't you working? He said you were supposed to go crabbing with him this morning."

"George?"

"Denise's husband."

His lips curved into a crooked smile. "The lady with the enchiladas?"

"Yes," I said, ignoring the double entendre. "They're our neighbors to the north. George is the guy with the boat. The guy you don't want to tick off—remember? Only he was plenty ticked off when he left here this morning. He got really upset when I informed him that you've lost your memory. Said he had to talk with you, that it was important."

"I think I did talk to him—big, burly guy. Gruff. Looks like someone you'd want with you if you were lost in the wilderness?"

I nodded. "That's George."

Voices on the golf course grabbed my attention. A couple of well-baked, middle-aged ladies in knee-length shorts, sleeveless tops, and visors pulled rolling golf carts. One of them stopped, drew a club, and swatted a ball while the other waited. I watched them walk away, chatting. A couple of golf carts whirred down the asphalt trail and passed them.

"He dropped by this morning. Evidently, I'm going crabbing with him tomorrow. I'm supposed to bring bait. He was pretty adamant about that. Do we have any?"

Stan's voice drew me back to our conversation. "I don't think so, but don't you have to work?"

"Work, huh? What do I do?" He looked totally confused.

"Construction. You're working on a restaurant down south of Newport—Seal Rock, I think. The cab of your truck is trashed with reams of paper and other stuff too gross to mention. Maybe you'll find a clue there. Your keys are on the desk in the kitchen.

"Oh, and don't forget to cancel with George, or he'll be ringing our doorbell before sunrise tomorrow morning, too."

He shut his lids and rubbed the bridge between his eyes. Sympathy pains bloomed inside me. With memory issues plaguing him, this had to be a lot to take in—acquaintances he doesn't recognize, shaky relationships, and unfamiliar job. "You do know how to saw a board and hammer a nail?" I hoped.

"I think I can handle it," he muttered. "Is there a computer I can use? The one in the office appears to be off limits."

"That's because it's mine. Yours is in your toy room."

His look said he didn't have a clue what I was talking about.

"One of the back bedrooms—the one that looks like it's home to a hoarder. Oh, and I found your phone in that hydrangea over there," I said, pointing. "Do you know how it got there?"

He studied the bush in question as if it held the secret to his mind-bending experience. "Nope," he finally uttered, shaking his head. "But I'm glad you found it. Maybe something on it will kick-start my memory."

"Maybe," I mumbled, praying it wouldn't. I thought it best not to mention that I'd snooped on his cell, then considered bringing up the waitress and the man who had acted so strange but decided against them, too. I didn't want to push Stan over the edge. "Do you have your wallet?"

He nodded, then huffed. "Well I guess I'll check out my truck. Then maybe I'll pick up some groceries, so I can eat." He pushed himself out of his recliner. "You gonna be around?"

I noticed he was back in baggy cargo shorts. He must've belted them tightly, because there was a big bulge circling his middle beneath his *Feelin' Clammy?* tee-shirt. His feet remained bare. He looked showered and shaved.

"Uh-huh. I have some work to do," I assured him. My eyes dropped to the check, and my stomach tightened. "But first I'm gonna run next door and find out what this check's all about."

"You want me to come with you?"

My throat tightened. I'd forgotten what it was like to have a man at my back. "No. It'd make things tense," I explained. "Phil and Javier like me. You, not so much. That's why this check makes no sense at all."

"I'm here if you need me."

My eyes burned. "Thanks. Oh, and don't worry about the groceries. I'll get them when the tourist infestation lets up. I brought you breakfast. It's on the kitchen counter."

He studied me long and hard. "Thank you."

I shrugged. "You're welcome."

When he disappeared into the house, I let out my breath. *Polly. Polly. Polly,* I warned myself, *don't get too attached to that guy. He could disappear at any moment.*

༝ ✿ ༝

Javier gazed at me through the French door, then opened it. His smile was too tight, his eyes too edgy.

"Polly, come here girl," he chirped, drawing me into a warm hug. "I hear you need some lovin'. Laura didn't go into detail, but according to her text, your life's a fiery hellhole." He pushed me away to arms' length and studied me, concern lining his freckled face. "I didn't think it could get any worse, but evidently, it has, huh?"

Fighting the threat of tears, I nodded and waved Phil's check. "I need to talk with Phil."

I didn't think Javier's face could be any paler than its natural hue, but it turned a deathly pallor. He took a step back, grasped his chest, and gasped, "Where did you get that?"

"From Stan. Phil gave it to him. Where is he?" I asked, shaky with the realization that this was going to be worse than I'd thought.

Javier's bright green eyes flicked the room like a darting hummingbird before they settled back on me. "He went to the shop to get some work done."

"Well, I guess you'll have to explain it then. And from that look on your face, my hellhole's about to get hotter."

He shook his head, an incredulous expression on his face. "I don't get it. Why did Stan give that to you? It doesn't make any sense at all."

As does my life of late, I wanted to confess. But where to start? "Stan's having memory issues," I finally admitted. "He doesn't recognize anyone, and he doesn't remember anything about his life before yesterday morning . . . except *maybe* me. Or so he says."

"Do you believe him?" Clearly, Javier didn't.

"I think so."

"So that's the reason for the ambulance ride?"

"Uh-huh. Well, part of it, anyway," I admitted, wondering how much Laura had told him.

"Come in," he said, motioning me into his artfully decorated living room and on into his over-the-top gourmet kitchen. Honestly, the place belonged between the covers of *House Beautiful*—all polished wood and leather and various forms of metal, much of it handcrafted by Phil. "As you can see, I'm making Phil a strawberry pie. He spotted them at a roadside stand on the drive back from Ashland. Gorgeous, aren't they?"

A flawless golden brown pie crust sat on the bronze countertop, and glossy, plump strawberries drained in a strainer in the copper sink. Javier picked up a paring knife and sliced strawberries into the crust. He looked like he belonged on one of those cooking shows on "Food Network" with his perfect hair, perfect body, and perfect clothes.

"Javier, did you leave some chocolate truffles by my front door on Friday?" I asked him.

"Truffles?" His eyes drifted up to probe mine. "You mean for your birthday? No. But I can't believe I didn't think of it. You love chocolate, and it's the one thing your gluttonous husband wouldn't devour before you got to them."

"That's just it. He did devour them—three of them—and they were loaded with Triazolam. It's a sedative. Just one put me out for hours, so you can imagine what three of them did to Stan."

His face literally sagged. "And you thought they were from me?"

"No," I assured him, relieved, choosing not to mention that it was Laura who'd planted the seed. "But the sheriff thinks they were homemade, and you're the only person I know who could've created those gorgeous truffles and packaged them so elegantly."

"Well, it's sweet of you to say that . . . I think," he mumbled before he returned to his slicing. "But who would leave something like that for you? I mean, that's just awful. No wonder Laura was so freaked out. Are you okay?"

I nodded. "I have no idea who did it. I hoped you'd made them, and someone else had seen them by my door and doctored them up. Maybe the sheriff will figure it out."

"If Stan ate three of the things—and I'm seriously wishing he'd eaten twice that many—for sure, he forgot he detests chocolate. But you think he's forgotten other things, too, huh?"

"Yeah, pretty much everything." When it came to Stan's memory loss, I really didn't expect Javier to take my word on it. He'd need some up-close time with Stan. Then he'd see the changes in Stan's behavior and maybe, like me, write them off as the aftereffects of a drug overdose. But what about Stan's appearance? I really didn't want to bring up his possible death and rebirth, so what might explain those improvements? Maybe Javier wouldn't notice.

Who was I kidding? Javier noticed when I retained a drop of water.

I took a deep breath and plunged in. "Okay, Javier. This is for your ears only. You can't even tell Phil. Promise."

His eyes shot up. "Oh, my. You're serious," he murmured, plopping a strawberry into his mouth. He raised his small finger. "Okay. Pinkie promise."

"You might think I'm nuts, but I'm gonna tell you anyway because you're my friend, and I need you to figure out what's going on." I paused to work up the nerve to ask him to believe in an incident when I wasn't even sure I did. Javier stuck another strawberry into his mouth and stared at me expectantly.

"Well, Friday night I woke up in the middle of the night, and I saw Stan in his recliner on the deck. I went out to wake him up, and I swear he was as dead as that sea lion we found on the beach last fall."

He blinked several times and worked his lips, ogling me far too long before he responded. "Yuck. That was so gross—bloated and smelly and covered with tiny little feasting creatures."

"Yes, well Stan was, too," I assured him. "Not quite that bad, but he was definitely kind of bloaty, and he felt cold and waxy. Not breathing. No pulse. I know he was dead."

"Well, now you're creeping me out 'cause that just can't be. I saw the dirty degenerate with my own two eyes, in his recliner on your deck, wearing one of his tacky tee-shirts and reading one of his fishy magazines. Just like every Sunday morning." He picked up another berry and seemed to consider it before he sliced it into the crust.

"I know. That's because the next morning he was alive—in rough shape but very much alive. But it's like he returned back to life a brand new man. Not only is his memory gone, but he's nice—really nice. And clueless. He doesn't know why Phil dropped this check in his lap."

The check! It had slipped my mind. "And speaking of this check, why *did* Phil give him a check for twenty-five-thousand dollars?"

Javier's lids dropped. He chewed on his lower lip and rubbed his chin with his free hand before he took a deep breath, studied me, and uttered, "Polly girl, do you honestly believe Stan's memory is gone?"

My head seemed to nod on its own accord. "Yes, I really do. I don't know why, but he seems totally lost."

"Do you think he'll get it back?"

I shrugged. "I hope not." At this point, it was more than hope. I was on a mission to keep this newer, improved version of my husband alive.

"What do the doctors say?"

"I don't think he told them. He seems happy to just float along in oblivion. And I'm not going to push any recollections. This might seem really naïve, but I like new Stan, and I'm going to do everything I can to keep him here."

Doubt still oozed from his features. "So, the check?" I prodded.

He huffed and shook the knife at me. "I'm putting my ass on the line here, so you have to promise that you won't say a word to anyone. Not Laura. Not Sara. Not this new Stan you seem so sure of. And especially not that blabbermouth Denise. I swear, if Phil finds out I snitched on him, I'll come after you with more than doctored truffles."

My insides clenched. What in the heck had Stan been up to? I raised my little finger. "Pinkie swear," I murmured.

"I mean it, Polly. You have to keep your mouth shut, no matter what happens. If your deadbeat husband gets his memory back or causes any flack about that check, you need to stay out of it and let him and Phil work things out."

"Okay, I promise."

He closed his eyes and huffed again, then blurted, "Stan was blackmailing Phil."

"Blackmailing him?" I gasped, breathless.

"Yes. When Phil was a kid, he lived in the L.A. area, and he was deeply involved in the gang culture—drugs, theft, violence, pretty much everything you think of when you think of gangs."

"Phil was in a gang? Wow. I would've never guessed." The whole notion clashed with everything I believed about gentle, soft-spoken, kind Phil.

"I know, but he was," he assured me, his tone now firm. "And he did a lot of horrible things, so revolting that he won't talk about it. That's why he spends so much time at his shop. Welding seems to be an outlet for his feelings of self-disgust. He's tried to put it all behind him, but it's a struggle.

"He was really making progress." He paused, and anger flickered in his eyes. When he spoke again, it was through clenched teeth. "Then a couple of months ago, that depraved monster you call your husband cornered Phil with a proposition he couldn't refuse—pay up or he'd spill the beans about Phil's past."

"Oh, dear lord," I whispered, suddenly lightheaded. "Poor Phil. Stan finally went too far."

"He went too far long before that, Polly. You just won't open your eyes and see what's right in front of you. Why do you think Phil has always detested Stan? It's because Stan's a living, breathing reminder of what he used to be—albeit Stan's much more conniving."

"He's my husband, Javier. I promised to stand by him." It was my standard comeback, and it had worn thin. Even I wasn't convinced.

He jabbed the knife again. "And when does it stop? When he finally kills someone, like Phil did?"

I grabbed the bronze counter for support. "Phil killed someone?"

"He did, and it's what finally knocked some sense into him." Javier sighed and returned to his berry slicing. "He was seventeen at the time, and he spent twenty-three years in prison, mastering the art of welding and figuring out how he was going to make a new life for himself once he got out.

"When he was free, he changed his name, moved up to Oregon, and settled here on the coast. In no time, he made a name for himself in the art world. He has respect, money, prestige . . . me. What more could a guy ask for, right?"

He gazed at me with sad eyes. "Only, somehow Stan found out about Phil's previous life and rubbed it in his face. Phil will do anything to keep his past a secret. If the truth comes out, he could lose everything, except me, of course—I'd never desert him. Thus, that check you have in your hand."

"I'm so sorry, Javier." Beyond sorry. Stan had been cruel and callous, and he'd tossed me onto a killer carnival ride that nauseated me. "I honestly had no idea. I don't think new Stan does either."

"Of course, you didn't. We knew that. But we couldn't risk telling you. If this got out, it'd spread faster than that flu bug that swept through here in February. Phil's life would be ruined." He jabbed the knife again to emphasize his words. "That's why you have to keep your promise and not breathe a word to anyone."

"I won't. Triple pinky swear," I promised, laying the check on the countertop. "The check is yours. Hide it. Burn it. Give it to Phil. Do what you think is best. For now, Stan and I know nothing about Phil's gang days or prison time. If old Stan returns—and please, please don't let that happen—we'll deal with whatever happens."

Javier studied the check, then nodded and sliced berries.

My stomach heaved with a new thought. "There weren't any other checks, were there?"

"No, but I'm sure this wouldn't have been the last one."

He sliced the last berry, then dropped the knife and walked to the refrigerator to pull a small saucepan from it. While I replayed Javier's words in my mind and wondered how this might play out if Stan's memory returned, I watched him carefully pour glistening red syrup over the mounded strawberries in the crust.

"Oh, lordy. What am I gonna do if old Stan does return?" I finally blurted.

His intense gaze slammed against mine. "You're gonna dump his ass, that's what you're gonna do," he commanded. "It's way past time to think about you instead of that worthless piece of shit."

"And I'll be alone," I whispered, fingers of fear clawing inside me. I couldn't go back to that—back to the time when I was so young, a widow and new mother with no close friends or family nearby. Back to the time when I was so alone.

"Not alone. Phil and I, Laura, Sara, and a lot of your other friends—we're all here for you."

"I know, but it's not the same." I knew I sounded pathetic. I knew Javier was right. Still, I grasped at straws. "If I divorce Stan, he gets half of everything I own, including my house. I'm not sure I can pull together enough money to buy him out, so I might have to move. And Sara, it's time for her to move on and live her own life."

"You're not dumping us, too, Polly. Whether you live here or somewhere else, we'll always be a part of your life, a life that'll be a hell of a lot better than the one you have now."

Javier scraped the sides of the pan with a spatula, then smoothed the top of the pie. He licked the spatula while he eyeballed me.

"But maybe the one I have now will get better," I implored.

"Well, it certainly couldn't get worse. You've got a husband who treats you like dirt, verbally abuses you, cheats on you, doesn't give a shit about your feelings, is a lazy slob, and has. . . ."

"Cheats on me?" I choked, grabbing my stomach to keep from hurling all over Javier's beautiful pie.

He shook his head and huffed. "Oh, dear lord. You're such a Pollyanna. You really didn't know?"

"Who is she?" I managed to whisper.

"Well I don't have a list of names, but Phil and I get out and about, and we see things. And even when we stay home, we have a clear view of your deck."

"Meaning?"

He just stood there and stared at me, licking his spoon, eyes sympathetic.

"Out with it," I begged, bracing myself.

"Denise. We've caught the two of them going at it several times."

"Stan and Denise?" Images of the two of them played through my mind. I closed my eyes and fought my heaving stomach. Anyone but Denise. Although, Javier had implied that it was everyone *and* Denise.

"I'm sorry. I honestly thought you knew," Javier offered.

I watched him walk the pie to the refrigerator and stuff it inside. "I didn't think he'd jeopardize his relationship with George," I reasoned. Suddenly, Denise's visit the previous evening made so much sense.

"Maybe George doesn't know, or maybe he just doesn't care," Javier offered.

"Of course, he cares. She's his wife."

He shook his head. "You're being Pollyanna again. You give them all way more credit than they deserve. Just because you have high moral standards, doesn't mean they do, too."

I knew he was right. It was in my nature to expect more from people than I usually got in return. It always led to hurt and disappointment, sometimes even anger. I never seemed to learn from it, though.

"I'm feeling kind of sick. I think I need to lie down for a while and process all of this," I told him.

With a sigh, he pulled me into a lengthy hug, then pushed back and gazed into my eyes. "Are you gonna be okay."

He looked so concerned that I wanted to reassure him. "Oh, yeah. It's just difficult to deal with what's been going on and accept that I've been oblivious to much of it. You're right; I am a Pollyanna. And now I have this brand new Stan who's just as oblivious as I was to the mess he created. I need to decide how I'm going to handle all of this."

CHAPTER 5

I clutched the steering wheel with both hands, leaning forward over it as if it would keep my Sonata from rolling back down the hill, and wove my way up the narrow, winding street. Sighting a widening in the road, I pulled as close to the curb as possible, then put the car in park. A black sports sedan and a white Mini Cooper sped past.

Portland stretched out below me in all its mid-morning splendor—bright sun reflecting off blocks of glass and steel and vehicles streaming down a network of streets like busy ants and crawling over the hodgepodge of bridges that arched over the shimmering Willamette River. Mt. Hood stood, snow-capped and serene, in the distance, keeping watch over its empire.

Frank Ellis probably took this breathtaking view for granted. After all, he'd grown up with it. He'd never been saddled with money worries or fear of being alone. He had it all—a mansion in prestigious Kings Heights, plenty of kinfolk, and enough money to do whatever the heck he felt like doing.

"Get over it, Polly," I muttered, sick to death of brooding about my pathetic life. At least it wasn't as boring as Frank's ho-hum life story. Today I needed to focus on digging something juicy out of his eighty-some-years-old recollections, not mooning over my own forty years.

The two-hour drive from Lincoln City to Portland had been an emotional roller coaster. My alarm had pulled me out of a troubled sleep early, and I'd showered and dressed hurriedly in navy slacks and a slinky white blouse, hoping to avoid contact with Stan, who was no longer my bedmate. I'd banished him to his toy room. Good riddance.

Breathing a sigh of relief when I didn't spot him that morning, I'd rushed to my car with a briefcase stuffed with interview paraphernalia and backed out of the garage.

It was the crunching sound that halted me. I gazed through my window at the open passenger door on Stan's flashy blue truck, then opened the door to get a better look. Sure enough, the window was now shattered chunks of glass on the driveway and passenger seat.

"*Grrr,*" I growled. Since Stan slept at the front of the house now, surely he'd heard the truck's alarm bellowing. Whatever the case, his battery was most likely dead.

I slid from my Sonata and crunched through the glass to inspect the cab. Except for the open glove compartment and a hefty metal toolbox, there wasn't much to see. Stan had cleaned several boxes of garbage out of it the previous day. I'd found him sorting through the clutter at the kitchen table when I'd returned from my visit with Javier. I hadn't asked what he'd discovered in the mess. I didn't want to talk to him, and I didn't want to know.

Huffing, thoroughly annoyed with the shattered window, I slammed the truck door shut and marched back into the house and down the hall to pound on Stan's cracked door. He tugged the door open and stood in baggy blue boxers with the kitten clutched in one hand, staring at me and rubbing his bleary eyes. My gaze gravitated to his bare chest and froze. New Stan had muscles—lots of them—and abs. What had happened to his man-boobs, pudgy belly, and love handles?

"You wanted something?" he groused.

I tugged my eyes up to meet his. "Uh . . . yes . . . uh, someone broke into your truck last night. The battery's probably dead, and you're missing a window. I've gotta get on the road, so you'll have to deal with it before you can go to work. We have Triple-A. There should be a card in your wallet." Out of air, I grabbed a breath before I asked, "Can you handle it?"

He smiled. "No problem."

The smile messed with my mind. "Remember to set the security alarm," I reminded him before I made my way back to my car.

But that was a couple of hours and a lot of miles ago. Now I gazed at the glistening peak in the distance and reflected on Stan's pearly whites. Even his smile was different, not conniving and sneering like old Stan's, but open and amused. It made me want to smile, too—sometimes.

Though not the previous afternoon, when I'd stomped into his toy room with his toothbrush, razor, and a week's worth of clothing. After an hour of lying on my bed replaying Javier's heart-wrenching words, I'd worked up an impressive rage. It didn't matter which Stan had done the dirty deeds, one of them was going to pay.

I'd dropped his supplies on the cluttered couch and turned to face him, hoping my look was as deadly as it felt. Hands poised over the computer keyboard, he studied me, brows arched high, questioning.

"New sleeping arrangements," I hissed. "You're here. I'm there. Don't cross the line."

His brows dropped into a frown. "And I did something to deserve this?"

"Uh-huh. You did Denise."

"Denise? The lady with the enchiladas?" At least, he had the good sense to blush.

"The highly enhanced enchiladas."

"Are you sure?"

"Darn sure. I saw her before she purchased them. Sure of the other, too, since Phil and Javier watched the two of you going at it on our deck . . . several times. Poor guys. Lord only knows how many other people got a peep show."

His lips curved into a smile. "Evidently, George didn't. I'm still his fishing buddy."

"And you need to keep it that way," I snapped. "No more Denise."

"No problem," he murmured.

I broke eye contact and scanned the room, biting my tongue against the urge to confront him about Phil's check. Fishing and hunting supplies dangled on the walls and lolled on shelves, overflowing onto the floor to join the empty beer bottles and food wrappers and the crusty dishes. My gaze zeroed in on his computer screen, and he moved to block my view. Still, I'd seen the email page. He might not remember anything else, but he certainly knew his password.

Fighting the urge to challenge him about that, too, I muttered, "If you clean that junk off the couch, it'll fold out into a bed. Hunt up your own bedding," and left his room.

And as I sat and gazed at Mt. Hood twenty-four hours later, I was still fried about Stan's infidelity. Dammit! I'd trusted the guy. After all the crap I'd taken from him, why'd he have to betray me like that . . . and with Denise?

Why couldn't I be more like that mountain—cool, composed,

regal? The ice queen. Just throw me whatever you've got. I'll weather it all and not feel a thing.

Why did I let Stan get to me? Even more important, why did I cling to something not worth clinging to—him?

I growled again and rubbed my face, trying to scrub my mind clean, to fill it with warm thoughts of Frank Ellis and his perfect home and family. A quick glance in the mirror assured me I hadn't smeared my mascara or blush, but my lips looked pastier than Denise's pie crust. I scribbled Denise from my mind, then pulled a tube of *Smoky Berry* lipstick from my purse and slathered it on.

Eyeing my straight, shoulder-length hair, a vision of Denise's thick, fiery red mane popped before my eyes. "Scratch that," I hissed, shaking the image away, then fluffing my locks with the tips of my fingers. I looked like I'd hiked ten miles through a windstorm, so I smoothed the tresses back into place. It was hopeless. I'd never be a Denise—not even close.

"Enough already, Polly. You *definitely* don't want to be Denise." I muttered as I shifted the car to drive and pulled onto the street to wind my way up the hill.

This area of Portland was plastered with a medley of upper end homes that clung to the steep hillside. In the early 1900s, the slope had been terraced. Then construction began. The paved streets running to and from the million-plus-dollar homes snaked up the incline, a tangle of curves and switchbacks held together by short straight stretches. Parking space on the narrow road was limited.

Focused on watching for street signs, I rounded my second switchback and nearly ran into the left taillight of a black sedan that was parked with its rear-end in the road. I honked loudly and glared at the man in the driver's seat as I drove past. Something about him sparked a memory, but I sloughed it off to mentally prepare myself for my upcoming interview with Frank.

His house was in the uppermost section of the neighborhood. Forest Park, the largest urban forest in the United States, stretched from his backyard. I spotted a house I recognized and made a left turn. Frank's Arts and Crafts style manse rose before me, three stories of gray wood and stone, unpretentious but impressive.

I pulled in beside a panel and keyed in the pass code I'd been given. Black iron gates swung inward. Pressing hard on the gas pedal, I climbed the steep driveway, then rounded the house to park in front of the five-car garage. A pristine silver Mercedes lounged next to me.

"Don't get any ideas," I warned my red Sonata. "He's too pretentious for us."

After a quick check for lipstick smudges in the mirror, I grabbed my purse and briefcase and strode purposefully to the front door. The air was ripe with the sweet, musky fragrance of rose blossoms. Bees buzzed around the bloom-laden bushes.

"Ah, Polly. Frank has been asking about you," Marta, the lady who always answered the door, greeted me with her deep, husky voice.

Having no experience with housekeepers and such, I still hadn't figured out who exactly she was. As always, she looked flawless in her coordinated slacks ensemble, with her silver hair sprayed into a compliant Pageboy. On previous visits, I'd caught her scrubbing a sink and dusting the front hall. I hadn't yet worked up the nerve to ask Frank if she was hired help or his special woman friend. Today, bakery smells clung to her.

Since promptness was something I prided myself on, I didn't respond to her comment. I knew I'd arrived right on time. "It's nice to see you, Marta," I said, noting that she didn't appear all that happy to see me. "And what a beautiful day to be up here. The view is amazing."

"Yes, we've been enjoying it," she uttered, her intense gaze studying me. "Did you have a nice birthday? Forty can be a tough one."

How in the world did Marta know I'd just turned forty? I hadn't mentioned it to Frank or anyone else in this house. Remembering the Mercedes, I glanced around. Hopefully, Brad Ellis wasn't here to interfere with my quest for scandal. There was no sign of him.

"It was fine," I lied.

Surprise flickered in those probing eyes. "Oh, good. Frank's in the family area. Nell's with him." She took off, and I followed, pondering why Frank's daughter picked this particular day for a visit.

As we walked through the bowels of the huge house, my gaze stroked the beautifully aged wood and the gorgeous antique furnishings. Frank's grandfather had built this house in 1922, and Frank and his father had grown up here. The place reeked of times gone by, of intrigue and secrets. If only I'd unearth them.

Muted voices grew louder as we stepped into a large room with a wall of windows that must've spanned a good portion of the front of the house. "Wow!" I whispered, riveted on the panoramic view before me. I stepped forward. If I reached out, I knew I could touch Mt. Hood's icy peak. It stood stark against the cerulean sky. Below it, verdant slopes trailed toward me to meld with manmade structures.

"Yes, the air's so clear today that everything's much brighter. More like it used to be," I heard Frank's voice say.

Heat rushed to my cheeks. I turned to face him and a woman who I knew was forty-six, though she could pass for ten years younger. She'd outfitted her trim body for yoga. Her blonde hair was pulled back in a tight ponytail. Her face screamed Botox. She and her father both stood a few feet from me.

"I'm sorry. I didn't mean to be rude. The view is just so incredible," I explained. "It's nice to see you Frank."

He smiled, and his blue eyes sparkled. "You, too, Polly. I've been looking forward to our session today. This is my daughter Nell, mother of my two beautiful granddaughters. Nell, Polly Morton."

"Nice to meet you," I murmured, unsure of her last name and not wanting to address her as "Nell."

She attempted a smile, but parts of her face didn't budge. "Likewise," she murmured, her voice silky smooth and cultured. "Dad seems to be enjoying his time with you. I hope he's not yammering on too much about our boring lives. Really, I can't imagine there's anything worth writing about."

There wasn't, but I couldn't tell her that. So I hedged. "Oh, you'd be surprised at what enthralls readers, especially when it involves one of the area's early lumber baron families. History buffs eat up this kind of stuff."

Her jaw dropped. Sparks flickered in her dark eyes. "History buffs? Surely you're not digging into the family archives? There's nothing back there that would interest anyone. Just the same old drudgery."

"Marta and I dug a box of stuff out of those old trunks in the attic—news clippings, correspondence, ledgers, that kind of stuff," Frank informed her, his eyes beaming. "Polly's going through it. Maybe she'll find something we don't know about."

Her fiery gaze flicked from Frank to me. "Well, if you do, I'd appreciate it if you run it by me before you include it in the book." She huffed and turned to Frank. "And we've already had that discussion about my namesake. If that comes out, my girls will never hear the end of it."

My ears perked up—her namesake? Finally, a hint of something that showed promise.

"Oh, pooh," Frank spat. "A little tarnish is appealing. No one's family is squeaky clean. Just ask that patron of all things Portland and your good friend, Breezy."

"Breezy has nothing to do with this, Dad," she snapped before she zeroed in on me. "I want to read this book before it's published."

"It's my life story, and I'll put anything I want into it," Frank stipulated in a "don't cross me or you'll regret it" voice.

It was my first glimpse of Frank Ellis, lumber baron extraordinaire, and it made me glad I wasn't the one butting up against him.

Frank was slender and probably not over five-feet-eight or so. He had a healthy head of white hair that had a life of its own, and he wore thick, wire-rimmed glasses. When he spoke, it was in hushed, gravelly tones. When he smiled, his whole face lit up. His chuckle was contagious.

Evidently, there was more to Frank than his grandfatherly persona. I took note.

And evidently, Nell had inherited her father's stubbornness. "We'll see about that," she argued, which resulted in a father-daughter faceoff.

Nell broke eye contact first. "I need to pick up the girls," she muttered, her jaw clenched. "Nice meeting you, Polly," she threw my way.

"You, too," I yelled after her as I watched her stride from the room.

Frank harrumphed. "Don't listen to her. She thinks, because I'm old and not as sharp as I once was, she can boss me around. I'm sure that day will come, but not yet."

That had been my previous assessment of Frank. Observing him take a stand with my own eyes and ears only reinforced it.

Before I could respond, Marta spoke. "I'm going to get back to my baking. Do you need anything?"

"How about something to drink?" Frank asked me, smiling.

"Sure. Whatever you have is fine."

"Iced tea, coffee, or lemonade?" Marta offered.

"Iced tea, please," I told her. "No sugar."

"Iced tea for me, too," he told her before turning to me. "With all of this beautiful sunshine, I think we'll sit in here today. Is that okay with you?" He stepped to a couple of oak chairs with cushioned seats and gestured for me to sit in one of them.

"Of course," I assured him as I stepped forward, dropped into the chair, and set my purse and briefcase on the polished dark hardwood floor.

Frank grasped his chair arms and carefully lowered himself into the seat, then swiped a hand through his mop of hair. "Did you get a chance to go through those family records I gave you?"

"Not yet. They're so old that I didn't want to handle them, so I had copies made. I just got them back. Next time we meet, I'll return the originals to you." I pulled my voice recorder and a notepad and pen from my briefcase and set the recorder on the small table between us.

"I'm anxious to hear what you find out, especially if there's anything that has to do with what happened to my great-grandmother, Nellie Ellis."

"Your daughter's namesake?" I asked, wondering what *had* happened to Nellie. Hopefully, something outrageous.

"Yes." His blue eyes sparkled. "I'm surprised Nell hasn't changed her name because of it. The truth is Nell should be flattered to share a name with such an adventurous and courageous lady. But she doesn't see it that way. For Nell, adventure means skipping the spa for one week."

Excitement bubbled inside me. I tried to contain it, to not appear overzealous. "I hope I get to hear about Nellie today?"

"I think so. We've pretty much covered her husband—Jesse. We might as well discuss the only colorful character on my family tree next."

"She sounds fascinating," I murmured. "Let me get this going, and we'll get started." I turned the machine on, pushed the *record* button and recorded the date, time, location, and Frank's name. "Today Frank's going to talk about his great-grandmother, Nellie Ellis," I dictated. "So Nellie was married to Jesse Ellis, Frank?"

"Yes, Jesse and Nellie tied the knot in 1875. He was close to fifty and had accrued a lot of land and money by then. Had a big house in the heart of Portland, up near the South Park Blocks. Nellie was only eighteen, and she was beautiful. Once we're through with our chats, we'll go through the old photograph albums. Then you'll see for yourself."

Marta arrived with a plate of cookies and our iced tea. She set the dewy glasses on coasters. "I put sugar in yours," she told Frank.

"Thank you, Marta," he murmured.

"Yes, thank you," I echoed.

She smiled stiffly and left the room.

"That's quite an age difference," I remarked, eyeing what had to be freshly baked cookies as whiffs of butter and vanilla floated around me.

"Yes, it is," he acknowledged. "But family lore has it that the two of them were devoted to each other and very much in love. Nellie came to Oregon with her parents the year before they met. Her parents died, and she was left to fend for herself. In a sense, Jesse rescued her."

He paused to sip tea, and I followed suit. As he appeared to be gathering his thoughts, I grabbed a cookie from the plate and nibbled. Marta definitely knew how to bake a tasty cookie.

At last, Frank sighed and continued. "I think you need to have an idea of what it was like in Portland back then. Not anything like it is nowadays. It was wild and seedy, especially the north side. Where Waterfront Park is today was a place of industry—docks, warehouses, and ships. Lots of ships. Sailing ships—schooners that required a lot of men working the decks. It was grueling work, and no one wanted to do it.

"Immigrants poured into the city and lived in cheap boarding houses, many of them with no funds or a job. They survived on credit, which created its own set of problems. Brothels, saloons, and gambling houses lined the streets, and shanghaiing of men to ship out on the schooners was an accepted practice. Those in charge of enforcing the laws were as corrupt as those breaking them. The city was dirty and smelly and plagued by floods and fires."

And I thought my life was miserable. I swallowed a bite of cookie while Frank sipped tea. "And Jesse and Nellie lived in the middle of this lawless pigsty?" I probed.

He smiled. "Not really. They lived on the respectable upper south side, well away from much of the squalor and vice, so they were mostly untouched by it. Course, with the lumber business, Jesse spent quite a bit of time down on the waterfront.

"Then Nellie got involved in the temperance movement, and she spent some time on the north side, too. I believe that's how the whole mess got started."

"Wow. She did have some spunk, didn't she," I ventured, anxious to learn about that mess.

"Yes, she did. The temperance ladies were very vocal at that time. Determined to clean up the city. You'd even find them in the saloons, preaching and singing. Some of them were arrested and spent time in jail, but that didn't stop them.

"Course, when she disappeared, Nellie was eight and a half months pregnant, so she wasn't actively participating. But it was probably those earlier trips to the north side that drew the kidnappers' attention and made her a target."

"Kidnappers?" I blurted, my pulse suddenly sprinting.

Frank nodded and selected a cookie from the plate. He bit into it and chewed for what seemed like minutes, studying me. By the time he spoke, my tongue throbbed.

"Yep," he acknowledged. "One night she vanished, right out of her house. Jesse was at a business dinner. When he got home, she was gone. Course, he called in the police, but they were pretty much worthless. Probably spent more time figuring out how they could make money off of the incident than they did looking for Nellie.

"A week went by, and nothing happened. Jesse spent most of that time cruising the streets and waterfront, especially on the north side, searching for news of Nellie. He was consumed with the need to find her. Not only had he lost her, he'd also lost their child."

Finally, I was getting my juicy story. So why did I feel so lousy? Maybe it was the sad look in Frank's eyes. Or maybe it was the vision of a distraught Jesse tearing through Portland's underbelly in search of his pregnant wife and unborn child. Whatever the case, my stomach squirmed. I sipped tea in an attempt to settle it and focused on Frank.

He swallowed another bite of cookie before he continued. "Then Jesse got a ransom note demanding money, way more than he could get his hands on in a short amount of time. Course, by then pretty much everyone knew about Nellie's disappearance, so Jesse couldn't be sure that the note was from someone who actually had Nellie. He kept it a secret and worked quietly to pull together some funds.

"Then one night a young woman showed up at his door. She begged Jesse to come with her. Said she knew where his wife was. He hitched a horse to his buggy and followed her lead."

"How did he know it wasn't a trap?" I asked. I'd pictured a Jesse that was too sharp to take a chance like that.

Frank shrugged. "By then he didn't care if he was walking into a trap or not. He'd do pretty much anything to get his wife and child back. She directed him down to the Willamette River, south of the city, where a rowboat waited. They'd just left shore when Jesse spotted a huge, two-story barge in the middle of the river and realized where the woman was taking him—Nancy Boggs' floating bordello."

I jerked forward. "Are you serious? There actually was a floating bordello on the Willamette?"

"Oh, yes. Nancy Boggs ran a thriving business right there in the middle of the Willamette River. She figured if she wasn't conducting business on soil in Portland, or East Portland, she didn't have to pay taxes to either one.

"Back then, they were two completely different cities, with two city governments, two police forces, and two sets of liquor laws. There were no bridges, so the only way to get from one city to the other was by boat. Course, the east side wasn't nearly as developed as the west side—mostly houses and small businesses. The two towns were constantly at war with each other, and Nancy could move her scow back and forth across the river as the need arose. For several years, her business flourished on that barge floating in the Willamette."

I shook my head. "Smart lady."

Marta appeared with a pitcher of iced tea. "Refills?" she asked.

"Please," I said. "Your cookies are delicious. You must like to cook."

"Marta can make anything taste good, even brussel sprouts," Frank confirmed, smiling up at her and winking.

"Why, thank you, Frank. And thank you, too, Polly. I'm glad you're enjoying the cookies." She filled our glasses and dropped a couple of sugar packets on the table, then stepped away.

Frank dumped sugar into his tea and sipped. He cleared his throat, then spoke. "Anyway, that's where Jesse was headed that night. Course, the family has always claimed that was his first visit to Nancy Boggs' place. Because of what I'll tell you next, I'm not so sure. There were so few women around here in those days that prostitution was pretty much accepted as a part of life. Course, that's just my opinion.

"Well, it turned out that Nellie was on that barge, and Jesse had two people to take home with him that night—his wife and newborn son. That baby was my grandfather."

I sighed. "So it does have a happy ending. For a while there, I was worried it might not. But how did Nellie get on the barge? Was she really kidnapped?"

He nodded, his face glum. "Oh, she was kidnapped all right, then stuffed into a dirty, musty basement down on Second Street for more than a week. When Jesse started searching for her, word spread quickly.

"Turns out, after her parents died, Nellie had spent some time on Nancy Boggs' scow. The family's always been adamant about the fact that she cooked and cleaned and that was the extent of her duties. Me, I'm not convinced. I'm hoping you might get a definitive answer from that box of papers I gave you."

"Would it matter to you?" I asked.

He chuckled and snatched another cookie. "Not in the least. I'd just like to know the truth about Great-grandma Nellie. I spent some time with her when I was a young boy. She was a bright spot in all our lives—chatty and always smiling and laughing. She loved to sing, and she spent many an hour filling my mind with tales of adventure. She and Jesse had three children, two sons and one daughter. They had many wonderful years together before he died in 1906."

He chewed a cookie, his eyes distant and a contented look on his face, as if remembering happier times. I gave him several moments before I broke into his reminiscences.

"So how did Nellie end up at the brothel?"

Frank blinked back to the present and pushed an errant lock of hair off his forehead. "Oh, well one of Nancy's customers consumed too much liquor one night and happened to mention to one of her girls that he knew where Nellie was being held. Nancy made the arrangements to rescue Nellie from her kidnappers. And just in time. Nellie was in labor when they found her. My grandfather was born not long after they got her to the brothel. In the end, thanks to Nancy's intervention, Nellie and her son returned home."

"Did they catch the kidnappers?"

"No. Since the guy who squealed was one of Nancy's loyal customers, she wouldn't give him up. All she said was that they found Nellie in a hellhole down on Second Street. Nellie was blindfolded, so she didn't see the kidnappers' faces and had no idea where she was, except that it was a basement. Most of the buildings in that area have basements, some of them connected to each other, so that was no help. The police weren't inclined to put any effort into a search, and Nellie refused to discuss her kidnapping. In the end, Jesse was happy to have her back and his son safe and healthy. He finally let it go."

I selected another cookie from the plate and thought about Frank's story and how it might fit into this tribute to his family. It would definitely spice it up. "That's quite a story. I hope you'll let me include it in the book?" I begged.

"Of course, I will. Great-grandma never did talk about it, so what I've told you was passed down through word-of-mouth from Jesse's recollections. He was dead long before I was born, but my grandfather often spoke of it. I think he was rather pleased with his birthplace."

He huffed and frowned, eyeing me intently. "If Brad and Nell have their way, tales of Jesse and Nellie will die when I do. That's one reason for this book. I want my grandchildren and their children to know their roots and to be proud of who they are and where they came from. Both Jesse and Nellie worked hard to dig their way out of severe circumstances and make a decent life for themselves and their progeny. Instead of excluding them, we should be thanking them."

Wow. Frank's sentiments had me all tingly. I glanced at the recorder to make sure it was doing its job. That last gush of words would make a touching quote in his book.

Still, Brad and Nell didn't seem to find Jesse and Nellie's adventure as alluring as Frank and I. A tiny voice inside me questioned if we might have to battle Frank's kids to honor his wish to commemorate Nellie's plight.

~~ ☼ ~~

The Willamette River flowed by me, sparkling ripples attesting to its swift progress toward the mighty Columbia, then on to the Pacific Ocean. To my left, the Burnside Bridge stretched from the west shore to the east. And down a ways to my right, the Morrison Bridge did the same.

I tried to imagine it as Frank had described it a couple of hours ago—no bridges, no motor-powered boats, and no concrete and steel structures reaching high into the sky. I gazed over the metal railing down to the seawall that extended along the west bank, then at the green grass and cement walkways that lined the shore. Scratch them out, too. I mentally replaced them with wooden docks and warehouses.

And mud. With Portland's rain, everything would be coated with dark, gooey mud down here by the river. Bulky wooden schooners would be secured to the docks and anchored out in the river, their masts piercing the blue sky, sails folded. And smaller boats, too—ferries, rowboats, and such. Oh, and men. Lots of lanky men in grubby clothing working their butts off for almost nothing.

Today a few people lounged on the grass and walked on the

paths. A couple of bicycles sped past. A man ran by in shorts, his chest bare and sweaty and an earphone stuck in his ear. Not far off, someone else appeared to be taking in the view, too. He wore a red tee-shirt and plaid shorts, his cap and sunglasses pretty much hiding his features. I glanced down at my slacks and shirt and wished I were wearing a pair of shorts and a tee.

"Quit whining," I whispered. "If it were the 1870s, you'd be cinched into a long gown with layers of undergarments weighing you down. Oh, and you'd be carrying a frilly little parasol." And back then, I definitely wouldn't be alone on the waterfront.

After my visit with Frank, I'd driven down here to get a sense of what it might've been like when Nellie was kidnapped. I'd walked Second Street—now Second Avenue—and found it lined with buildings, some old and some new, and parking lots. It was difficult to imagine it as it had once been, a haven for crime and transgressions, packed with those whose dreams were being crushed.

I turned back to the rippling river and watched a red-trimmed white sternwheeler paddle upriver. Passengers milled around on its three decks, several of them waving. My mind flashed to Nancy Boggs, and I tried to picture her two-story scow sitting smack dab in the middle of the Willamette. It would be quite a row to reach it from shore, especially when the wind blew.

Frank had told me that a few years after Nellie's abduction, Portland and East Portland had finally joined forces to put an end to Nancy's tax evasion. They cut her anchor in the middle of the night, which set the barge free to drift toward the Columbia and on to the Pacific. It was Nancy who saved her girls. She rowed a boat to Albina, the city just north of East Portland, and convinced the skipper of a sternwheeler to rescue her bordello. The next morning, it was back in the middle of the river. However, rather than risk another similar incident, she abandoned the scow and set up her booming business in East Portland. And she dutifully paid her taxes.

I had to hand it to Nancy. She was independent and resourceful. And she was resilient. Though I'd never known her personally, a little voice inside me suggested that I might learn something from her.

Which reminded me of the mess I had waiting at home. Just like that, it felt like I'd donned a fifty-pound backpack. *Nancy's predicament was far worse than yours, and she fixed it*, I reminded myself.

Yep, she didn't cling to something that no longer worked for her.

She adjusted. And when she was in a jam, she took action and dealt with it.

Well, wrapping my mind around all of the wackiness going on in my life is too much of a mindbender, I argued. My sleazy husband had blackmailed my neighbors—and lord only knows who else—cheated on me, and rifled my office. Not only that, but somehow he'd returned from the dead with no memory, reincarnated as a likeable version of his nasty, old self. And for some reason I couldn't fathom, someone had drugged us with doctored truffles. Now Stan's truck had been broken into. What was that all about?

And all I could think about is how nice it would be to just shove it all down the garbage disposal and move on to a blissful life with new Stan. He was nice. He was thoughtful. He had a sense of humor. And Laura was right—he was hot.

Yes, and how do you know old Stan won't return with a vengeance? What will you do then? that voice inside me screamed.

"Deal with it," I whispered.

Like you've dealt with it before? it challenged.

I rubbed the pressure between my eyes, an effort to silence the battle within. Truth be told, all of the strange goings-on appeared to be continuing. My only choice might be to deal with it.

"Well best get to it then," I muttered as I turned from the river to walk back to my car.

An hour and a half later, I cruised toward the Pacific on the Salmon River Highway, still wrestling with myself. Farmland lined both sides of the road, stretching to the forested hills beyond. As I traveled west, Portland's sunshine slowly turned to a moody gray drizzle.

I'd stopped for lunch at at an artsy winery-bistro place in Dundee, a small town known for its local vineyards, and consumed more than my share of iced tea, enough that I was now drowning in it. I pressed my knees together and squeezed. This being a safety corridor, I didn't dare drive much faster than the speed limit, but I was about to burst. The trickles hitting the windshield weren't helping.

Valley Junction was just ahead, Grand Ronde only a mile or so past it. And there was a casino in Grand Ronde, one with plenty of clean restrooms. The truck in front of me suddenly slowed to make a right turn off the highway. I glanced in my rearview mirror to make certain I wouldn't be rear-ended, a gut reaction ever since a Dodge truck with a massive iron grille welded to its front bumper had slammed into me a couple of years before. Nope. The black sedan still maintained a safe distance.

A couple of minutes later, Spirit Mountain Casino appeared, a sprawling mass of low, salmon-colored, brick buildings decorated with a white and blue Native American motif. It lay nestled in a valley along the South Yamhill River. I signaled right and pulled into the turn lane, then circled and passed under the highway. When I stopped in front of the casino, the black sedan was at my bumper. Whispers of unrest trickled through me. I went left into the parking lot and checked to see if it followed. It turned right.

"Get a grip, Polly. There are zillions of black cars out there," I muttered. "You've got enough problems without inventing new ones." I pulled into a parking space and shut off the engine. "And right now your biggest problem is to get into that building without peeing your pants."

I hadn't brought a jacket, which was fine. Everyone would assume I was dashing to get out of the rain that was now pelting my windshield noisily. Gritting my teeth, I grabbed my purse, scrambled out of the car, and made a mad dash for the row of front doors, not even slowing to admire the gorgeous gardens that always lined the walkway. Once inside, I strode purposefully to facilities I knew to be in the building to my left.

Greatly relieved, I emerged from the restroom, tugging on my damp white blouse. Hopefully, it would dry enough that it'd lose the Saran Wrap cling. My eyes cruised the busy room. Slot machines were everywhere, a mishmash of them, garish images bursting from their screens. They clung together in rows or huddled in circles, promising riches to the rapt patrons poking and punching at them. The noise was deafening—machines blaring and ringing, singing and uttering. Beneath that was the drone of human voices. Lights flashed. Cigarette smoke dusted the air.

The Confederated Tribes of Grand Ronde owned and operated the casino. I knew they donated a lot of money to worthy causes through grants and sponsorships. *Since I'm here, I might as well give to the cause*, I reasoned as I drew a twenty dollar bill from my wallet.

Still fanning my blouse, I followed my tracks back to the front entry and on into the main gambling area. It was a roiling sea of machines, people, and sounds. Experience had taught me that, if you didn't pay attention, you could get lost in the labyrinth. I stepped into it and wove my way toward the back of the room, waiting for a machine to speak to me.

About halfway I spotted an older slot decorated with cupids, hearts, and glossy chocolates. Portentous perhaps? I slid onto a stool and fed it my twenty, then watched it whirr to life.

"My husband dropped a wad of bills into that thing and didn't get much out of it, so it's ready to pay," a woman next to me said.

She was plump with deep wrinkles and tight white curls, flashy turquoise and silver earrings, and eyeglasses dotted with rhinestones. Jeweled rings adorned her pudgy fingers. Though she spoke to me, her eyes were glued to the images rolling by on her screen. I noticed the card dangling from her neck was plugged into a niche, and she was betting the maximum amount—a serious gambler.

"With my luck, it'll eat my twenty with one spin," I told her.

She shook her head. "Not your day, huh? I'm up several hundred, but it can suddenly turn on you. The trick is to walk away when it does." She grabbed a plastic cup with a lime slice and cherry floating in it and took a hefty sip.

"Ain't that the truth," I muttered, thinking more of my lousy marriage than my prospective gambling losses.

At that moment, something passed by behind her that sparked a memory. My stomach did a couple of flips, and my heart rate kicked up. "Would you mind holding this machine for me," I murmured as I slid off my stool.

"Sure thing, honey," she said, her eyes still on her screen.

I stepped behind her to peer around her machine and search the flashing slots and milling people. And there he stood, behind a man playing one of those towering video games, his shadowed eyes scanning the room. He wore the same plaid shorts, red shirt, and cap he'd worn several hours ago on the waterfront.

Just like that, images flashed before me—the black sedan at The Galley and again in Kings Heights that morning. The black sedan that had followed me here!

It wasn't my overactive imagination. That guy was tailing me. But why?

I squinted, trying to see him more clearly. He looked young, maybe in his twenties or early thirties, and he looked like he was in pretty good shape. With the cap shading his features, it was difficult to get a good look at his face. Still, I was certain I didn't know him.

My heart pounded so hard I feared it would burst. The designer salad I'd lunched on churned in my gut. His gaze slid my way, and I quickly darted behind bejeweled lady's slot.

"A stalker or an ex?" she asked.

"I don't know who he is, but I'm pretty sure he's following me." My voice quivered. I glanced at my hands; they trembled. I held my breath and took another peek. Suddenly, he headed toward me.

"Yikes," I squealed. Dropping onto my stool, I hunched forward and dropped my head.

"What's he look like?" the lady asked.

I felt something slide onto my shoulders and glanced up. She'd taken off her sparkly pink sweater and draped it around me. "About six feet, slender, plaid shorts and red tee-shirt. He's wearing a black baseball cap," I murmured as I slid my arms into the sweater and pulled it up to cover the ends of my shoulder-length hair.

She handed me her rhinestoned glasses. "Put these on."

I did, with hands so shaky I nearly put an eye out.

"Play the machine, honey," she advised. "I'll keep watch."

Breathing deeply, I lifted my eyes and studied the blurred screen. Then I lifted a hand and pressed the only button I could make out. Smudged shapes rolled by, then froze. A bell rang, rollicking notes sounded, and coins clinked—way too loud. I prayed for it to stop, but it blared on and on.

"I told you it was gonna blow," the lady chirped. "I'm glad it's you that won all of Clyde's dough. He'll be happy, too. And he has plenty where that came from, so don't think twice about taking it."

"I wish it would stop," I muttered.

"It's okay. He already walked by. Nice looking guy. Maybe he just wants to hook up."

I stared at her—or tried to anyway. Then I slipped off her glasses, and she slid into focus. "He followed me here from Portland."

"Oh. Well, he didn't glance at you twice. If you hurry, maybe you can sneak out of here."

I expelled pent-up air in a long sigh and handed her glasses to her. "You're sure it was him?"

"Oh, yeah. These are reading glasses, for up close." She pushed herself to her feet and walked to where she could see toward the lobby, then returned. "Yep, he's headed for the hotel."

My machine finally stopped screaming. I eyeballed it and blinked several times to make sure I was seeing right. Maybe my luck had changed. I'd just won one-thousand, one-hundred, and thirty-four dollars.

Feeling a bit rummy, my eyes flicked to my kinky-haired rescuer.

She'd returned to punching buttons. I slid off her sweater and placed it in her lap. "My name is Polly," I said. "You don't even know me. Still, you helped. Thank you so much."

Her bespectacled eyes slid my way, and her lips curved into a white-toothed smile. "Millie," she informed me. "And I was happy to help. We ladies have to stick together. My fourth husband turned out to be a real creep. Didn't take long for me to kick his sorry ass out the door. It infuriated him. He hounded me until I was forced to take out a restraining order against him. I probably should've killed the loser and stopped him right then and there. That way no other woman would've had to put up with his macho bullshit."

"Turns out, I have one of those at home," I told her. *And maybe you did kill him*, my mind whispered. "Once I figure out what's going on, I might be kicking his sorry ass out."

"You think he's the reason you're being tailed?"

I shrugged. "I don't know." And I didn't. Why would Stan have someone tail me? But then, why would someone tail me, period?

Millie opened a bulging red leather bag and burrowed inside it, then handed me a business card. "Here's my phone number. You need help, you give me a call. I can hook you up with a divorce attorney that'll rip the socks from his feet."

Of course, Stan rarely wore socks, but I got the idea. "Thank you," I told her, examining the card. It appeared that Millie was a practicing medium. I could see it. After all, she'd predicted my gambling win when I'd sat down beside her.

And speaking of that, I turned back to the slot to collect my spoils and grabbed my ticket.

Millie pressed a button, her eyes on the screen. "Don't forget to cash that in. And keep an eye out for that guy. He'll be heading back this way soon."

I studied her. How did she know that—women's intuition or her psychic abilities? "I will," I assured her. "And good luck."

"Oh, honey. I don't need luck. This baby's ready to hit," I heard her mutter as I walked away.

Clutching my winnings tightly I scoured the room, searching for a black baseball cap, as I sneaked toward the lobby. Afternoon was wearing on, and foot traffic had picked up as the evening crowd arrived. I shouldered my way through several gawking groups, then scrutinized the path to the hotel before I turned in the opposite direction, toward the front doors. A jumbled line of seniors trailed around the machine from which I'd planned to collect my winnings, so I hurried past and on to the cashiers' counter.

Turning from her conversation with a coworker, an official looking woman perused my ticket, then raised her eyebrows. "Lucky day," she said.

I wondered if it was a statement or a question. For all she knew, I'd lost far more cash than I'd won. "On the whole, no," I told her, my gaze nervously darting between her and the casino entrance.

"Well you don't have to fill out any tax forms. That's lucky," she informed me as she counted out my money.

This being my first big win, I hadn't even considered that. Perhaps I should secret my winnings away. I'd never before thought it necessary, but the past four days had given me a whole new perspective on my life and my marriage. Stan had access to every penny I owned and all of my credit cards. Maybe it was time I battened the hatches, so to speak.

"Thank you," I murmured as I stuffed the cash into the bottom of my purse.

The coast still looked clear. Of course, it was difficult to see through the blue hair group still waiting to claim their booty. I approached them and glanced around the last man in line. My stalker was headed my way, a determined look to him.

Panic immobilized me. Lunch gurgled in my stomach. I frantically searched for a hiding place. My eyes landed on the larger group of seniors that milled near the front doors, overflowing onto the outside sidewalk and probably waiting to board the white bus parked in the driveway.

Two ladies walked from the cash machine, too busy chatting to notice me. I stepped in beside them, making myself as small as possible. When we reached the group, I slowly wiggled my way to the middle and hunched down.

Steeling myself, I rose on my tiptoes and peeked out. He was standing a few yards from me, his eyes searching the area. I ducked just in time and wove my way through the shuffling bodies and out the front door. A few more healthy squirms, and I'd reached the bus. After one more quick look to make sure he wasn't gazing directly at me, I took a deep breath, darted around the bus, and sprinted through the pelting rain to my car.

When the locks clicked into place, I settled into the passenger seat and forced myself to breathe normally. *Deep and slow*, I told myself until my muscles began to relax and my head no longer felt like it was drifting faster than Nancy Boggs' scow. My eyes were glued to the parking lot entry. I expected him to suddenly appear, spot my car, and, like the villain did in all of those suspense thrillers, march doggedly toward me.

And of course the damsel in distress is so frightened that she drops her keys and can't find them. "Not me," I muttered, jamming my key into the ignition and turning it.

I grabbed the steering wheel with shaky hands, backed out, and rolled toward the exit. My whole body tensed as I drove past the bus parked at the front door. No one even glanced my way.

"Oh, dear lord. What's going on?" I whispered after I pulled onto the highway and checked my rearview mirror to make sure a sporty black sedan wasn't on my tail.

Stan was the only person I could think of who might hire someone to shadow me. Did he think I was cheating on him? I snickered at the thought. It hurt to admit it, but Stan wouldn't care.

He was having an affair with Denise. Perhaps they planned to ditch their spouses and move in together. Maybe he'd hired someone to get rid of me, so they'd have our house and whatever savings I'd managed to accumulate. Maybe Denise had left those truffles, knowing how much Stan hated chocolate and expecting me to eat all of them and die in my sleep. The thought burrowed deep in my gut, a hollow, empty feeling.

But it didn't feel right. Denise was too much of a ditz, even for Stan.

That didn't mean he didn't want our assets all to himself, though. He lied. He cheated. He blackmailed. Was he a murderer, too?

⩜ ✧ ⩜

A half hour later I was back on the Coast Highway, cruising south. The rain had let up, but a damp gray gloominess shrouded everything—Siletz Bay and the ocean beyond to my right, the tree-covered hills to my left. Me.

The closer I got to home, the more agitated I grew, like a too-tightly-wound clock, prepared to burst if someone pushed me one notch further. My eyes flicked to the rearview mirror. At least I'd ditched the guy in the black car. For now. If he knew where I lived—well, that was another matter.

I huffed. At the moment, he was the least of my worries. The fact that I had no idea who waited for me at home—old Stan or new Stan—had hounded me since that salty ocean smell touched my nostrils. Given a choice, I'd pick new Stan with bells and whistles, but whichever Stan I faced when I got home, I needed to deal with him.

Deep in my gut, I knew all of the weirdness in my life lately traced back to the man I'd married. With his return, I'd get answers. New Stan didn't have a clue what was going on. Still, I prayed the nicer version would be there when I stepped through my front door. Visions of a confrontation with an angry, hostile Stan had my insides jittering.

Shaking the images away, I rolled into the right turn lane and onto the paved road next to a sign that announced *Sandy Cove Estates and Golf Course.* The road wove toward the ocean, past upper-end houses and sections of the golf course, then jogged left into an entrance decorated with colorful flowerbeds and a massive rock waterfall. Drawing near to my house, I noticed Stan's truck wasn't in the driveway. My whole body melted.

Laura stood across the street next to a honkin' big, flashy motorcycle, visiting with a tall man sporting a salt-and-pepper ponytail and close-cropped beard. He wore black leather, top and bottom. A red kerchief covered the top of his head. Laura was a burst of lemon in her yellow skinny jeans and windbreaker. When I punched the garage door opener, the two of them looked my way. I waved and drove in.

They had crossed the street and waited for me when I crawled out of my car. Though all I wanted to do was rip my dressy clothes off and sit down in my comfy chair with a glass of wine and a Patsy Cline CD, I grabbed my briefcase and purse and stepped to meet them.

Laura's radiant smile turned to concern. "OMG, Pol. You look like an ocean breeze would topple you. Is everything okay?"

I sighed and pasted the best smile I could muster onto my face. "Oh, yeah. Long drive, and I was up early." I turned to the man and reached out a hand. "Polly Morton," I murmured.

His was large and calloused, engulfing mine when he shook it. "Harley Miller. It's nice to meet you." His pale blue eyes twinkled even in the dreary light. The creases lining his tanned face indicated he was in his late forties or early fifties. So who was he?

"Harley?" I asked, eyeing the motorcycle across the street.

He chuckled. "Yep, my dad was a bike freak. Loved his Harleys. With a name like that, how can I not own one?"

"I met Harley at the Whale's Spout Friday night," Laura informed me, face glowing. "Turns out, we both love to dance. They have live music on weekends, so we danced Saturday night, too. He was out on his bike, so he stopped by for a visit."

So Laura had a special man friend, huh? She hadn't mentioned that on Saturday. "Well, it's nice to meet you, too," I murmured, trying not to check him out too blatantly.

Tugging my gaze from his, I spotted Stan's blue truck charging toward us. My pulse skyrocketed. I moved over to give him room. Laura followed suit. Harley tagged along.

"Stan's truck was broken into last night," I told Laura. "They smashed a window. You didn't happen to hear the alarm or see someone around who didn't belong here, did you?"

She frowned and shook her head. "My golly, Polly. You've had more than your share of rotten luck lately. Did they take anything?"

Stan eyeballed us as he pulled into the driveway. His face looked more wary than growly, so chances were my prayers had been answered—thank you, God. A new window replaced the shattered one. The engine quieted. I tensed when I heard his door open.

"I don't think so," I replied, more focused on Stan than Laura. "Stan cleaned the cab out yesterday, so there wasn't much to take. His toolbox was in there, but it appeared to be untouched."

"The tools were all there," Stan announced when he joined us. "And some of them are worth a lot of money. I'm not sure what they were after, but it was a pain in the butt to get that window replaced." He wore faded jeans today—most likely cinched at the waist—a loose-fitting nylon jacket, and heavy leather boots, none of which were flecked with mud, wood shavings, grout, or any other form of building material. What in the heck had he been up to?

"Did you report it to the sheriff's office?" Laura asked tentatively. She was alert, studying Stan like she expected him to morph into one of those *Wesens* on "Grimm" at any moment. Harley stared at him rather oddly, too.

Stan shook his head. "Nah. They have more important things to worry about than my truck. It's no big deal."

"No big deal?" Laura echoed, giving me a "this is creeping me out" look.

"Stan, this is Laura's friend, Harley Miller," I said, hoping to change the subject before Laura's thoughts spewed out her mouth.

Stan reached a hand out. "Nice to meet you, Harley. And it's nice to see you again, too, Laura."

Harley's confused eyes darted back and forth from Stan to me. Finally, he grabbed Stan's outstretched hand and gave it a token shake.

Laura just stared at Stan, evidently too stunned to respond.

"I gotta get going," Harley told Laura. His smile was gone. In fact, he looked irritated. With that, he strode across the street.

Laura had noticed it, too. I saw it in her eyes. Brows raised, she eyeballed me and shrugged. "Oh, okay," she yelled after him. "See you later, Pol." She rolled her eyes and trailed after Harley.

When I turned back, Stan was staring at the two of them, frowning.

"Do you know that guy?" I asked.

His frown deepened, and he shook his head like he was thinking something through. "I don't think so. Maybe he doesn't like men talking to his woman."

"Laura just met the guy. He seemed so nice . . . until you came along."

The murmur of voices filtered to us and drew my attention. Harley and Laura were engrossed in a heated discussion. I watched them, knowing I should mind my own business, but she was my best friend, and I hoped her interest in this guy wasn't something she'd later regret. Every so often, she flicked me a concerned glance. Finally, the two of them retreated to the porch to continue their conversation.

I huffed and hauled myself inside the house, Stan trailing me. The kitten came scampering and tangled in my feet. I dropped my purse and briefcase on the kitchen table, picked up the screaming fluff ball, and punched off the screeching security alarm.

When I returned to the kitchen, Stan was rooting in the fridge. "Want anything?" he asked.

"Yes, please. Wine if there's a bottle open."

He emerged with a Diet Pepsi and a dewy bottle of Chardonnay. I grabbed a wineglass from a cabinet and held it out for him to fill. The kitten began a contented purr, working its prickly paws on my chest. I kicked off my wedge sandals and took a sip—perfect. It all seemed so natural, like a well-established routine perfected by years of harmonious marriage.

Only, it wasn't.

"Did you work today?" I pried, praying he would be truthful.

His face grew alert. "I tried. Turns out I was fired last Tuesday."

"Fired? From your job?" *Here we go again,* I wanted to add. Instead, I sipped wine to tamp my irritation.

"Uh-huh. They weren't any too happy to see me. Evidently, I didn't take the news well."

Well, that explained why he'd golfed with George on Friday. But how about the other three weekdays? "So what did you do today?"

"Got the window fixed. That ate up a couple of hours. Then I checked on other jobs." He leaned against the counter and crossed his feet while he appeared to mull something over. "It doesn't look promising. Turns out I've burned more than a few bridges."

"Maybe you'll have to pursue a different line of work," I snapped.

The look on his face made me wish I'd held my tongue. "I take it we need the money?"

"To maintain your previous lifestyle, yes. The house is paid for— no problem there. My father left it to me." Of course, with no prenuptial, he now owned half of it. What in the heck had I been thinking?

"Have you lived here long?"

It took me a few moments to digest his question and come to terms with the fact that new Stan didn't know much about me. My reaction must've flashed on my face, because he looked troubled.

"Eight years or so," I informed him, deciding that I might as well lay it all out there. "I grew up in Eastern Oregon. Laura did, too. We went through school together, including some time in college. We both married our high school sweethearts. I lived in Central Oregon— Bend. She moved to Lincoln City.

"My husband died in a ski accident right before my daughter, Sara, was born. I stayed in Bend, because I had the perfect job and was able to take classes and finish college."

"Where's Sara now?"

"Oh, she's at school—Oregon State. Took a summer internship there."

"The two of you get along?"

"Yes," I exclaimed. "You're the problem. My guess is she didn't want to relive the past two summers." For some reason, I needed to make that clear.

His look said he heard me loud and clear. "So . . . you lived in Bend?"

"Uh-huh, for thirteen years. When my mother passed away, my dad turned into a lost soul. He'd always wanted to live on the coast. Laura convinced him to buy this house across the street from her, and he invited Sara and me to move in with him.

"Then about three years ago, he died, too. You and I were dating at the time. You wanted to get married, and here we are." *Biggest mistake of my life,* I silently added.

He frowned. Obviously, something bothered him.

"You don't remember any of this?" I prodded.

He shook his head. "It's clear that I'm a lazy, lying, cheating jerk. You're beautiful, smart, and nice, and you seem gutsy enough, and independent. I doubt you love me. So why did you marry me?"

His words nearly knocked me over. My head felt light, my limbs weak. I set my wineglass down and leaned on the counter, clutching the kitten tightly to my chest. All of those old, hopeless feelings of being deserted and alone rushed in. He'd voiced my thoughts, the ones I was unable to say out loud. But what did it mean? Was this the end, then?

I struggled to pull myself together, to hide the fact that he could unhinge me like this. "I have my doubts, too," I answered honestly, my voice weak and shaky. "It seemed like the right thing to do at the time." Actually, it was more a matter of me convincing myself that it was the right thing to do. The prospect of being alone again had been too devastating.

"Well, I'm sorry I've been such a mean, unthoughtful son of a bitch. That's gonna change."

And that was it? No talk of one of us moving out. Or divorce. Or who gets custody of the kitty?

"And I'll start by cooking dinner," he offered.

The kitchen spun around me. I told myself to take slow, deep breaths, then set the kitten on the floor, afraid I would drop it. "You don't have to do that," I assured him. "Let me change my clothes, and I'll whip up something."

"No. You look beat. You shopped for groceries yesterday, and you worked today. Until I find a job, I can do the cooking and laundry and some of the other work around here."

Finally, the swirling images halted. My body showed signs of calming. But Stan cook? He lived on Twinkies, tortilla chips, ice cream, and hotdogs for a reason. "You sure you can cook?" I asked.

He smiled. "No problem."

"Well . . . thank you." I grabbed my wineglass, took a generous gulp, and headed for my bedroom to change into jeans and a sweatshirt.

When I returned twenty minutes later, he'd shed his boots and jacket. I had to admit that he looked pretty darn hot standing there in that cloud of steam pouring from a large pot. He didn't seem to notice the kitten clawing its way up his pants leg while he stirred something in a skillet. The air was fragrant with garlic and some familiar herb I couldn't identify. Placemats set for two and a yummy-looking green salad adorned the kitchen table.

I set my wineglass on the counter and grabbed my briefcase, purse, and shoes.

"Be ready in five," he told me as he tugged the kitten loose to set it on the floor and poured raw scallops and shrimp into the skillet."

"Smells heavenly," I yelled, heading for the bedroom.

The doorbell's chime stopped me. I detoured to open it, arms loaded.

It was George, dripping wet and looking like he'd been on a three-day bender. Behind him, raindrops pelted in the dreary dusk. I squinted across the street. Yep, Harley's Harley still stood in Laura's driveway, but they must've moved inside out of the rain.

"George," I huffed, hoping he would take the hint and go away.

He sniffed the air, then barked, "I need to talk to Stan."

"He's in the kitchen," I said, stepping back to let him pass and sniffing, too. He reeked of dead fish, not booze, so he probably wasn't drunk.

I watched him stomp toward Stan, leaving a muddy trail on the hardwood floor. Then I finished my trek to my bedroom.

George was really laying into Stan, no doubt about that. I heard his angry voice when I walked back down the hall. "What do you mean, you don't have the bait? You damn well do! And you better be outside my house tomorrow morning with it, or there's gonna be trouble. You're not getting out of this by playing dumb."

When I entered the kitchen, Stan's wary gaze slid from George to me. "Do we have some crab bait?" he asked. His knees were flexed, his arms at his sides, shoulders hunched, as if prepared to defend himself if George's heated threat turned physical.

One look at George told me that was a real possibility. My first thought was that he must be on drugs. The camo outfit he'd worn the previous morning was streaked with mud and grime. Tufts of greasy gray hair stood up on his head, and stubble nearly hid his cheeks and chin. But his eyes were the worst. They were red-rimmed, wild, and fuming.

I shook my head guardedly. "I don't think so. But we can certainly get some if you need it, George."

His furious gaze flashed to me, then back to Stan, where his anger swelled to the point that he puffed enraged bursts of air. Finally, he spit, "You heard me. Eight o'clock sharp. And bring the bait." With that, he stomped to the front door.

It slammed, and my eyes met Stan's. "You suppose he found out about you and Denise?"

He swallowed hard and shook his head slowly, clearly confused. "Could be, but why not just confront me and pound me to a pulp?"

"Well what else could it be about?"

He shrugged. "I guess it's my turn to bring bait." His gaze trailed toward the front door, and he sighed. "I hope we like crab, 'cause it looks like I'm going tomorrow. Though, I guess that won't matter if I don't survive my day with that lunatic."

CHAPTER 6

Stan bobbed up and down with the churning waves the wind had kicked up in Yaquina Bay. Just looking at him made my seasick tendencies kick in. He tossed another crab cage into the agitating water, and the coiled yards of white rope slid through his hands. Finally, he threw a fluorescent green float out of the boat.

I dropped the binoculars to my lap and sighed deeply. So far, nothing looked amiss. Hopefully, it would stay this way until high tide passed. If so, I'd have a pleasant morning in my car doing something I'd never before done—drink coffee, watch the puffy clouds float around in a brilliant blue sky, and observe the activity in the bay.

Of course, I wasn't up close and personal with George, so I could enjoy it. Poor Stan. He was trapped on a boat with the guy. And with George only a few marginally controlled breaths from becoming a raving maniac, who knew what might happen to Stan.

That's why I was here. I'd awakened in the middle of the night gasping for air, my heart thudding in my chest and sweat sticky on my body. In my dream, Stan and I were on a pristine, sandy beach, alone and holding hands. It was dusk, and the sunset was spectacular—brilliant shades of yellow, amber, orange, and crimson floating over the ocean to bathe us in their fiery mist. Though we walked near the water in our bare feet, an occasional wave crept up to caress our bare calves. All was peaceful contentment.

Then out of nowhere, a massive sneaker wave grabbed Stan. I felt its immense power tug at me and dug my heels into the sand to fight it, clinging to Stan's hand as I watched the water become a surging, roiling sea of rich, glossy, dark chocolate. It flowed seductively up my legs, tugging on them. Then ever so slowly Stan's fingers slipped from my wet grasp, and he was gone.

I'd shot up out of my sleep, and once I'd calmed down enough to think straight, I knew what I needed to do—shadow Stan.

Unable to shake the dream and relax back into sleep, I spent the rest of the night in my office typing up notes on my interview with Frank Ellis. At six-thirty, I showered and dressed in jeans and a knit top. Then I headed to the kitchen to whip up breakfast and enough strong coffee to fill a thermos and keep the two of us in a buzz. If Stan spent the morning hauling in crab traps, he'd need sustenance.

With the kitten purring contentedly on his lap, he downed three cups of coffee and enough pancakes and eggs to last him until dinner, if necessary. Then he tugged on a windbreaker and cap, grabbed the super-sized package of raw chicken backs he'd purchased the previous evening, and rushed out the door.

Keeping one eye out a front window, I slipped a baseball cap over my ponytailed hair and zipped a heavy sweatshirt over my torso, then grabbed my sunglasses and purse and a pair of binoculars. When I saw George's truck pull out of the driveway, boat in tow, I ran for the garage, grabbing the thermos on my way out the door.

And now here I sat, halfway through that thermos of coffee, wondering why I'd been so worried about Stan's crabbing trip with George. They appeared to be doing just that—crabbing.

I scanned the endless rows of trucks and boat trailers in the parking lot at the marina not far from where I'd parked. Still no suspicious-looking black cars in sight. Maybe I'd actually ditched the guy for good.

Across the bay, except for a smattering of tourists walking the docks, workers milling around the colorful canneries, and seagulls cruising for tasty morsels, the harbor appeared quiet. Most of the commercial fishing trawlers had already motored beneath the towering Yaquina Bay Bridge and out to sea. George was one of only a few crabbers who'd ventured out in the bay this morning, probably due to the stiff breeze blowing in from the west.

It looked like his boat had stopped. I picked up the binoculars and watched Stan drop another cage. That made five. They floated in a giant circular squiggle, marked by lime green floats.

Bobbing floats of various other colors dotted the blue water, too—orange, yellow, dirty white, and red. A small silver boat bounced so much it had difficulty getting near enough to a white float to get hold of it. Not far from it, two larger boats appeared to be biding time before they hauled in their catch. I turned the binoculars on them. I could make out a woman in the blue and white boat. She sat in the back, facing forward, a travel mug in her hand. Every so often she spoke to someone hidden under the canopy at the front of the boat. The second boat was much larger. Three men sat in it, perched in seats that swiveled.

Upriver a ways, almost hidden from view behind a wall of sea grass, was a black boat that rode low in the water and was more streamlined. I focused the binoculars on it and could barely make out movement in the forward covered portion of the boat.

Turning back to George and Stan, I noticed that George had fired up the big motor. They were jetting back to the marina with water gushing up around them and some serious wakes trailing behind. Maybe Stan's morning coffee caught up with him. I hoped their return to the dock was something as innocent as that.

I watched them until they disappeared in the maize of docks, then went back to caffeine sipping and voyeurism. With a lot of rolling and jostling, the young couple in the silver boat finally hauled in a couple of crab rings and several legal crab. They threw the crab into a Styrofoam ice chest and the rings into the bottom of the boat and struggled toward the far shore.

Before they reached the docks, the larger boat motored out to an orange float and maneuvered around it until one of the men hooked it with the pole he held in his hands. He lugged a crab pot into the boat, and the other two men donned rubber gloves and went to work sorting and tossing. When they were done, they tossed the pot into the water and moved on to their next float.

The deep rumble of a fishing trawler caught my attention. It rolled into the bay from the ocean and dodged toward the far shore to avoid the hodgepodge of floats and crabbers pulling in their catch.

Then the black boat zoomed from its hiding place. I watched to see which floats it would approach, betting on red. But it sped by red and slowed to circle a yellow float. I adjusted the binoculars, trying to see who was manning the boat, but the canopy over it was low and long and left only a small portion at the back of the boat open. Suddenly, a black shape darted out and hauled in a trap. I could see several large crab clinging to the cage, but he didn't separate them from the smaller ones. Just opened the cage and dumped the whole lot of them into the water before he disappeared from view. The boat sat still for several long moments, then jetted on.

"That's weird," I muttered, wondering why someone would

venture out in the bay on a windy day like today if they weren't going to feast from their efforts. I mean, crabbing wasn't exactly a fun time. It was work. Your arms and shoulders ached from hauling in loaded pots, and your hands and fingers got blistered, clawed, and pinched. Not only that, but when the wind blew, the waves knocked you around the boat, and you ended up wet, chilled, and bruised. For me, getting my land legs back once I was on solid ground was worse than the injuries.

The blue and white boat caught my attention. I expected it to head for the red floats, but it passed by them and headed for George's fluorescent green.

"What the heck?" I muttered as the woman hooked a float. She lugged in the trap, opened it and extracted a couple of large crab, after examining their undersides. The rest she left in the cage. The crab went into a bucket; the cage back into the water.

Poachers!

I glanced toward the marina, hoping I'd see George rush in to save his booty. No such luck. Whatever he and Stan were up to, it was more than a potty break. In the meantime, they were being robbed. One by one the woman pulled up George's traps, helped herself to a couple of crab from each, and returned the traps to the water. Then it motored up the bay and disappeared around a bend.

When I turned back to the pots, the larger boat was heading for its holding area, and the black boat raced up the bay in the other's wake. There was still no sign of George and Stan, and they'd been gone for more than thirty minutes. I scanned what I could see of the docks in the marina, but I didn't know George's boat well enough to distinguish it from too many others. George and Stan were nowhere in sight.

"So what's the plan, Polly?" I muttered, dropping the binoculars into my lap. Should I go look for them or stay put? If they saw me, I'd have to invent a plausible excuse for being here. I wasn't sure there was one.

A flash of white leaving the marina caught my attention. At first I thought it was George, but when I looked at it through the binoculars, I noticed the boat carried two older couples. I watched until they reached the red floats and hauled a pot in, then checked for George and Stan. Still no sign of them.

I huffed and considered my own screaming bladder. I'd driven off the pavement, so I could stay in my car out of the weather and still see out onto the bay. To avoid drawing attention to myself, it might be best if I walked to the marina. Still I'd need to move stealthily.

When I stepped out of my car, the wind caught my cap and nearly ripped it from my head. I pressed it down hard and zipped the binoculars up inside my sweatshirt. Harbor sounds filled the air—boat motors, seagull squawks, and shouting voices. The salty air was ripe with the smell of gasoline and diesel fumes and pungent sea life.

Pressing into the stiff breeze, I headed down the sandy path toward the parking lot. Before I crossed the pavement to the restroom, I paused to scour the area, searching for signs of George and Stan. There were none. In fact, there were very few people around today, just their trucks and trailers. A lone man leaned against a silver truck a few yards away, drinking from a large paper cup and studying me. He nodded, and I returned the greeting. Then I scurried to the restroom.

When I stepped back outside, the man was talking on his phone. Evidently, he'd lost interest in me, so I slid nonchalantly behind a white SUV and pulled out my binoculars to peruse the docks. In mere seconds I spotted Stan not far from me. He sat in George's boat, and he had his phone to his ear, too. If he'd truly lost his memory, who in the heck was on the other end of that conversation? George was nowhere in sight.

"Well, at least Stan's okay," I whispered as my eyes traveled the marina.

There wasn't much camo going on this morning, so it didn't take me long to spot George. He stood several steps from a small bait and tackle store, and it looked like he was in a heated argument with a rough-looking man twice his size and in much better shape. Leave it to George to pick on some guy who could pass for *King Kong*. Hopefully, he wouldn't pull Stan into his brouhaha.

I gazed at them through the binoculars. The man grabbed hold of George's jacket and shook him hard, nearly lifting him off the ground. He looked mean and angry and spit something at George through bared teeth. A black stocking cap was pulled low over his forehead, covering half of his face. For once, George didn't look full of himself. He looked scared shitless.

My heart pounded. I squinted at Stan. Would he sprint up the dock to George's rescue? No. Instead, he appeared to be snapping photos of the exchange with his cell phone. Not a bad idea I decided, as I pulled out my own phone and joined in the photo-op.

After manhandling George for a minute or so, gorilla guy let go of him, bared his teeth once more, and strode off, ape arms and massive shoulders swinging.

George still looked scared shitless. He shook himself hard and glanced around. Surprisingly, it seemed no one but Stan and I had observed the altercation. I glanced around the back of the SUV at the man with the paper cup. He had a clear view of George, but he seemed more interested in his phone conversation than some guy being pounded outside the market.

I watched George tug his camo jacket into place and march down to his boat. He uncoiled a rope tied to the dock and threw it onto the bow, then leveled a nasty glare at Stan and barked something. It didn't seem to faze Stan. He raised his eyebrows and said something back. George loosened the other line and pulled the boat close to climb on. Then he disappeared into the cabin. A few seconds later, the motor fired up, and George and Stan putted toward the marina entrance.

Before I headed back to my car, I took a few moments to pull myself together. It was a good thing I didn't make my living as a private eye, because I'd be a bad one. I'd wanted to jet out there and demand that those crab-poaching bozos return them. And though I knew George deserved to be taken down more than a few notches, I'd itched to confront that bully. Being a witness, yet unable to step in, was definitely not for me. But the *coup de grâce* was that I had to stay mum about my whole surveillance experience.

I stuffed the binoculars back into my sweatshirt and began the windy trek back to my car. Paper cup guy checked me out as I passed by him. Knowing it might be the highlight of my day, I flashed him a smile to thank him.

Away from the protection of the marina, mega force gusts pummeled me and tore at my car door when I opened it. The waves had definitely picked up out on the bay. George's large boat sprang up and down like a bouncing ball as it plowed through them. He made several circles around a float before he was close enough that Stan hooked it. Stan threw the rope over a pulley and pulled on it, all the while fighting the roiling motion of the boat.

The trap looked loaded when he lugged it into the boat. He sorted and measured and tossed quite a few crab back into the water. The rest went into a compartment at the back of the boat. Then he coiled the rope and threw it and the float into the trap. Evidently, after they pulled the rest of the traps, he and George were done for the day.

Stan leaned over to push the trap forward and George must've gunned the motor without warning him because Stan fell forward over the trap, his feet still planted on the floor. His loose jacket lifted with the breeze, and something flashed in the sun's rays.

I adjusted the binoculars to focus on what it was, and the bitter aftertaste of coffee hit my throat. Tucked into the back of Stan's belt was a very deadly-looking gun.

♒ ☼ ♒

Yaquina Bay was a pool of blue far below me when I crossed the bridge on my way home. George and Stan had most likely emptied all of the traps by now and were motoring back to the marina. If I dared take my eyes off the road for one second, I'd search for them. But the wind blasted even stronger way up here on this steel viaduct, making it difficult to stay on the road, even with my death grip on the steering wheel.

After I'd seen what was concealed beneath Stan's jacket, I'd washed my hands of my spying gig. If Stan carried that pistol around for protection, he certainly didn't need me watching out for him.

That gun had my insides twisted into fretting knots. I couldn't get past the fact that it was an old Stan thing to do. New Stan seemed as harmless as the kitten who'd attached itself to him. Although, now that I thought about it, that kitten had four sets of skin-piercing claws and teeth that could draw blood.

Was it only a ruse—Stan, not the kitten? Was he only pretending he'd changed? Only pretending that he'd lost his memory? And I, being the gullible Pollyanna Javier claimed me to be, had believed every lying morsel he fed me.

"Well, scratch that," I muttered, my lips twitching at my play on words. From now on, I would examine every word that man uttered, every little nuance in his actions and expressions.

I drove off the bridge and through the state park, then rolled past the stores of downtown Newport a ways before I turned left. Down one block, I went right. The dark stone exterior of the museum towered just ahead. I parked on the street and studied the building. It was built in the late 1800s and, with its large upper windows and turret, looked like it belonged on the edge of a steep cliff overlooking the ocean in some gothic novel.

Since I was in Newport, I'd decided to stop and settle up with Bev for the photocopying she'd done for me. She spent most of her days at the museum. Bev liked to gab—mostly about the history of the area—so if I wanted to beat Stan home, I'd need to avoid becoming embroiled in one of her lengthy lectures.

I tugged off the baseball cap and finger combed my smashed bangs futilely, then applied a coat of lipstick. Grabbing my purse, I slid from the car and sprinted up the steps. Bev sat at the front desk, her nose in a stack of yellowed newspapers. She looked up and gazed at me over the top of her reading glasses.

"Polly, so nice to see you," she murmured, worry touching her matronly features. "I hope the copies were okay?"

"Oh, I'm sure they are," I assured her, sniffing against the mildew smell wafting from the stack of old newsprint. "I just got them a couple of days ago, so I haven't had a chance to look through them yet."

Her elegant brows dropped into a frown. "*Hmmm.* I'm certain your husband picked them up last Monday. I remember because we had a busload of second graders in here. I was trying to deal with them, and he . . . well he seemed in a hurry to get the stuff and get out of here."

In other words, Stan had been his usual difficult self. Heat blossomed in my cheeks. "I'm sorry, Bev. Sometimes, he's not very patient."

She smiled. "Unfortunately, neither are most second graders. But that's old news. What can I help you with?"

"Actually, nothing. I was down this way, so I thought I'd pay you for the copies. I really appreciate you making them. Frank Ellis dug them out of his attic, and they looked so old and fragile that I was afraid they'd be a shredded mess by the time I finished with them. This way, I can return the originals to him. So thank you."

Noises in the back distracted her for several moments—voices, bumps, and footsteps on the old floors. When she turned back to me, she gave her head a quick shake and gazed at me intently. "Your husband did give you the packet of letters?"

Packet of letters? I thought back, trying to remember if Stan had said anything about some letters. He had asked me about the contents of the box and where they'd come from. At the time, I'd thought it odd since he'd never before been the least bit interested in my work. Was that why he'd searched my office Friday night? Did it have something to do with letters?

I slowly shook my head. "No."

She huffed and pulled off her glasses, her mouth set in a perturbed pucker. "Well, I specifically asked him to give those to you to read. I know I did. Even with all of those kids running around and touching everything and him chomping at the bit to be on his way, I remembered to do that."

"Sometimes Stan forgets things," I assured her. *And sometimes you need to chill*, I wanted to add. Bev could get *über* protective about her little kingdom here at the museum. "So why are the letters important?"

"They're correspondence between a woman named Nellie Ellis and another woman." Her eyes flitted around the room before she continued, this time speaking in a loud whisper. "It seems that one of Frank's ancestors was born in a brothel."

Which evidently, Bev seemed to find totally scandalous. I stared at her, wondering if being buried in all of this old stuff had kept her from taking that leap into the twenty-first century.

"Oh, I know all about that. Frank told me," I informed her.

She was speechless for several long seconds. "Well, okay then," she finally muttered. "I just thought it might be some big secret or something. Surely he doesn't want anyone to know about it?"

"Frank's pretty open about the whole thing. Although he doesn't care, his kids seem to want it kept quiet. Frank insists I include it in the book, and he's the one paying me, so. . . ."

Her dark eyes popped. "Hmmm. Well, I hope it doesn't cause any problems down the road for them. You know the Ellis family has a long history here on the coast, too, especially up around Tillamook. They still own a lot of land and harvest a lot of timber in this area. From what I hear, their construction business has really taken off, too."

And here we go, I silently warned myself. If I appeared the least bit interested, Stan would have the crab boiled and shelled by the time I got out of here—that is, if he was still new Stan.

I jumped in when she paused to take a breath. "You know, I'm not quite ready to explore the family's impact on this area yet, but when I am, I'll bring a voice recorder, and we can sit down for a visit. Would you be willing to do that, Bev?"

She glowed, and I almost heard the cogs turning in her head. "Of course. It'll give me time to do some research."

"Great. Now how much do I owe you?"

"Let me see. I've got it right here," she murmured, digging a file out of a stack on the corner of her desk. She handed me a bill that was inside. I wrote out the check quickly and traded it for a receipt she'd produced.

"I really do appreciate it, Bev. I'll give you a call when I'm ready for that interview. Have a nice week," I chirped as I turned to make a hasty retreat before she latched onto another topic.

"You, too," she yelled after me. "And if I come up with anything interesting in my research, I'll give you a call."

The quick stop had taken longer than I'd expected. I jogged to my car and fired it up, determined to be home and settled into my office, as if I'd spent the whole morning there, when Stan walked in the front door. Fortunately, it was a weekday, which meant the Coast Highway wasn't quite the slug stroll it was on the weekend.

For the most part, this section of the highway snaked along the Pacific's shoreline. It was a beautiful drive with sandy beaches, ocean waves, and imposing rock structures and dark cliffs to the west and forested hills to the east. The sky was sea blue, blotted with cotton candy clouds. The sun was late morning bright. If gusts of wind hadn't been blowing me all over the road, I might have enjoyed the twenty-five-mile scenic trip home.

By the time I pulled into my garage, my knuckles ached from clutching the steering wheel so tightly. I grabbed my things and made a beeline for my bedroom, dropping the thermos off in the kitchen and my purse in my office on my way through. My tennis shoes, cap, and binoculars went into my closet, and I stopped at the sink to wet and fluff my flattened bangs. Back in the kitchen, I emptied the rest of the thermos coffee into a mug, rinsed out the thermos, and stuffed it into a cupboard.

The kitten appeared from somewhere. It ambled to my feet and stood there looking up at me beseechingly and meowing.

"What's wrong? Do you miss new Stan?" I murmured picking it up. I walked over to look out a front window, then sighed. No sign of George yet. Maybe he'd decided to rinse his boat at the marina instead of in his driveway today. I carried the kitten into the laundry room and filled its food bowl, then gave it fresh water. It tore into its kibbles like it hadn't eaten in days.

Backtracking, I grabbed the mug of coffee off the kitchen counter and walked to my office, where I plopped into my leather desk chair and fired up the computer. Then I took a deep breath and settled in, relaxing into the chair.

Yep, Stan wouldn't have a clue I'd tailed him. In fact, if I really wanted to figure out what he was up to, maybe I should make a habit of shadowing my lying, cheating husband, just like those women did in all of those made for TV movies. After all, their suspicions were always right on.

I mulled over the pros and cons as I pulled up my *facebook* page. There were twelve new posts, plus a zillion ads. I always wondered how in the heck those got posted on *my* private page. Ignoring them, I scrolled through what was left to see who was up to what and paused on a pic of Sara. The caption read *Hiking Cultis Lakes—good weather, good friends, good times.* I studied the photo, wishing I were there with her.

When we'd lived in Bend, we hiked the Cultis trail every summer. Now she stood in front of what looked like Little Cultis with two other girls, arms around each other's shoulders, dressed in hiking boots and khaki shorts. Behind them, the lake and sky sparkled a clear, high-mountain blue.

I sniffed, and swallowed at the ache in my throat. "And I'll bet you're covered with mosquito bites," I murmured, fighting tears.

Looks like you're having fun. Enjoy! I typed.

And at that moment, I promised myself that whatever happened with new Stan or old Stan or any other Stan who showed up, I would do whatever it took to get my daughter back.

With a final sniff, I closed *facebook* and pulled up my email to scan my inbox. It was mostly ads and deals from companies that had somehow weaseled their way into my email account. I clicked on a message from Frank Ellis and read: *Hi, Polly. I enjoyed our visit yesterday and appreciate you driving in to Portland to meet with me. I thought you should know that my kids are on the warpath over what we discussed. They can moan and groan and make all the threats they want, I'm not going to change my mind. Just wanted you to know that. Frank*

I sighed. Hopefully, I wouldn't end up in the middle of a family feud over an incident that happened more than a century ago. I'd write Frank back later and tell him I knew who was signing my check.

Then I noticed that Brad, Frank's son, had also emailed me. I braced myself and pulled up his message: *Mrs. Morton, I'm wondering why you didn't let me know that you were meeting with my father yesterday, when I specifically asked you to do so. Please do not meet with him again unless my sister or I is present. Also, please know that you will need our approval before you publish your book. I hope it won't be necessary to get my attorney involved in this. Bradley F. Ellis*

"Bully!" I blurted, infuriated that Brad Ellis felt he had the right to address me in such a condescending, authoritative manner. Well, I wouldn't be writing him back. Let him sit and stew.

"Yes, bring it on, *Bradley*," I uttered. I couldn't wait to get a look at that packet of letters Bev had mentioned. Hopefully, I'd uncover something even more shocking to sleaze up *Frank's* family history.

I studied the two boxes I'd dropped against a bookcase. Since they'd bounced around with the garbage in Stan's truck for nearly a week, I was lucky I now had them. And lord knew what else I'd find hidden in them.

I shivered at the thought, then turned back to my email and clicked on a message from Laura: *Hey, Pol. OMG! Stan is freaking me out. We need to talk. BTW Harley's picking me up on his Harley to take me to lunch, so it'll have to be in the PM. Hang in there! Hugs*

The vision that popped into my mind brought a smile to my lips—Laura in skintight pink leather with a big gaudy turquoise decal sewn on the back of her jacket. And her boots would have to be stilettos. The helmet, rhinestoned. On a day like today, she'd be holding on for dear life, so she wouldn't blow off the back of the bike. I chuckled, then muttered, "Oh, Laura. You must really like that guy. Now I. . . ."

The front door opened, and I froze. It closed. My heart pounded, and my muscles stiffened. I tried to look relaxed, like I was totally engrossed in my work.

Five seconds later he stood at my office door. "What should I do with the crab?"

I glanced his way. He looked wind burned and pooped. "How'd it go?" I asked.

He tugged off his cap and rubbed his matted hair. "About like I expected. What I can't figure out is why I ever put up with that guy's macho bullshit."

Because you and he were two peas in a pod, I almost informed him. But I had the feeling he already knew that and wasn't thrilled with the knowledge.

"I'll get some water heating for the crab. You're wet and smelly. Go clean up."

He gave me a hard look, nodded, and ambled on. When he turned, I squinted at his butt to see if he was still packing, but his jacket was too loose to tell.

A big pot of water boiled on the stove when he lugged a large bucket into the kitchen. "There's a dozen," he informed me.

So even with poachers, they'd limited. I looked in the bucket. Though a couple of the orange creatures crawled around, beady eyes flashing, most of them were still. I reached down and grabbed one across its back. It wiggled and tried to reach my fingers with its pinchers, but I dropped it into the boiling water before it latched onto me. After I wrangled five more into the pot, I dropped the lid onto it and set the timer for twenty minutes, then sucked on a bruised finger and studied Stan.

He seemed to be studying me, too, while he leaned against the counter and nibbled on a slice of cheese. I noted that he was back in gathered shorts and a baggy tee-shirt, this time with a tiny deer's head and oversized antlers plastered across it. If he stuck around, we needed to shop for clothes that fit, preferably minus the wildlife theme.

"So nothing exciting happened, just the same old, same old?" I probed.

"I guess. We put the boat in. We crabbed. We took the boat out. Not much to report." His gaze grew more intense, but when he spoke, it was with an even voice. "How about you, same old, same old?"

"Yep." Why hadn't he mentioned George's confrontation? Like me, he'd witnessed the whole thing. I itched to call him on it. I settled for prodding. "So nothing unusual, huh?"

His eyes narrowed even further. "Not that I can think of. He trash talked my bait. Appears that's a trigger point for him."

"I've been wondering about that—your memory loss, about how much you do recall. For instance, did spending the morning with George help you remember other times you've gone out in his boat with him?"

"Nope."

"Did it seem familiar, you know, like you'd done it before?"

"No, not really."

"But you knew what to do?" Even more than the memory loss, it's what gnawed at me. Why did he know how to do so many things—work a computer and bring up his email, cook a gourmet meal, get his window fixed, load a gun . . .? The list went on and on.

He shrugged. "Mostly. If I didn't, George made sure I did."

"How about other things—like me, for instance? What do you remember about me?"

Sparks flickered in his eyes. His jaw clenched. "Look, I told you, I don't remember much of anything, about you or anyone else. Let's just leave it at that!" He stuffed the rest of the cheese into his mouth and stomped to his toy room.

I'd pushed too far, but darn it, he didn't add up. I liked this version of him, so it was easy to just let it slide and ride the waves. To forget how weird it was. But this time, I'd had the distinct feeling he was scrutinizing me as much as I was scrutinizing him. What was that all about?

〰 ☼ 〰

The kitten purred on my lap. At least *it* wasn't sulking. I hadn't heard a peep from Stan since our discussion earlier. He'd come out of his room about an hour ago to start a load of laundry. Then he'd disappeared out the front door. No truck noises followed his exit. I was pretty sure he wasn't with George, so maybe he'd headed to the beach to lick his wounds.

With a sigh, I flexed my neck back and forth to work out the cricks. I'd been working on a couple of chapters from Frank's book for several hours, and my brain was fried. They were about Frank's growing-up years and his life today, much of which was a snoozer, and I had to stretch my imagination to put some verve into the rather humdrum reality. It was time for a break and a glass of wine. I relaxed back into my chair and let my eyes wander the room. They landed on the box filled with Frank's old documents. Then I remembered—the letters.

I set the kitten on the floor and walked to the two boxes. One held the copies Bev had made, and the other, the real stuff. Bev had said she'd given Stan the packets of letters, so I expected to see them lying on top of the pile. There were no letters in either box.

Visions of the mountain of garbage in the back seat with the boxes sounded alarms. My stomach constricted painfully. Hopefully, those letters hadn't fallen out of one of the boxes and then been discarded when Stan cleaned out his truck.

Maybe Stan had set them somewhere, intending to hand them to me. The kitchen desk was the obvious place, but I knew they weren't there, and they weren't in our bedroom. I considered snooping in his toy room but nixed that since Stan might return at any moment. The only place left was his truck, and it was spiffier than when he'd purchased it. The garbage had been hauled away the previous day, so that wasn't an option either. It looked like I'd have to paw through the papers in both boxes.

"Please let them be here," I murmured as I dropped down onto my knees beside the box of Frank's original documents. The kitten stretched out on the carpet to watch me carefully examine the delicate pieces of yellowed paper.

I'd barely started when the doorbell chimed. The kitten hopped straight up in the air, its fur charged, and I stood up to shake my legs out and walk to the front door. When I opened it, Javier stood there in a stylish black and neon lime workout suit. The high tech athletic shoes on his feet matched his outfit. His bright red hair stood on end, and his freckled cheeks glowed pink.

He gasped dramatically and strutted inside. "Oh, Pollyanna, what's going on in your life *now*?"

"What isn't?" I muttered, shutting the door. Then I considered his wording. "Why? What's happened?"

"Stan, that's what's happened. Phil and I saw him sprinting on the beach. And I don't mean running; I mean sprinting. For at least an hour. I mean I haven't seen the guy do anything faster than a mosey since you met him, and he's down there channeling Jesse—*freakin' amazing*—Owens."

"I told you; he's changed," I reminded him, relieved that Stan working off his frustrations was Javier's only concern.

"Yes, but you didn't tell me he'd lost forty pounds and turned to muscle in only four days. You need a reality check, girl 'cause that's just not possible."

My sigh turned into a huff. "I know that, but it's staring me in the face, so there's not much I can do about it. Like I told you, he is Stan, but he's not Stan."

"You got that right—he's definitely your lousy husband," Javier carped, grimacing. "You think he's been on some miracle *weight-loss-workout-be-nice* program, and we didn't take notice? Not!"

That had been my reasoning, but Javier had just negated it. I might have tuned out a four-month makeover; not Javier.

"If he was, it didn't keep him from chowing down on his favorite foods," I agreed. "I swear, Javier, he had his pudgy belly when I saw him Friday night. The next morning it was gone. New Stan has abs of steel."

I headed for the kitchen, and Javier followed. "Wine?" I offered, pulling an open bottle from the fridge.

He shook his head and waved a hand, then leaned his back against the counter. "And he still claims he's lost his memory?"

"Yeah, and I haven't seen anything to indicate otherwise." I filled a glass and took a fortifying sip while I gathered data. "His whole personality has changed. He's kind and thoughtful. I mean, the guy cooked this amazing pasta dish last night. He started a load of laundry before he headed to the beach. That little kitten that I was hiding from him, well it spends most of its time curled up on Stan's lap. And if that doesn't freak you out, go look in his truck. It's spotless!"

His ginger eyebrows shot up, and a hand shot out, palm facing forward. "Hey, I'm freaked out enough, thank you. Maybe you should talk to the law about this?"

"And tell them what? Since my husband overdosed, he's been acting strange."

"Yeah. When you put it like that, it does sound kind of lame."

"Besides, the sheriff thinks I'm a nutcase already." A nutcase who was convinced her husband was dead—I still hadn't given up on that notion. "He didn't know Stan before the metamorphosis, so he won't see how really bizarre this whole thing is. You and I did. Laura, too; she sees it. She's concerned, but she doesn't have any answers either."

He gave me an intense look. "Girl, you gotta stay on point. And remember that Phil and I are only a scream away."

"How's Phil doing?" I asked, latching onto a less worrisome topic. Maybe then my taut nerves would ease a bit.

Javier facial muscles visibly relaxed. "Much better, thanks to you. But I can tell he's still angry and upset. When he saw Stan on the beach, he growled a few *bleep* words and headed home. He worries this is just a reprieve, that Stan will return even more conniving and nasty."

"That's my fear, too," I admitted.

"Good. Then you won't get complacent." He took a deep breath and shook his head. "But that's not why I'm here. Your text. You said to come get crab."

"I sure did. Stan went out with George this morning and limited, so I have more than we can eat."

"With George, huh?" He sniggered scornfully. "I'd loved to be a pigeon hanging over that boat. He has to know Stan's been getting it on with his wife."

His words squeezed at my insides. After all, my husband was the one "getting it on" with her. I tried not to care, but I did. George?

"I'm not sure he'd care," I reasoned. "Have you seen him lately? He looks like he's strung out on drugs or is nursing a permanent hangover or something equally as debilitating."

"If I lived with Denise, I'd probably turn to drugs and booze, too."

"Seriously, I'm worried about him. I get the feeling he's about to explode."

He shook his head and eyed me as if I were a gullible five-year-old. "The guy's an obnoxious jerk, Pollyanna. If he didn't have all of us to push around, he'd have exploded long ago. Steer clear of him."

"Easy for you to say. He's not standing on your doorstep everyday," I retorted, a bit miffed by his attitude.

His eyes narrowed. "So he and this *new* Stan are still friends?"

I shrugged. "I don't know. New Stan doesn't seem to like him any more than I do. I guess I just have to wait and see what happens."

"Like I said, Phil and I are only a scream away. Or a text, if that's easier."

The front door opened, and Javier shot me an anxious look. A couple of seconds later, Stan wandered into the kitchen in a pair of athletic shorts and a sweat-soaked tee-shirt with a giant mosquito and the word *sucker* printed on it. His hair was damp and windblown, his feet bare.

He eyed us both warily. "Mind if I get some water?"

Javier didn't say a word, too busy ogling Stan as if he really were a zombie.

"Help yourself," I muttered. "Javier stopped by to get some crab."

"Uh . . . yes, and I better hurry on home and get them shelled," he blurted.

I gulped the last of my wine, then opened the fridge, grabbed a large plastic bag filled with three crab packed in ice, and handed it to him. "They're already cleaned."

He gave Stan a final once over and scurried to the front door. I followed him outside where he hummed the theme from the "Twilight Zone," his bugged-out eyes probing mine.

"I must be getting used to him," I admitted. "He doesn't seem so strange anymore."

"Well watch every move he makes. If he's faking it, he'll slip up." He turned to leave, then looked back and murmured, "Thanks for the crab. My special Louies tonight, one of Phil's faves."

"Glad you could use them." I watched Javier stride away, then headed for the kitchen to drink a couple more glasses of wine. Hopefully, Stan had sprinted himself into a better mood.

Only he wasn't in the kitchen or the living room. I checked the garage and the deck. No Stan. The kitten was asleep on a pile of foxed newsprint on the floor in my office. I picked it up and replaced the papers in a box, then locked the office door and shut it.

"Find Stan," I told the ball of fur. It stared up at me and meowed plaintively. Stan's toy room door opened and he peeked out at me, then down at the kitten. It scampered down the hall toward him.

"If only I could solve all of my problems that easily," I muttered as I retraced my steps to the kitchen to grab another packet of crab and the open bottle of wine.

When I stepped outside, I noticed the wind no longer battered me. The gentle breeze wafting in from the west smelled damp and salty, like the ocean. Though it was approaching evening, the sky was so clear that sunset seemed hours away.

There was no Harley parked in front of Laura's house, so I hugged my provisions close and stepped cautiously across the street in my bare feet. She answered on the first ring. No pink leather clothed her ample body, only lavender cotton and denim. A radiant smile lit up her face, even more dazzling than usual. No doubt lunch with Harley had put it there.

"Oh, good. You brought wine," she chirped. "And is that crab I see in that bag."

"For you," I said, handing it over. "Caught this morning. And the shells are filled out, so they're full of meat."

"*Mmmm* . . . I can already taste it. Thanks, Pol."

She led me into her turquoise and pink fifties-era kitchen where she stuffed the crab into her fridge, then slid a couple of pink Depression wine glasses out of a cabinet. I filled them with the chilled Chardonnay. Then we settled into a couple of high-back vintage chairs in her living room.

Laura loved old stuff, especially if it was from the thirties, forties, and fifties. Her row of floor-to-ceiling windows that faced west was decorated with lurid, floral bark cloth, and knickknacks, pictures, and lamps that I remembered seeing in my grandparents' house decorated every available space. Oh, and crocheted doilies and embroidered runners were lying about—lots of them.

I relaxed into the chair, which was amazingly comfortable, gazed out at the beach grass, sand, and water and felt myself gradually unwind. The ocean's murmur was a steady lament on this side of her house. A couple strolled along the wet sand near the water, fingers entwined, and a gathering of adults sat on blankets higher up on the beach, three young children romping around them.

"Quiet out there today," I remarked.

"Yeah, but now that the wind's died down, things will pick up." She paused and gave me a searching, rather sad look. "Stan was down there playing Olympic speed racer. What's that all about?"

"Javier told me. I think he's ticked at me because I asked too many questions."

"Javier?"

"No, Stan." I took a sip of wine, pulling words together. I could tell Laura pretty much anything, but how could I explain to her what made no sense to me. "I don't know, Laura. It just doesn't feel right—his memory loss, I mean. There are too many other things that don't make sense, like the baffling changes in his appearance and personality.

"The most exercise old Stan ever got was reeling in a salmon. There's no way he could sprint for an hour. He'd keel over from a heart attack after thirty seconds. And now he can cook like a chef, and get this: he did his own laundry. But what really fries me is he carries a gun."

She blinked hard and jerked forward. "What?"

So I wasn't the only one who found that alarming. "Uh-huh. Here he is acting like the meekest, nicest guy around, and he has a pistol shoved in the back of his belt."

"You saw it?"

I nodded. "I followed him this morning when he went crabbing with George, who by the way is about one pinch from going totally whacko."

"You tailed them in your car?" she asked, disbelief written all over her pretty face.

"Yes, I had some binoculars and I parked where I could see their boat. Stan's jacket blew up, and I saw his gun. I also saw this huge, tough-looking guy rough up George. Stan just sat on the boat and watched it happen."

She shook her head, her blonde curls bobbing, and made a throaty noise. "OMG! That doesn't sound like you, Pol. You actually spied on Stan?"

"Well, my life's so zany that I had to do something," I reasoned. "Besides, new Stan is kind of a . . . wimp. And George has been such a hot wire in the past few days that I worried about Stan being alone with him." I thought it best to keep my chocolate sneaker wave dream to myself for now. After all, I had to appear sane.

Laura burst out laughing, but she looked more angry than amused. I sipped wine, wondering if she was getting weird on me, too.

She finally pulled herself together, and took a healthy gulp from her glass. "I'm sorry, Pol. But seriously, do you really believe Stan needs you watching over him? I don't care how he acts or looks right now. Deep down inside, he's still Stan. He's still a rotten-to-the-core asshole. And he's still that louse you should never have married."

Wow! I didn't know how to respond to her outburst, but it sure made me feel lousy. I took a healthy gulp of wine, too. Maybe I should just get the bottle and drink from it.

"I'm sorry. I'm just so ticked at that guy right now that if I could get my hand on his gun, I'd probably use it on him," she snapped, her jaw set, eyes fuming.

I gazed outside. Laura was right; people were gravitating to the beach for an evening stroll. If only I were out there with them, my only concern being if a renegade wave would drench my sneakers. Then I braced myself and faced Laura. "Did he do something to you?"

"Worse than that; he did something to you."

"In the last few days?" I asked, praying she would say no.

Her eyes narrowed. "I don't know. Does it matter?"

"What'd he do?"

"You remember Harley?"

"Of course." And his reaction to Stan had been bugging me.

"Well, when he saw Stan yesterday, he recognized him"

"I had a feeling that was the case," I acknowledged with a sinking feeling.

"Harley's been doing a lot of internet dating, so he gets out and about a lot. Of course, I'm hoping that will stop now that he's met me."

"Yep, I got that, too," I told her, wishing she'd get to the point.

"So where did Harley see Stan?"

"At the Whale's Spout and a couple of other bars."

"And they got into a fight or Stan was spouting off or what?"

She gulped wine, then took a deep breath, and that "poor Polly" look blossomed on her face. I closed my eyes and held my breath, prepared for the worst, hoping I'd already faced it.

"I'm sorry, Pol. He was with another woman," she blurted.

Air seeped through my lips, and I stared at her, relieved. "It's okay. Javier told me he's been getting it on with Denise."

Her eyes grew as round as the saucers in the teacup display behind her. "Really . . . Denise? I even gave Stan more credit than that. But it wasn't her. Harley said she's probably in her early thirties, and she's blonde. He said they're definitely an item, that it's been going on for several months. They were together Friday night at the Whale's Spout. Stan must've seen me and jetted out of there."

And just like that, tears leaked from my stinging eyes to tickle a trail down my cheeks. I covered them with a hand, as if it might obliterate the hurt, humiliation, and feelings of worthlessness gushing from deep inside me.

I'd spent a whole day getting ready to celebrate my fortieth birthday with a night on the town with my husband. He knew how important it was to me. I'd waited hours for him to get home, making excuses for his tardiness, giving him the benefit of the doubt, blaming myself. And while I was doing that, he was out on the town with his young, blonde girlfriend. Talk about a slap in the face.

He'd cheated on me, lied to me, treated me like dirt, blackmailed my friends, chased away my daughter, and most likely done a whole lot more despicable things. But the thing that kept reeling through my mind was my unbelievably awful fortieth birthday.

Maybe Laura was right. Maybe it didn't matter which Stan did what. Maybe it was time to cut my losses and get rid of Stan. Period.

CHAPTER 7

"**W**ant to talk about it?" Stan asked. He stood in my office doorway in his sprinting duds, oozing concern.

From my chair, I studied him, trying to sort through the conflicting emotions gushing through me. He was a stranger, yet somehow I felt close to him. I didn't like who he was, but I liked him. And quite frankly, I didn't trust him. Deep down, I knew he wasn't being entirely truthful.

"Since you don't remember anything, there's nothing to talk about," I told him, stroking the fluff ball asleep in my lap.

He frowned. "So this is about something I did?"

"Like I said, you claim to have no memory, so talking about your lousy, lying, cheating ways is a moot point." Obviously, I was still upset from my visit with Laura. I'd taken a clue from Stan and had run on the beach until I was too exhausted to stand up, thinking my heart wouldn't have the oomph to hurt. I was wrong.

"Agreed. But it might help if you get it off your chest," he argued.

Well, maybe I didn't want to get it off my chest. Maybe, for once, I wanted to wallow in my misery.

He wouldn't let it go. "Look, I'm as frustrated as you, but it doesn't help us figure out what's going on and work through this if you clam up."

"Oh, and you didn't?" I challenged.

"Point taken. Now what's the problem?"

"*You* are the problem," I snapped. "Why couldn't you just keep it in your pants?"

Enlightenment blossomed on his too appealing features. "*Ahhh . . . Denise.*"

"No, not Denise. I need to believe she pounced during your

drunker moments."

He frowned, clearly confused.

So I tried to explain. "It's just that I've made so many excuses for you, and I've blamed myself for your rotten behavior. I told myself that you were just being sidetracked, that I needed to accept you for who you are. The one thing I always came back to was the fact that you were a faithful husband. For me, that was proof that you at least cared about me."

"So there's someone else. Who?"

"I don't know," I admitted, though I sure as hell aimed to find out who she was. "But she's young and blonde, and you've been seeing her for a while."

"And you know this because?"

"Harley's seen you with her."

He harrumphed and eye shrugged. "Thus, the reason for that awkward moment."

"Uh-huh."

"Might her name be Amber?"

The name on his cell phone! Since I'd snooped on his property, I chose my next words carefully. "Why do you ask that?"

"Because I have a couple dozen texts from her on my cell, asking where I am, each of them sounding more desperate."

"And you didn't text her back?"

"I don't know who she is, so I thought it best to ignore them."

"Any phone calls or voicemails?"

"No."

"Email messages?'

"A few. Just more frantic pleas to contact her."

"When did her texting barrage begin?"

He looked at the phone clutched in his hand and punched buttons for several long moments. "Saturday, late afternoon."

So her name was Amber, which rang no bells. She was with Stan Friday night and had become worried the next afternoon. But how about Denise? She must've been curious about what was going on next door, yet I'd seen no texts from her on Stan's phone.

"Do you have anything from Denise?" I asked.

He shook his head. "No. Why?"

"Doesn't that seem odd?"

"Evidently, Amber doesn't know what's happened to me. Denise does."

"Yes, but she didn't know until she showed up here with her disgusting enchiladas," I reminded him. "For all she knew, you were dead."

His eyes dropped to his phone again. At last, he looked up and shrugged. "Nope. There's nothing from Denise on here, not even her phone number."

Which didn't make sense. Even if Denise hadn't successfully bagged Stan, she'd been pursuing him like a fox in heat. I'd heard the two of them conversing on the phone numerous times and had only rolled my eyes.

"Are there any other women's numbers?" I asked.

He consulted his phone again. "A few, but no more texts or phone calls."

That should've given me some relief. It didn't. "Well, if you don't know who Amber is, we have nothing to discuss," I murmured.

He took a deep breath, scrunched his mouth, and seemed to mull over something. "I shelled a crab for you and made a salad. They're in the fridge," he finally offered.

Which was thoughtful, but it didn't make up for all of his transgressions in his past life. "Thank you, but I'm not hungry."

"Well, I'm gonna take a shower and go to bed."

"Good night," I mumbled as I turned back to my computer screen.

The print was blurred, a sign that it was my bedtime, too. Besides, I'd done more soul searching than writing. I read through the last few paragraphs I'd typed and winced. Whatever I'd accomplished this evening would most likely need to be rewritten. Thank you, Stan!

I shut down the computer and eyed the television. Since Friday, I'd not been tempted to turn it on. "Guess all that drama loses its attraction when it's happening to me," I mumbled to the kitten as I cuddled it against my chest and stood. Tiny green eyes stared up at me. "You gonna sleep with me tonight?"

I locked my office and made the rounds to make certain all of the lights were off, the doors locked, and the alarm set. Since I'd taken a shower after my run on the beach, all I had to do was brush my teeth.

Gazing out through the wall of windows onto the deck and the golf course beyond, I thought back to Friday night when Stan had been out there in his recliner, and I'd been convinced he was dead. Had it only been five days ago? Perhaps it was turning forty or maybe it was an upshot of being on the receiving end of a five-day pounding, but I felt so much older and wiser than I had when I'd stood here Friday night.

I closed my eyes and visualized Stan in his cargo shorts and snug Guns N' Roses tee-shirt. His arms dangle free, and his legs are spread eagle. And there's his chubby belly peeking out between his waistband and where his shirt has scrunched up—not fat, but it soon would be if he didn't cut back on the carbs. He's not wearing a belt, and the shorts fit snuggly at the waist. His dark hair is shaggy and mussed, and his eyes are closed, mouth hanging open. Empty beer bottles rest in a messy pile beside his chair. Not far off, a lone pillow from our bed provokes suspicions.

Bracing myself, I reach out and touch his arm. It's cold and firm, like chilled melon rind. I fall to my knees and place my ear over his open mouth. No sound or warmth whispers from it. Nothing.

"He's dead," I vowed as the image evaporated.

But how could that be when I'd just spoken with him?

〰☼〰

I shot straight up in bed. My eyes darted, two determined laser beams searching the darkness. A loud siren blasted from somewhere, high-pitched and pounding. The security alarm!

"Oh, lordy, what now?" I gasped as air streamed through my lips. Pain pierced the skin on my abdomen.

I rubbed at my eyes to awaken them, then patted my heart to still its thumping with one hand while I pulled the kitty claws free with the other.

A shift in the air told me someone stood not far from me. I froze, straining to hear anything but the deafening screech, trying to calm the quivering feline.

"Are you okay," a male voice called.

Two beats later I realized who it was. "Yes. Did you open a door?"

"No."

And then Susan's sorrowful voice gushed from my phone. I felt for it on the nightstand, flicked it on, and held it to my ear.

"This is Global Security. We've been alerted that you have a security breach. Can I have your password, please?" a male voice inquired.

My password? Was he serious? I'm suffering a panic attack, and he expects me to come up with some word that had meaning eons ago. I searched my memory. Oh, yeah. "Pink roses," I told him, suddenly remembering all of those roses Stan hadn't given me.

"Do you require assistance?"

"Do we need assistance?" I asked Stan.

"No, I can handle it. Whoever it was, that racket must've chased them away."

We were yelling over the siren, which wailed so loud that it pounded in my head, right along with the pounding of my heart. "No. We'll take care of it," I told the guy on the other end of the line.

"Okay. I'll switch the alarm off. If you need help, call us or set off the alarm again. The Sheriff's Office will respond."

And miraculously, the noise ceased. "Thank you," I said, my voice shrill to my ears, before I punched the phone off.

I reached out a shaky hand and turned on a lamp. Stan materialized, clad only in a pair of baby blue boxers. I eyeballed his torso. No way was its perfection anything close to what I'd visualized earlier that night. Then I noticed the pistol dangling from his fingers and flinched.

"You have a handgun?" I probed, hoping to elicit some straight answers.

He studied it as if he'd forgotten it was there. "Evidently. It's one of the 'toys' from my 'toy room.'"

I didn't know it was possible to make air quotes with a gun in your hand, but I was wrong. When it dropped back down to his side, I breathed a sigh of relief. "Is it loaded?"

"Yep. I figure it's best to be prepared. I took it crabbing today. That George is dangling a little too far out there for my peace of mind. I didn't know what to expect from him. Thought I might end up being the crab bait."

Well, that didn't take much probing. Evidently, he didn't share my qualms about accessorizing with a handgun.

I pushed back the sheets and stood up, tucking the still trembling kitten close against me. Stan eyed the kitten, then me. Fortunately, I'd worn a classy cotton nightgown to bed instead of my usual mismatched flannels, so I didn't feel like a total loser next to his flawless physique.

"We need to check the house," I prodded, wondering why someone wanted inside my home.

"Uh . . . yeah. Stay here. I'll take care of it, starting with your bathroom and closet."

He disappeared, and I crept over to make sure the locks on the French doors were still secure. They were. "If he thinks we're staying here alone, he's dead wrong," I informed the kitten, then cringed at my choice of words. Whether Stan was now alive or dead or even of the living dead, one possibly dead body in a week was all I could handle.

When he returned, I waited at the door. He gave me a perturbed look and muttered, "Stay behind me."

Visions of a skulking shape grabbing me from behind, then dragging me and my panicky kitty off flashed before me. "Why? I thought you said it was safe," I reminded him.

He stared at me hard. "Humor me."

I nodded at his gun. "Okay, but watch where you point that thing."

"No problem."

With that, he turned and walked out the bedroom door with me nearly tiptoeing on his heels. We checked Sara's room and the spare bath. No one lurked in the shadows. My office door was still locked tight, as was the front door. The living area was ahead, a darkened, high-ceilinged area strewn with a couch, a couple of overstuffed chairs and a couple with no stuffing, several small stands, and Stan's Barcalounger. Stan flicked on a light, and the space became more welcoming. There really was no place to hide, so he stepped to the French doors and checked the locks. I noticed that the gun still hung at his side.

Next we passed through the kitchen and on into the laundry area. Since it appeared that no one hid in a dark corner, his intention to murder us, I set the kitten down and filled its dish with food. Like a starving mini panther, it tore into its vittles.

"This is the one," Stan uttered from behind me.

I twirled. "What? I checked it when I went to bed."

His brows rose. "It's unlocked now."

Shivers prickled my spine and shoulders. This was too real. "Why would someone want inside our house?" I wondered aloud.

I watched in awe as Stan morphed into *Robocop*. Tense and unwavering, he raised the gun in front of him and gripped it with two hands. "I don't know. I'm gonna check the garage. Stay here and lock the door behind me." This time it was an order.

He opened the door, flipped the light switch, and did the gun searching thing like they do on all of those cop shows, then disappeared. I shut the door and locked it but held off on the deadbolt in case Stan needed a quick exit.

Then I lived through the longest minutes in my life. I pressed my ear against the door, straining to hear through it. All was quiet. Pinpricks on my legs told me the kitten was through with its grub and clawing its way up my nightgown. I reached down, tugged it loose, and cradled it.

A loud knock sounded and I twitched. "It's me," Stan said.

I opened the door. He stood there looking more like his wimpy self. "He's gone now, but he sure made a mess of the garage."

"Seriously?" First my office, then Stan's truck. Now our garage. I couldn't come up with one reason anyone would want anything we had.

He nodded, an odd glint in his eyes. "You have a Twinkie fetish?"

"No. You do," I informed him, more annoyed than frightened by the invasion now that the danger was past. "And their shelf life can't last forever, so you better get to eating those babies."

I stepped around him and scanned the trashed space. My car was directly in front of me, the trunk lid up. I opened the front passenger door. Being the neat freak I was, it should've been spotless. Instead, the glove box was open—papers, owner's manuals, hand sanitizer, a couple of CDs, and a packet of towelettes strewn on the seat and floor. There really was nothing else to empty in there, so I stepped to the trunk. The floor mat was tossed to the side. A flashlight, paper towels, garbage bags, and a bottle of water had been pulled from the storage compartment, and the road assistance kit was unzipped.

No doubt about it, someone was definitely searching for something. But what?

My first instinct was to tidy up my car before I moved on, but I'd seen enough TV crime shows that I knew to swallow the urge to pull a couple of towelettes and scrub away the intruder's cooties, along with his fingerprints and DNA. Instead, I gritted my teeth and shuffled around the car.

It was a three-car garage, but the other two spaces were occupied by a battered '57 Chevy Stan pretended to be restoring and a hodgepodge of tools, outdoor playthings, and dusty exercise equipment, some of it Stan's, some of it inherited from my dad, and some of it Sara's and mine. The back corner was home to Stan's Twinkie stash—enough of them to keep a slew of kids' sports teams on a sugar high for a year. They were usually tightly bundled inside a tower of bulky cardboard boxes.

Not tonight. Tonight it looked like a freak Twinkie storm had swept through my garage and left a layer of the creamy, cellophane-wrapped cakes everywhere. They covered open containers and numerous other objects that had been swept off shelves, dusted the larger items and storage units, and were piled in drifts on the floor. As if strategically placed to lure passersby to come closer, a few even adorned Stan's rusting Chevy.

"We can always burn them for heat come winter," Stan murmured from somewhere behind me.

"It's a gas fireplace," I informed him. "Besides, all of that cellophane can't be good for the ozone. I'd planned to donate them, but now that they're out of their containers, I doubt anyone will take them."

"Why so many?"

"Word was the company was going to stop making them. You panicked."

Which was putting it nicely. Actually, it was more like he'd gone on a month-long tirade before he'd come up with the idea to squirrel away a lifetime supply.

As for new Stan, he ogled his sabotaged stockpile like it was worthless cake crumbs, probably trying to make peace with his former self. Finally, he took a deep breath, and let it seep through his lips in a long sigh. Gun dangling, he turned to me. "You want to call the cops?"

After the day I'd had, the mere mention of a midnight meeting with Sheriff Bronson made my empty stomach gyrate. "I can't deal with this right now. Let's wait until morning."

He gave me a facial nod and glanced around. "Any idea what they're looking for?"

I looked, too, my numbed mind searching for an answer that made sense. "I honestly can't think of anything, but if you had a memory, I bet you'd know."

"What does that mean?"

Apparently he didn't like my surmise. His features had gone hard, and an intense glint flickered in his eyes. "It means you must be involved in something shady. Otherwise, whoever did this would just ring the doorbell and ask for what they want," I explained.

"So I'm being blamed, huh. How do you know *you* didn't land smack dab in the middle of something fishy? Evidently, those drugged chocolates were meant for you."

He did have a point. And he didn't know my office had been searched, or that some guy had followed me. But what in the heck did I have that someone else might want enough to resort to break-ins? Nothing; that's what.

Of course, he also didn't know why Phil had written that check—I didn't want to consider how many others he might be blackmailing. I'd promised Javier I'd keep it on the QT, so I bit my tongue against the urge to throw it in his face.

Instead, I shrugged and shook my head. "I don't know, but I'll deal with it tomorrow." I paused to consider the trashed garage. "Plus, this mess."

ᨓ ☼ ᨓ

Waves pounded on my windows. Like a massive kettle drum, the steady vibrations shook the whole house. I gaped at the churning chocolate outside the French doors and watched in horror as streams of the dark, velvety liquid seeped into my bedroom around their edges. If I didn't leave the safety of my mattress island, I'd soon be drowning in the stuff.

I thrashed at the confining sheets, trying to free myself. To escape before the deadly chocolate smothered me.

The riotous ocean had already consumed one person. I barely discerned his voice calling for me to rescue him. I knew he was right outside the door, but if I opened it to let him in, I would be devoured, too.

"Help me . . . please."

There it was again—the insistent plea. I pushed the sheets aside and stood beside the bed, staring at the pleading face pressed to the glass, gooey chocolate oozing between my toes.

His features sparked alarms. I blinked and shook myself, trying to pull everything into focus.

Just like that, the chocolate receded, and I stood on my hardwood floor staring into George's desperate eyes. I blinked again and clutched my racing heart, shaking at the brain fog. Yes, it was definitely George, but something was wrong with him.

I stepped closer. He leaned against the door, his bloodied face smashed against its window. Scarlet squiggles trickled down the glass. As if he were a windup toy, his right hand hammered rhythmically against the doorframe.

"What the heck?" I whispered, concern slowly replacing the fear that had me shivering. Drawing light from the lamp I'd left on, I steeled myself and shuffled nearer. And he collapsed into a heap on the deck.

"Oh, lordy!" I gasped, rushing to the door, fumbling with the locks.

When I wrenched it open, the security siren blasted and sent my heart rate spiraling even higher. Ignoring it, I dropped to my knees beside George. His lids were closed, but I heard ragged breaths. Blood spewed from his flattened nose. Both eyes were puffy mounds of raw flesh.

Suddenly, George lay in a pool of bright light. I glanced up into Stan's anxious gaze. His darted back into the room. "I'll get it," he yelled.

I was too rattled to try and figure out what he'd gone to get. "Oh, George, what have you gotten yourself into?" I murmured. *And most likely Stan, too,* I silently conceded, growing even more alarmed when I noticed the amount of blood staining my deck.

My hands shook so hard it made my search for blood-gushing parts a lesson in determination. He'd crumbled onto his side, and I was hesitant to move him, but I didn't want him to bleed to death either. I figured he'd walked here, so his legs must be intact. I straightened them, then ran a shaky hand over his grimy camo gear, searching for dark, wet spots. They appeared to be isolated around his middle. I was tugging at his jacket when Stan dropped down across from me.

"The ambulance is on its way," he informed me.

"Thank you for calling." I'd been so focused on George that I hadn't noticed the alarm had stopped blaring, and I'd completely forgotten about the security company check-in.

"Can I help?" he asked, eyeing my bloody, quaking fingers as I tried to get inside George's jacket.

"If you can get these buttons free," I muttered, wrapping my arms around my chest and slipping my hands beneath them. Though I knew the temperature was in the high sixties, it felt like ice coursed through my veins, freezing my flesh.

I watched Stan unbutton George's jacket and open it. Then he lifted his blood-soaked tee-shirt. Three stark gashes on George's hairy belly oozed.

"Stab wounds?" I guessed.

"Appears to be. You have something cotton we can press on them to try and get the bleeding stopped?"

I did, but I wasn't sure my wobbly legs would get me to it. I eyed my cotton nightgown, now smeared with red blotches, then grabbed the hem. A few rips later, I handed Stan a folded square of cotton. He pressed it over one of the cuts. George moaned, and my eyes darted to his face. His lids remained closed.

Breathing a sigh of relief, I ripped two more squares, folded them, and placed them on the other two wounds. Then I hesitantly pushed on them with my palms. "You think that big guy at the marina did this?" I asked.

When I didn't get a reply, I looked up into Stan's cold stare. I swore I could feel him snooping in my mind, searching for something. But what?

"Darn it," I muttered when what had come out of my big mouth hit me. If it were possible, I shook even harder, glad my stomach was empty since it was threatening me, too.

The doorbell's chime broke some of the tension.

"I'll get it," he uttered through clenched teeth.

I watched him walk away in his baggy blue boxers. As he passed by the bed, he reached out and stuffed a metal object beneath my pillow. So he'd had his gun with him, hidden from me, the whole time. "And you think my behavior is suspicious," I murmured, shaking my head.

Moments later, the Saturday morning crew returned to my deck, gurney in tow. I wondered what they'd thought when Stan, the patient they'd carted away on their last visit, answered the door in his underwear. No doubt, we provided colorful stories for their get-togethers.

"We'll take it from here," one of the men said.

I struggled to my trembling feet and stepped back to give him access. His gaze slid down my bloody nightgown before he dropped to the deck and began to inspect George.

Taking my cue from him, I slipped past Stan without making eye contact and into my bathroom, where I stared into the mirror at my pasty, blood-smeared face. My stomach heaved. I grabbed it, lifted the toilet lid, and gagged several times, managing to wrench up only yellowish bile. It lit a fire in my throat. I rinsed my mouth and gargled several times with water, unable to get rid of the bitter taste.

With shaky hands, I scrubbed my face, arms, and hands. Then I tugged off my nightgown and slid into a pair of worn jeans and a heavy sweater. Still, I shivered uncontrollably. Even my teeth rattled.

"Get a grip," I told myself, gazing intently into my panic-stricken eyes in the mirror. "This isn't something you can ignore. Get your butt out there, and deal with it."

So I did. Reluctantly.

〰☼〰

"Here's your coffee." I set the steaming, half-filled mug in front of Sheriff Bronson, then slid another across the kitchen table to Stan and a third in front of my chair. The sheriff eyed it like it was poison. "Cream and sugar coming up," I promised before I turned to fetch them.

It was two in the morning. George had been hustled onto the gurney and was now speeding toward the hospital in Lincoln City, siren blaring. Hopefully, Denise wasn't far behind. With my help, the sheriff had rousted her from her bed, kicking and squawking like a disturbed hen. My guess was he didn't like her attitude because he'd informed her that he could either interview her at the station or the hospital. She'd chosen the latter.

Apparently, he'd meant after he'd spent some quality time with Stan and me.

I dropped the cream and sugar in the center of the table along with a couple of spoons, then remembered that new Stan consumed his caffeine black and pushed the additives closer to Sheriff Bronson before I settled into a wooden chair. The sheriff emptied half of the pitcher into his coffee along with several spoonfuls of sugar and set to stirring. He tasted it, raised his caterpillar brows over his horn rims, hummed, and nestled into his chair.

My stomach still roiled, so I curled my hands around the mug's warmth and held on. Not even a week had passed, and here we were again—Sheriff Bronson and I. And Stan sat across the table, steely eyes glued on me as if I'd confessed to planting surveillance cameras in his toy room and truck. The kitty purred in his lap, unaware of its master's acrimony. No doubt Stan had a weapon tucked beneath that loose hoodie in which kitty snuggled. Talk about a study in contradictions.

Just suck it up and get through this interrogation, I told myself. Then you can curl up in your nice, safe bed and sleep through the rest of this night from hell. Only it wasn't safe, was it? Fear churned in my gut.

Evidently, Sheriff Bronson planned to do some serious note taking this time. He had a voice recorder and a thick yellow legal pad laid out before him. While the ambulance crew did their job, he'd run through our recollections of George's baffling appearance with each of us. Now, pen in hand, he eyed Stan and me, then punched a button on the recorder, voiced the date and time in his gravelly voice, and asked, "How well did you know Mr. Seaver?"

I glanced at Stan, who was too caught up in being pissed off at me and my spying jaunt to hazard an answer. "Stan fishes and crabs with him. Occasionally, hunts and golfs, too," I told the sheriff. "Oh, and he's screwing his wife."

The sheriff blinked hard and studied Stan, then me. Stan's eyes simmered.

Well, too bad. If he wasn't going to participate here, I figured I might as well be the one to lay it out there. No doubt, Sheriff Bronson would chat with Laura and Javier, too. They'd welcome the opportunity to trash talk Stan's seedier moments, and I'd seen enough cop shows to know not to "hold back" my way into the suspect corner.

"I *had* a short fling with her," Stan admitted, throwing me a snarly look.

"And how long did that last?" the sheriff probed, his face flushed a rosy pink.

Stan shrugged.

"He has an alleged memory loss," I informed the sheriff, hoping it might explain Stan's shitty attitude.

This time he really scrutinized Stan through his bottle-thick eyeglasses. Stan lifted his brows and stared right back.

"Ever since he gorged on my truffles," I added. "Maybe it was the chocolate. Maybe he's allergic to it or something."

The sheriff scribbled on his notepad, then turned to me. "About that chocolate, we haven't come up with anything. You?"

I shook my head though the words *only in my dreams* flitted through my mind. "No one I spoke with saw anyone leave them."

He tapped several fingers, thoughtful, while he swigged coffee-laced cream and sugar. Finally, he turned to Stan. "You don't remember anything at all?"

"No, not even my hot, steamy affair," he avowed.

Sheriff Bronson's spectacles darted to me, then back to Stan. I was so numb that I barely felt the jab. I swallowed the hurt and any outward response, then mentally donned another layer of armor.

"But you did spend time with Mr. Seaver?" he probed.

"Yes, we went crabbing this morning. I remember that," Stan mumbled.

"And how did he seem?"

"Like a strung-out, macho asshole."

The sheriff flinched at Stan's words. "Strung-out, what do you mean by that?"

Before he spoke, Stan actually appeared to consider his response. "He was wired, really nervous. It didn't take much to set him off. And he seemed obsessed with the bait and the traps and where they were placed. He insisted on going crabbing, but he didn't seem to give a rip about the crab." He paused and eyeballed me. "But maybe that's normal for him. I really can't remember."

Sheriff Bronson turned to me, too, a questioning look on his pudgy face.

I sighed. "He's always been a macho asshole, but the strung-out part is new. Lately, I've felt like he's operating on the edge. Like he's about to blow."

Since Stan knew I'd tailed him, I figured there was no need to stop there. Maybe this was my chance to explain why I'd done it. "It was to the point that I was worried about Stan going out with him this morning, so I followed in my car and watched them in Yaquina Bay from the south marina side, in case something happened to Stan."

"And did you see anything unusual?" the sheriff asked.

I nodded and turned to Stan, willing him to speak up. He didn't, so I did. "Not while they were in the bay. But after they dropped the pots, they went back to the marina, and George got into a heated disagreement with a man."

"You saw it?"

"Yes. He was huge—tall with massive shoulders." I traveled back, pulling the harsh images from my brain. "George is a husky guy, but he towered over George. I didn't get a good look at his face because he had a black stocking cap pulled down over his forehead. At first the two of them were just arguing, but then he manhandled George for several minutes before he let him go."

"Could you hear what they were saying?"

"No, I was quite a ways away, watching them through binoculars."

The sheriff jotted notes and sipped from his mug, then turned to Stan. "Did you see it, too?"

He nodded, but his intent gaze was on me. "Yes. It was pretty much as Polly said. They were up by that little store at the marina."

"Did you hear anything?"

"No, the wind was blowing umpteen miles per hour through there, and I was more focused on keeping my breakfast in my gut than on those two." He paused and seemed to shift gears before his eyes landed on the sheriff. "I figured George asked for whatever the guy gave him. He really is an asshole."

"Did you get a good look at him?"

He shook his head. "Like Polly said, he was tall and muscular. And he was dressed all in black. He walked like a weight lifter. You know, kind of strutted with his arms swinging out from his body. I snapped a couple of pictures. You can't make out his face, but I'll send them to you."

"Ditto," I murmured.

The sheriff considered us both, then dropped his gaze. While he scribbled, Stan and I eyeballed each other circumspectly. He seemed to let go of some of his animosity. Still, there was wariness about him.

Sheriff Bronson's gruff voice blasted through the unease. "Was there anyone else around who might have seen their disagreement?"

I thought back to that morning—was it really only seventeen hours ago? I'd been surprised at how few bodies had milled around the marina. "There weren't many people, and no one seemed to pay any attention to them," I told him. "Oh, there was this one guy out by the restrooms where I was. He was leaning against a big white truck, drinking out of a paper cup, and talking on his cell. He might've seen something."

"Anything unusual about him?"

"No. Just your typical middle-aged man who hangs out at the marina—average height, average weight, a lot of outdoor gear covering his body." *Possibly hitting on me*, I silently added.

He scrawled, then asked, "Had you followed George and Stan before?"

"No," I blurted, offended by his insinuation and where it might take his sheriffy mind-ramblings. "But George was acting so erratic, and Stan with his memory loss is kind of . . . well, a bit of a Milquetoast. I was worried about what George might do to him," I explained. I would've shared my chocolate sneaker wave dream with him, but he didn't seem like the kind of guy who would grasp its significance.

"Has anything else unusual happened lately . . . other than what I don't already know about?"

My eyes slid to Stan to give him the go-ahead, but he was messing with something hidden beneath the table in his lap, which would've been a bit unsettling had I not known there was a kitten down there. So I rolled my eyes, took a deep breath, and dove into the next segment of this fiasco—my life.

"Someone's been trying to get into our house," I informed him. "I think he's searching for something. I just can't figure out what it is."

Either Sheriff Bronson's tricklings of caffeine had kicked in or I'd finally said something to uproot him, because his tubby torso actually bounced forward in his chair, beady eyes alert through his mega specs. "And you know this because," he demanded.

I blinked, surprised by his response. I mean, he probably dealt with several break-ins a day. "Stan's truck was broken into two nights ago," I told him. "Then a little before midnight tonight, someone broke into our garage. It's trashed. He tried to get into the house, too, but he activated the security alarm, and it must've scared him off. By the time we looked in the garage, he was gone." I didn't bring up the fact that my office had been searched, too. I still clung to the theory that it was Stan's doings.

"And you didn't let us know?" he groused.

Which led me to defend my actions. "Come morning, I planned to. I didn't know George was going to show up at my door stabbed and beaten."

"Could be it was him in your garage."

"Maybe," I agreed. "But I can't think of any reason he'd break in there. If he wants something, all he has to do is ask for it."

He shook his head resignedly and jotted notes, then drilled me with a scowl. "Did you check outside?"

"No. We kind of figured the guy was long gone." But maybe he'd stuck around, and George had heard the alarm and gone to investigate. Then maybe George had bumped into him and been beaten to a pulp and stabbed. Guilt gnawed at me.

"Once the men are done outside, they'll need to process the garage, too. In the meantime, don't touch anything in there."

"We didn't," Stan assured him. "But you might want to check George's garage. Maybe it was broken into, too."

The sheriff gave a jerky nod and pulled a cell phone from his pocket. For several long moments, he punched buttons, his plump features mirroring his emotional journey. Finally he set it on the table next to the recorder and swigged the rest of his coffee before his bespectacled eyes landed on Stan. "I doubt it. His wife's car was in there, and I didn't hear anything from her."

"Anything else you're not telling me?" he asked, glancing from Stan to me.

I eyed the two of them, wondering if it was worth bringing up. After all, I hadn't seen my stalker for two days, so could be, it was just my overactive imagination.

"What is it?" Stan prodded, concern warming his dark eyes.

"Some guy was following me," I murmured.

Shock transformed his passive features. "What? And you didn't tell me?"

Quite truthfully, I didn't think he'd care. But I couldn't admit that in front of Sheriff Bronson. So I shrugged and rationalized. "I didn't think it was a big deal. I saw him in the parking lot at The Galley on Sunday. Then on Monday, when I drove into Portland, he followed me up to Frank Ellis' house and down to the waterfront.

"I stopped at Spirit Mountain on the way home and noticed him inside the casino. That's when I figured out that he must've been tailing me all along. I managed to sneak out of there and haven't seen him since. Then when. . . ."

"*The* Frank Ellis?" the sheriff interjected.

"I guess," I murmured, surprised that Sheriff Bronson knew of him. "I'm writing his family history for him. I spent some time interviewing him Monday morning. Then I went down to Waterfront Park to get a feel for the area. The guy following me stood not more than twenty feet from me, so when I saw him in the casino, I recognized him."

"What did he look like?"

An image popped into my head, as clear as the sky had been that day on the waterfront. "Youngish. Tall and lanky. Dark hair, I think. He wore a baseball cap, so I didn't see much of his face. He drove a sporty type of black car, you know, with one of those wingy things on the back."

He and Stan shared a knowing glance before he scribbled notes, then asked, "Did you get his license number?"

So many times, I could have. If I'd only known. "No, but I will if I ever see him again."

Leaning forward, he gave me the same no nonsense look my mother had once leveled at me. "If you do see him again, you give me a call."

"Me, too," Stan uttered.

My eyes flicked between their solemn gazes. "Okay," I assured them.

Sheriff Bronson seemed to sigh several hours' worth of air while he settled back into his chair like a nesting robin. "Anything else you've kept to yourself?" he uttered.

Of course, there was. But I'd promised Javier I'd keep quiet about Stan's blackmail endeavor. I looked to Stan to see if he'd confess to his fling with Amber. He had an odd, contemplative look on his face, as if he'd mentally slipped from the room. I bit my tongue. No need to drag Amber into this until I'd identified her and was assured that Harley's vices didn't include spreading unsubstantiated rumors.

I pasted what I hoped was a sincere look on my face and said, "Not that I can think of."

So I suppose I was holding back information after all. I sure hoped it didn't come back to bite me.

ᨒ ✿ ᨒ

"Milquetoast?" he challenged.

Which was a long stretch from any label I'd tack onto him at the moment. We stood in the hall—Stan and I—so close that his warm breaths fluttered my bangs, and eyed each other warily. I was too disturbingly aware of his musky scent and his chiseled features, of the muscles that lurked beneath his gray sweatshirt, to call him anything but "manly."

Midst a flurry of packing and organizing the faux leather case he'd lugged into the house with him, Sheriff Bronson had instructed his men to clear out and return at eight sharp the next morning to process our garage and interview the neighbors.

With a stern look aimed at Stan and me, he'd barked, "And, you two, keep your noses out of there," before he scampered toward the door on his matchstick legs. As if he'd hit a brick wall, he stopped and looked back. "Your feet, too," he added gruffly.

And now, after being thoroughly trounced by the sheriff in the middle of the night, Stan was in my face and questioning my metaphors.

Steeling myself, I stuck my hands into my jean pockets, so they wouldn't reach out and touch him and made a feeble attempt to push aside the intense feelings his overpowering male aura had awakened inside me. The last thing I needed on my plate right now was a passionate liaison with a husband I barely knew.

"Yes, Milquetoast," I insisted. "Look it up—unassertive, timid, docile."

"I know what it means," he snapped, sparks in his eyes.

Evidently, I'd offended him. Was that what this huddled *tête-à-tête in* the dimmed hallway outside my bedroom door was all about— his attempt to prove his masculinity? If so, I had to admit it was working.

Still, I fought it. "Well, good for you because the old you wouldn't have a clue. He was more about action, and screw the consequences. You're the antithesis of him—content to let life happen around you and do whatever you're told, like a trusting child. Surely, there's a happy medium?"

"So get some balls, Stan. Is that what you're saying?"

Suddenly the heat was stifling. I didn't want to think about Stan's balls or any other parts of his anatomy. So I studied the "growing up" photos of Sara displayed on the taupe walls and tugged at the front of my sweatshirt while I waited for the flames in my cheeks to chill.

"I mean, George is being pummeled and you just sit there and watch?" I finally explained. "And you even had a gun." My eyes dropped, searching his waistline for signs that he was still carrying.

"Like I said, George probably egged that guy on. If he's gonna dish it out, he better be willing to take it, too," he argued.

He had a point. And in truth, he had taken control of the situation earlier when the alarm had blasted us both out of our beds. And he'd searched the garage alone, gun ready. Given his alleged situation, perhaps I was being a bit hard on him.

"Maybe so," I agreed. "But what about when the sheriff was grilling me, glaring at me from behind those thick glasses with those accusing eyes? You just sat there petting the kitten and let me sweat and do all of the work."

I paused to consider the lump of fear that had plagued me since my first visit with Sheriff Bronson. "I know he thinks I did it," I blurted.

He blinked hard; questions filled his eyes. "Did what?"

If only I could suck my words back. They weren't meant for anyone's ears but mine. "I don't know, but whatever it is, he does," I explained lamely.

His soft chuckle sent my bangs flying. My insides fluttered. Then he grew pensive, his eyes probing mine. "I'm sorry," he finally murmured. "Most of that stuff I just don't remember, so it doesn't mean anything to me. And when we sat down with the sheriff, I was trying to figure out why you tailed me today."

I shrugged, ready to move on to sleep or a new topic. I eyed the open doorway, and George's bloody, beaten face flashed before me. Prickles of fear raced through me. I shook the vision away and murmured, "Well now you know."

"Yeah, you were worried about me. That's sweet." He smiled, and his whole face lit up, making my heart do funny things. "Although I'm wondering what you planned to do if George did go berserk—swim out to the boat through that choppy water and rescue me?"

"*Ha. Ha*. Very funny. You took a gun with you, so evidently you were worried, too."

Just like that, he turned serious. He rubbed at one brow and chewed a lip, obviously thinking. "I was," he admitted. "And after what happened tonight, looks like we were right to worry. Any ideas on who might've done that to him?"

I shook my head. "Other than Denise, no."

"You really think she's capable of that?"

"No. It was too physical. She wouldn't take the chance of chipping a nail." I paused to seriously consider his question, not that it did much good. "George is a burly guy, so it had to be someone with some meat on his bones. As volatile as he's been lately, he's probably pissed off a lot of people. Case in point, that man at the marina. George makes a snide comment, and the guy doesn't let it slide."

"You think it was him in our garage?"

"Who? George?"

He nodded.

Sheriff Bronson had wondered the same thing. I still didn't see it. "Why? Unless he thinks we hide our stash of good bait in there, so we don't have to share it with him."

Something sparked in his eyes. "So it's not just me. You think he over obsesses about bait, too?"

It had been a flippant remark, but Stan was right. George seemed fixated on the bait Stan supplied for their fishing and crabbing trips. "Yeah, lately he seems to." A tiny seed sprouted in my brain and took root. "Do you think it's really something else?"

"What do you mean?"

"What if the word 'bait' is a code word you and George used?" So all right, maybe I did read more than my share of mystery novels and watched too many TV cop shows. It seemed plausible. And it would explain some of George's recent wacky behaviors.

"And when George tells me to bring the bait, he really means I'm supposed to bring something else," Stan added.

I studied his face. He appeared sincere. "But what is he telling you to bring?"

He shook his head, finger rubbing his eyebrow again. "When we were in the marina, did you watch the bay at all?" he finally asked.

"For a half hour or so."

"Did anything odd happen?"

I thought back to the previous morning and pictured those four boats out in the bay with George and Stan. "No, not really. There was this streamlined black boat that seemed out of place—more like a speedboat or one used for water skiing and such, you know. They raced it out there and emptied all of their pots. Didn't keep a single crab.

"And the people on this other inconspicuous boat poached your traps. They kept a couple of crab from each pot, then threw the traps back into the water. At the time, it really ticked me off. I mean, it was so sleazy to wait until you were gone and then sneak out there and steal from you. I guess it didn't matter. You still limited."

He shrugged, and a curious glint sparkled in his dark eyes. "Good thing George didn't see that. I might've had to use my gun."

I smiled and shook my head, wondering about men and their fascination with weapons. To sidetrack my mind from drifting to fascinating mind-wanderings about the man sharing my space, I mumbled, "By the way, what took you guys so long at the marina."

"I have no idea. As soon as we tied up at the dock, George disappeared into the parking lot. The next time I saw him he walked out of that market and that big guy grabbed him from behind."

A yawn appeared from nowhere. I tugged a hand from a pocket to stifle it, then glanced into my bedroom, which, in truth, was Stan's bedroom, too. Tonight the wall of windows seemed an open invitation to whatever evil lurked in the darkness beyond. The corners were too dark. The walk-in closet, alive with malevolence. The king-size bed, too large and empty.

The thought of going back into that room alone had my nerves twitching. I rubbed at the fear in my gut and swallowed the words I wanted to utter, then turned back to Stan and said, "Well, I guess I'll take another stab at sleep." I winced at my choice of words, then mumbled hopefully, "Surely, nothing else will happen before morning."

He glanced down the hall to his toy room, then studied my face closely. Reaching out, he idly traced an index finger down my cheek. "Thank you for covering my back today."

Sparks ignited. My heart raced. What was going on here? A touch from old Stan had *never* had this effect on me. "No problem," I whispered. "Turns out, you had it pretty well covered yourself."

His hand cradled my chin, and he fondled my cheek with his thumb. I stared into his intense gaze, wondering if our minds were channeling the same path. I mean, he was my husband, and I was his wife. Sure, technically, he'd cheated on me, but it wasn't actually *him* who'd done it.

"Maybe we should stop analyzing it, and just let it happen," he murmured.

Mesmerized by him, I stood there like a spellbound adolescent, the pros and cons swirling in my mind. He lifted my chin and raised an eyebrow. My head barely nodded.

Flames ignited in his dark eyes, and he lowered his lips to mine and kissed me gently, soothingly, for long, mind-muddling moments. My lips responded; my limbs melted. But my mind whispered that Stan had never *ever* kissed me like this before. His approach had always been more like an all out frontal attack.

Stan's hands slid to my waist, and he drew me up against his body. It felt like it looked—hard, solid. Unfamiliar. He deepened the kiss and ran his tongue along the crease of my lips. A satisfied murmur oozed from somewhere deep in my throat. I slipped my arms up around his neck and opened my mouth to his, feeling lethargic, yet wired, and all gooey inside, as if I were embraced in one of those massive chocolate sneaker waves from my dream, the rich, velvety chocolate caressing me, sapping my strength.

It was a dream come true—yet foreign. The fantasy romance novels are made of.

Fiction, something inside me whispered.

He pulled me even closer, lifting me onto my toes and guiding me backward into our bedroom, his tongue stroking mine in a leisurely ballet.

Oh, lordy, was my last thought before the fervor consuming my body stifled my qualms. With a contented murmur, I relaxed into my husband's very capable arms.

CHAPTER 8

"Oh, Pollyanna, what have you gotten yourself into?" I muttered, numbed by the truths I'd been battling for over an hour now. A fact was a fact—there was no way around that—and I was facing too many.

At last you've reached a point where you can't rationalize your way out of this deep pit you've dug yourself into, I told myself, hoping I'd be convinced to give up trying.

I tightened the quilt around my shoulders, then snuggled deeper into the cushion on the cedar recliner, seeking comfort of any kind. Most likely, Sheriff Bronson would chew me out for invading his crime scene, but he hadn't said to stay off the deck, and no yellow cop tape floated about.

So until I heard otherwise, here I sat, staring across the burnished golf course to where a vermillion sun reached out to wash the morning in hues of orange and red. Cirrus cloud wisps floated in the fiery creation. There was no damp haze this morning, just dewdrops sparkling like brilliant cut diamonds on the deck and plants and every blade of grass on that perfectly manicured course.

From somewhere, a mower revved. My heart rate revved with it. Instinctively, my eyes shot to the bedroom door, and my breathing stopped. *Not yet,* I begged, dreading what was to come. The blazing sunrise reflected from the wall of windows, making it impossible to see what was going on behind them.

No one walked through the door, so I breathed easier until my gaze slid to the pool of dried blood—George's—from earlier that morning. Shivers zipped along my bones. With a shake of my head, I squelched the images flashing in my mind and glanced at the mug of cold coffee next to my chair. I considered getting a fresh cup but knew it was a waste of time, something to keep my mind off the inevitable. My stomach wouldn't accept a drop of water, let alone a few sips of acidic coffee. It felt like snakes were in there slithering around and entangling with each other.

"Oh, lordy. What were you thinking?" I moaned.

And therein was the problem: I hadn't been thinking. I'd silenced my common sense and my good judgment. I'd surrendered to passion. Now I had to suffer the consequences.

The squeak of a door warned me my time had come. Every muscle in my body flexed. Blood pounded in my head. Beneath the quilt, I pressed on my stomach to quiet it.

He approached from the living room. Our eyes met and held, and with all of the chaos churning through my body, a warm burst of joy poured through me. Was it love? If so, it would only complicate things.

I saw the uncertainty in his eyes and steeled myself against the urge to take the easier route. He dropped into the other recliner and stretched his denim-clad legs out on the navy and lime cushion, a mug of steaming coffee cupped in his hands. My eyes automatically dropped to his waist. Was a gun concealed beneath his gray hoodie? Yesterday the thought had piqued my interest. Today it frightened me.

"Was it that bad?" he asked.

Unable to pull together words, I gaped. Why did he ask me that? He knew the answer as well as I.

He lifted a questioning eyebrow and nodded toward the bedroom.

"No," I murmured.

"Then what's the problem?"

"That *is* the problem," I informed him, cringing with the knowledge that this was only the beginning of a long, difficult conversation, one that would change my life forever.

Confusion clouded his features. "You're kidding?"

I studied him in that chair and thought back to Friday night—to Stan's lifeless body—and I wondered what had really taken place on this deck. "Who are you?" I demanded.

Shock flashed in his dark eyes. His jaw tightened, and I felt him pull away. "What do you mean?"

"Let's just can the crap," I snapped, springing forward like a freed bunny. "There's no way on God's green earth that the guy I shared a bed with last night was the man I've slept with for three very long years. I'll spare you the intimate details, but believe me, my evidence is conclusive. You are *not* Stan. So who are you?"

He blinked hard and held my unrelenting stare. I swore I heard him sorting through and casting aside possible explanations, which only made me more determined to wrangle the truth out of him. Finally, he breathed a long sigh of resignation and murmured, "Stan's brother."

His brother! Did he think I was an idiot? Stan didn't have a brother. "Nice try," I uttered. "Now try the truth."

"It is the truth. Stan's my little brother."

"Then why didn't he tell me about you?"

"From what I've learned in the past few days, he didn't tell you a lot of things."

He had me there. Still. . . . "Prove it," I challenged.

"No problem," he claimed.

He set his mug on the damp deck and disappeared through the bedroom door before I considered the fact that he might not return. What would I do then? I'd have no Stan. Period. How would I ever explain that to Sheriff Bronson?

I eyed the door, growing more agitated as seconds ticked. And just as I was about to chase after him, he reappeared to drop several cards into my lap. I pulled my hands from the quilt folds and examined the one on top. It was a copy of a birth certificate for Colton Reginald Morton, born in Westport, Washington, which would explain how he knew about crabbing. I examined the birthdate and calculated him to be a couple of years older than Stan.

Glancing at the man across from me—maybe Colton—I noticed that he observed me closely. I picked up the second card, a California driver's license, and compared the photo to the face that had been a part of my life for five days now. It looked younger, but the features were the same. No doubt, Stan could've passed it off as his. As for the other information on it, it jibed with the birth certificate.

The third card contained an image of a blue and copper-toned badge. *United States Secret Service* was written on it, as was Colton's name and some other information. I turned my focus to him, still coming to terms with the fact that Stan had a brother, one who was so different from him. "You work for the government?" I asked.

He nodded. "Yes. I'm stationed in San Francisco. Most of the time I'm on assignment, I'm required to work under the radar, so it worked out best for Stan and me to keep our relationship between the two of us."

I caught his use of the past tense, and felt something within me wither. "He's dead, isn't he?" I whispered, barely able to get the words out.

As if I'd gut punched him, his face crumpled. Sadness filled his eyes. At last, he nodded. "Uh-huh."

"What happened?"

He shook his head slowly, a faraway look to him. "I don't know. That's why I'm here." He gave me a "don't-you-dare-cross-me" look and added, "And I won't leave until I find out, even now that you know the truth. Stan might've had his faults, but he was still my little brother. I'm gonna catch his killer."

My heart stopped as that word killer seemed to reverberate in the air around us. Just like that, another kind of fear claimed precedence in my emotional mayhem. "So he was murdered?" I gasped.

"Oh, yeah. Asphyxiated. Someone held something over his face. There were no signs of a struggle. No bruises. No scratches. Nothing."

All of a sudden, it was late Friday night, and I saw myself bent over Stan's dead body, eyeing that pillow that had somehow found its way onto the deck. I'd picked it up and stuffed it back onto our bed.

But had I taken it out there, too, my intent to suffocate him in its down stuffing while he was too drunk to comprehend what was happening?

"I gotta have some time to myself, to process all of this," I muttered as I pushed the quilt aside and stood.

My lids dropped against a sudden dizzy spell, and I forced myself to take deep breaths. I had to escape, to find an empty space and think this thing through. But with very little sleep, my mind and body were sluggish.

You'd know if you did something like that, I assured myself. But another voice reminded me of how angry and hurt I'd been that night.

Had I done something really horrible, so repulsive that I'd wiped it from my memory altogether?

≈ ✿ ≈

Couples and clusters strolled on the wide strip of damp, packed sand, many of them harnessing a rambunctious dog or two. Caught up in my own private misery, they were a blur of shifting shapes when I raced by them.

My lungs screamed. My legs were mushy spaghetti. Sweat

tickled my face and pasted my sweatshirt to my drained body. Dried tears itched my cheeks. And after a nearly sleepless night and twenty-four hours without food, my body sputtered on fumes. And still I pumped my arms and legs, determined to rid myself of this emotional firestorm, so I could deal with this crazy predicament rationally.

Stan was dead—murdered. This time there would be no reneges. He really was gone. For good. Somehow I had to come to terms with that fact.

In truth, it wasn't that I grieved his death or the end of our turbulent life together. No, my grief had more to do with the inane fantasies I'd clung to of what our life would be once we'd weathered the rough times. Besides, this new guy was not Stan, which meant that I truly was alone.

"Quit whining," I wheezed. "You still have Sara. And what about Laura, Javier, and Phil? They're always there for you."

A young couple glanced at me like I was a raving psychopath and veered away from my path, toward the lapping ocean water. *Enough, already*, my mind shrieked. *This whining and self abuse isn't solving any of your problems. If anything, it's keeping you from resolving them.*

I planted my aching feet, bent at the waist, braced my hands on my wobbly thighs, and sucked air for a couple of minutes. When each breath wasn't a chore, I straightened and raised my face to the light breeze, then shivered as it cooled the perspiration coating me.

After drawing one more deep breath, I stood on shaky legs and searched the landscape for familiar landmarks. The sky was a lazy blue, feathered with translucent clouds. Hovering above the tree-swathed hills to the east, the sun reached out its early morning rays to warm the sand that stretched to the grassy berm separating the beach from the houses beyond. Water-ravaged logs, some of them charred black, littered the endless stretch of gray. And not far down the beach, a familiar stump reached three gnarled limbs high into the air. I'd run up the beach as far as I could, then turned and retraced my footsteps. Now I was almost home.

My stomach churned, and I clenched my jaw against the urge to escape. I had questions—lots of questions—and I needed answers. I aimed to begin my search for those answers with Colton or whatever the heck his name was.

I untied my shoes, then tugged them and my socks off to wiggle hot toes into the cold dampness. The wet sand massaged my aching arches. Then I stepped close to the licking waves and let them flow over my tired feet and higher up onto my calves, relishing the numbness.

Not far away, a German shepherd lunged into a frothy wave to retrieve a chunk of wood. I watched the animal shake, water droplets shooting from its glossy fur, and proudly carry the stick to a laughing barefoot boy. He smiled up at the man next to him and petted the dog.

"If only life were that simple," I mumbled before I dragged my tired feet across the wet sand, then slogged through the deeper, drier stuff.

As I drew nearer to the familiar marker and the path beside it, I noticed a man in jeans and a gray sweatshirt not far from it, sitting just below the swaying beach grass. He watched me intently as I approached. Even exhausted, my heart rate kicked up, and nervous jitters unsettled me. I tried to ignore the warm glow that settled somewhere near my heart.

"You and I have something in common," he said after I plopped down facing him.

I set my shoes beside me and brushed at the sand clinging to my wet jeans. "Yep. I try to run away from my problems, too."

"And how's that working for you?"

"It's not," I muttered, studying the shadows under his dark eyes, the stubble on his cheeks. "I thought that's what you might do."

Surprise settled onto his features. "What—abandon you?"

I nodded.

"And leave that for you to explain to Sheriff Bronson—no husband, no body?"

"Uh-huh." I dug my cell phone from a pocket, flicked it on, and checked the time—seven-twenty-five—then dropped it into a shoe. "And he and his men will soon be here to do their sleuthing. The neighbors and the golf course powers-that-be are gonna love that."

Our eyes caught and held. His were filled with questions, with emotions I didn't want to explore. I glanced away, toward the ocean, and muttered, "Did you see Denise this morning?"

"No. Why?"

"I wondered how George is doing. Maybe the sheriff will know."

For long moments, the only sounds were the roar of the curling waves, muted voices, and the piercing screech of seagulls. I closed my eyes, drawing energy from the cooling breeze to confront a painful topic. "Where's Stan?" I murmured.

I felt his hand on my arm, squeezing it gently.

"He's in a safe place," he assured me. "They did an autopsy to determine the cause of death, then cremated him. I know that's what he'd want. If you want them, the ashes are yours."

Tears pooled in my eyes, burning. I blinked them back and tried to swallow the lump of hurt lodged in my throat. "What about Sheriff Bronson? Shouldn't you tell him?"

"I will when the time is right. When I figure out what Stan was messed up in. If I let him in on it now, he'll take control. He's got a whole county swarming with summer tourists to watch over, so he won't be able to give it the focus it needs. Besides, if everyone thinks Stan's still alive, we have a better chance of catching his killer. Someone will slip up."

Familiar male voices filtered from the path not far from us. Colton's hand vanished from my arm. I glanced at where it'd been, missing its comfort. Then I looked up as Phil and Javier walked over the berm. They wore top-of-the-line running shorts and windbreakers, Nikes on their feet.

Surprise registered on both of their faces when they saw me, transforming quickly to delight. It appeared they were stepping closer for a visit until Colton turned to see what had drawn my attention, and they froze as one. Phil's dark features turned stormy. He breathed raspy breaths, clenching his fists repeatedly, before he swiveled toward the ocean and jogged off.

Javier watched him go, then turned back, his brows arched in query, no smile.

"Good morning, Javier," I said, mostly to break the tension.

"Good morning to you . . . two," he muttered, scrutinizing me so closely that I felt myself squirm. "You had some excitement last night . . . again."

So that's why he'd stayed behind. Was it curiosity or did he want to make sure I was okay? "Yep," I told him. "George showed up on our deck in the middle of the night. He'd been beaten and stabbed. He's in the hospital."

His white skin turned pasty. His eyes flicked from me to Stan. "Is he okay?"

"I don't know. He was unconscious when the ambulance arrived."

"I guess we better keep our doors locked and pack a weapon if we leave the house," he muttered as his eyes drifted off to where Phil waited for him near the water. When he turned back, he scrutinized

Colton, then leveled a grave look at me and added, "You be careful, Pollyanna. You're too trusting," before he took off to join Phil.

"Obviously, they adore me," Colton cooed.

"They have their reasons," I informed him.

"Care to elaborate?"

A promise was a promise, and I planned to honor it, hopefully throughout this ordeal. "You thought George was an asshole. Well, you should've spent some quality time with your brother."

Hurt clouded his eyes, but he quickly deflected it. "Hey, those two guys would've happily gutted and stuffed me the other day. Maybe one of them decided the neighborhood would be a better place to live without Stan."

"They disliked Stan, but not to the point they'd murder him. Besides, they were in southern Oregon Friday night," I argued.

"And that check?"

I'd hoped he'd forgotten about that. "It was nothing, just a misunderstanding."

"Has anyone ever told you that you don't lie well?"

Heat radiated from my cheeks. "It's between me and them and has nothing to do with what's going on here," I avowed. At least, I hoped it didn't. Laura claimed Phil and Javier had delivered a sculpture to Ashland, that they'd been gone all day Friday and stayed the night. My visit with Javier on Sunday had affirmed what she'd told me, which dropped the two of them from my prospective list of suspects.

I watched Phil and Javier carry on an animated conversation. They glanced at Colton and me before Phil jogged up the beach. Javier gave us a final look and ran after him.

"So why were you here Friday night?" I asked, hoping to draw his focus from my two friends.

He sighed and rubbed his brow. "Stan left me a voice mail. Said he was caught up in something he couldn't get out of, so he was gonna be out of touch for a while—like me."

A whimper escaped. I held my breath, willing myself to react later, not here. "So he planned to leave me?"

"If you weren't in on it, I suppose so," he admitted. "It sounded like he was desperate to get away from a dangerous predicament, not you—if that helps."

Nothing would help. I'd put up with all of that crap from him while all the time he was plotting to ditch me—just disappear. I forced myself to take a step back, to become an observer. "I wonder what it was." I offered.

"He didn't say. But he did say he had some funds coming in, so he'd be set for a while, and when he got settled, he'd contact me."

Yes, twenty-five thousand dollars of Phil's hard-earned money. Most likely, there were others he'd blackmailed, too. And I didn't want to contemplate how much he'd planned to snatch out of my savings accounts—not that he'd earned any of it.

I swallowed the pain and plodded on. "So you sneaked here in the middle of the night to check up on him?"

"Pretty much. He's my little brother, and I feel responsible for him. As you know, he can be a huge pain in the butt, and he's caused more than his share of trouble." He scooped up a handful of sand and watched it sift through his fingers. "You know, when he married you, I thought he was finally pulling it together. Then about a year ago, I saw signs he was getting restless again. I knew it was just a matter of time, so when I got his text, I wasn't surprised.

"I contacted him around nine Friday night. He was ticked that I was here and wouldn't tell me what he'd gotten himself into, but he agreed to meet me at one in the morning at our usual spot."

"Which was?"

"Right here. I waited for a half hour, and when he didn't show, I went up to your house. You were sleeping in the bedroom. I thought Stan was asleep, too—until I touched him."

I wiggled my toes in the damp sand, contemplating timeframes. "That was around one-thirty?"

He nodded. "He hadn't been dead long. Since your security alarm wasn't set, I searched around the deck and inside your house, but I didn't come up with anything that answered any of my questions, except for a pillow. Then I grabbed one of those chocolates and headed back to the beach to think. It wasn't easy with that Triazolam slowing me down. At the time, I thought it was due to shock and grief.

"Long story, short, I decided to take his place, and the powers-that-be put their stamp on it. We'd done it before, when we were young kids, and had gotten away with it. I guess I didn't take into account how age can change a person. You suspected something was off right away."

"Yes, but I couldn't come up with a logical explanation for it, other than your memory loss. Still, I had my doubts," I muttered, my mind back on the pillow he'd mentioned. Of course, he'd known about it since he'd discovered Stan's dead body before I did. So why didn't he ask me if I'd picked it up?

Instead, he smiled and said, "I know. That's why I tried to lie low and keep my mouth shut—your basic Milquetoast move."

A young couple with two small girls appeared on the path. Still thinking about that pillow, I watched the adults plod through the deep sand while the children frolicked back and forth in front of them, squealing with joy. They dropped towels and buckets with shovels before they headed for the water.

I glanced at Colton. He was still running sand through his fingers. So he had found Stan at one thirty, and Stan was still there at three-thirty when I'd seen him. "Where did you put Stan?" I blurted.

He stopped playing in the sand and frowned at me. "I told you; we cremated him."

"Friday night—you were there the next morning, not him. What did you do with him?"

"I made arrangements to have him picked up and the scene processed. But when I got back to your house, you were on the deck, kneeling down beside him."

My mind flitted to the dark shape I'd seen on the golf course that night. Was it Colton who lurked in those shadows?

"I was ready to scrap my plan and take off—thought you'd call the sheriff," he admitted. "Then you picked up that pillow and put it on your bed, and when I looked in on you, you were in the living room sound asleep. I figured then that you were the one who'd killed him."

I froze, my insides churning. "And now?" I whispered, imploring him to relieve my agony.

"If you ate two of those chocolates that night, you wouldn't have had what it'd take to hold that pillow over his face." He chuckled, then smiled. "Besides, I can't picture you swatting a mosquito, no matter how much it annoyed you."

I prayed he was right. I didn't want to be a murderer. Breathing easier, I moved us on. "So while I'm asleep, Stan is whisked away and the crime scene investigators do their thing. No one noticed all of that activity?"

"It was before sunrise, and we're trained in stealth. It took one man to cart Stan away and one to process the scene. One vehicle. In quietly, then out quietly. As far as I know, no one asked any questions."

"Lucky for you, the neighborhood's on summer break," I informed him. "So, after they left, you decided you were hungry and ate two more truffles?"

He nodded. "Basically, yes. Except that I'd had a business meeting earlier that day, so I was wearing a pair of slacks and a dress shirt. I knew those had to go, so I dug through Stan's dresser drawers and found some shorts and a tee-shirt to put on." He harrumphed and shook his head, eyeing his baggy clothes. "I didn't realize he'd put on so much weight.

"My stomach felt queasy. I thought it was because I'd skipped dinner, so I grabbed two more of those chocolates—huge mistake—and headed for the deck to strategize. The next thing I knew, the sheriff was shaking me."

"Uh-huh. Once the drugs wore off, I called him. I'd sure like to know who left those ghastly things on my front porch. And why."

"It might answer some of our other questions."

A red dragon kite leapt off the sand down toward the water. The breeze caught it, carrying it higher until it suddenly jetted upward with its long tail flapping behind it. Bobbing with the currents, it gazed down on us like an avenging beast.

"Now it's your turn," Colton murmured.

"What?" I asked, pulled from the dragon's grip.

"Tell me what you recall about Friday night."

I shrugged. "There's not much to tell. It was my fortieth birthday, and we were supposed to go out and celebrate. Unfortunately, Stan didn't show up for the celebration, so there was none," I admitted, trying not to sound too pathetic.

My mind traveled back to that night, to how furious I'd been, and how hurt. I figured that was a given, so I didn't bring it up. "Around ten, I decided to lie down. On the way, I grabbed a truffle. It put me to sleep before I got out of my clothes. Something woke me up around three-thirty. That's when I saw Stan on the deck and went out to wake him up. I couldn't, of course."

An image of that darn pillow popped up again. I considered passing over it, then said, "I snatched the pillow, so it wouldn't get damp and headed into the house to get my phone and call 9-1-1. That's when I grabbed another truffle and sat down in the chair, planning to make the call. Around seven, a lawnmower woke me up. I glanced outside. Stan was still there. Still dead. I called the sheriff."

"And he shook me out of a drugged sleep," Colton added.

"I was shocked and totally confused when I walked outside and saw you there—alive," I told him. "I couldn't figure out what was going on."

He nodded. "I noticed. Any idea what time Stan got home?"

"No, only that it was after I fell asleep. I figured he'd come home eventually, so I didn't set the security alarm. If I had, we might be able to pull the exact time from it."

He shrugged. "Well, we know it was after ten, right?"

I nodded. "And he was supposed to meet you at one."

"So some time between ten and one—according to the autopsy, closer to one—someone killed him. Any idea who?"

Before I responded, I thought hard about his question. I'd scratched Phil and Javier from my suspect list. As much as Laura disliked Stan, she didn't belong there either. And I refused to place my name on that list until I had some hard evidence.

"No," I answered honestly. "He didn't exactly have an endearing personality, so I'm sure he's made some enemies." *Especially if he's been blackmailing people,* I silently added,

Then I considered the old love triangle scenario—or whatever they call it when four people were involved. "If Denise found out Stan was messing around with another woman, I could see her going ballistic. Or maybe the other woman if she learned about Denise. Perhaps George, if he discovered what was going on between Denise and Stan."

He shook his head, frowning. "I get the feeling Stan had something else in the works with George. Maybe something he couldn't wiggle his way out of. Any ideas on what the two of them could've been involved in?"

"No." Other than blackmail, of course. "Stan's been very closed-mouth in the last year or so. I really have no idea what he's been up to outside of our house. Maybe the guy who attacked George also killed Stan."

"Could be. Hopefully, the sheriff will track him down."

I turned back to the flying dragon, pondering what I knew and didn't know and trying to piece it together as the kite zipped across the sky. Then I searched up the beach for Phil and Javier and spotted them in the distance, two tiny figures running back this way.

"How about your friend Laura's boyfriend?" Colton asked.

I stared at him. "Harley?"

"Yeah. Clearly, he knew Stan, and he'd have decked me right there in your driveway if the two of you hadn't been there. How well do you know him?"

"I don't," I admitted. "Laura hooked up with him when she went dancing Friday night."

Something sparked in his eyes. "When I spoke with Stan, it sounded like there was live music in the background. Do you know where Laura was?"

"The Whale's Spout. It's a popular bar and dance spot in Lincoln City, in the center of town. Laura told me Harley saw Stan and his sleazy girlfriend there Friday night. Evidently, they weren't there long."

"You ever been there?"

"Yes. I should've been there Friday night, but. . . ."

Music blasted, cutting off my words. My focus turned to my shoes. I dug my phone from one of them and flipped it on. "This is Polly Morton," I murmured.

"Sheriff Bronson here," a gruff voice replied. "Say, we're at your house and need to get into the garage. You nearby?"

"I'll be there in a couple of minutes," I promised.

"Thanks," he uttered before he broke the connection.

I brushed at a sandy foot, then pushed it into a shoe. "The cops are here," I told Colton.

That intent look returned to his eyes. "And we're in agreement that I'm still Stan, right?"

Just thinking about the alternative made me feel like I was in the throes of a deadly bug. Colton would leave, and I would be left in that house alone, clueless as to who was doing what around me. For all I knew, someone close to me might be a murderer. And other than blackmail, I had no idea what other shady deals Stan might've wriggled his greedy fingers into or how many other women claimed him as their lover.

If I was going to get to the bottom of this fiasco, Colton appeared to be my best bet. I nodded. "For now," I told him before I pulled on my other shoe.

I eyeballed him as I stood up, thinking that we were now co-conspirators. "But I'm trusting you to get me out of this when the time comes," I added, hoping he would.

~~~ ✿ ~~~

Since she'd plopped into a chair at my kitchen table, Laura hadn't taken her rapt gaze off Colton. Her blue eyes had landed on him, and shock had flashed on her beautiful features. Obviously, he was very much at home in my kitchen, hands flying as he poached eggs and toasted English muffins, which was one reason Laura scrutinized his every move. I relaxed and sipped coffee, bushed and famished. If I hadn't figured out who the guy really was, she wouldn't either.

Voices trickled in from the garage where Sheriff Bronson and his men sorted through Twinkies. The look on his face when he'd seen Stan's stash had been photo worthy. It was too bad I hadn't had the courage to flash one to post on my *facebook* page. No doubt, he'd sniff breakfast smells soon and step into the kitchen to brief us on the latest goings-on or ask questions.

Plaintive meows and door scratching noises came from the laundry room. Poor kitty. It was used to having the run of the house. I'd locked it away this morning to keep it from being underfoot.

At long last, Laura's eyes turned from Colton to me, her expression saying, *this just gets creepier and creepier.*

"Your coffee's getting cold," I told her.

She eyed it as if it might be infested with Stan cooties, then took a cautious sip. "Those officers are going door-to-door, asking questions. They even searched around the outside of my house," she muttered. "First someone leaves you those doctored truffles. Then you know. . . ." She paused to give me a meaningful look and nod toward Colton before she continued. "Your truck is broken into, and now your garage. Last night George was attacked. Do they think someone is terrorizing our neighborhood?"

"I think they're just covering their bases," I assured her. "All of those things happened here at this house, so if anyone's being terrorized, it's us."

Her eyes flicked to Colton. Mine followed suit, and warm, fuzzy feelings nearly made me sigh aloud as I watched him fill three small glasses with orange juice. He'd removed his hoodie, and a tee-shirt printed with labeled fishing lures now displayed his fit body nicely. I glanced down at my sandy jeans and baggy sweatshirt and wished I'd taken the time to clean up before breakfast. Laura, as usual, looked gorgeous in a daffodil yellow ensemble, blonde curls beguiling, makeup perfect. I pulled out my scrunchie and smoothed my hair back from my face into a new ponytail, then swiped at the salty residue on my face. For now, that would have to do.

Colton set the orange juice on the table, flashing an angelic smile at Laura.

"No breakfast for me," she told him. "I just came over to make sure you're okay." Which translated *to I couldn't wait any longer; I had to know what's going on.*

"Make her a plate," I said to Colton, and to Laura I murmured, "You'll thank me later. New Stan can cook." Dealing with his two names kept me on my toes.

Laura returned to Stan staring. I noticed she didn't talk much when Colton was around, but it seemed like the opportune moment to open a certain discussion while he was within earshot. "Are you and Harley getting together today?" I asked.

Her face brightened, and her lips curved into a smile. "Oh, yeah. He's coming over this evening. A light wine. Fresh crab with summer greens and sourdough bread. Sinfully decadent dessert. We'll probably practice our dance moves. Then a leisurely stroll on the beach at sunset. Can't get much more romantic than that."

"Wow. You really like this guy, don't you?" Alarms blared in my head. Laura barely knew the man, and already she sounded love-smitten. What if he really was mired up to his kerchief-covered pate in one of Stan's messes? I didn't want to play mother hen, but I also didn't want her to get hurt. "Does he live around here?" I probed.

"In Depoe Bay." Her eyes turned dreamy. "He has the most amazing log house, on a hill overlooking the ocean."

Dollar signs flashed before my eyes. "What does he do for a living?"

"OMG, Pol. You're gonna love this. I mean, the guy looks like he spends his days tinkering in car bellies, right? But not Harley. No. He owns a bakery in downtown Depoe Bay. He makes the most amazing breads and pies and pastries. And he designs cakes and cupcakes, you know, for weddings and birthdays and such. Oh, and he's kind of famous for the candy he makes from scratch and sells in his shop."

My eyes flicked to Colton as more alarms unsettled me. He stopped spooning yellow stuff onto plates to give me an intrigued look. "What kinds of candy?" I asked.

"Pretty much everything—fudge, chocolates, caramels, stuff like that."

"Does he run the place by himself?"

She waved five perfectly manicured lavender fingertips at me. "Oh, no. He spends most of his time managing the company now. There's an online business, too, and they supply goodies for a lot of local stores and restaurants."

Colton set two plates on the table and slid them across to us.

"And he still finds time for romance," he murmured. "Good for him."

Laura blinked and eyed Colton as if he'd materialized from the air in front of her. "Oh, yeah. It's his number one priority," she mumbled, studying the enticing Eggs Benedict on her plate. "That's why he took up internet dating. The guy's never been married—can you imagine that? I mean, he's great looking, he's nice, he's fun to be with, and he has his own money. He even picks up the tab when we go out. Refuses to let me pay for anything. And he likes my nicely padded curves. He's almost too perfect."

I couldn't agree more. I wanted to believe Laura had landed a man with all of those very fine qualities, but I couldn't help but wonder what in the heck Harley might be up to.

Laura sniffed at the steam wafting off the plate, then picked up a fork, cut off a bite, and slid it into her mouth. Surprise shone in her eyes as she chewed. "*Mmmm. . . .* I like it with the crab," she purred.

"Thank you. Enjoy, ladies," Colton said before he returned to his preparations.

I forked a bite of egg, crab, and bread into my mouth and nearly swooned. The Hollandaise sauce blanketing it was perfect—creamy and buttery with a lemon kick. "Well, just keep in mind that you've only known him six days," I reminded Laura, trying to disregard the fact that I'd only known Colton five days.

Fork in midair, she fixed me with a determined look. "FYI, Pol, Harley's the first man I've met who even comes close to being the man Benny was. He's a keeper, and I'm gonna do my best to hold onto him."

I reached out to touch her arm. "I hope it works out for you, Laura," I told her. And I meant it. Still, the fact that he made chocolates niggled at me. I prayed it was only a coincidence.

The garage door slammed, and a heartbeat later Sheriff Bronson stood before us. He looked as done in as I felt. Puffy dark shadows lurked behind his horn rims, and crevices lined his saggy features. His uniform had always appeared neat and tidy. Today it was wrinkled, and the front of his shirt was spotted with whatever he'd nibbled on.

His gaze gravitated to the Eggs Benedict, then flashed to Colton. "You're quite the cook," he said.

Colton smiled. "I dabble. Sit down. I'll get you some coffee."

The sheriff dropped into a chair and set his case on the floor. Then he placed two packets of folded paper on the table. "These yours?" he asked.

"Yes," I murmured, studying the packet of yellowed letters. They were tied with a faded pink ribbon, just as they must've been when Frank Ellis had given them to me. I assumed the other packet contained the copies Bev had made for me. "Where did you find them?"

"Underneath a mountain of Twinkies. Figured they didn't belong out there."

"Thank you. I wondered what happened to them."

Stan must've gotten sidetracked and left them in the garage. But why not just leave them in the boxes in his truck, with the other documents? Perhaps because Bev had pointed out their importance, and he'd planned to mention that to me. It didn't sound like something Stan would do in a zillion years, but it was the only explanation I could come up with.

"You missing anything else?" Sheriff Bronson asked.

I thought back to the previous night. I'd only given the garage a cursory look. Who knew what was lurking beneath those Twinkies? "I don't think so," I told him. "When I straighten up the garage, I'll know more. Last night I didn't look very closely."

"Well, let me know," he muttered, his attention settling on the coffee and condiments in front of him.

"Would you like some breakfast?" Colton offered.

He eyed my plate and seemed to fight an inner battle, then sighed. "Maybe half of what these ladies are eating."

Colton grabbed a plate from a cabinet and scooted half of his breakfast onto it before he poured more Hollandaise sauce over the top. The sheriff doctored his coffee. Laura gobbled her Benedict when she wasn't eyeballing the sheriff.

Which reminded me of my manners. "Sheriff Bronson, this is my friend, Laura. Laura, Sheriff Bronson," I muttered.

He stopped stirring to study Laura. "Nice to meet you. You live across the street, right?"

Laura swallowed. "Yep."

"So you must know the Seavers?" he asked.

"Double yep."

"Any idea why someone would want to kill Mr. Seaver?"

"Kill him!" I gasped, grabbing my stomach to keep that yummy Hollandaise there. "Is George dead?"

Sheriff Bronson shook his head. "No. Most likely thanks to you and your husband. He's still in a coma, though. Sounds like it's touch-

and-go right now."

"You think the guy meant to kill him?" My mind didn't want to go there. One murder was enough.

His gaze dropped to the plate Colton had set in front of him. "He was stabbed three times. That's way past roughing him up. Although, it appears whoever did it beat the crap out of Mr. Seaver before he started slicing." His blurred eyes turned to Laura and me. "Could be, Mr. Seaver had some information the guy wanted. The three of you have any ideas on that?"

I looked at Colton. He shook his head. Laura and I followed suit. "Did you talk with Denise?" I asked.

"Sure did. She doesn't seem too broken up about the whole thing. She claims that, except for a few hunting trips, her husband spent all of his time either golfing or out in his boat." He fixed his bespectacled eyes on Colton, who leaned against the counter, eating what was left of his breakfast. "Claims the two of you ended your affair a while ago, Mr. Morton. Also claims you and her husband were buddies."

"That's what I've been told," Colton admitted. "Quite truthfully, I'm not all that fond of the guy."

His look turned skeptical. "So you're still saying your memory's gone, huh?"

Colton met his stare. "No, I'm not just saying it. It *is* gone. If I get it back, I promise you'll be one of the first to know. Until then, I have no idea who'd want to kill George. Clearly, it wasn't me since I was inside this house with the alarm set while George was being attacked." He set his plate on the counter, stepped to the table, and held out both of his hands, palms down. "As you can see, I haven't pounded on anyone recently."

Since they were right there in front of me, I examined them, too. The nails were clean and nicely manicured. A few nicks and small cuts marred the skin—most likely crabbing battle scars—but the knuckles weren't swollen and bruised like they would be if he'd been punching someone as much as George had been punched.

The sheriff lifted his bushy brows, shrugged, and turned to Laura. "Did you notice anything unusual around here last night?"

She dropped her fork and seemed to give it serious thought. "No. I went to bed early and slept through the night. My bedroom faces the beach, so I don't hear much of anything that happens in the street."

"Any idea why someone would want Mr. Seaver dead?"

Her eyes flicked mine with her "is he serious?" look. "Other than the fact that he's a loud, offensive, foul-mouth jerk, no," she enlightened him.

"I'm getting a lot of that," he muttered. "You see him hanging out with anyone in particular?"

"Just Stan."

The sheriff sighed. Clearly exasperated, he picked up his fork and dug into his grub.

I felt Colton's eyes on me and met his troubled look. Was he thinking the same thing as I? All of the evidence seemed to support the notion that Stan and George had been mixed up in something together, and whatever it was, it had to be bad. Someone had murdered Stan and had tried to off George, too.

Did the murderer get what he was after, or was he still searching? If he was, Colton was surely his next target. After all, I was the only person who knew he wasn't Stan.

≋ ✵ ≋

"This is not a good time," I muttered at the computer screen, knots of anxiety settling in my gut. I reread the email message to make certain I'd interpreted it correctly, then leaned back in my desk chair, rubbing at the headache behind my tired eyes. Yep, I had. Sara planned to come home for the weekend.

At any other time, I would've shrieked with joy, thrilled that my daughter wished to spend time with me. But not now. Not when another man charaded as my dead husband. Not when someone was trying to break into our house. Not when I was possibly being followed. And especially not when a murderer was on the loose in the neighborhood.

Unlike me, when it came to Stan, Sara didn't cling to any fantasies or make excuses for his bad behavior. No. Her radar would shift to high alert the moment she set eyes on Colton. She'd demand to know what was going on, and I didn't want her involved in the whole sticky mess. It was best that she stayed away, out of danger.

But what could I tell her? I didn't want to lie. Maybe a partial truth would do the trick.

I sat forward and composed a message, explaining the circumstances involved in George's battle for his life. Then I explained that our garage had been ransacked. Finally, I begged her to wait and come home once it was safe. Besides, I rationalized, I had a busy weekend planned and wouldn't be able to spend quality time with her—which was mostly true. My heart twisted when I hit the *send* button. I would've so loved to spend several days with my daughter.

So quit sulking, and get out there and find some answers, my mind hollered.

I sighed and sank back into the chair, playing over the past twenty-four hours in my mind, searching for clues—the break-ins, George's pounding, the best sex of my life, Stan's actual death, my beach run and discussion with Colton, and Sheriff Bronson's breakfast visit.

After he and Laura had left, Colton and I had spent hours stuffing Twinkies back into cartons and paraphernalia into containers to be reshelved. Every vessel had been opened, every hidey hole searched. Clearly, the person who'd breached my security alarm was hunting for a particular item. From what I'd surmised, he hadn't found it in my garage.

The only benefit I'd reaped from those hours of labor was the pile of stuff I'd culled to haul to Goodwill—mostly Stan's junk. That rusted Chevy would've been added to the heap, too, if I hadn't caught Colton caressing it with stars in his eyes.

My eyes flicked to the letters the sheriff had discovered, now neatly boxed where they belonged. Stan had to have dropped them in the garage. But why? Over a week ago, he'd questioned me about them. At the time, I'd thought it odd, since he'd never shown any interest in my work before. Whatever Bev had mentioned when he'd picked them up at the museum, it must've piqued his interest.

Still, why were they left in the garage? Had he actually intended to read them? If so, why? I'd never seen Stan read anything more challenging than a hunting or fishing magazine.

I turned off my computer, then stepped to the boxes and selected the packet of aged letters. According to Frank, they had belonged to his great-grandmother, Nellie Ellis. Bev had said they documented his grandfather's birth on Nancy Boggs' floating brothel. Of course, that wasn't news to me since Frank had already told me all about it.

After wiping my hands on my shorts, I untied the faded ribbon and unfolded the fragile paper. A musty smell tickled my nostrils. The words were tiny and faded, almost blurred, and the penmanship was scrawled with fancy flourishes. My eyes screamed from just looking at it. Reading them tonight was out of the question. It would require rested eyes and a lot of natural light.

I quickly retied the ribbon and dropped the packet in the box, then checked the clock—only nine-thirty. I eyed the TV and didn't feel any urge to turn it on. What in the heck was up with that? In the past few days, I hadn't watched any of my "Who done it?" TV shows, and I really didn't care.

"So just go to bed," I told myself, which sounded like a great idea.

It'd been a long day. Once the garage was cleaned, I'd showered and dressed in clean clothes, then shut myself in my office to check my bank accounts and work on Frank's book. After he'd armed the house alarm, Colton had driven off in Stan's truck. A couple of hours later, he'd returned, hauling a quart of clam chowder and a couple of bulging bags that looked to contain clothing. He'd added crab to the chowder, and we'd slurped it on the deck with a loaf of garlic bread and a couple of glasses of wine. It'd been so perfect that I'd repeatedly pinched myself as a reminder that he was only playing a role, one that was short-term.

No wonder I was so bushed. It'd been a long, stressful day. I grabbed my cell, turned off the office lights, and made my rounds, checking to make certain the alarm was set and doors and windows were locked. When I reached the kitchen window, I watched Denise's car drive away. More than likely, she was taking advantage of George's absence to party. I said a quick prayer for George's recovery, then glanced across the street and noticed that Harley's bike was still parked in Laura's driveway. Kitty was nowhere in sight, which meant it was with Colton.

My bedroom was nearly dark when I walked into it. I dropped my phone on the bedside table and reached out to turn on a lamp. The soft drone of nighttime breathing stopped me. I gazed at the lump on the far edge of the king-size bed and froze. I hadn't thought to discuss sleeping arrangements with the man. I'd assumed he'd know he was back in Stan's toy room.

Still, after last night's scare fest, it was comforting to have him here. And in truth, the bed was an island, large enough to sleep four comfortably. If he stayed on his side and I on mine, all would be fine. Besides, he was already sound asleep. It would be ridiculous to rouse him from a deep sleep and banish him to the lumpy hide-a-bed down the hall.

I rubbed my aching forehead, too pooped to care. *I'll deal with it tomorrow*, I promised myself as I headed for the bathroom to brush my teeth and wash my face. Just as I got my face lathered, there was a knock on the sliding door. I dried my hands on a towel and peeked out.

Colton stood there, bleary-eyed, my cell phone in his hand. "Your daughter," he mumbled.

My headache kicked up a notch, as did my heart rate. In hindsight, I realized I should've waited until the next day to respond to her email message. Now I would have to match wits with her while I was too exhausted to think straight. I grabbed the phone and muttered, "Thank you." He slid the door shut.

I took a fortifying breath, and plastered the cell screen against my soapy face. "Hi, sweetie," I murmured.

"Hi, Mom," blasted into my ear. "What the hell's going on there? And where's Stan? Are you having an affair or something? Is that why you don't want me to come home?"

Honestly, the girl had extra sensory powers. And she'd never had a flair for tact. I wasn't actually having an affair. Or was I? Whatever the case, I didn't want to think about it right now, much less talk about it. My sluggish brain wouldn't formulate a response.

"Mom, are you okay?" she prodded, decibels rising.

"Yes, I'm fine," I assured her. Maybe if I chose my words carefully, I could avoid the whole Stan charade altogether. "I've just had a rough couple of days. I didn't get much sleep last night because of the break-in and George, and I'm exhausted. I'm headed to bed. Could we maybe have this conversation in the morning when I can think straight?"

"So someone really did break into your garage and beat up George?"

Did she actually believe I'd invent a story like that? "Yes, they tried to get into our house, too, but the alarm went off. Then later during the night, George showed up on our deck. He'd been beaten and stabbed. He's in serious condition, still unconscious. By the time the sheriff left, there wasn't much sleep time left." *So can we please do this tomorrow?* I silently pleaded, scratching at the itchy lather congealing on my face.

"Did they catch the guy?"

I sighed and sat down on the side of the soaking tub, surrendering to my daughter's tenacity. "No, not yet. That's why I don't want you here. I don't know who it is or why it's happening. I just know I want you to be safe, and at the moment, this doesn't feel like a safe place to be."

Long, silent moments followed my plea. When she spoke, there was a quiver to her voice. "Well, maybe you should get away from there for a few days. I don't want you to get hurt, either."

Tears pooled in my eyes and burned my throat. "I know, sweetie, but we're being really careful," I assured her. "When we're in the house, the alarm is set, and Stan and I are sticking together like glue. He has a gun."

"Oh, dear lord, Mom. Are you nuts? Get that gun away from him and hide it before he shoots someone. And what's with him, anyway? He sounds weird."

"Just a cold," I lied. "You woke him up; he was half asleep."

"Well, promise me you'll let me know if anything else happens," she demanded. "And text me several times a day, so I'll know you're okay."

A smile touched my lips. I wondered if she realized how much she sounded like me. "I promise. And I'm sorry about your visit. Once things settle down here, I'll set aside a whole weekend, so we can spend it together."

"That'd be great, Mom."

She paused, and I sensed her gathering forces for a new onslaught. "I swear I'm being overly cautious, Sara," I pledged. "I spend most of my time locked up in my office working on a family history I'm writing. And if I need help, Javier and Phil are right next door and Laura, across the street."

Her sigh of resignation whispered into my ear. "Well, okay. But be careful. I love you."

"I love you, too," I murmured before I clicked off the phone.

I eyed the soap scum on my phone screen and wiped it off onto my khaki shorts while I pondered the promises I'd made to Sara. As much as I wanted to believe them, I felt about as safe as a Chinook salmon at a fishing derby.

CHAPTER 9

"Nothing there," I muttered as I climbed down the stepladder and scrutinized Stan's walk-in closet one last time.

Frustrated didn't begin to cover what I felt. I'd searched every possible hiding place in this whole house, except Stan's toy room, and had discovered nothing amiss, not even a stray photo of his girlfriend. So why was someone trying to get into my house?

I grabbed the ladder and carried it into my bedroom, then sat on the bed next to the kitten to think. I'd handed Colton several empty boxes and a container of cleaning supplies, and he'd disappeared into Stan's toy room. I'd yet to hear anything more than vacuuming sounds from the room, so his search must be as fruitless as mine.

I ran my fingertips over the kitty's silky black fur and listened to it purr while I replayed several hours of cleaning and hunting in my head. There had to be something here. I felt it like I felt a bad storm rolling in over the Pacific. But what? And where?

"If I were Stan, where would I hide something?" I whispered.

The answer was obvious: either his toy room or the garage. The garage had been so crammed with junk that I'd closed my eyes to it, and I'd made it a policy to not set foot in Stan's toy room, mostly because the need to straighten and scrub would send me into a cleaning frenzy that would have Stan in an uproar. Poor Colton; that room had probably not been cleaned since Stan took possession of it. Maybe I should check on him.

Sighing, I left the ladder, grabbed the kitten, and trekked down the hall. The boxes I'd given Colton sat against the wall, mounded with a hodgepodge of items—clothing, magazines, shoes and slippers, bedding, CDs and DVDs, fishing gear, deer antlers. One box was loaded with empty bottles and cans, another with food wrappers and scraps of paper.

When I peeked inside the room, Colton was down on all fours, digging around inside the closet. "Any luck," I asked, gazing around at the transformed space to keep from ogling his very nice behind.

"Not yet," his muffled voice replied. His head appeared, and he sat on the floor and leaned against the sliding doors, legs outstretched and crossed, slapping gunk from his hands. Cobwebs clung to his short, dark hair; dust smudged his face. "The crawlspace access door is in there. I've just about got it uncovered, so I can open it. Maybe he stashed something down there. If not, I'm out of places to search in here. How about you?"

I shook my head. "Nothing. My house is clean, though, and I added to the Goodwill pile in the garage. If you're through with that vacuum, I'll sweep the hardwood floors."

"This floor will need swept well after I'm through, too. Stan was always a packrat, but the garbage I just pawed through went way beyond that. His truck was just as bad. I hate to trash talk the dead, but my brother was a damn slob. Did he ever clean up after himself?"

"Not really," I muttered, remembering my frustration—actually, it was more like irritation, sometimes fury—with Stan's slacker attitude.

I scrutinized the room. The carpet was clear of debris but needed a good shampooing. Shelves and tabletops were neat and tidy. Weapons lay in a row on the couch, and fishing equipment dangled from hooks on the walls. Colton cooked like a five-star chef, knew his way around a laundry room, and shopped for his own clothes. Not only that, but the guy had mastered the art of house cleaning. He truly was a gem.

My mind drifted to another thing he'd mastered, and heat blossomed in my cheeks.

"You okay?" he asked.

"Yes, just warm," I lied, setting kitty on the floor, so I could shake the front of my blouse to cool the flames.

The kitten trotted to Colton, climbed into his lap, and clawed its way up the skull and guitars printed on his Def Leppard tee-shirt. He stroked a lean finger down its black back and set it in his lap, then petted it gently. "So what's her name?" he asked.

"*She*, huh? You sure?" Evidently, he knew more about cats than I did.

"Yep."

"She doesn't have a name, but I suppose I can give her one

now."

"Why's that?"

"Because she can stay," I explained. "She's a stray, just showed up on my doorstep a couple of weeks ago. Stan hated cats, so I hid her from him. I knew I couldn't keep her, and I didn't want to get too attached. So, no name."

He narrowed his eyes, giving me an intense look. "It's your house, too. If you wanted to keep the kitten, you should've stood firm on the issue."

"I doubt she would've survived my stand," I blurted, hoping the truth wasn't too blunt.

"You really believe that?"

Evidently, he had his doubts. "I do." In truth, I didn't just believe it; I knew it. But I wasn't going to engage in a debate on the issue, so I nodded at the kitten. "I'm thinking I'll name her Nellie because she's a survivor."

"Nellie?"

"Uh-huh." Of course, he had no idea who Nellie was, so I launched into a seriously abridged version of Nellie's life. "The man I'm writing the book for, Frank Ellis—you met his son Brad at Mo's on the way home from the hospital—had a great-grandmother named Nellie. At a low point in her life, she worked on a floating bordello on the Willamette River—maybe only as a housekeeper, not that it matters.

"Anyway, Frank's great-grandfather, Jesse Ellis, married her. They were quite wealthy, and one day Nellie was kidnapped and held in a damp, dirty, cold basement for a couple of weeks. At the time, she was nearly nine months pregnant. The lady who owned the bordello rescued her. When Jesse rowed out to the vessel to pick his wife up, he discovered that his son was born in that brothel in the middle of the Willamette."

A dubious frown furled his brows. "And he wants you to record that in his family chronicles?"

"Actually, he seems proud of it," I assured him. "Nellie was a strong woman—a survivor, like that kitten. She plowed through difficult times and moved on with her life. According to Frank, even in old age, she was going strong."

I paused to consider what I found so compelling about Nellie. "I'd be satisfied to have half of her strength and resilience," I finally explained.

He studied me long and hard, then leaned forward and said,

"You need to give yourself more credit."

His words surprised me. "What do you mean?"

"You raised your daughter alone, right?"

"Yes."

"Then nursed your dad through a difficult illness. What you put up with from Stan would've driven most women to drink, drugs, or divorce—maybe all three—but not you. Now you're caught in the middle of some kind of killing spree and who the hell knows what else, and you're holding it together better than I am." His gaze became even more intense. "That's what I mean."

Guilt gnawed at me and made me shift uncomfortably on my feet. "I should never have married Stan," I confessed. "And when I realized what a big mistake it was, I didn't have the courage to get out of it."

He smiled and slowly shook his head. "You know, I've only known you a few days. Still, it's clear to me that there was something in Stan that you loved, something you clung to."

I closed my eyes, fighting tears so hard I trembled. If I lost control, it felt like my insides would explode all over Stan's newly cleaned toy room. Colton was right, of course. The truth was staring me in the face, and I hadn't seen it. I opened my eyes, nodded, and finally choked out, "I don't know how he could be such an ass and still be endearing at times, but he was."

"He had plenty of practice. Our parents wanted more kids but had to be content with Stan and me, which meant that Stan remained the baby of the family. He could do no wrong . . . ever. They made excuses for his bad behavior and never held him accountable for his actions. Both of them passed away when Stan was in his early thirties, too late for him to grow up, I guess."

"And I followed in their footsteps," I muttered, remembering all of the slack I'd cut him, the endless excuses I'd concocted. A tear tickled its way down my cheek, and I brushed it away. "I am gonna miss him, you know."

He nodded and sniffed. "Me, too."

"And I want to find out who killed him"

"We will," he assured me. The set jaw, the steely eyes, the edge to his voice, all said he meant it.

I swallowed the burning rock in my throat and let my misty eyes wander the room. If we were serious about figuring out who murdered Stan and uncovering his dealings, we needed to move past this touchy-feely moment and get on with it.

"You didn't find anything unusual in here, huh?" I murmured.

His gaze traveled the room, too. "Nothing."

"Doesn't that seem odd to you?"

"Yeah, it does," he admitted. "I expected to find some personal notes and photos. Maybe some pornography. At least some bookkeeping, receipts, stuff like that. Except for a box of extra checks for your joint account, there's nothing here. And not much on his computer or cell phone either. He must've erased as he went along. Makes me wonder why."

Something twisted inside me. "If he was planning to leave right away, maybe he cleared all of his personal stuff out of here. Maybe it's at his girlfriend's house."

He sighed resignedly. "Could be. But someone's searching for something, and they think it's in this house. If it isn't something of yours, then it had to belong to Stan."

"Unless there's a priceless mystery novel buried on a shelf in my office, it's not something of mine," I assured him. "I'm sure you've noticed that I don't own any expensive jewelry, art, antiques, clothing, knickknacks, or whatever."

"Here," he said, handing the kitten to me. "I'm gonna check out the crawlspace, and I don't want to spend the rest of my day dodging spiders while I chase her around beneath the house."

I gave Nellie a couple of quick pets and set her down in the hall, then shut the bedroom door. Colton was already on his hands and knees, head inside the closet. He tossed out a pair of rubber chest waders and a loaded fishing vest. A pair of insulated camo hunting pants joined the fishing gear. Finally, he set a pair of heavy leather boots on the floor next to the pile. All were caked with dried mud. I was tempted to haul the whole disgusting heap out to the boxes in the hallway, but the plaintiff meows and scratching sounds from the other side of the door stopped me.

A muffled thump sounded from inside the closet, and an earthy smell made my nose twitch. Colton dropped down onto his stomach. A few seconds later, I heard a grunt and rustling sounds. Then he dragged a black plastic garbage bag out onto the carpet.

"What an idiot!" he growled, folding back the layered flaps to expose what was inside. "What in the hell was he up to?"

I eyed the heap of money inside the inner bag and sank to the floor, my legs too mushy to support me. The room spun, my heart pounded, and a dull numbness made thinking a chore.

Colton dug through the rubber banded packets of currency. "There must be several hundred thousand dollars here." His focus turned to me, his eyes intense. "Do you know where it came from?"

Phil's distraught face popped into my head. How far had Stan's greedy blackmailing tentacles stretched—and to how many people? I clamped my teeth together to keep from spilling secrets. Javier was a dear friend, and I'd made him a promise. I tried my best to meet Colton's suspicious gaze without flinching and shook my head.

"Could he have taken it out of one of your bank accounts?"

Again, I shook my head.

He lowered his forehead and leaned forward, questioning.

I swallowed hard, fighting the urge to run from the room and keep right on running, to put all of this behind me. "I checked all of my accounts online last night," I murmured, my voice shaky. "Nothing was missing from them. We had a joint account that we both contributed to for household expenses. It's fine, too. He had his own credit cards. I don't know anything about them."

"I'll check into it. Do you know if he had any other accounts anywhere?"

"No, but I seriously doubt it. He had a hard time holding onto a job, and to be quite truthful, he rarely had his share of the money to contribute to our account."

Of course, he'd had no problems spending money—his new blue truck, fishing and hunting gear, golf trips with George. The list went on. I'd assumed they were the reason he'd snubbed his household obligations, but looking back, I had to wonder where all of that spending money came from.

I scrutinized Stan's treasure trove, and a weak, helpless sensation ran through me once again. Where *did* all of that money come from?

CHAPTER 10

I shivered inside my red windbreaker and tugged the hood up over my damp hair, then zipped the front up to my chin and stuck my hands into my pockets. Somewhere behind the early morning mist, the sun had risen, but only a few rays penetrated the thick wall of fog that enveloped the overgrown yard a half block from the beach. The quiet murmur of conversation drowned out all but a whisper of ocean sounds.

My eyes dropped to the cement walkway where grass etched a verdant patchwork in the jagged cracks. A pair of manly-size, knee-high rubber boots stood in front of my navy clogs. I traced them up legs and torso to a scruffy cap of graying hair. The man was tall and bent-shouldered, clad in a heavy olive jacket that looked several sizes too large. A hefty canvas bag dangled from his shoulder. Laura had huffed agitatedly when she'd seen him.

Of course, Laura was also irritated by the half dozen people standing in line in front of him. She liked to be the first to pass the threshold into estate sale bliss. The first to sprint from room to room, snatching up treasures before rival hunters spotted them. This morning, she'd have to suffice with being eighth. It didn't sit well.

When she'd asked me to accompany her on her Friday morning hunt, I'd welcomed the distraction—anything to get that bag of dough Colton had pulled from the crawlspace off my mind. It was wreaking havoc on my mental and emotional wellbeing. After discussing what we should do with it until we were spinning in circles, we'd agreed to put it back in the crawlspace and pile bulging boxes from the hallway on top of it. If it was what the burglar sought, it was doubtful he'd find it there.

As for the source of the money, Colton planned to spend the day snooping for possibilities. I'd spent a nearly sleepless night, tossing and turning and playing scenarios over and over in my mind—theft, blackmail, marijuana sales, swindling, pimping. . . . Whatever it was, it had probably led to Stan's murder and, most likely, George was involved up to his comatose eyeballs in it, too.

"Okay. My name's on the list, Pol," Laura muttered as she settled in beside me in her fluorescent tangerine jacket. "Here's your basket. You take the bathroom and bedrooms, and I'll cover the living areas and kitchen. Let's meet in the garage."

I grasped the hefty basket she handed me. "Jewelry, then purses, shoes, and clothing, right?" I confirmed, already dreading the mad scramble from room-to-room.

This was far from my first antiquing foray with Laura. Still, I wasn't nearly as adept as she at spotting something she'd profit from on one of the many internet sites she used to sell her finds. Before she paid and we moved on to the next sale, she'd sort through my haul and toss out what she didn't want.

She nodded. "Yeah. You know the ropes. If it's something you think I might be able to sell, grab it. I'll check the prices later. Stand your ground. Those two innocent-looking, white-haired ladies at the front of the line will snatch something out of your hands if you let them." She lifted her brows and jerked her head toward the man in front of us. "And carry that basket in front of you or it'll be empty when we meet up."

I nodded and glanced behind me. Already, the line stretched out of the yard and into the street. With luck, we'd be in the first group to enter the tiny, rundown house. Hopefully, they'd only let a few people in at a time, or we'd be tripping over each other's feet.

"I caught Denise when she got home last night. She said George is still in a coma."

Laura's murmured words drew me back to her. "Did she say anything about his prognosis?" I was worried we'd never find out what George and Stan were involved in if George didn't regain consciousness. How long could Colton and I go on with this pretense, playing husband and wife, seeking answers and only becoming more confused?

She glanced around, then leaned in close to me as if she feared eavesdroppers. "No. I got the feeling she isn't all that interested in whether he lives or dies. If George wasn't such a jerk, I'd feel sorry for him. Denise is gone more than she's at home, and the way she's dressed, I doubt she's hanging out at George's bedside."

I lowered my voice to match hers. "You think she has a boyfriend?"

"Well, that Stan you're living with now isn't giving her what she needs, is he?"

"I doubt it." From what I'd observed, Colton wasn't all that awed by Denise's many ample assets.

"Well, you know Denise; she needs to be the Barbie doll on the birthday cake," Laura muttered, rolling her blue eyes derisively.

Yes, she did. And she also wouldn't take it well if another woman were to take her place on that cake. It made me wonder how she'd dealt with Stan's girlfriend—Amber. I'd watched Denise salivate over Stan for months, mostly wondering if she was deaf and blind or what. Finally, she'd lured him in, only to lose him. Was Denise somehow caught up in this labyrinth, too?

Suddenly, it was quiet. Anticipation charged the air. Laura twirled, and her eyes shot to the frazzled-looking lady who stood on the rickety porch. "It's pretty tight quarters in here, so we'll only let ten of you in at a time," she announced. Several groans drifted forward from behind me. "Please select your items and pay quickly, so we can get those who are waiting inside in a timely manner."

She gazed at the list posted beside the door and called off ten names, Laura's and mine included, and we shuffled forward into the crowded entry. Laura darted off, shopping bags in tow, and I wove my way to the back of the house where I suspected I would find the bedrooms.

There were two of them. I joined a couple of ladies who pawed through cardboard lids piled with jewelry and snatched several sparkly clips and brooches, a couple of Bakelite bracelets, and a cameo pendant that looked like it might be the real deal. Then I grabbed three purses, two pair of fancy dress gloves, and several hats that screamed "the fifties." I wiggled my way around the man in the rubber boots to seize two plaid Pendleton jackets and a lacey tablecloth from a rack. He gave me a dirty look and nudged me aside with his brawny body.

Glancing up at his face, sparks of recognition niggled me. I couldn't place where I'd seen him before, so I flashed him a syrupy smile and made my way into the bathroom, only to discover why I was the only person there. My eyes roamed the worn towels and collection of bottles and jars before I headed for the second bedroom, where a man and woman were arguing over a scrapbook that looked as ragged as I felt. Figuring I had enough drama in my life without getting involved in their fracas, I swerved and headed for the garage.

Laura had beaten me there. Her bags bulged, and her eyes dropped to scrutinize the items I'd collected. She picked each one up to check its price and examine it more closely before she dropped it back into the basket. "My golly, Polly," she chirped. "You're getting pretty darn good at this. I might have to promote you from minion-in-training to my personal assistant."

"Gee thanks," I muttered. "Does that mean I don't have to drive or buy coffee anymore?"

She smiled. "Maybe I need to think this through." She stepped toward two middle-aged ladies in *Madge's Estate Sales*-emblazoned pink sweatshirts who were conversing behind a long table when rubber boot man barged in front of us and dropped his loaded satchel and an armful of items onto the table.

"Excuse you," Laura snapped.

He turned and gave us a haughty look, then curled his upper lip disdainfully and dismissed us to dicker with the ladies. In the end, he didn't get the deals he wanted and threw most of his stash on the cracked floor in a huff before he stomped out the door.

Laura rolled her eyes again and shook her head. "Louis Eastman," she murmured. "He's hovering up there at the top of the jerk meter with George, maybe because the two of them spend time together. I don't know two guys who are more deserving of each other."

My eyes slid to the door, but he was already gone. So he was one of George's friends—maybe even Stan's. That's why he'd seemed familiar. I must've seen them together somewhere.

When I turned back, Laura was on her knees on the grimy cement examining the pile of discards Louis had dumped. She quickly sorted them into two piles. One went to the ladies, who were busy bagging my finds, and the other was set on the far end of the table.

"Do you know what he does for a living?" I asked.

"Who, Louis?" she asked, pulling colorful pottery bowls from a bag and setting them on the table. "He has an antique shop in Lincoln City. Imports most of his stuff, then claims it's American. I think he shops the estate and garage sales, auctions, and flea markets to annoy other buyers. Unless he can get something for a fraction of what it's worth, he doesn't buy."

"Madge keeps threatening to ban him from her sales," one of the ladies told us. "I think she's afraid he'll sue her or something."

"I'd be afraid he'd do more than that. That man has a mean streak, and I know he hides things under that huge coat he always wears," the other lady added.

The two of them eyeballed each other and nodded in agreement, then returned to their bagging. Laura handed them a cocktail shaker etched with starfish, several glass flower frogs, and a handful of small kitchen tools with wooden handles.

"Where did you see him with George?" I probed.

She gave me a searching look, then pulled more items from her bags. "I know George golfs with him. I've seen Louis drive by to pick up George and his clubs, and I've seen the two of them together at the clubhouse. Seems like Stan was with them at times, too. I don't know much more than that. When I spotted them, I ran the other way."

"The total comes to two-hundred-fifty-four dollars. How about we call it an even two-hundred-twenty?" one of the ladies asked.

"Sounds good to me," Laura chirped, pulling a wad of bills from her jacket pocket and peeling off twenties.

An elderly couple stepped into the damp garage and perused a table covered with tools. While Laura took care of her payment, I grabbed several of the bulging bags and stepped outside. The sun's rays now pierced the dense fog in places, promising blue skies and sunshine. I eyed the twenty or so people who still waited to get inside the house and silently thanked Laura for being an obsessive early bird.

When Laura caught up with me, my bags were already stowed in the trunk of my car, and I waited in the driver's seat. She added hers to the pile and slid in beside me. A radiant smile lit up her beautiful face. "Well that was definitely worth the early morning rising," she twittered. "What a haul. Processing it will keep me busy for a while."

"Where to next?" I asked.

"None of the other estate sales looked all that promising, and by now, they'll be picked over. There's a garage sale at Roads End that looks interesting. Let's head there. Then I'll treat you to breakfast at The Galley."

We were at Gleneden Beach, only a mile or so, as the seagulls fly, from where we lived. To get to Roads End, we'd need to travel around Siletz Bay, then through Lincoln City to the very most northern tip, a good twelve-mile trip.

As we crept north on the Coast Highway, Laura chattered excitedly about her purchases and what she planned to do with each of them. I listened with half an ear, my mind replaying this past week's craziness like an old thirty-five millimeter film that won't end.

One week ago today, I'd turned forty. Laura and I had spent the day being pampered at Saunia's Spassage. And I had been so naive—yes, more like stupid. In my mind, Stan was faithful to our marriage. Though I'd known he had his faults—yes, more than his fair share—I hadn't known he was blackmailing Phil, or that he was squirreling away a fortune under our house through his many shady dealings.

Stan had plans to leave me, just disappear from my life without an explanation or a goodbye or a "thanks for putting up with all of my crap," and that hurt worse than all of his other lousy, lowlife actions. It felt like he was stabbing one of his fish filleting knives into my heart and twisting it back and forth, back and forth, until I longed to wail with the agony.

I pressed my hand over my mouth to hold the pain inside and glanced at Laura. Fortunately, she was too busy examining the jewelry I'd found to notice my misery. She didn't know about Stan's murder or his unlawful endeavors, and now was not the time to let her in on the whole sordid mess.

So I tried to focus on the road in front of me. It was closing in on eight o'clock, and traffic had picked up. Lincoln City sprawled along Highway 101 for several endless miles. Restaurants, shops, and other businesses lined both sides of the highway, which snaked along, sometimes nearly touching the beach and sometimes curving in toward the lush hills and Devils Lake.

In places, the road turned from four lanes to two for a mile or so. I was approaching one of those places when I checked my rearview mirror, then nearly swerved into a car merging in front of me. I pressed on the brake, righted the steering wheel, and glanced behind me to confirm what I was certain I'd seen—a familiar-looking black car. If it was still there, it was hiding several cars back.

"Is everything okay?" Laura asked.

My eyes met hers fleetingly. "Yeah. I just wasn't paying attention. Sorry."

That worried look on her face said she hadn't bought it. "You sure?" she probed. "You're awfully quiet this morning."

I forced a smile and peeked to my rear again. "Of course. With all that's been going on, I have a lot on my mind. Sara wanted to come home for the weekend, and I nixed it. I don't want her around all of this zaniness. I feel bad about it. I want to get closer to her. Instead, I pushed her away."

"I'm sorry, Pol. But you know you had no choice. Some maniac is terrorizing you, and Stan's acting weirder than that loony who kept streaking the golf course in silver stilettos and a rhinestone tiara last spring. Once things settle down, Sara will be here with you."

"I know," I agreed, wondering if things would ever settle down. For sure, they'd never return to normal. Stan was dead.

We were back to four lanes, and I still hadn't sighted the black car behind me. We passed the outlet mall, and soon colorful kites dotted the nearly clear sky. The ocean and beach stretched out to my left; the turn to Devils Lake to my right. Even at this early hour, beachgoers were scattered along the sand—walking, sitting, and playing.

Wishing I were that carefree, I sighed in resignation and followed the curve in the road inland. Still, there was no familiar-looking black car in my rearview mirror. Maybe I'd only imagined it.

I glanced at Laura. She was digging in her jacket pockets. "OMG. I know that address is in here somewhere," she muttered. "Turn left at the light. I'll find it."

A couple of minutes later, we'd passed by Chinook Winds, a rambling, tribe-owned casino and hotel overlooking the Pacific, and were still cruising north.

"Got it," she chirped triumphantly. "Pass by the State Recreation Site, and turn right on Sixty-fourth, then left."

Out here there was no traffic, and the road was a straight stretch. I scrutinized the pavement behind me, searching for anything black that moved. Nothing.

Give it up, Polly, I told myself. *You're being paranoid. There are thousands of black sporty-looking cars on the road, and they are not all following you.* By the time I parked across the street from the two-story house that was Laura's next shopping spot, I'd nearly convinced myself that was true. Besides, something else had grabbed my attention.

"We can do this one together," Laura murmured as she gathered her canvas shopping bags.

"You go ahead; I'll catch up," I told her, eyeing the man who'd just exited the house and was trudging across the street.

She gave me a funny look, blinked hard, and said, "Okay. See you in a few," before she slid from the car and hurried off to peruse the loaded tables across the street.

I grabbed the keys and my purse and climbed out, too. Normally,

I didn't approach strangers, but Laura had piqued my interest, and now was as good a time as any to talk with the guy. Besides, we'd locked eyes less than an hour ago, so technically we weren't strangers, were we?

I took a deep breath and patted my racing heart, then approached him. "Mr. Eastman," I yelled as he reached for his door handle.

His eyes darted up and zeroed in on me. Irritation blossomed on his hawkish features, and he turned away.

With a sudden spurt, I managed to settle in front of the door to his Lexus before he got it open. "I just have a couple of questions," I begged.

He glared down his long nose and curled an upper lip disgustedly. My eyes darted around, searching for onlookers. At the sale, a young couple pulled drawers from a wooden desk, and a woman fidgeted with apparel hanging from a ladder. I spotted Laura inside the garage. She stared at me as if I'd lost my mind, which I was beginning to think I had. Louis Eastman looked like he wanted to beat me to a pulp and run over me with his shiny, luxury car.

"My friend Laura said you know George Seaver," I managed to squeak.

"So what?" he snarled.

"So I was wondering if you're aware that he's in the hospital in a coma. Someone stabbed him and left him to die."

Something flickered in his eyes, but it was as if his facial features were carved in granite. "What's that got to do with me?" he growled.

I glanced at Laura, gathering strength. "Well, since you knew him, I thought you might have some ideas as to who might want him dead?"

His frown deepened. "Well, I don't. You want to know about George, you talk to Stan Morton. Not me."

My limbs turned to jelly; my insides churned. So Louis *had* known Stan. "Well, you see, uh," I stammered. "Uh, Stan's my husband. He doesn't know George all that well."

His steely gaze slid down and back up my body. "You must be a total bitch or a dud in the sack."

A slug in the gut would've felt better. "What's that got to do with George?" I gasped.

"You're decent looking, so I figured there's another reason your husband wanders."

Anger burned in my throat. "That's between Stan and me and none of your business," I snapped.

He snorted contemptuously. "Just thought you might like to know. And by the way, your husband's a damn liar."

"What do you mean?"

"He knows George well enough." He leaned forward and jabbed an index finger at me. "But I don't, so keep me out of this. If I hear you've mentioned my name to anyone, I'm gonna come looking for you and your lying husband. Got it?" With that, he jerked the car door open, shoving me aside, and climbed into the driver's seat.

I wobbled into the street on shaky legs and watched him speed away, certain that Louis Eastman was a liar, too. I was also now thoroughly convinced that George and Stan had been in cahoots and that their partnership was far more sinister than crabbing and fishing.

〰 ☼ 〰

"I need coffee," I mumbled, still rickety from my encounter with Louis Eastman. Desperate, I scanned the crowded restaurant and spotted a few empty tables.

Laura eyeballed me and huffed, exasperated. "OMG, Pol. What were you thinking? That guy is evil incarnate. He'd sell his mother to make a buck. Stay away from him."

"No problem," I assured her. "I just wanted to ask him some questions about George."

"And you honestly thought he'd give you some straight answers. Whatever George was mixed up in, Louis was probably right there beside him. Like I said 'two peas in a pod.'"

My insides knotted. "Don't you mean three?"

She shrugged and glanced away. "Hopefully, that's changed."

"How many in your party?" a waitress I recognized as Ginger asked.

"Two," I told her.

She led us to a booth overlooking the highway and beyond it, ocean water to the horizon.

"Coffee for me, please," I murmured, sliding onto the cushy, plastic seat to enjoy a short reprieve from the more snarled portions of my life.

"Me, too," Laura added.

Ginger flashed a toothy, professional smile and set menus and water in front of us. "I'll let Amber know. She'll be your waitress."

Amber! Suddenly faint, I closed my eyes and leaned against the cushioned back. I'd just confronted the scariest man I'd ever met, and now I had to face my murdered husband's girlfriend. What had I done to deserve this?

"Here, drink this," Laura ordered.

I lifted an eyelid and grasped the glass she held out to me, then took a couple of sips. "Thank you."

"Maybe we should stop at Saunia's and get you a massage on the way home. I'm worried about you, Pol. You're wired." She looked worried, all frown lines and sad eyes.

"I know. Once I get some food and coffee in me, I'll relax." I sniffed the air and attempted a smile. "*Ahhh*, those breakfast smells—bacon, maple syrup, cinnamon, pastries. I could devour the Captain's Grub platter all by myself this morning."

She smiled. "You're not fooling me, but I'll play along, mostly because I'm starving and craving caffeine, too. And because you're my best friend, and I appreciate you coming out with me this morning."

"Well, I appreciate you asking me. I suppose Harley will soon be carrying the sacred bedroom and bathroom plunder basket in my place." And I sincerely hoped he was the wonderful, innocent man she thought him to be.

Two coffee cups landed on the table, and I looked up into a pair of familiar green eyes. Only this time those eyes weren't anxious; they were fuming. I studied her strawberry tinged blonde bangs and ponytail and her flawless face. Yes, she was probably in her early thirties, and she was beautiful.

She filled our cups, sloshing coffee over the side of mine. "You know what you want?" she asked, narrowing those lethal eyes at me.

"Yes," I muttered. "I want my husband."

At least she had the decency to blush. She regained her composure quickly, then studied a wide-eyed Laura and checked for eavesdroppers before she stepped closer and said in a quiet voice, "So you know, huh? Is that why he hasn't contacted me?"

I decided to go with it. It was certainly less complicated than warped versions of the truth. "Yes. Did you really think he would leave me, just disappear, and take you with him?"

She tensed and curled a plump lip, which made her look downright mean. "We had it all planned out. So what happened? Did you find out about the money?"

I nodded. "That, too."

"If he hadn't had those last three big business payments coming in, we'd be gone, and I wouldn't be stuck here waiting tables."

Phil's was most likely one of those payments, but what were the other two? I glanced at Laura. She sat speechless, shock frozen on her face. "And what kind of business would that be?" I probed.

She snorted disgustedly. "You know, his online investment business."

"Oh, that. Well, I think it crumbled. He's pretty strapped for cash right now."

"You took his money?" she snarled, dropping the glass coffee pot onto the table so hard I was surprised it didn't shatter. Her eyes quickly scanned the room, then returned to me.

I gave her my most sincere smile. "What's his is mine. It's a husband and wife thing."

"So that's the hold you have over him."

If only, I thought. The truth was that I'd had no hold over Stan whatsoever. Even without a penny to his name, he would've taken off with Amber. "And how long were you and he involved in your adulterous fling?" I asked.

She stuck her perfectly pointed chin out, a challenge. "Long enough to know it wasn't a fling. He loves me."

At one time, I'd been certain that he loved me, too. Maybe I wasn't the idiot I thought I was. Amber was young and beautiful and totally infatuated with Stan, and Denise had the hots for him, too. How many other women had he captivated with his machinations?

For sure, not Laura. My eyes shifted to her. Had Stan ever come on to her? She'd never mentioned it.

She gave me a flustered look, eyeballed Amber, and said, "I hear you were with Stan last Friday night."

Amber eyed her warily. "Yeah."

"Dancing?" Laura probed.

With an insinuating smile, Amber's eyes swung to me. "And other stuff."

"It was my birthday," I told her. "Did he happen to mention that?"

"Yes, but he didn't care."

I pushed aside the hurt and pressed on. "Do you know when he headed home?"

She shrugged. "He left my place a little after eleven."

"Seems kind of early. You two have a fight?"

"No," she snapped, her glare even more heated. "I had to be here at six the next morning." She paused and seemed to consider something before she spoke. "Oh, I see. He got home, and you were ticked because he skipped out on your big *'four-oh,'* so you had it out with him. That's why he didn't return any of my messages the next day."

"And he hasn't returned any since, has he?"

Tears glistened in her eyes. I almost felt sorry for her. Almost.

"He will . . . eventually," she murmured, picking up the coffee decanter. After a quick scan of the room, she snarled, "I need to get back to work. You gonna order?"

Oh, yeah, so she could cough on my waffle and drop my bacon on the germy kitchen floor. "I've lost my appetite," I told her, digging my wallet from my purse. I pulled out a five dollar bill and dropped it on the table.

She grabbed it and walked off.

I relaxed against the seat, feeling like I'd gone a round with a pro wrestler. It hadn't been my finest moment, but I had culled a few tidbits from Amber, tidbits that might help me figure out what had happened to Stan on the night he was murdered.

My eyes met Laura's. She still had a possum-in-the-headlights look about her.

"At least we got our coffee," she muttered, reaching for her mug.

"I wouldn't do that," I warned her. "She probably spit in the mugs."

CHAPTER 11

Heavy Saturday morning traffic crawled south on the Coast Highway. Unfortunately, I crept along in it. Sunlight streamed in through the windshield, and a light breeze stirred the branches on the trees lining the road.

My eyes flicked to Colton, who sat beside me in the passenger seat clothed in khaki shorts and a cotton, short-sleeved shirt that looked pretty darn good on him, probably because they were two sizes smaller than what he'd been wearing. Dark stubble glistened appealingly on his cheeks, something that had always looked slovenly on Stan. Just looking at him made me mushy.

Get a grip, I told myself, pulling my eyes back to the road. *Circumstance is the only thing keeping the two of you together. Nothing more.*

We were headed to Depoe Bay to check out Harley's bakery—specifically, his chocolate candy. If it looked anything like the Triazolam-laced truffles left at my front door, Harley had some serious explaining to do. And then I'd have to sit down with Laura for an anguishing heart-to-heart. I dreaded the prospect.

Still, I had to know if Harley was an innocent suitor or a manipulative player in George and Stan's money-making schemes.

We left the sandy beaches behind and climbed up to Boiler Bay viewpoint. Steep dark cliffs to our right dropped to the churning ocean. I checked the string of cars in my rearview mirror and swore the black sedan three cars back was "the one."

"So you think this Louis guy might be involved in whatever George and Stan were up to?" Colton asked.

I shelved my black car phobia and glanced at Colton. "I wouldn't be surprised. The way he threatened to come after me if I get him involved in George's stabbing, he has to be hiding something."

"Well, hopefully George will come out of the coma soon, and he'll be scared enough to talk. Then if Louis is mixed up in it, George'll be the one who squeals on him."

That would suit me. I had absolutely no desire to meet up with Louis Eastman again. Or Amber.

I'd replayed my visit with Amber for Colton earlier that morning. Now we were both wondering about those payments Stan had been expecting. Of course, I knew Phil was supposed to deliver one of them. But how about the other two? Surely, at least one of them was connected to our break-ins.

Colton had spent most of the previous day in Portland, trying to track down Stan's business dealings and had come up with zilch. As far as he could determine, Stan had no extra bank or investment accounts, and evidently, he didn't conduct business on his computer or his cell phone. No safety deposit box and no trail of cashed checks. *Nada*. Evidently, he dealt in cash and banked it beneath his toy room. He had one credit card, on which he owed a little over three hundred dollars, spent on gasoline for his truck. Either Stan had earned his stockpile honestly and just didn't trust the system, or he was a whole lot smarter than I'd realized.

"And you don't think Amber might've murdered Stan, huh?"

During the last twenty-four hours, I'd replayed Amber's words and actions over and over in my mind, and I'd always drawn the same conclusion. "I really don't," I assured him. "She was angry yesterday, but when I saw her last weekend, she was upset, almost frantic with worry. I can't come up with a reason she'd want him dead. He was her ticket out. I asked her if they'd had a fight since he left her house so early that night. She denied it. Said she had to be at work at six the next morning. And since you found Stan dead at one-thirty, her timing works. If he left her house a little after eleven. . . ."

That black car popped into my rearview mirror again, three cars back. I pulled off my sunglasses and squinted, trying to see it more clearly, but it was too far away.

"Is something wrong?" Colton asked.

Just me being paranoid, I admitted silently. I had to get a handle on this black car thing before someone noticed how wacky I was becoming.

The highway curved down, and a stunning panorama appeared—dark, sheer precipices dropping into the endless blue ocean, waves crashing into them. "Just love the view from up here," I told him, slipping my sunglasses back on and tracking back through my train of thought to the conversation we'd been having.

"Anyway, if Stan left Amber's a little after eleven," I recapped, "he'd be home by eleven-thirty. That would give him time to drink his six-pack and be murdered before you showed up. Besides, why would Amber follow him to his house to murder him? If she wanted him dead, she could've done it before he took off."

I glanced at Colton. He seemed lost in thought, staring at the array of bumper stickers covering the rear of the beat-up minivan in front of us. Like me, he was probably obsessed with trying to figure out who had killed Stan. I turned back to my driving, praying I wasn't on his list of suspects.

Just like that, traffic slowed to snail speed. Depoe Bay was just ahead. As if it might be possible to speed through town, a cop sat in his cruiser at the side of the road.

"You think Amber'll be at that dancing place tonight?"

My eyes darted to Colton. "The Whale's Spout?"

"Yeah. Any chance she'll be there?"

"Maybe . . . if she thinks Stan might show up. Why?"

"I'd like to see what happens if she runs into me."

A sick feeling settled inside me. It was ridiculous, but I didn't want Colton and Amber to meet. She was young and beautiful, and she would think he was Stan. Who knew where that might lead? "So you're going dancing tonight?" I probed.

"*We're* going dancing tonight."

My eyes met his. "Won't I put a crimp in your plans?"

He smiled and shrugged. "Could make it more interesting. You in?"

"Sure," I murmured, searching for a place to park. To my right, ocean water splashed on the far side of the sidewalk wall. A hodgepodge of vehicles faced toward the walkway at an angle. It was a typical summer Saturday in Depoe Bay—lots of people milling about and no parking.

Storefronts lined the other side of the highway—cafes, souvenir shops, clothing stores, an ice cream parlor. And there was Harley's Bakery, painted a beach blue with white trim. Large picture windows added a homey touch.

I opened my mouth to point it out to Colton when I noticed a set of rear lights flash. "Maybe my luck is finally changing," I muttered as I pressed on the brake and waited for a silver SUV to back out. I could almost hear profanities spewing from the drivers behind me as I pulled into the space. Most likely, I'd claimed the only empty parking spot in town.

When we climbed out of the car, the wind had picked up a bit. After sitting in the sun-warmed vehicle, it felt invigorating to stand on the sidewalk and gaze down over the massive rocks at the water roiling, churning, and gushing, to smell the ocean breeze and feel its coolness on my face and bare arms.

"I saw the bakery not too far back, on the other side of the street," I told Colton.

"Yeah. I saw it, too." He stared into my eyes, smiled, and draped an arm around my shoulder, pulling me up next to the low rock wall. "But what say we take a few to enjoy the moment?"

I went all soft on the inside, but panic stiffened my limbs and spine. More than anything, I longed to nestle into his strength, to lean on him for support. Maybe sneak a kiss. He gave me a questioning look.

"It's complicated," I murmured.

"That it is," he agreed, rubbing my arm soothingly. "But you're wound tighter than a bowstring. Relax and enjoy the view. That bakery's not going anywhere."

So I faced the ocean and watched the waves crash up onto the rocks, felt the salt water mist my face, and tried to shut out all of the people milling around us and their people noises—kids' shouting, garbled chatter, and carefree laughter. I told myself to let it all go—Stan's death, George's botched murder attempt, my schoolgirl crush on Colton, the break-ins, and all of the other weird things going on in my life.

And it only emphasized the fact that the drama in my life was spiraling, totally out of control. Each time Colton and I tried to solve a piece of the puzzle, it only became more complex—like our relationship.

I hadn't had the heart to send him back to the lumpy hide-a-bed in Stan's spotlessly clean toy room, so he still slept beside me every night. Though, truth be told, he was clear on the other side of the bed, and he'd never once crossed over to my side. Occasionally, some wanton, weak part of me wished he would. Then guilt gnawed at me for my wayward thoughts. Stan was barely in his grave—or urn, in his case—and I was drooling over his brother. Talk about sleazy.

A quick peek at Colton told me he gazed out at the blue horizon.

He looked relaxed, not tangled into tight knots like me at the prospect of Harley's deception. I should be at home working on Frank's book, and here I was playing private eye, something that was definitely more alluring on screen or paper than in real life.

Which reminded me of my latest correspondence from Brad Ellis. I'd received another disturbing email message from him that morning—*I was to do this and that or else . . . blah, blah, blah*—as if I didn't have enough going on in my life right now without his threats and abuse. Well his great-great-grandfather was born in a brothel, and other than he and his sister, who the hell cared? No one, that's who.

"I see the cogs turning. You're winding yourself even tighter, aren't you?"

I eyeballed Colton. "Guilty," I muttered. "I was thinking about Brad Ellis, the guy you met at Mo's that day. He's such an ass."

He squeezed my shoulder, then let go of me and leaned his side against the stones. "What'd he do?"

I hunkered close to the rock wall, too, to give folks ample room to pass behind me. "He wants control over the book I'm writing for his father, Frank. He and his sister seem convinced that I'm going to disclose some deep, dark family secret that will blacklist them from high society."

"Are you?"

In today's world, one had to do something downright appalling to be ostracized. I couldn't imagine that Brad's ancestors' actions would have any effect on his standings with the elite.

So I shrugged and launched into an abbreviated explanation. "I told you about Nellie. She's Brad's great-great-grandmother. Well, Frank wants the truth about the birth of her child in the book. My guess is that Brad and his sister, Nell, don't. But I find it difficult to believe they'd be so upset about something as trivial as that."

"Maybe it's something else."

Though I seriously doubted it, I considered his point before I responded. "Could be, I suppose. Frank gave me a box of old papers—news articles, ledgers, letters, stuff like that," I explained. "The packet of letters Sheriff Bronson found in the garage was from that box. I had copies made, so I wouldn't have to handle the originals, and Stan picked them up at the museum in Newport for me. He must've dropped the letters in the garage and then forgot about them.

"Anyway, I haven't had a chance to go through everything in the box yet, but I doubt there's anything that scandalous in there. Frank would've mentioned it . . . or Bev, my friend who made the copies. That's why I'm so miffed at Brad. He plans to pick the box of papers up on Monday. He's just letting me know he's top dog. It's his way of controlling me."

He frowned. "So he called you?"

I shook my head. Thankfully, I'd been spared that trauma. "No. He emails me, but I refuse to acknowledge his messages until he can be civil."

A sudden idea made me pause to ponder it. "I think I'll respond to his latest one, though," I told him, feeling pounds lighter. "I'm going to take that box of papers to Frank Monday morning. If Brad wants them, he can deal with his dad. I'd pay to be a fly on that wall. Frank may be in his eighties, but he's still one tough *honcho*."

"Well, if you drive to Portland, be care. . . ."

Sudden shrieks drew my attention. A gush of icy water drenched my front. I froze, gasping, and pulled off my sunglasses to wipe the water from my eyes. Beside me a wiry-haired mutt shook, peppering my bare legs. Around me, shocked faces turned to smiles. Laughter and excited voices filled the air.

"Sleeper wave," the guy with the dog said. "They're deceiving— just trailing along with the other waves; looking like something they're not. When you least expect them, they sneak up on you and *wham!* If you're not prepared, they can get you."

I glanced up at his grizzled features, fanned my wet blouse, and considered his words. *Sounds like my life*, I wanted to tell him, *riddled with deceit.*

Instead I studied Colton's dripping features. "Maybe we better visit the bakery before we get washed out of town," I muttered.

≈ ✿ ≈

Mouth-watering smells enfolded us when we stepped into Harley's Bakery—chocolate and cinnamon, butter and baking dough. Every counter and case overflowed with decadent offerings. Baguettes two feet long peeked from apple baskets while a wire rack was loaded with every other kind of bread imaginable. Cookies, bars, pastries, and luscious-looking cakes and pies beckoned from inside a wall of glass cases. Off to our right, several people waited to pay at a counter. Through the spattering of customers I sighted the sheen of candy in a smaller glass cabinet that stood not far from the cash register.

I watched a couple of teenage girls tug a number from a stand beside the door and reached out to procure my place in line. If nothing else, I planned to devour one of those maple bars calling to me from behind glass.

"Suddenly, I'm starving," Colton said from beside me.

"I could definitely be a human caterpillar and eat my way through this place," I muttered. "Poor Laura. If my boyfriend owned this place, I'd either be plumping up or frustrated beyond belief. I'm surprised Harley's stayed so lean and fit."

"Must be the thought of replacing all that leather. It ain't cheap."

Back on the clock, so to speak, I scanned the room, searching for Harley. A middle-aged lady manned the cash while a trio of younger women stuffed baked treats into bags for customers. All wore jeans and baby blue polos with a *Harley's Bakery* logo on the right shoulder.

"No Harley," I murmured.

"Not that we can see. Maybe he's baking," Colton offered.

"Laura said he doesn't work here, just runs the business end of things," I informed him. "Could be he has an office in the back, though."

One of the women called out a number, and I checked mine and uttered. "Six more in front of us."

"Gives us time to check out the candy," he said, placing his hand on my lower back to guide me toward the cabinet I'd already spotted.

Behind its glass doors, slabs of fudge lounged on tan trays—chocolate, vanilla, peanut butter, penuche, orange, and nearly every other flavor imaginable. There was not a truffle in sight.

I hadn't realized how tense I was until I felt my muscles loosen. Relief flowed through me as my eyes met Colton's. He raised his brows and shrugged.

"Polly?" a female voice tweeted.

I glanced around and into a familiar face. If only I could place it. My mind scrambled—short and round, white curls, kind eyes, lots of bling and turquoise—and visions of screaming slot machines flashed before me.

"Millie," I guessed.

"In the flesh," she confirmed. "Fancy meeting you here. This is Clyde, my sugar daddy," she added, tugging an ancient-looking man with a cane forward with a ring-laden hand. "He got a hankering for one of Harley's caramel rolls, so we hopped in the Bimmer and headed down here."

"Nice to meet you, Clyde," I told him. "This is . . . uh, my husband, Stan. Stan, Millie and Clyde. I met Millie at the casino last week."

"A pleasure," Colton murmured, fidgeting a bit under Millie's astute stare.

"I doubt it," she muttered derisively before she turned to me and added, "You okay, honey?"

I nodded hesitantly while I tried to recall what I'd disclosed to Millie about Stan's and my marriage. Her look told me I'd blabbed more than I should have. "Of course. We got a hankering, too—for Harley's fudge," I assured her.

"And this guy's your husband, right?"

"Yes. Why?"

"I've got the creepy crawlies, which usually means something fishy's going on."

Of course; I'd forgotten. "Millie's a medium," I informed Colton.

He gave me a "you've got to be kidding" look, then seemed to get it together enough to smile sweetly. "Well, rest assured, Millie. There might be all kinds of fishy things going on around here— after all, the Pacific's right across the street—but we came for candy. Period."

She narrowed her eyes at him. He crossed his arms and met her glare, not even blinking.

Millie was the first to back down. She sniffled, then slipped on the rhinestoned glasses dangling from her neck and turned to scrutinize me. "I don't know what's going on here, honey. I just hope you're not in any trouble," she finally said, concern etched in her deep wrinkles. "You do know that guy is still following you?"

"What?" I gasped. Was she relaying a psychic vision of some kind?

"Clyde and I walked right past him. Clyde's not as quick on his feet as he once was, so I got a good look at him. He's definitely the guy from the casino."

Knots of tension returned. My heart rate soared. "Where is he?" I managed to ask.

"Across the street—tan shorts, navy shirt, sunglasses. He's just standing there staring at this bakery."

I darted for the door but was halted by a hand on my upper arm. "He'll see you if you run out there. Look out a window," Colton suggested.

He was right, of course. If I went tearing outside, the guy would be gone before I got close enough to confront him. I took a couple of deep breaths, told myself to get a grip, and stepped to a window to gaze across the street. People of every shape and size milled about, but there was no tall young man in tan shorts and a navy shirt. My gaze traveled north, searching painstakingly, then south.

"Do you see him?" Colton asked from beside me.

"No, but people keep walking by and obstructing my view," I muttered, heading for the door.

I walked to the curb and renewed my search. Still no stalker.

"Maybe Millie was wrong," Colton offered.

"Yeah, maybe," I conceded, swallowing my disappointment. "She did only see him the one time." Still, a little voice inside me asserted that Millie was one sharp lady, and if she said she saw the guy tailing me, she did. After all, hadn't I thought I'd spotted his car three times in the last couple of days? I'd blown it off and blamed it on nerves. Maybe my imagination wasn't as wild as I'd thought.

Colton draped an arm around my shoulder and squeezed. "I'm sorry," he murmured.

I shrugged when what I really wanted to do was bury my face in his chest and sob until I was so spent that I couldn't feel the frustration and fear and fury living inside me. "Let's go check out the candy," I suggested instead.

Millie and Clyde were ogling pastries. She glanced back at me, questions in her look. I shook my head, and she frowned and scrutinized Stan before she turned back to the calorie-laden goodies.

A couple of minutes later, our number was called, and I stepped forward to greet a brunette with a bright, toothy smile. "We're interested in the candy," I told her, handing the number over the counter.

"Good choice. Harley's famous for his fudge," she said as she headed toward Colton and the candy display. "What kind would you like?"

I stared through the glass as if contemplating a choice. "Actually, we heard that you have some incredible truffles?"

She looked puzzled. "No. I've never seen truffles in here. Just fudge. We make it ourselves. Would you like a sample?"

Why not? "Maybe just a tiny bite of the dark chocolate," I told her.

She opened the case and cut two minuscule slices off the slab, dropped them on parchment paper, and handed one to Colton and one to me. I put it in my mouth and, as it melted across my tongue, purred silently. It was rich. It was velvety smooth. It was everything chocolate should be. And it tasted distinctly different from my birthday truffles.

I glanced at Colton. Pleasure radiated from his features, but he shook his head enough to let me know we were in agreement. "Do you know if Harley makes any other kinds of chocolate?" he asked.

Her smile tightened; her eyes were not so welcoming. "Not that I know of," she muttered. "Do you want some of the fudge?"

"Yes. Do you have a small box you can put it in? It's a gift," I fibbed, hoping she didn't pull out a perfect cream-colored box with a gold liner.

The box was white and generic, nothing special. She patted a piece of parchment paper into it and waited. Her smile had crept back.

I eyed Colton and murmured. "What do you think—maybe a couple of pieces of the dark chocolate and two of the milk chocolate?"

He nodded. "Sounds good. And stick in two pieces of the sour cream and maybe two of the raspberry."

Evidently, Colton had a sweet tooth. If we ate all of that candy, we could easily hike home and, most likely, faster than we'd make it in the weekend traffic.

"I don't suppose Harley's here today?" Colton asked, as the young woman stretched a black band around the closed box and pushed it into a white paper sack.

"You know Harley?" she asked, her eyes a bit troubled.

"We've met," I informed her. "Just thought we'd say hello if he was here."

She leaned forward and murmured, "He has a girlfriend now, and they're pretty tight. I think he's with her today."

Harley seemed like the kind of guy who would frown on his employees disclosing his personal information to customers, but I chose not to bring that up to the young woman. "Good for him," I avowed. "Everyone needs a little love in their lives."

Her smile went tight again. "If you say so," she mumbled stiffly, handing the bag to me, then taking the twenty dollar bill Colton handed her.

"Must be having relationship issues," Colton whispered when she went to get his change.

"Aren't we all?" I threw out there. Before he could respond I added, "This was a bust. Have you noticed that we're making zero progress on solving even one itty-bitty part of this puzzle? Maybe we should turn it over to the sheriff."

He sighed. "I know, but I don't want to give it to him yet. I think we're close. Maybe tonight we'll get a break."

"Yes, and more than likely, it will be Amber breaking some part of me," I muttered, seriously worried that some of Millie's psychic powers might have rubbed off on me, and my prediction would come true.

∼∼ ☼ ∼∼

"We're gonna crash before we reach home," I warned Colton as we inched along behind a tractor-trailer rig loaded with a stack of logs.

"Then you better keep consuming sugar," he suggested, holding the box of fudge out to me.

After devouring a couple of the large chocolate chunks while we strolled around Depoe Bay, I nearly gagged at the sight of it. "*Ugh.* Hide that stuff, and slap my hands if I reach for another piece. It's more dangerous than those deadly truffles. Might be yummier, too."

He pushed the lid back on the box and dropped it into the bag. "Yep, Harley's definitely got it figured out. Looks like Laura made a good catch."

"I'm so glad. Relieved, too. She just met the guy, and I think she's already picturing that antique diamond on her finger. It would've devastated her if Harley was mixed up in Stan's mess."

"He still could be. I doubt he left those chocolates, though."

We were climbing, and the monster vehicle in front of us was trucking along at a sluggish twenty-five miles per hour. I gritted my teeth and glanced in my rearview mirror to see if steam was rising from any of the other drivers. Back four cars, I spotted *him.*

"Gotcha," I yelped triumphantly, hyped on nervous energy and too much sucrose. "Thank you, Millie."

"Your stalker?" Colton asked, turning around to look through the rear window.

I checked again. No, I hadn't imagined it. "Four cars back, behind the cranberry Cruiser."

"Well, now that we've got him, we can't let him get away," he muttered. We passed a sign, and I noticed his eyes zero in on it.

"What's Boiler Bay?"

"It's a scenic wayside, a place to watch the ocean from the cliff tops." My voice was a bit shaky. Trailing Colton had been one thing, but cornering a stalker was a whole lot more gouges up the totem pole. I glanced at Colton's tighter-fitting clothing, hoping he had his gun hidden under there somewhere.

"Pull in there—just ahead," he instructed. "If there's a restroom, drop me off at it. Then park and wait for me. Lock the doors, and don't get out of your car. Let's see if this fellow follows us."

I signaled a left turn and tried to patiently wait for a break in oncoming traffic, limbs twitching and pulse racing. Finally I made the turn, and we cruised down a paved road along the top of a series of sea cliffs that seemed to drop forever to jagged, jutting rocks and the churning ocean. I pulled over next to a trail that led to the restroom. Colton reached beneath the seat and pulled out his pistol. He stuck it into the back of his shorts, then pulled his shirt over it, jumped out of the car, and hauled ass up the trail.

My eyes darted from him to the rearview mirror. My breath hitched. The black car had stopped back a ways.

"Oh, lordy," I whispered, so shaky my breaths were choppy. "You're gonna get yourself killed, Pollyanna." With trembling hands, I parked away from other people and vehicles and locked my doors. The black car didn't budge.

Time crawled and my sugar high slowly waned. I sat in my hot car with the ocean swelling and crashing far below me and stared in my rearview mirror at that motionless vehicle. Sunrays pinked my arms and thighs, and wind bursts jiggled the vehicle. Sightseers came and went. Still, I sat—until my eyes grew dry and blurry from gazing into that blasted mirror, and all I wanted to do was close them and nap.

"Yikes!" I shrieked, suddenly alert, when the car did move. I blinked several times. Yes, it was drawing nearer.

To my surprise, it pulled in behind me, and Colton slid out of the passenger seat. He didn't have his gun in his hand. He didn't walk around and tug the jerk out of the car by his collar. He didn't even look threatening. In fact, he looked rather pleasant when he gazed in my window, a set of keys dangling from an index finger.

I unlocked the door and climbed out, my stiff legs and lower back complaining. Then I checked out the man in the black car. He leaned back in the seat, sunglasses shading his eyes and a sullen look on his face. "Who is he?" I asked.

"Some college kid. He said his father's paying him to keep an eye on you. I hoped you might provide some insight. Any idea who Dan Hunt is?"

"Dan Hunt?" The name didn't even sound familiar. Why would he have his son following me? I shook my head. "No. Does he know why his father wants me tailed?"

He eye shrugged. "Claims he doesn't. We put in a call to his dad. He should be here soon."

Oh, great, I thought, gazing down the steep precipice at the water crashing onto craggy rocks. *A showdown at the top of Boiler Bay.* How many times had I watched a scene like this in a movie or TV show? Someone always plunged off the ledge and ended up dead at the bottom of the cliff. And it wasn't always the bad guy.

I banished the gory images from my mind and tried to focus on the fact that we might finally get some answers. "Does he know anything?" I asked.

"Oh, I'm sure he knows a lot, just not about what's going on here. Dad ordered him to do it, so he did. He claims he didn't do anything wrong, that he didn't threaten you or get near you."

"That doesn't make it less scary," I argued, irritated that the kid thought it was okay to traumatize others.

Colton leaned against my car and crossed his ankles, face to the wind and sun. "Hey, his words, not mine. I'm just the messenger."

"Well, maybe I should talk to him then," I snapped.

I'd taken two steps when I noticed a monstrous white pickup truck charging down the road toward us. Brakes squealed, and it slid to a stop behind the black car. A brown logo on the side of the truck read *D. Hunt & Sons Construction.*

"Looks like you'll get to chat with his dad first," Colton muttered, "and he doesn't look happy."

In truth, he looked furious. Fixing his ominous glare on Colton, he stomped up to him in a pair of heavy work boots that stopped just inches from Colton's water sandals.

And suddenly, it hit me that I'd dealt with this guy before—in The Galley—and he'd been a loaded cannon then, too. I stared at his familiar features and wondered why in the heck Dan Hunt cared what I did.

Colton pushed himself up off my car, which forced the guy to step back. Then he folded his arms over his chest and said very calmly,

"Looks like you have a problem with something I did."

Hunt's puffy face blossomed beet red. He wagged a beefy index finger in Colton's face and growled, "I warned you, Morton. You think you can threaten me and get away with it? Well, think again. I told you to stay the hell away from me and my company, but you couldn't keep your dirty nose out of my business dealings, could you? And now you're messing with my son? Well, I think it's time I turned this over to the law; let them deal with you."

I hoped he'd follow through on his threat, but he dropped his arm and stood there fuming, flexing his hands and working his jaw. I also hoped my CPR training would come back to me if the guy got any more worked up. He was a heart attack waiting to happen—hefty, with a bulky belly hanging over his belt.

Colton pulled a cell phone from his pocket. "I'll make the call for you. I just happen to have Sheriff Bronson on speed dial. He and I have developed a close relationship this past week. I wonder what he's gonna say about you sending your son out to stalk my wife."

Hunt's eyes darted to me. He curled a lip and dismissed me with a nasty look. "You're the one who got her involved, not me. It's just like you to make your wife do your dirty work. All I'm doing is protecting my interests."

Fire sparked in Colton's dark eyes. "First of all, her name is Polly," he retorted. "Second, I don't *make* her do anything. And third, I don't know what in the hell you're talking about. So I suggest we put our anger aside and talk this thing out before we call in the cops."

Though he looked like he might explode, Hunt glanced back at his son and appeared to be considering Colton's suggestion. Finally, he expelled a long gust of air and took a couple of steps back.

In response, Colton relaxed against my car. "So what is it that you think I did?" Colton asked.

"What you threatened to do when I fired your lazy butt, that's what: you're trying to take me down," Hunt snapped.

Oh, lordy. Stan and his big mouth. Dan Hunt's construction company must've been building that restaurant in Seal Rock, the one Stan was working on. Then Hunt had fired him, no doubt with good cause, and Stan hadn't taken it well. Evidently, he'd threatened to do something to Hunt or his business or whatever. But he hadn't followed through on it, had he?

"Ruin your business?" Colton probed.

"Yes, ruin my business. But it's not gonna happen 'cause I caught you at it, and I know what you're up to."

Colton looked to me, questioning. I shrugged and shook my head. If Stan was settling a score with his ex boss, he'd left me out of the loop.

"Well, I doubt you do since I'm not up to anything," Colton informed Hunt.

"Sure you are," Hunt spluttered, growing more agitated. "I saw the two of you in Mo's last Saturday. As usual, you looked like you'd been on a long bender." His heated gaze darted to me. "You had quite a conversation with Brad Ellis, and I have a good idea what you were promising him."

Huh? What did Brad Ellis have to do with Stan's revenge threat? I studied a vintage Mustang as it passed by while I pieced together scenarios. None fit. "I didn't promise him anything," I finally muttered truthfully. "I wanted him to know that his dad's the one in control,"

"Of course, he is," Hunt barked. "He always has been. And you went straight to Frank once you got the information, didn't you? I wouldn't have known that if Jase hadn't been following you."

"What are you talking about? What information?" I asked, even more confused.

"All the stuff you recorded the next morning—at The Galley. You really lucked out, didn't you? You snuck into that booth while I was in the can, and you got everything we said on tape. How'd you know we'd be discussing that Pacific City project? Did you follow us to the restaurant?"

I glanced at Colton. He looked as bewildered as I. What a muddle! "You thought I was recording your conversation?"

"Of course, you were. I saw the recorder sitting right there on your table. You didn't even try to hide it."

"That's because I wasn't recording you. I was listening to a tape."

His jaw dropped, and for long moments he stared at me, eyes narrowed. "I'm supposed to believe that?"

I huffed, irritated that Dan Hunt had jumped to crazy conclusions without anything to corroborate them. "Believe what you want," I told him. "Why would I care about you guys plotting some construction project?"

"To give the information to Frank Ellis. I'm sure he paid you well for it."

"Why would Frank want it?"

"Like you said, it might look like Brad and his son are running their construction company, but Frank's still the head honcho."

Suddenly it all slipped into place. I understood. "Your company and Frank's construction company are both bidding on the Pacific City thing, right? Is that why you assumed I was recording your meeting?"

"Yes, except I didn't assume it. You did record it," he insisted.

"And if that doesn't prove how small this world is," I whispered, gazing at the people milling about at the picnic and viewing areas farther down the road, wondering how many of them had bumped elbows with me—somewhere, sometime.

"Okay, Dan, listen closely," I advised. "Here's what really went down: I'm a self-employed, professional writer. Frank Ellis hired me to write a history on his family. His son, Brad, knew that and stopped by my table at Mo's to introduce himself and let me know that he has the final say on what's in Frank's book. He doesn't; Frank does.

"The next morning, I had breakfast at The Galley. Evidently, you didn't notice, but I was already in my booth when the three of you were seated. I was alone, so I listened to a recording of Frank telling me about his great-grandfather, with an earphone in my ear most of the time."

I paused to gulp air and glance at Colton. He needed to get this, too. "Early the next morning, I drove to Portland to meet with Frank. We discussed his great-grandmother, not his construction business or your construction business or any other construction business.

"To be quite frank, I have no interest in the construction industry or in getting vengeance because you canned Stan—something I'm certain he deserved. My only interest here is getting your son off my tail. And I *will* call Sheriff Bronson if that doesn't happen."

Feeling like I'd dove off the sea cliff and swam all the way back to Depoe Bay in the churning ocean, I wilted. If I didn't get off my feet, I knew I'd crumble down onto the grass and sit there like a sunburned, concrete yard ornament.

"And now, as far as I'm concerned, you can hash out the rest of your absurd allegations with Stan. I'll be in my car," I mumbled, grasping the door handle.

CHAPTER 12

The night was perfect. An attractive man sitting across the bar table from me—ogling me, not the other women. A Piña Colada to sip. Pleasant conversation and a few laughs. Maybe some dancing.

Too perfect. Because Colton sat on the other side of that table, not Stan. And Colton was not my husband. Unfortunately, I had to keep reminding myself of that fact.

Why couldn't you give me this, Stan? I asked his lousy legacy. *Then maybe you wouldn't be dead, I wouldn't be here searching for your murderer and cleaning up your mess, and this night wouldn't be so bittersweet.*

I glanced around the eighties-era lounge. Thanks to low lighting and an overflowing crowd of mostly middle-agers and Boomers, the frayed upholstery and scuffed tables and walls went unnoticed. A halfway decent band played tonight—mostly rock tunes from the previous century with some country thrown in. Couples wiggled and gyrated on the hardwood dance floor. Some actually danced, and by danced I mean the real stuff—swings and waltzes, cha-chas and two-steps.

Though I hadn't spotted Amber in the crowd, I had noticed a few familiar faces. Maybe she wouldn't show up. Maybe she'd switch to a dance spot that catered to a younger crowd. Maybe she'd given up on luring Stan back. Maybe . . . Maybe . . . Maybe . . . My life was riddled with "maybes."

But Colton didn't seem that concerned about Amber's absence. Tonight he was fishing for clues, hoping some of Stan's acquaintances would show up. Not just Amber, but anyone. He wanted to see how they reacted to his presence. A few had, too, with nods and beer salutes and crude greetings, but the moment they spotted me, they backed off.

However, the night was young. We'd solved one mystery today. Maybe we'd solve another tonight—another big "maybe."

"Still no Amber?" Colton asked, drawing me back to him. Fortunately, the music wasn't blasting so loud that we couldn't visit.

I shook my head. "No, she'll stick out like a ten-year-old at Senior Prom here, and I'm struggling with the fact that I do fit in. When did I get so old?"

He patted my hand reassuringly. "Don't be so hard on yourself. You look smokin' hot in that red dress."

"Opposed to how I usually look, you mean?"

Humor shone in his eyes. He gulped beer and stared hard at me. "You always look hot. Tonight it's super hot."

Which made the effort it took to salvage my fortieth birthday dress worth it. I smiled, my cheeks burning. Unfortunately, he looked hot, too, in classy jeans and an olive green silk shirt. "Always the diplomat," I pointed out. "Do you ever get the urge to just lay into someone?"

"Of course. I wanted to throttle Dan Hunt this morning, so he won't be around to jump to any more ludicrous conclusions and harass other poor souls."

"Well, I'm glad you guys talked it out and shook hands. And he did apologize. That's worth something . . . I guess." I'd actually been shocked when he'd opened my car door and admitted he was sorry for the misunderstanding. Of course, his son hadn't apologized for scaring me to the point that I had to have sprouted several new gray hairs.

Count your blessings, Polly, I reminded myself.

So I did. "It's nice to no longer worry about being tailed and to know why it was happening. I was convinced it was somehow connected to Stan's death," I told Colton.

"Yeah, me, too. But I don't think so. Until he thought you were spying on him, Hunt didn't have a motive to kill Stan."

"He is kind of paranoid," I pointed out. "Maybe he took Stan's threat seriously and did something about it."

"He didn't seem surprised when he saw me today."

"Of course, not. He saw you at Mo's a week ago. If he was shocked, it would've been then."

He frowned and seemed to consider what I'd said. "Nah. It doesn't feel right."

"Then who?" I challenged.

And my phone sang. "I'm sorry, but it might be Sara, and I don't want her to worry." I dug my cell from my jacket pocket and checked the screen—Laura. She was supposed to be with Harley, so why was she calling me?

I glanced at Colton. He was scanning the room, so I answered. "What's up?"

"Look right," she said, "over by the bar."

My eyes slid toward the bar and locked on Amber's lethal glare. "Oh, lordy," I muttered. "If looks could kill, you'd be planning my funeral."

"I might be, anyway, if you don't steer clear of her. What are you doing here?"

"Dancing. I even have my red dress on."

Amber's glare slid to Stan and transformed into dreamy-eyed yearning. She smiled seductively, licked her glossy lips, and ran fingers through her loose, flowing tresses. My eyes darted to Colton. Yep. He'd found Amber on his own.

"OMG, Pol. Looks like Stan is reverting to his wicked ways. Maybe you should dance on out of here . . . and take him with you. I don't have a good feeling about this. Denise is wandering around here, too. When we came in, I saw her in the parking lot with some guy, guzzling straight from a bottle."

A sick feeling settled in my stomach. Like Cinderella, my perfect night was turning to dust—radioactive dust. Why hadn't I listened to my screaming gut and stayed home?

"Where are you?" I asked Laura, thanking my lucky stars she was here to watch my back.

"Left of the dance floor."

Pulling my eyes from Colton and Amber's little scene, I searched until I spotted Laura at a table with Harley, who was gazing at the dancers. He'd shed his leather and looked rather dashing in a tan polo and dark slacks, his long hair pulled back into a neat tail. As always, Laura was a splash of vibrant color topped with blonde curls. She'd poured herself into a flowered sundress that displayed her ample cleavage nicely.

I waved, and she unwound a couple of fingers from her wineglass and wiggled them. "You're welcome to join us," I offered.

She eyed Harley, then me. "We would, but I don't want to ruin your night out. Harley has this thing about people who cheat on their spouses. He and Stan would probably end up in each other's face."

It seemed like an over-the-top response to infidelity, but I didn't know anything about Harley's life experiences, so who was I to judge? I sincerely hoped there hadn't been more going on between him and Stan than that.

"Okay. Thanks for warning me about Amber," I said. "Have fun."

"You, too. And, Pol?"

"Yeah"

"Be careful."

"Always," I whispered as I clicked off the phone.

When I glanced across the table, Colton seemed to be considering something. "I take it that's Amber," he said, nodding his head slightly in her direction.

"Yep. You interested? 'Cause I'd say she'll trample me to get to you."

"No, but if I get the chance, she and I are gonna talk." He downed the rest of his beer and huffed. "You ready to dance?"

"You do realize that Stan was a *really* good dancer?" I warned him. And if Colton wasn't, would anyone notice and wonder?

He smiled. "I think I can handle it."

I stood, balanced on my skinny, four-inch heels, and tugged the skirt of my dress down into place. Baggy and cotton described my usual attire, not something this fitted and revealing. A quick glance at Amber told me her dream of annihilating me still thrived. Colton held out his hand, and I clasped it.

When we reached the crowded dance floor, he stopped near the outside edge, then swung me around and led me through a series of quick twirls and turns. I must've looked surprised because he laughed and coiled me into him. "Told you I could handle it," he murmured into my ear, sparking shivers across my shoulders.

Yes, clearly he danced as well as Stan, if not better. He was lighter on his feet—smoother—as if it were second nature to move to music. "Where'd you learn?" I asked.

"Mom loved to dance; Dad didn't. Once we were tall enough, Stan and I were Mom's dance partners. She even dragged us to dance lessons."

"Thank you, Mom," I exclaimed as he looped me out, then under his arm. Through the rest of the pounding rock tune, it took all of my focus to follow his lead and keep from tipping over on my high heels. The room swirled around me, the tacky disco ball overhead sparkled, and Bob Seger's tribute to "Old Time Rock and Roll" held me captive.

With a final blast, the clamor died and morphed into a rendition of "I Want to Know What Love Is," a song I remembered from my prepubescent years. Colton pulled me close—too close. "Relax. We're married, remember?" he murmured curling his hand around mine and holding it next to him.

Only we weren't, and being clasped against his muscular body, his head touching mine, while the words to the song struck too many chords was torture. I set my jaw and studied people as they slid by with our slower turns. Not far off, Laura danced with Harley, her cheek resting below his shoulder, eyelids closed, dreamy look on her face. Amber was plastered against a guy in a sleeveless tee-shirt with tattooed arms, and she didn't look happy about it. Of course, those dirty looks might be aimed at me.

My eyes landed on a couple of men. I'd caught them staring at Colton several times tonight, and they were at it again. "Two men sitting at the bar," I said, "big guy in the Hawaiian print and the weaselly-looking one next to him, in the black tee-shirt."

He danced a turn, then asked, "What about them?"

"They seem overly interested in you. The big one reminds me of the dude George had the scuffle with at the Marina. You think it's him?"

"Could be. He looks like he could bench-press a semi." He drew back and gave me a hard look. "You know how to shoot a gun?"

"I used to." Years and years ago.

"It's in the car, and it's loaded. If those two decide to do anything more than glare at me, get it." With that, he pulled me back against him.

My night out deteriorated a bit more. If I tried to point a gun at someone, I'd shake so hard it'd probably discharge. Someone would get hurt, probably Colton or an innocent bystander. I eyeballed the two men, willing them to keep right on guzzling those beers at that bar all night long. Maybe *they'd* killed Stan and pummeled George. The larger one met my stare, his eyes cold and sinister. Icy shivers zipped through me.

Colton clasped me even closer. I closed my eyes, blocked out the "maybes," and surrendered to the music and the feel of our bodies moving as one to the unhurried beat.

"It's gonna be okay," Colton murmured into my ear.

And tears burned in my throat, turning to moisture behind my eyelids. I gritted against the onrush of emotion, fighting the urge to wrap my arms around Colton's neck and kiss him—to acknowledge these fervent longings that refused to be ignored. In truth, they were growing more intense. And the guy on stage crooning his desire for love wasn't helping.

At last, the song ended. I sniffed and mumbled something about needing to visit the restroom before I wobbled off in search of it on my stilettos. Once there, I hid in a stall and felt tears trickle down my cheeks, swiping at them with a hand, so they wouldn't leave spots on my dress.

It was a confusing, snarled mess. Initially, I'd thought Colton was Stan—my husband. Assuming that, I'd engaged in a rather spectacular night of passion with him, only to find out the following morning that he wasn't my husband. In fact, he was my husband's brother. Now, though to the world we were husband and wife, in reality, we were merely two strangers trying to clean up a nasty mess and track down a murderer.

Every time I looked at him, I saw Stan, only a different Stan. Colton was the Stan I'd dreamed of having for my partner. He was perfect in every way. He was all that I wanted and needed.

He's not Stan, I reminded myself for the umpteenth time. *He's not your husband, and after his work is done here, he'll be gone. So get a grip, Polly. This is reality, not your fairytale. Get your butt out there and do what you need to do to figure out what your murdered husband was up to. And if you need to point a gun at someone, you'll do it. Period.*

I tore off a wad of toilet paper and dabbed at my cheeks and eyes, hoping mascara wasn't smeared all over my face. After flushing it down the john, I stepped out, washed my hands, and peeked in the mirror. A white-haired woman with layers of blue eye shadow slathered on red lipstick next to me. Under the bright lights, I looked like "the next morning," after I'd had a few too many and hit the bed in full makeup. Figuring I might pass in the low lounge lighting, I headed back to my table.

Only Colton wasn't there. My insides clenched, and I glanced around the room, searching for him. Harley and Laura were two-stepping to a lively country tune, but I didn't spot Colton on the dance floor. Or Amber. My eyes slid toward the bar. Amber wasn't at her table either, and the two glaring men had disappeared. I scanned the rest of the room. Lots of people, but no Colton.

Just great! While I hid in the restroom, wallowing in self-pity, those two goons had probably dragged Colton somewhere to torture him. But where? The restroom? Maybe outside?

I circled the room, searching every darkened corner, and caught several couples necking. But no Colton. Then I toddled to the men's restroom and pounded on the door. "Anyone in there?" I yelled.

A tall, gray-haired man in a suit pulled the door open; a urine odor wafted out. "Emergency?" he asked, checking me out with a suggestive smile.

"Yes. Is there anyone else in there? I'm looking for my husband."

His smile flattened. "What's his name?"

"Stan."

He half turned. "Anyone named Stan in here?" he hollered.

"If it's Stan Morton, he went outside," a masculine voice replied.

I murmured, "Thank you." Then I headed for the front door, wishing I had worn my sneakers.

When I walked outside, the two goons stood in my path. Evidently, they'd stepped out for a smoke since the smell clung to them like bad cologne. My pulse skyrocketed. My limbs tingled. My lungs went haywire. I sidestepped to let them pass by. The larger of the two moved in front of me. He was a steel wall—at least six and a half feet of bulging, solid muscle. Unless he moved, I was going nowhere.

You can do this, Polly, I told myself. *Just play it cool.* I stiffened my spine a bit and looked each of them in their creepy eyes.

"Your husband has something of ours," the smaller guy uttered in a surprisingly deep, resonant voice. "Either he gives it to us, or we're gonna come get it." He shook his head and gave me a hard look. "You don't want that to happen."

No, I didn't want Colton lying in a hospital bed next to George, tubes running from his mangled body, monitors beeping. "What is it . . . money?" I probed.

They stood there and stared at me like I'd asked them if they moisturized daily.

I huffed and attempted to outstare them, but it was two to one, and my trembling would've been hard to miss. "Well, Stan is having some memory issues," I explained. "If I know what you want, maybe I can find it and give it to you."

"Just give him the message," muscle man muttered gruffly. Then they stepped around me and disappeared into the building.

As if someone had pulled my plug, I wilted against the side of the building. So Stan did have something that someone wanted. His truck and our garage—maybe my office, too—had been searched because of that. They hadn't reacted to my money suggestion, so it probably wasn't Stan's crawlspace stash. So what were they looking for?

The door opened, and a chatting couple walked out. They eyed me curiously. "Are you okay?" the lady asked.

"Yes," I assured her. And I would be—someday. Right now I needed to pull myself together and find Colton. If those two guys hadn't cornered him, then where was he?

Drawing on the strength I had left, I straightened and tugged my dress into place, then fluffed my hair. Feeling a bit more confident, I stepped forward and inspected the dimly lit parking lot. Vehicles sat in several straight lines. A car at the far end of the lot backed out and drove away. Other than it and the few cars passing by on the highway, there were no signs of life.

Except that I swore I heard a woman giggle. I froze and strained to hear. There it was again, and it seemed to come from my right. I squinted into the deep shadows, then reached down to tug off my shoes. With a sigh, I followed the sidewalk to the end of the building and peeked around the corner.

Colton and Amber were not six feet from me, locked in an embrace, playing kissy face.

My Piña Colada hit my throat, and I grabbed my mouth and swallowed hard as fear spiraled inside me. I pulled back and flattened my back against the front of the building.

What was going on here? Was I being played? Were Colton and Stan the same man and all of this some elaborate plan to drive me crazy? Or get me incarcerated? Or what?

CHAPTER 13

Colton trailed me—still. The ocean's roar drowned out his labored breathing, but I felt his presence. And I didn't like it.

He'd followed me here, insistent that I not run alone this late at night. But if I didn't wear off the nervous energy poking and prodding me, I wouldn't sleep a wink. It felt like a colony of busy bees was inside me—buzzing here, buzzing there, fluttering their tiny wings. I had to get relief soon, or I really might go crazy.

After last night's fiasco at the Whale's Spout, I'd vowed to take today off. And I'd given it a good effort: first a fervent, prayerful stint at church, then lunch at one of my favorite eating spots overlooking the ocean. I'd buried my feet in the sand on the busy downtown beach while I watched a medley of colorful kites soar and dive overhead and shopped at the outlet mall to spend some of my gambling winnings on a red leather purse. Finally, I'd driven to Chinook Winds to punch a few slots. Luck wasn't with me, so I'd headed home, waylaid only by a sinfully delicious bowl of strawberry cheesecake ice cream.

It hadn't worked. All day long images and snippets, conundrums and insights nagged me. Was Stan really dead? Was Colton who he claimed to be? How did Amber fit into this muddle? Should I spill my guts to Sheriff Bronson? And what were those thugs searching for? The mind-prattle droned on and on.

Even now, as my arms pumped and my feet pounded silently on the wet sand, it pestered me. I'd been running for a good forty-five minutes and felt the burn in my legs and lungs. Sweat glued my running gear to me and trickled down my face.

I lifted my nose and breathed deeply of the cool, salty air. It was a perfect night for a run on the beach—low neap tide, a light breeze, moonlight reflecting off the water. And except for the waves, so silent. With all of the chatter going on in my head, I savored the silence.

Eyeing the berm, I spotted the craggy stump's dark silhouette and paused to catch my breath before I waded through the deep, dry sand further away from the water. Deep shadows darkened the area beyond it. A series of shivers prickled my back and shoulders. *Don't be ridiculous,* I told myself. *Laura's house isn't far off, and Colton's riding your tail.*

"All better?" Colton asked, stopping beside me. He didn't even seem winded.

"No," I muttered, still pulling air. "But at least now I'm exhausted, so I might get some sleep tonight. I have to drive into Portland early tomorrow morning."

"Mind if I ride along with you? I have some things to check out at the Portland office."

I studied his shadowy features, then strode off muttering, "I told you; I need some time to myself."

He caught up. "I thought you did that today."

"I need more." A lot more. Until I figured out what was going on, I wouldn't spend any more quality time with Colton, Stan, or whatever the heck his name was.

"Fine," he retorted. "At least I won't have to worry about you leaving me stranded."

I stopped and located his eyes in the gloom. In truth, I probably shouldn't have taken off and left him at the Whale's Spout, but I'd been so upset and confused. Besides, he'd deserved it. "I didn't feel well, and you weren't around," I informed him. "I figured you'd get a ride home with someone—maybe Laura . . . or Amber."

"Amber?"

So that's how he was going to play it. I shook my head, disgusted, and plodded through the deeper sand. "That blonde you were with out behind the building," I threw over my shoulder.

He grabbed that shoulder and stepped in front of me. "Is that what you're pissed about? I told you I planned to talk with her."

"And she talks better with her tongue down your throat?" I snapped.

"What?" Even in the dimness, I watched him flounder, deciding where to go next, wondering how much I'd witnessed.

"Don't play innocent with me," I advised. "The lighting might've been dim back there, but I know what I saw." With that, I headed for the berm, arms pumping.

"Okay," he admitted, keeping pace. "So I played along with her for a while, but just until it became clear that she doesn't know a damn thing about where Stan was getting his money or what he was mixed up in. Believe me, it wasn't fun."

"Poor baby. The sacrifices you make," I cooed.

"You sound jealous."

More hurt than jealous—much more. "You're supposed to be my husband, and while I'm in the restroom, you're out in the parking lot making out with another woman. I felt like pond scum."

"Which is exactly what Stan would've done, right?"

I winced, too many old wounds too close to the surface. "That doesn't justify you treating me like that."

"You're right, and I'm sorry. It's my job. That's all."

My insides knotted. "Getting it on with women you don't know?"

"If that's what it takes, yes."

Which would explain him "getting it on" with me. Thank you, Colton; I now felt *lower* than pond scum. "I'll keep that in mind," I muttered, pumping harder.

Out of excuses, he turned it on me. "You scared me. I looked everywhere and couldn't find you."

"I sent you a text. I can't help it if you were too busy playing tongue tag to hear it."

Again, he stepped in front of me. "I'm serious. Don't ever do that again. I thought those two guys had taken you somewhere."

He did look serious, his face all stark ridges and crevices in the moonlight. "I'm sorry," I murmured, "I really didn't feel well, and part of the reason was those two guys. They cornered me outside the front door. They told me to tell Stan that he has something of theirs, and if he doesn't return it, they're coming after him."

The ridges grew harder, the crevices deeper. "Did they hurt you?"

I closed my eyes, that suffocating fear still with me. "No, but I was so scared that I couldn't think straight. I thought my legs would crumble," I admitted, shaky from the memory. Suddenly, all I wanted was my bed and sleep. I eyed the darkened berm and passed around Colton to approach it.

"You think they want the bag of money?" he asked.

"No. I mentioned money, and they looked at me like I was nuts."

"Evidently, they're not after you."

"No, they're after Stan or whatever he had of theirs."

At last, he was silent. I marched hurriedly on for long moments, my calves screaming.

"Well, we know that for certain now," he said, falling behind me as I started down the dark incline through the beach grass. "And if that big guy's the one who roughed up George at the Marina, we know George and Stan were involved in something together."

I stopped and turned but could barely make out his face. We were in a slight furrow between the beach and the golf course community, and it was deeply shadowed. "Yes, and we know who's been searching," I added. "We just don't know who, exactly, they are or what they want. I wish I'd snapped a photo of them last night."

"More than likely, they put George in the hospital, but they don't seem to want Stan dead. So who killed him?"

"And who left those truffles?" I muttered as I turned to follow the path.

Shuffling noises from my right startled me. I froze, then turned just as something plowed into my side and knocked me to the ground.

"What the . . .?" I heard Colton mutter, then a loud *whoosh*. *Thuds* and grunting sounds followed.

Something shoved me onto my stomach, face in the sand. It felt like King Kong landed on my back. He knocked air from my lungs and squashed my body into the grittiness. I fought the urge to breathe. Slowly, I forced my head sideways and gasped, drawing in air and sand. My eyes popped open to darkness.

Numbed by the pounding, I lay there long moments, listening to my labored breathing and the grisly noises from nearby. I tried to understand, but it was like searching through molasses.

Suddenly, my left arm was wrenched behind me, onto my back. Pain ripped through my shoulder. I winced. My body jerked to life, twisting and heaving, trying to get him off.

He pulled harder. The pain increased, nauseatingly so. "Lay still, bitch," he growled, "or I'll hurt you."

As if he weren't? I stilled, and fear became a living, breathing part of me. It pounded in my head and churned in my gut. My body shook uncontrollably.

Urging myself past the fear and pain, I focused on jumpstarting my brain. With my face smashed into the ground, a barely visible view of sand and grass was all I could see, but the *thumps* and *smacks*, the *grunts* and *groans*, still reached my ears. I lay perfectly still, concentrating on the sounds, trying to figure out who was doing what, praying Colton would survive.

Then all was still. I strained to hear through the ocean's purr. There was movement—I felt it—and loud breathing.

"What's going on here?" someone shouted from not too far off. I knew that voice—male, melodic, hint of a Spanish accent. Phil!

The body on top of me went rigid. My arm was tugged even tighter. A scream gathered in my throat and burst from my mouth. It pierced the silence.

Just like that, he was gone. My throbbing arm dropped forward, and I moaned.

"This is your last warning," a deep male voice barked before I heard the swishing sounds of movement in the sand.

Then I was flipped over, and Phil's murky features floated above me. "Are you hurt?" he asked.

"Just my arm and shoulder. I think they're okay, just sore," I assured him. No doubt, my middle would ache the next day, but it would be nothing compared to what Colton would endure. I squinted into the darkness. He sat several yards from me, hunched over, breathing hard—alive. "I need to help him," I muttered, struggling to sit.

Phil slipped an arm beneath my shoulders and lifted me forward. I closed my eyes against a spinning sensation. "I'll help him. You stay right here," he ordered.

I raised my lids and watched him step to Colton and crouch down beside him. "You need an ambulance?" he asked in a curt voice.

"No, I'm okay," Colton uttered. "Lucky thing you came along when you did. He'd just pulled a knife. I'm not sure how long I would've lasted against that. The guy's a ripped beast." He spoke in bursts, his voice pierced by pain.

A knife! Yikes. These guys were serious trouble. If Phil hadn't happened along, Colton might be dead or well on his way to it—like George. We had to figure out what they wanted and give it to them.

"Who are they?" Phil demanded gruffly.

"I don't know. They're probably the ones who went after George." Colton winced and took a deep breath, then asked, "You think she's okay?"

Phil glanced my way. "She says she is. Can you walk?"

"Yeah." Shuffling noises were followed by a gasp. "Maybe help me up. Then help Polly."

"Polly doesn't need any help. She can make it on her own," I told them. "You two, get along for however long it takes us to hobble to the house. Then you can go back to being hostile neighbors."

Not that I blamed Phil for his bad attitude. I'd feel the same if someone tried to blackmail me. It was a pain in the butt to hold onto big secrets that, if revealed, would make this so much easier.

I gathered my legs beneath me, gritted against the pain, and managed to push myself up onto my feet. Swaying slightly, I cradled my sore arm, took several deep breaths, and watched Phil lift Colton and support him. Then we struggled up the slight incline to the neighborhood on the other side, the two men in the lead, me trailing.

A couple of minutes later, we passed by Laura's darkened house, then traipsed across the street. I pulled the key from the waistband pocket of my running pants and unlocked the front door. "We'll put him on the bed," I murmured as I headed down the hall.

Phil lowered Colton onto the edge of the bed and turned to examine me. Colton scrutinized me, too, his arm cradling his middle. Except for several rosy abrasions, his face didn't look bad. I couldn't say that about his hands, though. They were red and swollen, bleeding in places.

"I really am okay," I assured them both. "The guy just sat on me and twisted my arm—literally. My shoulder is throbbing, but my arm moves just fine. See." To my surprise, through the pain, it did move on its own.

I studied Colton, then Phil, then Nellie as she clawed her way to the top of the bed. If I took Colton to the emergency room, would the county sheriff be notified? And then would Phil's past life be plastered across the media—journaled, televised, tweeted, and posted? I couldn't let that happen. I also couldn't talk with him about it in front of Colton.

In truth, I knew I should phone Sheriff Bronson. It was way past time to tell him the whole truth, before someone else was killed. But something told me I was in too deep now, that I needed to see this through. With Phil present, I couldn't discuss it with Colton.

In the end, I knelt and tugged Colton's sandy shoes off, my hands shaking uncontrollably. I didn't know if it was remnants from that paralyzing fear or relief that he was alive. "You should see a doctor," I murmured.

He shook his head. "No, I'll be fine. Would you help me get my shirt off?"

Fortunately, it was one of Stan's loose fitting tees. I grabbed the bottom. With a grimace, he lifted his arms, and I pulled the shirt over his head. When I glanced at his torso, I winced. It was a mottled abstract in hues of red and purple.

"You're not okay?" I gasped.

He stroked Nellie and attempted a smile. "It's just surface stuff. I can breathe fine, and there's no sharp pain inside me. It'll look bad and hurt like hell for a few days, but it'll mend." He glanced behind me at Phil. "Thank you. Things wouldn't have ended this well if you hadn't stepped in."

Phil nodded, his eyes narrowed, studying Colton closely.

It was time to get Phil out of here because, for sure, this bruised man wasn't Stan. Once, Phil had helped me get Stan into my car when Stan had stubbed his big toe. What a crybaby! There'd been tears and swear words that I'd never heard before and a trip to the emergency room. Stan had been laid up in his Barcalounger, popping pills, for a week, because his toe hurt when he walked.

Whereas Javier had reluctantly accepted the changes in Stan, Phil was far too worldly wise to not question them and then pursue those questions. I forced a quivery smile. "Yes, thank you, Phil. I'm sure I can handle it from here."

His intense gaze slid between us. "Do you plan to report this?"

Did we? My eyes locked with Colton's for endless moments, then flicked back to Phil.

"No," I assured him.

With a terse nod, he strode toward the French doors and disappeared into the night.

"You don't think we should let the sheriff know about this?" Colton argued.

"Where do we stop?" I reasoned. "We've kept too much from him. Are you ready to confess to withholding evidence and charading as your murdered brother and then let Sheriff Bronson take over your search for Stan's killer while we hang out in the slammer?"

He gazed into my eyes intently, then slowly shook his head. "Not yet," he whispered.

Then when? I wondered. Would we both have to die to solve this tangled puzzle?

CHAPTER 14

Marta's alabaster skin faded to ashen. She stood at the door and stared at Colton as if he were one of Frank Ellis' long dead relatives come back to give a firsthand recounting of his life in Portland's early days. Her body swayed, and a shaky hand reached out to clasp the door frame. Marta—always the stalwart, reticent professional—appeared to be having a rough moment.

My eyes drifted to Colton. Surely he wasn't the cause of her little breakdown?

With a loose shirt covering most of his injuries, he really didn't look that bad—just a couple of liver-colored bruises on his face and red, swollen knuckles. He'd spent the night on ice, but had insisted on riding shotgun with me today in case I ran into more trouble. So far, I hadn't. He'd swallowed some Advil, laid back his seat, and slept the whole drive to Portland. He still had that "been sleeping" look to him—droopy eyelids, vacant eyes, flaccid skin. With an arm across his aching abs, he gazed back at Marta as if he were trying to figure out where he was and what he was doing here.

I shifted the box I carried, my shoulder screaming, just wanting to get this jaunt over and get home for a nap. "This is my husband, Stan," I told Marta, hoping it might calm her enough to get us inside before another rain shower hit, so I could empty my arms. "He has some business to take care of here in Portland, so he rode with me today. I hope Frank won't mind. Stan, this is Marta. She . . . uh"—actually, I had no idea what, exactly, Marta did—"she's Frank's assistant."

"It's nice to meet you, Marta," Colton murmured with a vague smile as he stepped forward and stuck out a puffy hand.

Marta set her mouth and glowered. As if she were inflating, she drew a long, deep breath and grew a good five inches, reverting to her normal ramrod rigid self. "Follow me," she ordered in her husky voice, turning her back to us.

Colton's eyes met mine, and his eyebrows lifted in question. I shook my head. I had no idea what was eating at Marta today. In the past, she'd always been distant but cordial. Today she was downright rude. With the heavy box clutched against my sore midriff, I struggled to keep up with her trim figure as we wound our way through the house. Colton trailed behind me.

When I saw the wall of windows, I knew I'd arrived. Intermittent showers had drifted in overnight, so the view wasn't as spectacular as last time I was here. Still, there was something to be said for standing in the clouds.

I dragged my eyes from them and turned to Frank. Unlike Marta, he was beaming. "Hi, Frank. As always, it's nice to see you. Thank you for seeing me on such short notice. I wanted to return your family records, so I can quit worrying that something's going to happen to them." *Like your bully son confiscating them*, I wanted to add. I set the box on the coffee table and rubbed my injured arm.

"I'll take care of those," Marta announced, striding toward them in her sensible flats.

"No, leave them," Frank told her. "Since Polly knows what's in there, she can enlighten me. We might want to look at some of the documents."

Marta chewed her lower lip and didn't budge, resolute eyes on the box.

"Actually, I haven't had a chance to look at any of that stuff," I confessed. "I had copies made. Old paper is fragile. The less it's handled, the better. I'll shred the copies when I'm done with them."

Now Marta gaped at me as if I'd confessed to keying Frank's gorgeous heirloom furniture on my walk down the hall. What was her problem?

She huffed irately and grabbed the box. "Then you won't need this," she snapped.

"Leave it," Frank said sternly.

Which stopped Marta in her tracks. For long moments, she stared at Frank, her lips working as if she had a whole lot to say that couldn't be said. Finally, she dropped the box back onto the coffee table.

I glanced around the tastefully decorated room. Everything looked neat, tidy, and classy—even Marta. Not a speck of dust marred a surface. Maybe Marta was a neat freak who would obsess over that box cluttering her coffee table if she didn't tuck it away somewhere.

"I'm Stan Morton, Polly's husband."

Colton's voice drew me back. Frank was on his feet, shaking hands with him. "Frank Ellis," he said, eyeing Colton closely.

"I'm sorry," I muttered. "I should've introduced you two. Stan rode into Portland with me today. I hope you don't mind? I don't plan to stay, just drop off the papers."

"It's fine," Frank assured me, waving it off. "But after that long drive, surely you can visit a while? Have some refreshments?" His curious gaze turned to Colton. "Does the other guy look worse than you?"

Colton attempted a smile. "I like to think so. It was too dark to tell for sure."

"We were running on the beach last night, and two men attacked us. Stan got the worst of it," I clarified. I didn't want Frank to think I was married to a hothead who went around picking fights. Though, truth be told, Stan had been a hothead who'd hightailed it away from the scene before the fight started.

"So they got away?" Frank asked.

"Yep," Colton muttered.

"Well, no need to stand there looking miserable. Have a seat," Frank offered.

"Mind if I use your bathroom first?"

Frank nodded toward the entrance. A tuft of thick white hair fell across his forehead, and he brushed at it. "Sure. Turn left. It's just past the dining room. Would you like something to drink?"

"Coffee, please—black," Colton told him before he ambled off, clutching his middle.

Like a dog on point, Marta watched him go, then shot off after him.

"Marta," Frank barked. I noticed that beneath his thick wire-rims, his sky blue eyes had turned stormy. I hoped he never, ever gazed at me like that.

As if on cue, giant raindrops pelted the windows, pattering like a band of snare drums. Marta froze and slowly turned. "Yes?"

"We have guests," he sternly reminded her. "Perhaps you could get us some beverages."

Her eyes crept after Colton one last time before she sighed and muttered, "Of course."

Frank eyed her closely, concern replacing irritation on his features. "Thank you. Polly, what would you like?"

"Coffee would be nice. Black for me, too, please." With icing our injuries, it'd been another nearly sleepless night, and I was gradually slipping toward catatonic. Hopefully, some caffeine would put some verve back into me.

"Looks like it's three black coffees," he informed Marta before he turned to me and indicated the chair I'd sat in on our last visit. "Have a seat."

Bracing myself against a stab of pain, I slid into the well-padded chair and relaxed into it.

"Any idea who the guys were?" he asked after he sat, worry furrowing his bushy brows.

"No," I lied. "They were there; then they were gone."

"What's this world coming to, when you aren't safe running on an Oregon beach? In my day, we left our doors unlocked. As kids we tore around the neighborhood at all hours of the day and night without a care in the world." He paused and shook his head disgustedly. "Nowadays you have to check both ways before you step out your front door. It's a sad commentary on how degenerate we've become."

I thought about reminding him that his pregnant great-grandmother was kidnapped from her home and held in a frigid, mildewy pigsty for days on end but thought it best to keep that thought to myself. Fortunately, Colton shuffled back into the room—eating something.

Had he been in the kitchen with Marta? Squinting hard, I tried to make out what was in his hand.

"Ah, I see you talked Marta out of one of her homemade chocolates. When I'm very, very good, she shares them with me," Frank said. Then he chuckled and added, "Probably won't be getting any today, though, will I?"

"They're amazing," Colton agreed, giving me a meaningful look. "You have to try this, Polly."

He handed me a glob of brown goo. I eyed it, then popped it into my mouth and licked my sticky fingers. Rich, sweet chocolate melted across my tongue. But there was something else, something too familiar—a hint of liqueur. I closed my eyes, my heart hammering louder than the rain on the windows. Uneasy prickles zapped through me.

Why would Frank—maybe Marta—give me truffles laced with Triazolam? It made no sense at all. I stared at Colton, then Frank, speechless.

"Well?" Frank prodded. "Amazing, aren't they?"

Was this some kind of weird psycho game Frank was playing? "Marta gave you this?" I asked Colton.

"No, there was a fancy bowl filled with them on the dining room table. You know me and chocolate; I can't pass by one without tasting it," he rationalized, lowering himself cautiously into a plush armchair kitty-corner from mine.

"Let's hope Marta didn't have plans for that truffle," I gabbed, my mind furtively formulating a means to learn the motive behind the doctored truffles.

At that moment, Marta entered the room, face pinched, loaded tray in her arms. I studied her every move as she handed Frank, then me a steaming mug. When she reached Colton, her eyes turned deadly. If Colton hadn't reached out and grabbed it, she would've dumped the steaming coffee down his front.

And then I knew: Stan had done something terrible to either Frank or Marta—maybe both. I hadn't a clue what it was, but it was the only way to explain Marta's uncharacteristic behaviors since she'd encountered Colton. It seemed no matter where I went or what I did, I couldn't escape Stan's destructive ways. So I might as well try to make amends.

I sipped a bit of hot coffee to fortify myself, then made a request with what I hoped came off as innocent. "Marta, Stan just had one of your delicious truffles. I was hoping you might have an extra to share with me?"

Her jaw dropped, and she paled to the point that I was prepared to rush to her aid. Then she plopped onto the edge of the facing couch, dropped the tray, and buried her face in her hands. "You know," she whimpered, shoulders shaking.

"Yes," I admitted, "but I don't know why you did it."

She sniffled and rubbed her eyes, then glared at Colton with tearstains on her cheeks. "Because of him. All I wanted was the letters. He had no. . . ."

"Marta?" Frank interrupted. "What's going on here?"

I faced Frank's puzzled expression, and relief flowed through me. Clearly, he was clueless, so I took another sip of fortitude, set my mug on the side table, and enlightened him. "Marta left six of her amazing truffles in a beautiful box at my front door ten days ago, along with an unsigned birthday card. There was nothing to indicate who they were from, but since it was my birthday, I assumed it was a gift for me. Turns out they were loaded with Triazolam, a strong sedative."

Frank's bewildered gaze darted to Marta.

I turned to Marta, too, and gave her a hard stare. "You're lucky no one died or you'd be a murderer. Although I ate two of them, fortunately, it was hours apart, so all they did was put me to sleep. Stan here devoured three of the things and had to go to the emergency room. He was so sick he lost his memory . . . completely." The lies were slipping off my tongue as easily as that chocolate. It had to stop.

"Why would you do something like that?" Frank asked Marta. He looked years older, his skin loose and translucent, eyes dreary. His hands shook, sloshing the coffee around in the mug he clasped in them.

Marta looked miserable, too, unbearably so. If I didn't need answers, I'd have shooed her from the room until she pulled herself together. "I'm so sorry," she murmured. "I had to get those letters back, and I didn't know what else to do. Brad came up with the idea."

"Brad?" Frank and I uttered as one.

"Yes." She examined Colton, frowning. "He doesn't remember anything?"

Like a zombie, Colton stared at the squall going on outside and gulped coffee. More than likely, he'd popped a few Advil during his trip to the bathroom, and they were kicking in.

"No," I assured her.

"He, your husband, called me—actually, he called Frank, but I took the call. I often do that for Frank—pretend I'm him to screen his calls. I have a somewhat deep voice normally, so I just lower it a bit. No one questions it.

"Anyway, he claimed he had a couple of old letters that would prove that Frank wasn't who he claims to be. That he isn't any blood relation to Jesse and Nellie Ellis, and that it means he has no claim to the Ellis fortune. That it should've gone to Jesse and Nellie's *real* son and should now belong to *his* descendants."

"That's outrageous—a flat out lie!" Frank stormed, glowering at Colton now. "You believed *him*?"

A nagging, sick feeling had settled inside me. I thought back to the day I'd stopped by the museum. Bev had alluded to something concerning Frank's past that I'd been too hurried to hear. Had Stan listened to her and then turned that knowledge into another blackmail attempt? Was that why Sheriff Bronson had found the letters in the garage. Had Stan hidden them in his Twinkie stash?

My eyes met Colton's. He looked like a guy in the crosshairs—and wounded, too.

"He mailed you copies of the letters," Marta informed Frank. "It was in writing right there on paper. I couldn't argue with that, could I? Nellie's baby was stillborn, but there was a woman who worked at the brothel—a prostitute named Clara—who'd given birth to a baby boy. She talked Nellie into taking the baby and raising it as her own.

"Clara wrote those two letters to Nellie, or maybe someone wrote them for her. Anyway, in one of them, she thanked Nellie for taking her baby. The other was written several years later. She was dying, and she wanted Nellie to know how much she appreciated the opportunities Nellie had given her to spend time with her little boy."

Oh, lordy. What a heart-wrenching story, a tidbit that would kick Frank's family history from mind-numbing to enthralling. But the less I knew about it, the better. No doubt, it would never make it into Frank's book.

"With your health problems, I didn't want you getting upset over the news and the money, so I showed them to Brad," Marta told Frank.

"Health problems?" I asked. Was that why Frank was so determined to get his family history on paper and get it right?

"It's nothing, just some heart issues that need to be ironed out," Frank claimed. He dropped his mug on the side table and ran a hand through his thick, snowy hair. "And you should've come to me with this," he spat at Marta. "I still run things around here, not my kids!"

"I know, but I couldn't live with myself if I caused your . . . something to happen to you," she said, tears glistening in her eyes. "We just needed to get those original letters back. Brad said the copies wouldn't prove a thing."

"Why didn't you ask me for them?" I wondered aloud.

She turned a lethal look on Colton. "*He* said you hadn't read the letters and didn't know what he was doing, and you wouldn't if we did what he said. He wanted a hundred thousand dollars, but it would be double that if we mentioned anything to you about it."

Oh, lordy, Polly. You were married to a greedy, heartless, conniving crook. And he used you in his schemes. It can't get much worse than that, I acknowledged, feeling like I might lose the few drops of coffee I'd sipped.

Suddenly, the rain's tattoo ended. Bright sunlight streamed into the room. I blinked hard and glanced out the windows. Several sunbeams penetrated the thick, dark clouds. *Focus on the sunbeams, not those gloomy, ominous clouds,* something inside me whispered.

I swallowed at the bitter taste in my throat and turned back to Marta. She sat erect on the edge of the plush couch, legs sideways and knees together, hands neatly folded in her lap. As always, her slacks outfit was color-coordinated, every hair on her head combed perfectly into place. I tried to picture her sneaking around my house in the middle of the night, but the two images—Marta and the prowler—didn't fit.

"So the chocolate was meant to sedate us long enough for you to sneak into my house and search for the letters?" I questioned.

"Yes." She stared at me for endless moments, then took a deep breath and continued. "I tried to get into your house a couple of days earlier, but the alarm went off. I figured it was your birthday so the two of you would be together, and before, or after, you celebrated, you'd have a chocolate. I put one dose into each truffle, so I knew you'd be asleep for several hours. With you both home, I didn't think you'd set the alarm until much later, when you went to bed."

She scowled at me. "Then you were the only one there. I parked down the street and waited and waited for *him* to get home. When the sun went down, I crouched in a dark corner on your deck. Finally, you fell asleep on your bed. Then I came inside and searched."

And she hadn't found anything. Frank's box of old documents was in Stan's truck, and he'd hidden the letters in the garage. Evidently, a couple of the copies had been sent to Frank, then confiscated by Marta, before Frank saw them.

Like a sneaky tsunami, it hit me: Marta had been inside my house the night Stan was murdered, and unlike me, she'd been awake. "Were you there when Stan got home?" I probed.

She nodded, eyes wary. "Yes. He returned about an hour after I'd started searching. I heard his truck pull up and hid in the guest room."

"What time was that?"

"Around eleven thirty."

Which aligned with what Amber had told me. "What did he do?"

"He sat on your deck and drank beer." She studied Colton, a

disgusted twist to her mouth. "Lots of it. I kept an eye on him and finished my searching, but he didn't leave the deck, just sat there guzzling beer. Oh, and he had a couple of visitors. They didn't come through the house, though."

I wanted to glance at Colton but thought it best to keep this conversation as low key as possible, and keep it moving. So far, Marta didn't appear to notice she was being interrogated. Fortunately, I was a cop show junkie, so I could handle it.

"Visitors, huh? Did you get a good look at them?" I asked.

"Yes. First there was a woman. I couldn't hear what she was saying, but she looked angry, and she was shouting. Finally, she got up close, in his face. I got the idea she was going to kiss him, but he shoved her away. She shook her fist at him and left."

"What color was her hair?" I crossed my toes and prayed she would say red or blonde.

"Bright red—red enough that I could see it in the dim light—lots of it."

So Denise had been there that night—no big surprise. "What did the other person look like?"

"He was a man, maybe mid thirties, tall and slender." She turned to Colton. "Do you have any friends at all? That guy was mad at you, too. He didn't yell, but I could tell from the look on his face and the way he wagged his finger at you and flipped his head, his red hair flying. Finally, he left, too."

This time my eyes did dart to Colton. Red hair? Javier? But he and Phil were in Ashland that night—or so they claimed. Again, my stomach churned.

"I left right after that," she said, "a little after midnight. And there were still five truffles in the box. I knew I should've taken them with me, but then you would've known someone was in your house." Her eyes flicked Colton's with an accusing look. "If you ate three of them after drinking all of that beer, it's no wonder you got sick."

"That doesn't make it all right," I snapped. "What if I'd eaten all of them? I'd be dead."

She closed her eyes. I noticed her knees shook, and she was wringing her hands. I waited. Finally, she lifted her lids. "I'm so sorry. I hope you'll forgive me?"

"Fortunately, no one died," I murmured.

And the truth was that Stan had started this whole fiasco with his blackmail threat. Both Stan and Marta had broken the law, but of the two of them, Stan's was probably the most serious crime. I glanced at Frank. He'd been so quiet, probably processing the news that he might not be genetically linked to Jesse and Nellie, his heroes. How could I despise Marta for only wanting to prevent his demise?

But Colton was the one sickened by her brainless scheme. Our eyes met, and he gave a barely discernible nod.

I sighed resignedly and muttered, "With no memory, Stan's actually a much nicer, improved version of his old self. Since he caused all of this, let's call it even and try to forget about it." Unless, of course, it turned out that Marta or Brad actually did kill Stan. "But don't ever do that again," I warned Marta. *And I'm still really upset and angry about it,* I silently added.

"Never, I promise."

She looked sincere. She also looked relieved. I rubbed at the throbbing I'd just now noticed in my forehead, hoping I'd done the right thing and that Marta didn't make a habit of sneaking pharmaceuticals into people's diets.

Frank was rubbing too—his lower lip—and obviously pondering what he'd just heard. "And the letters?" he finally asked.

"The originals should be in that bundle of letters there in the box. It sounds like Stan sent you the copies. I haven't read them, and I don't want to. As far as I'm concerned, it's up to you to decide what you do with the information in them," I told him. I meant it, too.

His weary eyes flitted to Colton, questioning. Colton nodded and said, "I'm really sorry I caused this whole mess. Like Polly said, I have no memory of it, but I do know that it wouldn't have happened if I hadn't been such a greedy son-of-a-bitch. This is your family business, and I have no intention of getting involved in it again."

"Thank you," Frank murmured. "I have a lot to think about and some decisions to make. I do want to go ahead with the book, Polly, so please keep on with your writing. I just need to decide what's going to be included and what's going to be left out."

Yes, and if it turns out that either Marta or your son murdered my disgusting husband, we might need to add a new chapter. I thought the words, but I didn't voice them.

~~ ✿ ~~

Should I? Or shouldn't I? I gazed at Colton through the French door. He lounged in Stan's cedar recliner, staring out onto the lush golf course. Gray clouds sagged overhead, but he didn't appear to mind. Maybe he was asleep.

After our mind-blowing visit with Frank and Marta, I'd driven into downtown Portland and dropped him off on Broadway, where the local Secret Service office was located. Though he'd planned to ride home with me, his work had taken longer than expected, so I'd returned alone and, fortunately, without incident. A coworker had dropped him off here a little over an hour ago.

It was slipping into evening. I knew I should head to the kitchen and cook dinner, but something had pestered me since I'd left Frank's house, something I needed to take care of before I burst. I needed to know why Javier had lied to me about his whereabouts on the night Stan was killed.

Before I did that, I needed to spill my guts to Colton and, in so doing, betray Javier's trust in me. Of course, he'd betrayed my trust in him, so maybe it wasn't as big a deal as I felt it to be. Oh, what a tangled web—Stan's web. I was the one ensnared in it.

I'd be devastated if my big mouth jeopardized Phil's career or the life he'd worked so hard to establish. No doubt, Javier had sugarcoated his rendition of what Stan held over Phil's head. I suspected there was a whole lot more to tell, some of which might land Phil back behind bars. I figured the less I knew of it, the better. To me, Phil had always been a standup guy. Heck, he'd saved Colton's and my butts the previous night.

Would Colton share my feelings on the matter? After all, when you got right down to it, he was a cop. Still, he'd agreed to keep Marta's culinary death-bombs a secret.

I reached for the doorknob, and he cautiously sat up and turned around. Expecting him to make his way into the house, I waited, but he just sat there in his jeans and hoodie and stared at me, looking as exhausted as I felt. Behind him, a golfer whacked at a golf ball hidden in the grass.

After a long while, I opened the door and asked, "Are you coming inside?"

He smiled. "I was waiting for you to come out. You've been standing there for twenty minutes. I figured you had something you wanted to talk over."

So he had eyes in the back of his head. Or was he psychic, like Millie? What did it matter? I did have something to discuss. I dragged another recliner next to his and sat down on it sideways, facing him. A furtive glance next door assured me no one was eavesdropping, not that they'd hear anything if they did. "I need to tell you something. I promised to keep it a secret, so I hope you'll keep it between us?"

He nodded. "I'll try."

"Thank you. Amber told me Stan was waiting for three big payments to come in. I learned today that one of those was the hundred thousand dollars from Frank." I paused, guilt gnawing at me. Hopefully, Javier would understand. "I also know what another one was."

His brows dropped into a frown. "Okay."

"That check Phil gave you was a payoff. Stan was blackmailing him, too," I blurted.

"No wonder when I look him in the eye, I see visions of me being gutted with his hunting knife," he muttered flippantly, but he hadn't masked the shocked look on his face. "So what did Stan have on him?"

"Let's just say Phil has a less than stellar past. I don't know the details, but it must be bad."

"And you're telling me this now because . . . ?"

"Javier spread the word that he and Phil were in Ashland the night of my birthday—the night Stan was killed. From what Marta told us, Stan spoke with Javier that night right here on this deck. Why did Javier lie about where he was?"

His gaze slid behind me, to the deck next door. "You think he might've killed Stan?"

"Oh lordy, I hope not," I breathed, my insides twisting with the thought. "Javier would do almost anything for Phil but hopefully, not kill someone. I need to go next door and talk with him, but I wanted to tell you about Stan's blackmail attempt first."

He leaned forward, inches from my face, and gave me a stern look. "You're not going next door alone. If Javier was involved in Stan's death, it could be dangerous, especially if Phil's there, too."

I hadn't thought of that. "But if you're along, he won't open up to me. It's tricky, anyway, because he and Phil think Stan's still alive, so they'll be wondering why it matters whether they were in Ashland that night or at home? And it wouldn't. Unless one of them *did* press that pillow over Stan's face, and they're afraid you—thinking you're Stan—will remember and. . . ."

A jarring *thump* blasted from somewhere behind me, followed by a zinging whine. I froze, my heart racing, then gazed into Colton's stunned eyes. "Golf ball," I assured him. "They bounce off the roof all the time. Someone needs to give up golf or take some lessons."

I thought back to what I'd been saying and realized I'd been rambling—thinking aloud. "Maybe I'll invite Javier over here. With you in the house, he won't try anything," I told Colton.

Colton gave a curt nod, but his thoughts seemed elsewhere. "Let's say Javier didn't kill Stan. Who do you think did?" he asked.

"I really don't know. Marta was here, and Stan was probably feeling no pain after six beers. Since she didn't find the letters, maybe she couldn't pass up the opportunity to solve her problem for good. She didn't have second thoughts about infusing sedatives into our truffles and sneaking around my house in the middle of the night.

"Or Brad. He's a choice piece of manly, corporate supremacy—a real power junkie! I wouldn't put it past him to interlope on Marta's drugging venture and make a killing. I doubt he'd give it a second thought. I mean, how dare Stan the peon threaten his family's wealth and prestige."

He smiled. "You have feelings about him, do you?"

Heat bloomed in my cheeks. It wasn't like me to go on a rampage. I had, which testified to how worked up I was over the morning's unveilings. "I'm sorry," I murmured. "I truly believe Marta's heart was in the right place, but I wonder where she'd stop to protect Frank. As for Brad, I find it hard to believe he descended from Frank's loins. Nell's nearly as bad—Frank's daughter—and who's to say she didn't know about the letters, too?"

"How about Denise?"

Ah yes, Denise. We now knew she'd been around that night. "She was ticked at Stan, probably because of Amber. Maybe she went away and got even more riled up, then came back to teach him a lesson.

"Or maybe his death is all about that third payment Stan was waiting for."

"Which brings us to the two thugs. That payment might have something to do with them."

"And George. Maybe he killed Stan?"

He reached out with his injured hands and clasped mine. His eyes darkened, probing mine. "Or maybe it was you."

"Me?" I gasped, yanking my hands free, struggling for air. "Do you really believe that?"

"No, but I want to hear you say it."

My heart pounded so hard it surely would burst. I pressed on it, my eyes locked on Colton's. Sick feelings wrestled around inside me. The urge to run and hide consumed me.

Then fury reared its ugly head. "I didn't kill Stan," I seethed. "He was the lousiest of lousy husbands. He ignored me, he humiliated me, and he hurt me over and over and over again. Now I know he also had no qualms about sleeping with other women or blackmailing my friends. He was totally disgusting, and I was married to him. But I didn't kill him. In fact—and this is just to show you what a total dim-wit I *was*—I was sad that morning when I thought he was dead."

And I knew I'd spoken the truth. I really hadn't killed Stan. Like a punctured tire, I crumpled. Tears stung my eyes.

"Why'd you pick up the pillow?" Colton asked.

"Everyone knew what an asshole he was and how awful he treated me. He was supposed to take me out to celebrate my fortieth birthday, but he didn't come home. I was upset—really upset. I knew I'd get blamed for his death." By the time I finished, tears streamed down my face. I swiped at them and turned away to stare out at the golf course.

"Come here," Colton murmured, pulling me forward and drawing my head against his shoulder.

I don't know how long I sat there like that, tears dribbling from my eyes and Colton rubbing my back and assuring me everything would be okay, but it felt darn good to finally let go and be comforted by someone other than myself. Eventually, the tears dried. I realized that awful feeling hanging out in the pit of my stomach was gone. I sniffled and wiped my wet cheeks, then pulled away from Colton, feeling renewed but totally wasted. "Were you really certain I didn't kill him?" I asked.

He nodded, a tender smile curving his lips. "I knew you didn't, but you needed to know it."

"I did. I really did," I whispered. "Thank you."

Male voices from the golf course penetrated our cozy interlude. I gazed right and watched two guys search the grass for a ball, probably the one that had bounced off my roof. Then I turned back to Colton. "You know, on the drive home today I did a lot of thinking. Maybe it's time to be honest with Sheriff Bronson. He might cut us some slack."

"Or he might fulfill your prediction and arrest you for Stan's murder. As you pointed out, you had several good motives."

Yes, there was that, too. "Well, if we don't figure out what those two guys want, we might wind up dead. I'd rather end up in prison than in a casket."

He sighed deeply and stared fixedly into my eyes. "We're close; I can feel it. Let's give it a couple more days and see what happens."

And what if we don't survive those two days? I wondered. With us gone, would Sheriff Bronson ever catch Stan's killer? Would he even figure out that Stan was dead?

"Okay, two more days, but that's it," I muttered. "On Thursday we talk with the sheriff." Then a couple of glitches hit me. "We just delete Marta and Phil from the conversation . . . for now, anyway.""

"So we're not going to tell the sheriff about Stan's extortion attempts?"

"I guess not, unless we have to."

He snorted. "The sheriff'll love that."

"What?"

"Us, spilling our guts but holding back information."

"Oh, this is so confusing," I moaned as I pushed myself to my feet. "Where do the truths stop and the lies begin? The problem is they're all tangled into one giant knot, and Stan's at the core of the whole snarled mess."

He stood, too, hesitantly and with a couple of moans. "Well, we have two days to think about it. Why don't you get Javier over here, and I'll fix us some dinner."

"With those hands, no way. You need to ice up. Let me talk with Javier, then I'll cook or run get takeout." I shooed him away with my hands. "You take some Advil and climb into the Barcalounger. I'll get your frozen veggies."

"Yes, ma'am," he replied before he shuffled into the house.

Fifteen minutes later, Colton lay stretched out in the living room with bags of frozen peas plastered to his abs, face, and hands and a kitten nestled between his thighs. Javier stood in the kitchen with me, staring at him.

"Phil told me all about it—gruesome . . . and scary. You don't know who it was, huh?" he asked.

I shook my head, gritting against the glut of lies to come. "No. Just bullies letting off steam, I guess."

His eyes scanned me, probably reclothing me in some trendy mini dress with matching accessories. "You look okay," he murmured.

"Oh, yeah. I just got the wind knocked out of me and my shoulder wrenched a bit. I'm fine, but my arm and hand are sore." I eyed the pot of steaming water, the Italian sausage browning in the frying pan, the box of spaghetti, and the *Prego.* It was perfect staging. "That's why I needed you. As you can see, Stan's hands are a mess, so if you can open this, I'd really appreciate it." I handed him the jar of spaghetti sauce.

"Of course." He twisted the lid, then huffed, scrunched up his face, and twisted again. Finally, the lid popped off, and he set the jar on the counter.

"You know, Polly girl. I want to thank you for not running your little skirmish by the cops. Phil was in one of his blue funks about it. He said you didn't plan to report it, but one never knows. We didn't have any county cops storming our front door today. Thank you for that."

"It's no big deal," I assured him. "Phil's the one who saved our butts. It's the least I could do after that. And Stan refused to see a doctor."

He frowned and eyeballed Stan as if he were examining some weird, alien creature. "Yeah, what's with that? He's the guy who had a tizzy-fit when that bee stung him last month—couldn't have happened to a more deserving guy, by the way. And remember when he fell asleep at the pool and rubied up like a boiled lobster? The whining coming from your deck was ceaseless. Though, it was pure bliss to know he was suffering. And. . . ."

"Yes, well, he's changed," I reminded Javier, hoping to get his mind from questioning Stan's metamorphosis to the night it happened. "Which reminds me, you and Phil were in Ashland the night Stan ate those life-changing chocolates, right?"

He stilled, and his eyes darted here and there, head nodding briskly. "You need to chop up this sausage or you'll have big chunks in your sauce," he blurted, grabbing the wooden spoon to hack at the sizzling meat.

"Well, I was just wondering, because someone mentioned that they'd seen you on my deck talking with Stan that night. I told them it wasn't possible, but they assured me it was you. Was it?"

He stopped chopping and locked eyes with mine, a determined set to his jaw. "Does it really matter whether I was here or there?"

"Yes," I assured him. "Something happened to Stan that night. It might've been those truffles, or it might've been something else. If you talked with him, saw someone else with him, or saw him do something odd, I need to know about it. Someone's trying to break into our house. George was beaten and stabbed. I'm trying to figure out what's going on."

With a deep sigh, he dropped the spoon. "Okay. You're right. I was home that night. Phil had to have the money to Stan by Sunday, so he hauled the sculpture down to Ashland on Friday. I planned to go with him. We were going to spend the night in a cute little bed and breakfast, treat ourselves to a nice dinner out. At the last minute, I changed my mind.

"Phil refused to let me get involved in Stan's depraved threat, so I pretended my stomach was on the fritz—my 'go to' ploy. I knew Stan would keep asking for more money. I wanted to do what I could to help."

He snorted contemptuously. "I was the Pollyanna, Polly. I honestly thought I could talk Stan out of it. He laughed at me and called me filthy names that I refuse to repeat to anyone, even myself. And if they ever call me to testify in court, I won't say them there, either." He curled his lip, picked up the spoon with a shaky hand, and stirred the sausage listlessly. "I went home and drank a bottle and a half of Prosecco, and when Phil got home Saturday afternoon, I really was hugging the loo. End of story."

"Why did you lie about it?"

Tears filled his eyes, startling me. "Do you have any idea how your husband's callous, repulsive, hurtful words made me feel?"

"I think so," I murmured, my heart aching for him. "I'm so sorry."

"Well, I just wanted to forget that horrid encounter. Then when I found out about all the problems you'd had during the night and the next morning, I opted to stay far away from them. I couldn't stomach the thought of having to relive those degrading minutes with *him*. I'd stayed in the house, so everyone assumed I'd gone with Phil. Fine with me."

"I'm sorry I made you relive that. Never again, I promise."

He sniffed and studied the cooking meat. "Thank you."

I dumped the spaghetti sauce into the pan; he stirred. "Did you see anyone else with Stan that night? Anyone in or around the house?" I probed.

His freckled face scrunched, like he was really thinking about it. "No. No one. Not even you. I figured your lousy, rotten husband had finally followed through on something and taken you out to celebrate your birthday, like you'd planned. I noticed him on your deck a little before midnight. That's when I wandered over. After that I was drowning my agony."

I reached out and hugged him. "I'm sorry Stan said those horrible things to you."

"Me, too. Someday, maybe it'll be a dull memory. You're the one who lives with the slime ball."

"He really has changed," I argued.

"For now, maybe." He spooned some sauce and tasted it, then made a face and stuck out his tongue. "Where's your garlic and herbs, girl. This stuff's begging for help."

"Garlic's in the pantry. Fresh herbs are on the deck. But I'll take care of it. You get home to Phil. Tell him not to worry, that Polly will do everything she can to make certain his past stays right where it is. I promise."

I sincerely hoped I'd keep that promise.

CHAPTER 15

It was as murky as a pot of hot cocoa, which made perfect sense since chocolate was everywhere—plopping in large globs from the sky and surging up over the sides of the lurching barge on which I stood. The current was strong, too strong to fight it. It pulled us along while strong wind gusts blew at our back, whipping the chocolate drops into a frothy frenzy.

I swiped at my sticky face, trying to clear the goo from my eyes, so I could squint through the deluge to the distant shore. A raging river of roiling, rushing, dark chocolate thwarted a safe landing. All of this furor, yet there was not a sound.

We clung to the slippery railings I couldn't see their faces, but I felt their cries and knew I had to save them from certain death. The Pacific Ocean lay ahead, but before it, a hazardous bar to pass over. Nancy Boggs' bordello was a river barge, not an ocean schooner. It wouldn't survive the pummeling from the heaving, cresting waves in this squall, if we made it that far.

Fear lived and breathed inside me, devouring, impeding coherent thought. I was on a runaway boat, and I couldn't control it.

Suddenly a scream pierced the silence—shrill and clear like a baby's—and I knew: Nellie's baby was gone, an innocent victim of the decadent chocolate. My heart wrenched, and a sob burned in my throat, then broke through my lips. Another cry followed, this time a man's—Stan. Then George. I waited, my heart pounding. Who would be next?

Colton's face emerged through the cocoa haze, worry clouding his dripping features, eyes pleading. "No," I shrieked, grabbing his arm. "Not you, too."

"Polly, wake up."

Huh? I heard his voice, but it made no sense. "Hold on tight," I told him. "Don't let go."

"You're dreaming. Wake up."

A dream? No, his words were a ruse. "It will devour you," I pleaded. "Please hold on."

Hands squeezed my face. "It's a dream. You're right here in bed with me."

I rubbed at the cocoa clouding my vision, then blinked hard. Ever so slowly the raging chocolate melted away. Nancy's boat vanished. I jerked up, searching for it with my hands, gasping for air. No boat. No chocolate. Just Colton's hairy leg. I stared at it in the subdued light from his bedside lamp.

"Oh, lordy," I whispered. "It was so real."

"Just a dream," he murmured, pulling me close against his shoulder and rubbing my back. "Either too much spice in your spaghetti or your life, maybe both."

The dream might be gone, but a heavy, panicky feeling clung to me. Something bad was going to happen—I felt it deep in my bones—and I had no control over it.

"Want to talk about it?" Colton asked.

"No, I just need a few moments to get it out of my mind. That darn chocolate. It belongs in soothing, sensual dreams, not horrific nightmares. If Marta's doctored truffles end up trashing my love affair with chocolate, I won't be a happy camper."

A chuckle vibrated against my ear. "I think you're safe. After my Triazolam hangover, I thought I'd never be able to look at a piece of the stuff without retching. Not so. It's the one thing I still can't pass up."

"Me, too," I murmured, relaxing against him, "it and a glass of perfectly chilled champagne, the more expensive, the better. That's why I stick with chocolate. A Snickers bar, Belgium chocolate, Harley's fudge—I love it all."

He stilled. "Is there any chocolate in the house?"

I laughed. "There's some of that fudge left, but we devoured the chocolate pieces first."

"Well, I guess I'll have to settle for my next favorite thing then."

"And that would be?"

His hand slid to my neck, and he tilted my head up to meet his heated gaze.

"Oh," I whispered. Yikes! I'd been so busy banishing that ghastly nightmare that I'd missed the clues. A warm glow blossomed in my gut and spread, turning my limbs to hot mush. My heart trilled.

He flashed a devilish smile and dropped his lips to mine, covering them with soft kisses. My sore shoulder screamed. I turned toward him and placed a hand against his bare chest. He winced.

It was a wakeup call. I pulled back and sat facing him in my flannel pajamas, cross-legged and frustrated. "We can't do this," I moaned.

The seductive smile returned. "We can be creative. I have a pretty good tolerance for pain."

Which made me smile, too, and shake my head. "That's not the point. My husband died a little over a week ago. He was your brother," I reminded him. But that wasn't the only reason. "Besides, I'm having a tough enough time coping with what's going on in my life right now. I don't have the wherewithal to deal with whatever's going on, or not going on, between us, and I'm not blindly jumping into another relationship. This time I'm going to know what I'm getting into."

He huffed. "You're right. I'm sorry." Something flickered in his eyes. "You do know that I like you, right? I like you a lot."

"I like you, too—a lot." *More than a lot*, a voice inside me clarified. "It's just not the right time."

"Okay." He looked so dejected, like I'd confiscated his gun and banished him to the toy room.

Maybe I could cheer him up. "So what's your third favorite thing?"

"Right now sleep sounds good."

Light filtered in through the windows facing the golf course. It had to be early morning. I glanced at the clock—five-forty-six. "You're in luck then," I told him. "I'll leave you to it. I'm gonna make coffee and spend some time on Frank's book. At the rate I'm going, he'll be in his grave before it's published."

"You sure? You haven't had a good night's sleep in a while. We promise to leave you alone." He reached behind him, lifted Nellie in a hand, and nestled her against his bruised abdomen.

I smiled and crawled off of the bed. "I slept most of the afternoon away before you got home yesterday. The bed's all yours."

Twenty minutes later I sat in my office staring at Brad Ellis' latest email barrage while I attempted to drown my irritation with sips of caffeine. The guy was a tyrant, a mega control freak. The first rant had been written the previous morning, probably after he'd read my notice that I planned to return the box of papers to Frank that morning: how dare I ignore his orders, and if I planned to work for others, I'd damn well better learn to take direction. Not only that, but if he had his way, my services were terminated . . . blah, blah, blah!

The second message was written late the previous night. According to Brad, photocopying his family's personal records was a crime punishable by torture, if not death. He *personally* would collect those copies from me, and tattling to his father would put me at risk of another torture session. Oh, and by the way, since I'd dragged my corrupt husband along on my last visit with Frank, as far as he was concerned, I was fired.

I stared at the computer screen, futilely attempting to staunch the fury building inside me. What was Brad's problem? His behavior was overkill. Yes, Stan had tried to extort money from Frank, and yes, that was appalling. But he and Marta had given me Triazolam-laced truffles, an act that could easily have killed me and landed them in prison.

Was that it? Were his messages a reminder to me that I was a drudge, a menial worker bee, and that I better remember my place and keep my big mouth shut? Or was he freaked out about something else?

I eyed the box of copies Bev had prepared. I'd carried them from Stan's truck, set them on the floor of my office, and not touched them since. Was there something in there that had Brad firing the big guns?

After a fortifying gulp of caffeine, I approached them and stared down at the jumbled papers. It appeared someone had haphazardly thrown them into the box rather than organizing them into two neat piles—Stan? It was definitely not Bev's handiwork. If she'd seen this disarray, she'd be on her knees right now, sorting and stacking, her lips and eyes twitching tetchily.

I thought back to when I'd placed them there. Had they been tampered with then, too? I'd been in a rush to get to breakfast that morning and had been searching for Stan's cell phone. A vision blossomed before me: the two boxes on the backseat midst piles of garbage and junk. And paper—lots of paper. I hadn't taken a close look at that paper. Then Colton had cleaned out the truck. He would've assumed it was just more trash.

"Yikes," I breathed, dropping to my knees. Hopefully, he only threw away copies and not any originals.

I grabbed a handful of papers. Fortunately, Bev had stapled groupings together. Still, news clippings were clumped with business records, and personal papers with legal documents. Corners were folded, and pages were wrinkled. It was a mixed-up mess.

"Take a deep breath," I told myself. "Empty the box to make sure there aren't any of Frank's older documents in there. Then you can see what you have and what might be missing." Of course, the only way I could be certain was to look through the box of papers I'd returned to Frank. "Won't Brad have fun with that," I muttered.

Grabbing the box by its sides, I tipped it over, and the photocopies fell into an untidy pile. I blinked hard to make sure I wasn't seeing things. Sure enough, nestled in the mess was a package wrapped in a white plastic garbage bag. Was this what those two thugs were after?

My heart did a mad pitter-patter when I reached out to pick it up. With trembling hands, I unrolled the parcel and peeked inside, then dropped it in revulsion.

My stomach dropped, too. "Oh, lordy, Stan. What did you get yourself into?" I whispered. "And now I have to deal with it."

I wouldn't know meth from heroin or cocaine from PCP, but I did know one thing: the bag I held contained some form of illegal drug, enough of it that someone wouldn't think twice about killing to get it back. They'd tried, hadn't they—George.

This had to be the "bait" George had demanded. No wonder he was such a wreck; his life was on the line. Maybe Stan's had been, too. Maybe he'd died because he wouldn't give up what was inside this bag. Maybe he'd planned to disappear with it. Was the sale of it that third payment he'd expected?

Pressure built inside me until I knew I would burst into a zillion pieces if I didn't do something quick. I fell back onto my seat, crossed my legs, and lowered my head, fighting the wooziness. "It'll be okay," became my mantra. Like a child's talking toy, I repeated it over and over until the frantic voices in my head calmed.

"So on top of everything else, your husband was also a drug dealer or runner or user—maybe all three," I acknowledged. Whatever the case, he'd done his part to keep the destructive trade thriving. Colton might not like it, but I'd reached my breaking point. It was time to call Sheriff Bronson.

With a resigned sigh that wouldn't end, I pushed myself to my feet and gazed around my office, wondering if I'd ever work here again. Would I end this day behind bars, an accomplice in a cover-up or maybe even charged with the murder of my vile, degenerate husband?

"It beats ending up dead," I reminded myself. Bolstered by a final gulp of coffee, I headed down the hall, my lead feet dragging.

To my surprise, Colton was wide awake, eyes glued to the ceiling, stiff fingers stroking the kitten curled up next to him. "Too many problems to solve," he muttered, turning his perturbed gaze on me.

"Yeah. Well, I have one more for you," I informed him. "I'll get you a dose of caffeine and meet you in my office."

His eyes darkened. "Sounds like I'm being summoned by the principal—not good memories."

I doubted today would be either. "Only the start of what is not gonna be a good day," I promised.

"That bad, huh?"

"Uh-huh. We may need to make a chocolate run." With that, I shuffled to the kitchen and poured two fresh cups of coffee.

When I reached my office, Colton held the plastic bag open with the tips of his fingers and stared down into it. "Shit," he hissed.

"Exactly," I snapped. "That's shit. Stan was shit. And I'm left dealing with all of his *shit*!" I dropped the coffee mugs onto the desk corner, ready to blow. "Well, I'm through messing with his pile of shit. I'm calling Sheriff Bronson."

I grabbed my cell phone from the desktop and glared at him. "Don't even try to talk me out of it."

He dropped the bag and held out a hand, palm facing me. "You're right. It's time to involve the local law, but we need to sit down and discuss it first. You don't want your friend Phil involved, and we promised to keep Marta's killer chocolates a secret. So do we tell the sheriff about the extortion attempts or not? And what about that kid who followed you? Or that little scuffle on the beach?"

"Oh, lordy. This mess has too many tentacles," I murmured. He was right. Before I blabbed everything, we needed to strategize. I grabbed my coffee and plopped down into my chair, then set my phone next to the keyboard, within reach.

Colton sat in the armchair and gulped coffee, studying me. Finally, he huffed dejectedly, then spoke. "I knew there was drug activity in the area. DEA is on it. When Stan told me he was involved in something he couldn't wiggle out of—that he had to disappear—I was afraid it might be related to drugs. That's why I was here. I thought he might be willing to talk with authorities in exchange for some help." He rubbed at his left eye, then shook his head. "If only I'd been an hour earlier."

Yes, if only. Then I probably wouldn't be sitting here flogging myself over Stan's depraved deeds. This new drug thing was, by far, the most painful lash. "You suspected drugs, yet you didn't think to mention it to me?" I scolded.

"I couldn't. It's a hush-hush operation, and you could be sitting smack-dab in the middle of it. If I told you, and you let it slip to the wrong person, months of hard work would go down the drain."

"The wrong person? You think my friends are involved, too?"

"No, I don't. But I can't be certain. How well do you know Harley? And Phil does have a shady past, right? Then there's Denise, who's out partying while her husband's at death's door."

"Denise is not my friend," I informed him, "nor was George."

"Well, he was certainly Stan's friend, and it's a given that the two of them were involved in this together. Maybe Denise, too. We're hoping he'll come out of his coma and talk with us soon."

"So why didn't you have that talk with George when you were on the boat with him? Then he wouldn't be lying in that coma," I challenged.

At that moment, Nellie pranced into the room, meowing plaintively. Colton reached down, scooped her up, and set her in his lap. She licked a front paw and swiped her face with it. I sipped coffee and wondered how Nellie would handle Colton's absence when he exited our lives. The thought twisted into a painful knot near my heart.

"After I found Stan, it was decided that I'd take his place," Colton told me. "Those truffles screwed up our plans. You were suspicious of me right away, and I was, more or less, out of it for a day or so. The loss of memory charade evolved, so I went with it—just played it as a low-key and nonthreatening version of Stan."

"A Milquetoast." It'd been such a pleasant change.

"Exactly—observe and listen." His gaze suddenly became heated. A seductive smile curled his lips. "It worked, too, until I was called on to perform my marital duties, and my enthusiasm got the best of me."

I tried not to respond, but that smile did naughty things to my insides. "Enthusiasm, huh? Is that what you call it?"

"Passion. Lust. Desire. Call it what you want. It was most definitely worth the sacrifice."

Those gooey feelings vanished. "Gee, thanks," I muttered. "Fortunately, you won't be called upon to make that grueling *sacrifice* again."

He sat forward and nailed me with a stare. "I was referring to the fact that I blew my cover. In the end, I think it's turned out for the best. You've been a big help."

Help? Heck, I'd done a good share of the work while Milquetoast observed and listened. "It's nice to know the knowledge I've gleaned hasn't been wasted," I cooed.

"You've had law enforcement training?"

"Even better. I'm a mystery and suspense junkie—books, TV, movies."

His brows dropped into a skeptical frown. "I've never seen you watch TV or read a book."

"Probably because I'm up to my eyeballs in my own mystery and suspense." And speaking of that, it was time to get this conversation off me and back on track. "So what do you think Stan was up to?" I probed.

He sipped coffee and stared at the plastic bag, then seemed to pull himself back from somewhere. "We suspect he and George were trafficking heroin from Southeast Asia, funneling it upriver to dealers."

Heroin! Oh, lordy. It couldn't get much worse than that. "Upriver? In boats?"

"What could look more innocent than a couple of guys out in the bay crabbing, right there in full view to anyone who cares to look? They leave the packaged heroin in the traps with some bait, and it looks like they really are after crab. The packages are picked up by other boaters, but with a bunch of traps out there, who's gonna notice?"

"I witnessed that when I tailed you that day, didn't I?" I gasped, my heart racing with the knowledge that I was that close to drug runners. What if they'd seen me looking through my binoculars? "Only you didn't take the drugs—that bait George kept demanding—so there were no packages to pick up. No wonder what those boats did seemed so weird."

"Yep. And by the way, that was news to us. We had a couple of guys on surveillance, but they followed me to the marina. We thought something might go down there."

Nellie finished her toiletries and settled into Colton's lap. He absently ran a finger down her tiny neck.

I thought back to that day at Yaquina Bay, to the lone man I'd passed chatting on his cell phone. Was he one of the agents watching over Colton? Had he witnessed George's confrontation, too? "So why not arrest the guy roughing up George and convince him to talk?" I asked

"We're more interested in how the heroin's coming into the country. Right now we're in watch-and-wait mode, but that might change now that you've found that." He nodded at the package, then gave me a searching look. "Before we talk with Sheriff Bronson, I'm gonna need to make some phone calls. You okay with that?"

I eyed my cell phone, then nodded. I'd keep it with me. Come hell or high water, I would talk with the sheriff today.

"Let's make sure we've got our stories straight," I advised. "We don't mention Stan's blackmailing schemes or that Marta made the doctored truffles to anyone. It's obvious you've been in some kind of skirmish, so we tell the sheriff about being ambushed on the beach. Only we don't mention Phil's involvement, right?"

"Sounds good. I see no reason to involve the kid who tailed you in this either."

"Fine with me. So basically, we can talk with the sheriff about Stan's death and his involvement in drug trafficking, right?" Which wasn't much when you considered all that had taken place in the last week and a half.

"Yes, the sheriff. But at this point, no one else," he clarified. "If someone gets nosy, tell them the security alarm went off again during the night."

That someone being Laura, for sure. I cringed at the thought of telling her another lie. I stood, grabbed my phone, and stepped toward the door. "I'm gonna go take a long, hot shower. It might be my last for a while. I'm not sure I can handle the public bathing thing if I end up in prison."

Just like that, he was on his feet, and Nellie was on the chair. He took hold of my shoulder with his free hand and locked eyes with mine. "Trust me. You'll get through this just fine. No jail and no prison, I promise."

"He said with doubt in his eyes."

"It's not doubt; it's concern," he asserted. "The shit's gonna hit the fan soon, and the drug trade's about as nasty as it gets. You add an irritated sheriff to the mix, and things aren't pleasant. I don't want you involved in any of it."

"I can do that," I assured him, touched that he cared. My eyes flicked to the paper clutter on the floor. Would Sheriff Bronson impound it as evidence? If so, I was screwed. "Maybe I'll even get some writing done on Frank's book. Let me know when I can call Sheriff Bronson," I added as I headed out the door.

"Oh, you won't need to call him," he called after me. "As soon as he finds out what's been going on in his county and that he's been kept out of the loop, he'll be storming your front door."

∼∽ ✿ ∼∽

Two golf carts whizzed by on their way to the green—kids racing. Their shouts carried across the dew-covered grass to the deck where I stood. I thumbed off the spray nozzle in my hands, shaded my eyes against the blinding sunrays, and watched them. Oh, to be so carefree.

"Oh, to be so young," I muttered, fingering my damp hair. I'd sloughed my usual denim and tee for red capris with a red and white polka-dot blouse, something bright to offset my doldrums. I'd even brushed on some mascara and blush. And once my hair dried, maybe I'd curl it. Heck, Sheriff Bronson might be so busy ogling me that he'd forget to be outraged. *Fat chance, Polly*, a voice inside me asserted.

Movement to my left caught my attention—Denise. She'd dressed for sunshine in too short shorts and a camisole, sans bra. I swallowed a snarl and sheathed the fangs and claws that begged to be unleashed. Either she'd had a rough night or she'd been crying. *Even with red, swollen eyes, she'd distract the sheriff*, that pesky voice inside me claimed.

Denise sniffled, then said, "I rang your doorbell, but no one answered. Then I saw you out my kitchen window."

"Col . . . uh, Stan must be in the shower," I told her, hoping it was him she sought, so she'd be on her way. I had flowers to water, then a sheriff to unruffle.

"Well, I just wanted to let you know that George passed away during the night."

I heard a whimper, then realized it was mine. There was very little I'd liked about George, but he had been a fixture in my life for several years. I pictured him peering into my bedroom—bloody, beaten, and stabbed—eyes pleading. Those eyes had closed that night and would now never open again. The urge to sit in a dark corner and cry for George and Stan was overwhelming. They'd both had so much possibility, and, in the end, had thrown away their lives. Would anyone remember them with fondness?

Not me. And probably not Denise. I studied her as she stood there, barely clothed and with that perturbed look on her face. She must be feeling something—maybe remorse?

"I'm sorry," I murmured, eyeing the hose in my hands.

She shrugged. "He probably asked for it. I knew someday he'd tick off the wrong guy."

I blinked, surprised she hadn't even made a stab at playing the grieving widow. "I'll let Stan know," I promised, wanting her gone.

Instead, she stood there, an unwelcome guest who wouldn't take a hint. Finally, she said, "I know you don't like me. But you and me, we're a lot alike, you know. We both have lousy husbands who treat us like shit—or I did have one."

"Our husbands might've shared some traits, but the similarities end there," I informed her.

"What do you mean?"

"Well for one thing, I wasn't screwing your husband," I snapped.

She took a step back, and shock altered her pretty face. "Who told you?" she demanded.

No way was I going to sick her on Javier. "That's irrelevant. You did it. I know. Period."

"We were so careful. It had to be Stan. I thought you said he didn't remember anything?"

Careful? You were going at it on my deck, I almost screamed. Maybe even in my bed—*ick*! But I couldn't point a finger at Javier, so I just uttered, "I didn't say it was permanent."

Her face paled. "So I was right. He is getting his memory back."

I didn't want to go there, so I opted for what I did want. "Time for you to leave."

"You don't have to be so snippy. I was just trying to be a good friend."

"Friends don't sleep with their friend's husbands," I pointed out.

She flashed me a snide smile. "Well, maybe if those friends kept their husbands happy, their husbands wouldn't be getting it somewhere else."

Which hurt. I'd done everything I could to make Stan happy with our marriage. None of it had worked. I wanted to tell her that, but what was the point? I was through with Denise. "I'm really sorry about what happened to George. Thank you for letting me know," I told her. "As for you, you're no longer welcome at my house." With that, I dropped the hose, turned my back on her, and hurried inside, locking the door behind me.

Colton walked out of the bathroom. He'd made a token effort, too, and looked passably professional in jeans and a neatly pressed white dress shirt. "What'd Denise want?" he asked.

"George passed away during the night," I informed him.

He huffed and his expression turned grim. "So I hear. We were counting on him to wake up soon and talk. Someone's gonna be nailed on a double murder rap. Hopefully, that someone'll feel like talking."

"You think the same person killed both of them?"

"Probably, but we won't know until we find him . . . or her."

I took a quick peek outside. Denise had left, thank goodness. "It doesn't feel right," I told him. "Why would they kill Stan before they got what they wanted? And beating and stabbing someone to death is a long way from holding a pillow over his mouth."

He shrugged. "You might be right. But the sheriff's in your office being a pest, so let's focus on him right now. He's been briefed on Stan's murder and the drug investigation, so he's gonna have a lot of questions."

I eyed the deck, my stomach churning from hunger and anxiety. Would Sheriff Bronson miss me if I slipped out the back and escaped to the beach?

"He'll hunt you down," Colton warned. Evidently, he could see out the back of his head *and* read minds.

"I wish I had a dozen donuts or a cinnamon roll from The Galley to sweeten him up," I told him. "Maybe I should make a run. I'd pick up chocolate, too."

Colton chuckled. "He loads his coffee with more than enough sugar, and I made a fresh pot to keep him happy." He paused, clasped my shoulders, and peered into my eyes. "Everything is going to be all right. I won't let anything happen to you; I promise."

"Then why do I feel like my life is about to shatter."

"Because it is, but for the better. Stan will finally be dead—for good. No more pretending."

Tears welled in my throat and eyes. After all Stan had put me through, I was tearing up over my loss. Evidently, my feelings weren't governed by my good sense.

"I know," Colton said, his eyes watery, too. "He was a huge pain in the butt, totally self-absorbed, and his decision-making skills sucked. But he was my little brother, and I loved him. I want to hug him and at the same time, I want to knock some sense into him. I'm so angry and disgusted at him, but his death hurts like hell."

Words wouldn't come out without a deluge of tears, so I nodded.

"You can do this."

"I know," I whispered. All I had to do was get through the next hour or so. Then I'd be much better.

"Good. Let's get it over," he said, guiding me ahead of him out of the bedroom and down the hall.

When I got to my office, I paused to look inside. Sheriff Bronson stood beside my desk, sipping his cream-and-sugar-drowned-coffee. He watched a younger man in jeans and a black tee-shirt who knelt on the floor and searched through my pile of papers with gloved hands.

"Good morning," I greeted the two men.

Sheriff Bronson started and jerked around. Coffee sloshed over the side of his mug to spot the front of his beige shirt. He absently brushed at it with his free hand while he scowled at me. "Maybe for some people," he muttered ominously.

Colton and I shared an insightful look. "I'll be in the living room," I informed the sheriff before I scurried away.

"Yikes," I muttered when I reached the kitchen. "He's after blood."

I poured myself a glass of tomato juice and sipped it while I gazed out the window. Beyond Laura's house, the sky was a swath of endless blue. Seagulls soared and dived, and beach grass glistened in the morning rays. Closer in, Denise stood motionless, scrutinizing the two official vehicles parked outside my house. No doubt, she wasn't the only person staring at my house and concocting scenarios. This was the fifth time the law had paid a visit in the last eleven days, which made me wonder if I should peruse my homeowners' association manual to make certain I couldn't be fined or kicked out of the neighborhood for such a heinous offense.

While I was trying to remember where I'd last seen it, Harley cruised into Laura's driveway on his Harley. He whipped off his helmet and gave the two black SUVs a hard look, then strode over to Denise in his black leather and spoke with her. Several searching glances my way told me I was the subject of their conversation.

I thought about hustling out to inform him he was conversing with an adulteress but decided to keep my catty thoughts to myself. Instead, I set my glass on the counter and shuffled to the laundry room to feed Nellie. The door was closed. Colton must've put her inside out of the way.

Approaching voices drew me back to the kitchen. Colton watched Sheriff Bronson fortify a fresh mug of coffee. "You want to sit in here?" he asked.

"How about the living room. It's more comfortable," I suggested, already heading there. I plopped into my comfy chair, thinking I might get through this unscathed with its arms enfolding me.

Sheriff Bronson avoided the recliner and sat in a straight back chair closer to the ground. Still the soles of his black boots didn't lie flat on the floor. He wiggled a bit, set his leather bag next to him, pulled a pen from his shirt pocket, and dropped a notepad onto his lap. Colton set the sheriff's coffee on the small table next to his chair and slid into the Barcalounger. Together, we made a nice, neat equilateral triangle.

"I'm heading out." We all turned to look at the young man who'd been crawling around on my office floor. *DEA* was plastered across the front of his tee-shirt in gold letters.

"Keep in touch!" the sheriff barked.

The guy nodded curtly and locked eyes with Colton for several telling moments, then exited through the front door with my cardboard box in his gloved hands. No doubt, the bag of heroin was inside it. I wondered if he'd also confiscated my research materials. If so, I had a tussle with Brad Ellis to look forward to.

"I've been warned that this is just a friendly chat, so I can't tape it," the sheriff grumbled. "But I'm sure as hell gonna take notes." He turned his stormy eyes on Colton. "You have a problem with that?"

"No," Colton drawled. He looked as cool as a glass of iced sun tea sitting there with his radiant face and pleasant smile.

I felt more like coffee dregs—bitter, gritty, and wasted.

"Let's start with the night your *real* husband was murdered," the sheriff growled at me. "It was your birthday, right? And he didn't come home and take you out like he was supposed to, so you were spittin' mad. So mad you forgot to call 9-1-1 as I recall."

Heck, why didn't he just slap on the handcuffs and haul me away? Thank goodness Colton was over there flashing me an encouraging smile. I stiffened my spine. I'd gone over this enough times in my head that speaking it should be a leisurely walk on the beach. "It's like I told you before—remember the Triazolam-laced truffles? Stan didn't come home, so I ate one of those and fell asleep on my bed. That was around ten o'clock.

"The next thing I remember is waking up in the middle of the night. I went to look for Stan and found him dead on the deck, in his recliner. My cell phone was in the kitchen. I went to get it, planning to call for help. My stomach was upset, and I thought it was because I hadn't eaten dinner, so I ate another truffle. Then I sat down in this chair. But before I got the call made, I fell asleep again.

"I woke up early the next morning. Stan was still on the deck and still looked dead, so I called 9-1-1. That's when you showed up and informed me that Stan was alive. Only, he wasn't alive; he was actually dead, and it was Colton who was lying in that chair—a severely drugged Colton."

"And at that time, you were convinced he was your husband?" From behind those thick lenses, Sheriff Bronson's beady eyes seemed to pierce my skull and peek into my mind.

I shrugged off the creepy feeling. "I had my doubts, but I couldn't figure out another explanation. I was so certain Stan was dead that night, but after three of those truffles, Colton looked half dead. Stan's clothes were too big on Colton, and Colton's much more put together than Stan ever thought of being. Other than that, they could pass for twins. The new Stan's personality was completely changed, though. I tallied that up to his alleged memory loss."

"You didn't ever think he might be your husband's brother?"

"I didn't know Stan had a brother. I'd never seen Colton before that morning."

His bushy eyebrows skyrocketed. His jaw dropped and dangled. He jotted a few notes, then asked, "So when did you first know that the man you were living with was your husband's brother?"

Warmth in my cheeks warned me to keep my eyes on the sheriff, not Colton. Sheriff Bronson didn't miss much. Unless I wanted to confess to a night of wild passion with my husband's brother and, in so doing, cast more suspicion upon myself, I had to remain cool.

"Last Wednesday," I told him in a surprisingly calm voice. "Suddenly, I just knew. There was no doubt in my mind. I confronted Colton, and he told me Stan was dead. He said he worked for the Secret Service, that he'd have a better chance of uncovering Stan's killer if he pretended to be Stan."

Sheriff Bronson's eyes dipped, and he scribbled madly on his notepad.

My gaze locked with Colton's. His lips curled into an evocative smile, making me squirm in my chair and blurt, "I didn't know anything about the drugs or that investigation until this morning."

"Neither did I," Sheriff Bronson spat, throwing a glare at Colton before he turned it on me. "So you didn't think about maybe giving the law a call once you knew the truth?"

"Colton is the law," I informed him.

"That's a matter of opinion," he retorted gruffly before he grabbed his mug for a hefty chug. He flipped pages on his notepad and gulped coffee, then nailed me with a stern look. "So I was told someone held a pillow over Morton's face. You still have that pillow?"

Oh, lordy, the pillow. I was so hoping he wouldn't bring it up. "I stuffed it in a garbage bag and put it in my closet," I muttered, praying he would move on to another topic, so my poor racing heart would get relief.

"And when was that?"

"When I found out Stan was killed, and it was the murder weapon. I saw it on the deck that night and threw it back on my bed, so it wouldn't get wet from the dew," I confessed.

He blinked hard and stared at me as if my nose had grown several inches with that tiny lie I'd just spoken. "You didn't think maybe someone might've used it to kill your husband?" he challenged.

"I didn't know Stan was murdered," I explained. "I figured he'd had a heart attack or something. Moseying to the fridge was his exercise of choice, and he ate garbage. You saw his stash of Twinkies. My pantry's loaded with his chili, chips, and queso dip, and there are several gallons of his ice cream in my freezer. You saw his pile of empty beer bottles. That was a nightly ritual."

It was the truth. I'd just neglected to mention my fear that I'd been the one who wielded that cushy weapon. I studied Sheriff Bronson, praying my rant on Stan's eating habits had diverted him.

He wiggled a bit and sipped at his cold coffee while he consulted his notes. Finally, he uttered, "Did you see anyone around your house that night, maybe out on your deck or in your front yard?"

"No, no one at all." And I hadn't. Of course, I now knew that Javier and Denise had been on the deck with Stan, and Marta had been sneaking around inside my house. I ground my teeth together, determined to keep my secrets hushed.

The sheriff turned to Colton. "How about you."

Colton shook his head. "Other than Polly, no."

"Well, can you think of anyone who might've wanted your husband dead?" he uttered irritably.

A list of who didn't want him dead would be quicker—and much shorter. No way would I pull my friends into Stan's disgusting mess, and I'd made a promise to Marta that I planned to keep. Denise was a long shot. Besides, with a dead husband, she had enough on her plate right now. "It must be related to the drugs," I offered.

"But you had no idea your husband was trafficking drugs?"

"Absolutely not," I declared adamantly, irritated that the sheriff had asked. "Even now, I find it hard to believe he had anything to do with that." My stomach clenched with thoughts of the active role Stan had played in making money off of others' destroyed lives.

"Let's talk about that day you tailed Mr. Mor . . . uh Colton here. Did you know what was going down out there in the bay?"

I rubbed my stomach and turned my focus from Stan's rotten judgment to that morning on Yaquina Bay. I pictured Colton throwing out the traps and George motoring to the marina, then those other four boats. "No. I just thought it was weird," I told him. "Oh, and I was really irritated at the people who stole the crab from George's traps."

"You think you'd recognize them?"

"I might—the boats, not the people on board. But I haven't lived here all that long, so I really don't know that much about boats."

Once again, he consulted his notes. "The night your garage was broken into, what did you think they were looking for?"

"I really had no idea," I answered truthfully. "Maybe money? The next day, we searched this whole house, and we did find a garbage bag with money in the crawl space."

He shot forward, almost toppling out of his chair. "How much money?"

I shrugged. "I don't know. Lots."

"I'll need to take that with me."

"It's already been turned in," Colton informed us.

I eyed Colton. I'd watched him place that bag back in the crawlspace. Evidently, he hadn't kept me in the loop on that either.

The sheriff huffed tetchily and snapped, "Figures." Without missing a beat, he laid into me. "Hear you were attacked."

Another scene switch threw me off balance. I gazed out the window at the vibrant blossoms I needed to finish watering and thought back a couple of days. "Yes, Sunday night. We were walking up from the beach. There's a little gully there before you get to the development. Two guys attacked us there. One held me down, and the other hammered on Colton. He fought back. Then Phi . . . uh, finally they took off."

Yikes! I'd nearly blown it. And now I needed to get my blood pressure under control before my head exploded and set Sheriff Bronson to probing further.

"That who messed up your face and hands?" he asked Colton.

"Yep."

"You ever see them before?"

Colton's eyes met mine, and worry creased his forehead. My head pounded, and my stomach heaved. Clearly, the strain from trying to appear calm, collected, and truthful had gotten to me. This interrogation needed to be over. Soon.

"I think one of them was the guy who gave George a hard time at the marina," Colton told him. "Polly and I texted you the photos we took of him. We were at the Whale's Spout Saturday night, and two men cornered Polly and warned her that they wanted their stuff back or something would happen to her husband. We're almost certain they were the two who attacked us."

Sheriff Bronson's gaze flitted to me, then back to Colton. "Would you recognize them if you saw them again."

"I think so. How about you, Polly?"

All I could do was nod and rub my throbbing temple.

"Is someone still following you?"

I was aware of the silence, but it took a few moments to realize that the sheriff had addressed me. "I'm sorry; what did you ask?" I murmured.

"Is someone still following you?"

"Oh . . . uh, no. With everything else that was going on, I might've imagined that."

His look said he wasn't surprised—just another irrational female. "How about those chocolates? Any idea where they came from?"

Well, yes. As a matter of fact, I did. Only I couldn't tell him. I pressed on the pain in my head and pieced words together that made sense. "Maybe someone wanted me out of the picture for a while—or longer—so they could deal with Stan. Everyone knew Stan detested chocolate."

"You think a couple of drug thugs are gonna sit around filling chocolates with prescription drugs to get rid of you for a few hours?" he harrumphed.

"How would I know?"

"It's doubtful," he muttered, shaking his head. "Did your

husband and Mr. Seaver hang out with anyone?"

"Not that I can think of." Of course, they didn't hang out with me either, so how in the heck would I know?

Then I remembered my Friday morning antiquing stint with Laura. "There is this one guy. My friend, Laura, told me she'd seen George and Stan with him. His name is Louis Eastman. Evidently, he has an antique shop in Lincoln City. I've only seen him a couple of times—two times too many."

"Why's that?"

"He's rude and pushy—a total jerk." *A perfect match for George,* I almost said, but I thought it best to not speak ill of the dead. "Laura mentioned that he purchases cheap antiques from overseas and sells them as American made."

"And you think he's involved in drug trafficking, too?" Clearly, the sheriff didn't.

"Probably not. But he's the only person who comes to mind right now," I admitted.

And at that moment, I reached my limit. "It's been a rough week and a half. I'm exhausted, and my head feels like a pile of grenades are detonating inside it. So unless you're going to arrest me for whatever, I need to take a handful of aspirin and lie down," I informed the sheriff.

He glared at me like I'd requested an all expense paid trip to Fiji. I stared right back and pushed myself unsteadily to my feet. The room swayed, or maybe I did. Whatever the case, Colton grabbed me under my arms and helped me to the hallway.

"I'm not going anywhere, Morton. I still need to hear your side of the story," Sheriff Bronson barked after us.

"Just give me a few," Colton yelled back.

I settled onto my back on the unmade bed and stared at the twirling ceiling while I clasped my unsettled stomach and thanked my lucky stars I was still a free woman.

Colton looked down on me, worry clouding his handsome features. "This isn't a ploy, is it?"

"No, I feel like hell."

"I'll get you some aspirin," he murmured. "Then I gotta go pacify the sheriff. You gonna be okay?"

At that moment, I really didn't know. Or care.

CHAPTER 16

I was on the deck with my nose in a juicy mystery novel when Colton handed me a dripping margarita and plopped into the recliner next to mine.

"So you really do read that smut," he quipped, nodding at my book.

It's right up there with chocolate and champagne—brain candy.

He set his drink down and pulled off his oxfords and socks, then his belt, and tugged the tail of his shirt from his jeans. "It's been one hell of a day," he muttered, relaxing into the chair.

"Ditto," I told him. "Slept until early afternoon, went for a run on the beach, reassured my daughter that I'm still alive, and now I'm doing my darnedest to lose myself in some fictitious lady's gut-wrenching plight—not mine." I held up the margarita and sipped. "*Mmmm* . . . this'll help. Thank you."

He smiled and toasted me with his frosty glass. "You're welcome. I'm jealous—except for the far-fetched book. I spent my day in meetings and running around talking with people. You want to hear about it, or would you rather not?"

Rather not, I almost said. But then I watched Colton rub at the fatigue on his face and gulp his slushy drink. My headache had faded, and my stomach sat quiet. Even my heart had settled into a slow, steady beat. Colton looked like he'd eaten a couple of Marta's doctored truffles. It might help him to talk about his day.

"Sure; go ahead," I murmured.

He searched right, left, and out onto the golf course, then leaned closer to me and murmured. "We put together a plan to catch those boaters in the bay. We'll use George's boat. I'll be out there alone. I'm not too crazy about that, but as long as everyone does their job, I should be fine."

"Denise is okay with you using George's boat?"

"With luck, she won't know. One of the guys volunteered to keep her occupied."

"Poor man. But can you do that—just take George's boat?"

Colton shrugged. "Turns out George was up to that foul mouth of his in debt. The boat's on the docket to be repossessed. We just hurried up the process a bit."

I sipped tequila and lime juice and thought about Colton alone on that boat in the middle of the bay. I didn't like it. Hopefully, he'd wear his Kevlar vest . . . and hat, if there was such a thing. "How are you gonna take care of the traps *and* drive the boat?" I wondered aloud.

"I'll have to make it work. They won't buy me pulling someone new into this."

"Well I'm not new," I told him. "Maybe I could help." The words were out of my mouth before I'd contemplated the ramifications. It was too late to take them back.

"Absolutely not!" Colton stormed, jerking forward and swinging his legs over the side of the chair to face me. "You are not to go near Yaquina Bay tomorrow . . . or Newport. That means no tailing me. Got it?"

Dumbfounded by his reaction, I just stared.

"I can't do what I need to if I'm worrying about you," he argued.

Which made sense. "Okay."

"Okay what?"

"Okay. I'll let you do your job."

"And?"

"And I won't go near Newport." I smiled and sipped my margarita. With luck, he wouldn't notice that I'd omitted the most important word.

He narrowed his eyes, and slowly shook his head. "Tomorrow."

Darn. I honestly didn't know if I'd tail him or not, but I wanted the option left open. "Okay," I muttered. "I won't follow you or go near Newport tomorrow. But you've gotta promise to call me as soon as it's over."

"I promise." With a sigh, he relaxed back into his chair.

"What makes you think they'll even show up?" I asked.

"We had a chat with the bartender and several other employees at the Whale's Spout. Turns out, Stan didn't ever talk with those two goons. He sent them a couple of beers every so often. My guess is that's the signal. I'm heading there tonight to see if I can set something up. If all goes as planned, tomorrow morning I'll be crabbing."

I didn't like that either. Those two goons wouldn't think twice about beating him to a pulp out behind the building. But I'd learned to play it cool, so I sipped and stared nonchalantly at a couple of men moseying along in the middle of the fairway, golf bags hanging from their shoulders.

Then it hit me: the charade hadn't stopped. "I take it you're still Stan," I murmured.

He nodded. "For now. Just until this all comes down."

Which might be never. "I thought you wanted to catch the guy in charge?"

"We do." He saluted me with his half empty glass. "And thanks to you, we might have a lead on that."

"Me?"

"Yeah. Turns out Louis Eastman might not be the long shot you thought he was."

"Seriously?" The guy seemed too much of a hothead to run a major drug trafficking business.

"We're still looking into it," he admitted. "No matter what, he's a fishy character. There's a whole lot that doesn't add up about him, and importing antiques is the perfect cover."

"It couldn't happen to a more deserving man," I carped. And I wasn't sorry I'd said it.

Next door, Javier appeared and headed for his Traeger grill. He fiddled with it for several moments, then turned and, spotting me, waved. I lifted my glass to him. He smiled and headed back inside his house.

"You do realize you need to keep all of this quiet," Colton reminded me.

"Uh-huh," I assured him. "No arrests for murder yet?"

"No, but hopefully that'll fall into place once everything else does."

It was wishful thinking. Something kept telling me it was more complicated than that. But maybe the sheriff's nose was sniffing on it. "And how's Sheriff Bronson adjusting?" I inquired.

"Now that he's being included, his attitude has improved, but that just means he's a little less cantankerous. I have to say, though, it's nice to have his department on board instead of trying to run everything from the Portland offices."

He gulped the rest of his drink and set it on the deck. "And how about you—doin' all right?"

I thought back to that morning when I'd finally reached my breaking point. He'd been worried about me. While I'd been sleeping, he'd taken off to do his job. "I think so," I assured him. "I'm sorry I lost it this morning. Just like that, I knew I couldn't sit there and stretch the truth or lie or whatever it was I was doing."

"Hey, give yourself credit. You handled that interview very well. Bronson was a cranky bear, one determined to rip you to shreds. You held it together and told him what he needed to know—nothing more and nothing less."

Funny, I didn't remember it like that—except for the "cranky bear" part, that is. "And then I had a meltdown."

"You were due one."

"Thanks. It helped." And it had. I'd awakened feeling calm and renewed, like I could see this mess through.

Barbecue burn-off smells drifting from next door reminded me that Colton might be hungry. "You want some dinner before you go dancing?" I offered.

He chuckled. "No dancing, just business. And thanks, but I've been eating carbs and grease all day. It feels good to just sit here and visit, maybe squeeze in a catnap with Nellie a little later."

"Then I'll get refills," I told him, pushing myself to my feet and grabbing his glass.

"A guy could get used to this, you know," he murmured, his gaze intense.

I broke eye contact and scurried off. I was already too used to it. No doubt about it, Colton was going to break my heart.

మ ✿ మ

Yikes! What happened in the parking lot at the Whale's Spout needed to stay in the parking lot . . . or even better, behind closed doors. The rhythmic rocking of the blue hatchback in front of me left little to my imagination. A hefty middle-aged couple had crawled into its back seat not more than ten minutes ago. I figured they'd wanted a quiet place to visit or have a smoke. Guess I'd figured wrong.

I dragged my eyes from the bouncing car and gazed around the crowded parking lot. It was Tuesday, so there was no live music, just a DJ. Evidently, canned music wasn't a problem. Several streetlights provided pools of bright light that filtered out to darkened corners. I searched those corners and the rows of cars, hoping to find a dark human shape that might be watching over Colton. So far, I hadn't spotted one.

Fortunately, he had me to keep an eye out. Not that he knew it. In truth, he'd be furious if he knew I was here. But I hadn't promised I wouldn't tail him tonight.

I pulled the hood of Stan's black sweatshirt further down over my forehead, then checked the locks on the car doors and my cell phone battery for the umpteenth time. What would I do if someone dragged Colton out that door?

"You're just here to watch, Polly," I reminded myself. "No matter what happens, you're not going to haul that gun from under the passenger seat, then get out of this car and mess up their investigation. Even if it looks bad, they have it under control."

But did they really? I scrutinized the parking lot again. Surely some guy was stationed out here to keep an eye out for any action.

My eyes drifted back to the blue hatchback. It had stilled. A vision of those two rearranging clothing and spiffing themselves up in that small car nearly made me giggle. But this was serious business, and I was getting more worried.

The decision to follow Colton tonight had been spur-of-the-moment. He'd driven off in Stan's truck, and I'd sat in my comfy chair and read the same paragraph in my novel about fifty times before I'd finally tossed it aside. A niggling feeling in my gut told me something was off. That's when I'd hurried into my closet in search of a surveillance outfit.

And now I sat here in my red Sonata, dressed from head to toe in black, staring at Stan's blue truck and munching on a jumbo bag of M&Ms I'd picked up at a gas station market. He'd been inside the bar for a good hour and a half. It didn't take that long to order a couple of beers for a couple of thugs. What was he doing in there?

As if she were the answer to my question, Amber stepped out the door in a skimpy little sundress. She dug in her shoulder bag, then stuck a cigarette between her lips and lit it. Slouching behind my steering wheel, I watched her breathe smoke into the air and gaze around the lot. Every so often, she glanced behind her.

The couple in the hatchback suddenly popped out. After a good deal of tugging and fluffing, they smacked lips and headed for the bar, arms encircling each other. At the door, they said something to Amber.

She flicked her cigarette at them and stepped away from the building. Evidently, parking lot sex trumped secondhand smoke when it came to lounge etiquette.

Several minutes later, a young man in sagging cargo shorts walked out. He ambled over to Amber, and the two of them seemed to converse. Still, Amber shot searching glances at the front door. Suddenly, both of their gazes flew to the door.

I nearly dropped my M&Ms when the two goons appeared. They stood beneath the light and stared at Amber and her friend before their eyes turned to the parking lot. For endless moments, they scanned the rows of vehicles. I scrunched down as far as I could and peeked out, my heart beating madly. Finally, they strode to a souped up black truck, climbed in, and sped out of the lot with a lot of motor noise.

Headlights came to life several cars over from me, and a black sedan tore out after them, which made me think this place might be crawling with cops after all.

When I glanced at Amber, the young man was gone. After a final drag on her cigarette, she threw the butt on the ground, gave a final heated stare at the front door, and marched to the driver's door of Stan's truck. She seemed to fiddle with something in her hand, then walked toward the bumper. When she reached the truck bed, I saw what she held—a key.

In my mind, I heard that screeching sound and had to grip the steering wheel to keep from jetting out of my car to confront her and demand money for a paint job. She'd keyed the entire length of that nearly new truck. Thank you, Amber! With a crude finger salute, she disappeared from view. Taillights trailing out of the lot a few minutes later confirmed that she'd given up on Colton and called it a night.

"If that was a cop who followed those goons, there are more around," I murmured, examining the now quiet parking lot. Nothing moved, not even a shadow. This surveillance stuff was growing old. I yawned and grabbed another handful of M&Ms to munch on, willing Colton to appear, so I could go home and crawl into bed.

And he did. As if he'd read my brain waves, he walked out the door and glanced around, then hightailed it to the truck. The interior brightened, then the head and taillights.

I breathed a huge sigh of relief and started my engine but waited until he was out of the parking lot before I flipped on my headlights and followed him.

"See, he's fine," I muttered. "And now you need to come up with a good excuse for being out in this Ninja outfit so late at night." I shook my head, keeping an eye on his taillights as we headed south. He'd take one look at me and know what I'd been up to.

When I popped another M&M into my mouth, it hit me. I'd tell him I made a chocolate run. That, he would understand.

We were rolling down the hill to Siletz Bay—almost home—and I was feeling confident about my excuse when his right turn signal flashed. "What the heck?" I whispered. If he was craving chowder, he was out of luck. Mo's had closed hours ago.

I let up on the gas, debating whether to follow him or go on home. He turned onto Fifty-First Street, headed straight for the beach. It dead ended. If he made the circle and came back this way, he'd have to be blind to miss me.

The light turned red, and I stopped, still deliberating. Maybe he and the other undercover guys were having a rendezvous. I glanced in my rearview mirror. There were no vehicles behind me, or in front, for that matter. In fact, it was eerily quiet. Shivers raced across my shoulders, and my eyes darted to the clock—eleven-twenty. It wasn't all that late, but the streets rolled up early on weekdays.

The green light signaled that I needed to decide. "Oh, what the heck," I muttered as I followed in Colton's tread marks.

I flicked off my headlights and crept past housing and small businesses, then my chowder paradise, Mo's. The long beach parking lot stretched out before me, a pool of murky light and muddy blobs. Except for Stan's dark truck at the far end, it was empty. I stopped in the shadow of some bushes and stared at the truck. Other than muted surf sounds, there were no signs of life. Then I scrutinized the surrounding area. Nothing. Prickles on my arms confirmed that it was downright creepy.

Where was Colton?

Maybe this was a part of his plan—to meet the drug dealers here, not at the bay. If so, I was probably sitting in the middle of their setup. I pictured them stationed all around me, gazing through their night vision goggles, swearing under their breaths and silently yelling at me to get out of here before I ruined their carefully laid out plot.

I gazed around. "You can't see them, Polly, because they don't want to be seen. That's what they do." I murmured. I crunched on a handful of M&Ms and considered my options. Probably, I should just cruise on out of here.

But what if that nagging voice inside me was correct? What if Colton was in trouble?

There was one way to find out. My stomach somersaulted at the thought. If I stepped out of this car, would a platoon of undercover guys storm into the parking lot and chew me out?

I eyed the bushes that formed a barrier between the beach and pavement. It might be possible to reach the truck unseen if I used them for cover. I stuffed my cell phone and keys into my pocket and switched off the interior lights, then zipped the sweatshirt to my chin and tied the hood so tight that only my nose and eyes were uncovered. Blood pounding in my ears drowned out all other sounds until I opened the car door and slipped to my knees on the rough surface. I thought about locking the car but decided it best to leave it like it was. I might need to make a quick getaway.

For long moments I knelt there, silent, half expecting someone with a blow horn to yell at me, not that I would hear them. The waves crashing onto the beach roared in my ears. I crouched, sprinted to the bushes, and pushed my way through their grasping branches. Moonlight cast a sheen over the water rushing out of Siletz Bay into the Pacific. The tide was high. The current was strong. And there were no boogiemen or lawmen in sight.

Dropping onto the sand, I breathed slowly and deep while I studied the path that lay ahead. "Piece of cake," I assured myself. Just a quick dash down the beach to the end of the parking lot.

I pushed myself onto the balls of my feet and raced in the shadows of the bushes until there were no more. Stan's truck sat before me, ominously silent. No dark shapes moved about inside it. I tiptoed to the driver's door, stepped onto the running board, and peered inside. Empty.

"Where are you?" I whispered, pulling the door open. Light filled the cab. I glanced quickly around the interior. No keys. Nothing appeared amiss except for a faint floral scent that triggered memories I couldn't quite grasp. Not Colton's or Stan's. I'd never smelled fragrance on either of them.

And still no cops to castigate me for ruining their investigation. Where were they?

I closed the door as quietly as possible and eyed the murky trail ahead. I'd been here before and knew at high tide, it could be treacherous. Water hurtled from the depths up onto the sand, spraying high into the air and bouncing the plethora of weathered logs around like deadly bath toys. If you didn't stay far up on the beach, a sneaker wave might catch you off guard and drag you out to sea.

Visions of killer chocolate swells, upsurges, and undertows filled my mind. My insides churned. Painful shivers zipped along my nerves. Was I the psychic one here—my dreams about to come to fruition?

Get a grip, Polly, I told myself. *This is not some TV reality show, and you are not psychic. You are not going to be towed away by some deadly chocolate current. And you are not going to talk yourself out of finishing what you started. So get going, girl.*

Before I changed my mind, I hunkered down and crept along the path until I rounded the corner. It was darker here, with only moonlight and muted beams from a couple of buildings on the tree-covered hill to my right. The ocean's rumble was deafening. A fine salty mist tickled my nose. I squatted behind a large hunk of worn-smooth wood and squinted out over the log-infested beach, searching for signs of life.

Then I saw it—a shifting silhouette too near the water, then another. Colton? If so, who was with him?

Once more, I searched the hill and beach. Where were his gun-toting buddies?

"Oh, lordy," I whispered. Reading about this was a treat; living it was pure hell.

I reached into my pocket and fingered my cell phone. Should I call for help? But what if this really was part of a well-planned investigation? Calling in the troops could ruin several months of hard work, and because of my interference, the guilty parties might never be caught.

Or maybe Colton was meeting with a colleague, and they were in the mood for a risky wade in the Pacific. Whatever the case, I should probably find out what was going on before I rousted Sheriff Bronson from his bed. After a deep breath to fortify myself, I stayed low and crawled from log to log, working my way toward the two shadowy figures.

Finally, I plopped into the damp sand behind a hefty, gnarled chunk of wood. I paused to catch my breath and strained to hear voices, but the surging ocean sounds drowned out all but the whiff of a sporadic shout. Rising onto my knees, I peeped over the top. A splash of icy water drenched my face and stung my eyes. I swiped at it and squinted.

Colton and some woman stood not more than forty feet from

me. He stood in water up to his knees, facing me, his face shadowed. The woman was a murky shape, her back to me, but I could make out longish hair and a short dress.

Amber? Was I spying on their little *tête-á-tête*? Maybe she'd phoned him to apologize for her keying tantrum, and he'd agreed to meet her here.

A surge of water reached up to tug at Colton, engulfing him to his hips. His arms shot straight out and he leaned forward, fighting the pull. The woman was far enough up on the beach that only her feet and calves got wet.

"What the heck?" I whispered. Was he nuts or what?

The woman's arm jerked out. Something glimmered in her hand. I squinted so hard my head hurt. She waved it, and it glistened in the moonlight—a gun!

"Oh, lordy," I muttered. Secondhand chocolate smoldered in my throat. My whole body trembled. I glanced frantically around. Where were the troops?

Amber's arms were forward now, her shoulders high. Did she have that gun clutched in both hands now, prepared to shoot him?

Another massive wave flooded Colton. He pitched forward, then righted himself and stood firm. If she didn't pull the trigger, the current would soon drag him under. I had to do something. Now!

But what? I fingered my phone. By the time help arrived, Colton would be dead. A vision of that pistol Colton had stuffed under my passenger seat flashed before me. Why hadn't I brought it with me? I scanned the darkened beach and black patches, madly searching for a weapon—anything. Sand and dead wood were all there was.

My eyes shot back to the two figures. Colton was still upright. Amber's back was to me. Maybe I could sneak up and tackle her? But if her finger was on the trigger, the gun might go off. How about if I caught her from the side . . . maybe with a piece of drift wood?

I scoured the heavily shadowed area around me in the dim light. Nothing was the right size. I took a deep breath and crawled out of my hidey hole and toward the water, frenetically seeking a long, solid stick. Another gush of water rushed in. It soaked my hands and legs. My eyes darted up, and I swore they locked with Colton's for a nanosecond. I was so close now. If Amber turned, I was dead.

The water streamed back toward the ocean. As if God had reached down to hand it to me, a stout club floated by. I grabbed it and pushed myself up onto my feet.

"Step back," Amber screamed.

Colton took a step back. His eyes were focused on her, but I knew he saw me. I grasped the four-foot club in both hands and shuffled toward Amber's back.

"More!" she shrieked.

A massive wave hit Colton, knocking him over. I raised the bat over my right shoulder and swung it with all of my might at Amber's shoulder. A gun blast boomed, muffled by the roar of the upsurge. Amber fell sideways. Water whipped around my knees and calves, yanking. Sand washed from under my feet, unsettling me.

Colton was gone!

Something grabbed my ankle. I glanced down. Only it wasn't Amber's murky face I gazed at. It was Denise's. Her eyes flashed terror. She held on for dear life as the Pacific tugged at us. I stuck the stick into the sand and braced against it. Still, the water yanked.

I lifted my eyes to search for Colton in the murky, agitating mess. There was no sign of him. Panic shattered me. I lifted my leg and shook Denise free, then stepped forward.

Finally, the roiling water receded. Still, no Colton.

My gaze flicked to Denise. She was on her back, cradling an arm, hands empty. I scanned the sand for a flash of metal. None. Then I plodded a couple more steps, scrutinizing every square inch of obscure water for a dark shape. It was like searching for a blackberry in an agitating sea of indigo ink.

Another wave hit, this one not as strong. I planted the stick to buttress myself. Something shoved me from behind. I pitched forward, teetered, then caught myself. With a mighty shriek, I turned, raised the bat, and swung. This time it connected with her gut. Shock flashed in her eyes. She doubled over and fell backwards.

My feet slid from beneath me, and I dropped into several inches of icy water. I twisted toward the ocean and pushed my heels into the shifting sand, fighting the pull on my wet clothing. When I glanced up, Colton was on his hands and knees a couple of yards from me, fighting to crawl forward.

Images whisked through my mind, of glistening dark chocolate, swelling and surging, dragging and pulling. Killer chocolate. I shook them away. It wouldn't snatch Colton from me.

I slid forward, braced my feet, and reached out with the stick. Colton grabbed it with one hand, then the other. The force yanked at my shoulders, and I slid forward several inches, holding onto the slippery wood for dear life.

Finally, the battle ceased. Colton wriggled to me. "We need to move higher," he yelled.

I pushed myself onto my wobbly legs and hauled him up beside me. Using the branch as a cane, we staggered to higher ground. Gasping for breath I plopped onto my seat and leaned my back against a massive log. My eyes landed on Denise. She lay curled on her side in a fetal position, still in danger of the undertow.

"You don't deserve this," I muttered as I struggled up onto my feet.

My sweatshirt was an icy, fifty-pound backpack. I unzipped it and let it drop, then trudged to Denise. When I reached under her arms, she jerked and glanced up at me. Ignoring her hateful look, I used the last of my strength to drag her out of danger.

Then I drew from my extensive knowledge garnered from years of reading about and viewing mystery and detective TV programs. I used my shoelaces to secure Denise's hands behind her back. And thanks to the riotous ocean, I didn't hear her moans and groans. She sat against the log, eyes closed and knees curled up next to her body.

Thoroughly zapped, I turned to Colton. "You got your cell?" he yelled.

If it wasn't fried from the salt water. I grabbed my sopping sweatshirt, pulled the phone from the pocket, and flicked it on. Light radiated from the screen—praise the Lord. I wouldn't have to hike for help; it would come to us. I handed it to Colton and plopped down onto my butt, relaxing against the solid log.

That's when the trembling started—my limbs, my shoulders, my head. Even my teeth chattered uncontrollably. Prickly shivers raced through me, and it wasn't only because I was chilled. I pulled my knees to my chin and hugged them, fighting the urge to vomit a stream of chocolate.

What if I hadn't tailed Colton to the Whale's Spout? Would he now be dead, towed out to sea by the frenzied ocean waters? And Denise, would she have gotten away with murder?

And speaking of Denise, why in the world did she want Colton dead?

CHAPTER 17

Noises from somewhere roused me. I lifted my lazy lids and fought the urge to shut them. Fog clogged my mind.

There it was again—the sound of a door closing, then the annoying security alarm shriek. With considerable effort, I raised my heavy head and gazed around me. I sat in my living room in my comfy chair. Had I drifted off to sleep here?

Like a jolt of electricity, memory shocked some sense into me. Images flashed before my eyes, a speeding slide show—me watching for Colton outside the Whale's Spout, following him to the eerie parking lot at Siletz Bay, and Denise's botched murder attempt. I'd expected the cavalry to rush in with sirens screaming and strobe lights flashing. Instead, a couple of lackluster men in jeans and black windbreakers had marched in. One had whisked me to his SUV for a lengthy and harrowing retelling of the night's events. A short while later, a silent ambulance hauled Denise away. Then Colton drove out of the lot in Stan's truck.

I'd been sent home with a stern warning that none of what I'd just recounted had ever happened. The guy's rotten attitude almost made me awaken Sheriff Bronson from a deep sleep to be annoyed along with me. Almost.

But that was several hours ago. Now Colton stepped into the room, and I scrutinized him in the lamp's light. He looked worse than he had after his Triazolam incident—pasty skin, sink hole eyes, bed hair, and droopy shoulders. At least, someone had given him a pair of dry sweats, even if they were several sizes too large. I thought of the flannel pajamas I wore and remembered how wonderful it had felt to nestle into them after I'd scrubbed off all of the sticky, saltwater dregs in the shower.

Behind him, the outside world was a fuzzy auburn, waking up to a new—and hopefully better—day. "What time is it?" I murmured, stroking the meowing fur ball on my lap.

"Somewhere around five," he said, pulling a wooden chair up to face me. He sat down, leaned forward, and clasped my hands. "Thank you for saving my life."

Still groggy, I shrugged. "Eh, what the heck? Who's gonna catch the bad guys if you become fish food?"

His gaze grew intense. "I'm serious. If you hadn't stepped in, I'd be dead. I thought I could swim my way out of there, but the current was too strong. Denise was one determined lady. If the undertow hadn't killed me, she would've."

"But why?"

He dropped my hands and gave Nellie a couple of leisurely pets, then leaned back in his chair. "To her, I was Stan. I tried to convince her otherwise, but she didn't believe me. Like you, she saw me behind the Whale's Spout with Amber Saturday night and assumed that, since I'd snuck out back with Amber, my memory was back, too. Something you said to her yesterday confirmed her suspicions. She panicked. Decided she had to get rid of me before I remembered she'd tried to kill me—to kill Stan, that is."

I nodded and watched Nellie leap to the floor, my mind piecing together tidbits. So my "off the cuff" remark to Denise the previous day had set her on a mission to murder. Just goes to show how a little white lie can come back to bite you. Even more mind-boggling, Denise actually *had* murdered Stan. I wondered if anyone had shared that news with her.

Nellie stuck her sharp claws into Colton's sweatpants and began to climb. "The night of my birthday, Denise came back?" I wondered aloud.

Colton winced and grabbed the kitten to cradle her in a hand close to his chest and pet her back. "Seems so. From what I gathered, Stan had promised her they would go away together. Then she saw him at the Whale's Spout with Amber that night. When he got home, she marched over here to confront him about it, and he blew her off. She left, but the more she thought about it, the angrier she got. She was really gonna let him have it.

"When she arrived back here, it seems Stan was drunk and downright insulting. She was so furious that she came into your bedroom, grabbed a pillow, and held it over his face. She dropped the pillow on the deck and erased everything that had to do with her from his cell phone. You found that in the bushes, remember?"

"Uh-huh." I pictured Denise in her yard the following day, with puffy, red eyes. Then she'd paid us a visit with that ghastly casserole. "She must've really freaked out when she saw you and thought Stan was still alive." More so than I, if that were possible.

"And worried," Colton added. "But I suppose the memory loss thing relieved some of the pressure, that and the fact that Stan had been drunk."

Colton had known Denise was a ding-a-ling on the prowl *and* that she'd been angry at Stan the night of his murder, so there was one thing I still didn't understand: "Why did you meet her at the beach . . . alone?"

He frowned and cocked his head. "I didn't. She was hiding in the backseat of the truck. As soon as I was on the highway, she pointed that gun at my head."

"She must've been in there for a long time," I informed him. "I was in the parking lot for nearly two hours, right behind Stan's truck. I saw Amber key it, but I didn't see Denise climb into it."

With a derisive huff, he stretched out his legs and set Nellie in his lap. "Yeah, that Amber's a real piece of work. Stan sure knew how to pick 'em—except for you, of course." He paused and seemed to think something through before he continued. "As for Denise, she was in the bar when I first got to the Whale's Spout last night. I don't remember seeing her after that. She must carry a gun in her car."

Why was I not surprised? Then an image of another gun popped into my mind. "Speaking of guns," I murmured, "I wish I'd remembered to pocket the one you hid in my car before I headed to the beach last night."

"I wish I'd remembered to put it in the truck," he muttered, shaking his head disgustedly. "I'm so exhausted I'm not thinking straight. Heading to that bar without a weapon was careless, something I'm not. Good thing you can swing a bat."

"Yeah. All those years of softball practice finally paid off." It was an aloof remark. In truth, the revolting feel of that club hitting Denise haunted me. I fidgeted uncomfortably. "Is Denise gonna be okay?" I asked, praying she was.

"Oh, yeah," he assured me, concern written in the creases on his face. "A cracked humerous is the worst of her injuries. The rest are superficial. She can't complain too loud. You saved her from going in the drink, too."

"I feel kind of sorry for her," I confessed, which was crazy considering the lady had slept with my husband, used a pillow off my bed to suffocate him, *and* tried to kill me. "I know she begged for it, but both George and Stan treated her like bad dirt. Then George died. From what you told me, she's been left with debt problems. And now she'll probably spend the rest of her life in prison. It couldn't get much worse than that."

He shrugged and arched a dark brow. "Unless it turns out she's involved in drug trafficking, too."

"You think she might be?" I gasped.

"No, nothing points to that."

Which was probably a good thing in view of how easily she went berserk and reached for a weapon. I couldn't help but wonder how many other people would've died had Denise been working with the bad guys. "What's goin' on with that? Are you still going crabbing?" I asked, hoping the drug investigation had been wrapped up in a tidy little package during the night, so Colton wouldn't be out in that boat alone.

"Yeah, later. When the tide's in," he grumbled. "I'm hoping to catch a few winks before I head out."

Poor guy. He was still recuperating from a beating. Now he'd nearly drowned, then been up all night, probably placating Sheriff Bronson, among other things. "Maybe they won't show up," I hoped.

He shrugged. "The two goons were there last night. I tried to act like Stan and sent them their beers. They left not long after that. They didn't beat the hell out of me, so I must've done something right."

"I saw them come out and drive off. I take it the guy who followed them was one of your comrades?"

"Oh, yeah. He tailed them down to Newport and up the bay to Toledo."

My cell phone chimed, and I glanced down, then dug around in the cushion until I felt it. Laura's name appeared when I flicked it on. With a weary sigh, I turned back to Colton. "So where was the rest of your team? Aren't they supposed to have your back, and all that?"

"A couple of them were inside. When Dean took off after those two guys, we had one left in the parking lot. We all assumed the action was over. As far as everyone was concerned, I was headed home for the night."

Me, too. Still, I'd tailed him. "I hope they don't shirk their jobs today," I carped.

He set Nellie on the floor and leaned toward me, dropping his elbows onto his knees, and stared into my eyes with a hard look. "They'll be crawling all over that bay. And you better remember your promise. You are not to go anywhere near Newport today."

"Don't worry. I've had all the excitement I can handle," I assured him. And I had.

Still, I'd give almost anything to be watching over that bay with my binoculars. Sitting here and waiting for news of the outcome would be pure agony. "If you need me, I'll be in my office working on Frank's book. And for the record, it's a relief to know that neither Brad Ellis nor Marta had anything to do with Stan's death. Once you return that box of copies to me, I can finish the Ellis family history and move on."

"Good. I'm holding you to your promise—no excuses. None. I promise to call and let you know how it went down as soon as I can." He started to rise, then halted and added, "Until then, I need you to keep all of this under wraps. As far as anyone knows, I'm Stan, and I'm going crabbing in George's boat. Nothing about Denise, either. She's in jail, but no one can know that."

"Fine," I snapped, irritated that after all I'd been through, I still couldn't be honest with my friends and daughter. "I'll just ignore the hundred plus texts and voicemails I have on my phone from Laura and Javier and hide out from them. I'm through lying."

He stood and looked down at me. "Let's hope so," he murmured.

〰 ✿ 〰

"OMG, Pol. We were getting ready to march over there and drag you out of that house for an intervention. It's like that movie about the *Stepford Wives*, except that he's the creepy one, not you," Laura declared, her narrowed eyes studying Colton, who stood behind me— poor guy. "I was worried sick something had happened to you. Guess not, huh?"

"No," I assured her. "As you can see, I'm fine." And once I'd spilled my guts, I really would be.

Her eyes dropped to the casserole dish I clasped between two oven mitts. "Baked crab dip?"

"Uh-huh, with a couple of fresh baguettes . . . and Chardonnay."

"You think that's gonna make up for the misery you've put us through?"

Probably not, but hopefully, it would be a start. Laura adored my baked crab dip. "Us?" I questioned.

"Phil and Javier," she muttered, nodding to the rear of the housed. "They came over here an hour ago. And I wasn't kidding. We've been strategizing how to get to you. You didn't acknowledge any of our calls, texts, or emails. You didn't even answer your damn door. And the cops were there yesterday . . . again."

She paused and nailed Colton with a lethal look. "You've been around—even had the gall to take George's boat out, probably with Denise's blessing. What'd you do, kill George to get his boat and his wife?" Her eyes darted to me. "And not a peep from you?"

I smiled beseechingly. "I'm sorry, but I've kind of had my hands tied. If you let me in, I'll explain."

She glared at Colton again.

"Figuratively speaking," I explained. "No one has tied me up."

With an emphatic huff, she stepped back to let me pass by her. I feared she'd block Colton, but when I glanced back, he was on my tail. We walked into her turquoise and pink kitchen, and I set the crab dip on her treasured fifties-era refabbed stove.

Colton placed the wine and bread on the tile countertop. "You go ahead. I'll slice the bread and bring it and the dip in," he said, probably seeking a break from Laura's frostiness.

Laura eyeballed him as if he'd offered to wipe out the human race. "We'll take the wine," she snapped, grabbing it and an empty wineglass. On her way past me she whispered, "*Stepford*, for sure."

I flashed Colton a "thank you" look and followed Laura into the living room where Javier and Phil perched on a vintage rose mohair couch, clutching pink depression wineglasses. Phil looked like a buffalo lost in a 1950s TV sitcom, dark muscles bulging on his bare arms and calves and his thick mane of black hair brushing his shoulders. His worried eyes locked with mine, then traveled past me to where he knew Colton to be.

Javier scampered across the room and drew me into a tight hug. Pulling back, his fussy gaze scanned down my body, then up—surely *tut-tutting* over my faded jeans and sweatshirt—before he sighed and scolded, "Do you have any idea what we've been going through? Phil and I were ready to storm your backdoors. We were sure your lowlife husband finally did you in." Tears glistened like emeralds in his eyes.

"I'm sorry," I spluttered, so touched by his concern that my words burned in my throat. I gave him a quick hug and added, "As you can see, I'm fine—more than fine. For the first time in nearly two weeks, I'm not trembling in my flip flops, wondering if I'm going to survive. And finally, I can talk about it. If you sit down, I'll get started."

Curiosity blossomed on Javier's freckled features. He glanced at his empty glass and held it out to Laura. "It's turned into a three-glass evening—maybe four, or five," he murmured.

Laura grabbed a bottle from a cluttered side table and emptied it into his glass. Then she set to work uncorking Colton's bottle.

I plopped into my usual armchair, stared out the wall of windows at the sun's glorious ocean exodus and let myself melt a bit. Surrounded by my dear friends, the knots and coils inside me started to unwind. *Everything is okay.* I had to keep repeating it to myself until it finally sank in.

Stan was gone, and Colton would soon be on his way, but the rest of my life would continue as it had once been—minus George and Denise, of course. I'd now have time to focus on Frank Ellis' book. No doubt, Javier, Phil, and Laura would pick up any slack left by Stan's demise, silently applauding Denise for murdering him. Heck, Harley might even be my friend. There would now be nothing to prevent Sara from spending more time at home. Hopefully, she'd take advantage of my nearly empty house.

But for the first time in my life, I would live alone. I still hadn't wrapped myself around that jarring fact. And right now, I didn't want to think about it.

Laura handed me a wineglass. I took a healthy sip and plotted my confession while she and the two men stared at me. Thankfully, Colton chose that moment to enter with food. He pushed aside several colorful ceramic birds on the coffee table and set the bread and dip on a lacy doily, along with a stack of turquoise plates and some paper napkins printed with seashells. His eyes locked with mine for a brief second before he pulled an uncomfortable-looking pressed-back chair next to mine and gingerly sat in it. He stretched his legs out in front of him and crossed his ankles, then nodded at the two glaring men.

"Your crab dip, Pollyanna? Must be quite a story for you to resort to bribery," Javier chided. "Not that it's gonna stop me from eating it," he added, setting his wineglass on the table.

I watched him load a plate for Phil and then himself. Laura stepped over and filled one of her own. They "*oohed*" and "*awed*" and seemed to forget that Colton and I were there for a couple of minutes.

Suddenly, Javier eyeballed Colton suspiciously. "Where'd you get the fresh crab?" he asked.

"We'll get to that," I assured him. I took a stiff gulp of wine and dove in. "First of all, you need to know that Stan is dead, so please quit flinging death wishes at this poor guy." I pleaded, nodding at Colton.

Mouths and hands froze. Stunned eyes fixed on Colton. Then the doorbell rang.

"Be right back," Laura muttered, throwing me a "so he has brainwashed you" look.

Moments later, Harley, clothed in black leather and a Grateful Dead tee-shirt, trailed Laura into the painful silence in her living room. Obviously, he'd been briefed, as he skewered Colton with a lethal look, then grabbed a chair from the dining room and sat in the shadows, as far from Colton as possible to still hear the conversation. Shoulders hunched, he swished amber liquid around in the highball glass clutched in his hand.

All eyes turned to me, concerned, yet probing. I braced myself with another slug of alcohol. My retelling would be tricky. All references to Stan's blackmail attempts and Marta's role in doctoring chocolate and searching my house must remain mum.

"Stan *really* is dead," I asserted. "This is Colton. He's Stan's brother."

A tick of silence was followed by a flood of demanding voices: "You expect us to believe that?" "How'd he die?" "Why didn't you tell us?" "So he finally got what he deserved, huh?" The questions went on and on.

A shrill whistle quieted them. We all turned to Colton. "If you give us a chance, we'll try to answer all of your questions," he stated. "And yes, I am most definitely not Stan; I'm his older brother. Polly claims you're her friends, so please give her the courtesy of hearing what she has to say before you make your judgments."

Thoroughly scolded, their eyes narrowed on Colton, scrutinizing him closely. I felt a flush in my cheeks, and my heart did a silly little dance. Colton had my back—probably my heart, too, but I couldn't go there. Laura's guilt-ridden gaze met mine briefly. Then she stood and made the rounds, filling wineglasses.

When everyone was seated with filled plates and glasses, and I had their rapt attention, I continued. "You all remember my disastrous fortieth birthday." My eyes skimmed their nodding heads and landed on Harley's puzzled look. Laura gabbed; surely, she'd filled him in on the minutiae of my less than perfect life. I shrugged it off. I barely knew Harley.

"Well, thanks to that beautiful box of doctored truffles someone left at my front door, I woke up in the middle of the night to find Stan on the deck . . . dead. My brain was fuzzy from the drugs, but I knew I needed to call for help, so I went into the house to get my phone. That's when I ate another chocolate. I sat down in the living room and fell asleep before I made the call.

"When I woke up the next morning, I looked out, and there was Stan, still dead on the deck, so I called 9-1-1. The sheriff arrived, and that's when the confusion began. He informed me that Stan was very much alive. Sure enough, when I went outside, Stan was bundled up on a gurney, but he looked me squarely in the eyes, though I must admit his looked like a couple of empty black holes."

I paused to sip wine and peruse the group. They appeared to be with me. "I went to the hospital to pick up Stan and immediately noticed that he was different. His clothes were falling off him. He looked too fit, not scruffy enough. He was spacey, but nice. He'd lost his memory.

"And he ate oysters for lunch. As you know all too well, Stan detested oysters. Chocolate, too. And I was told he'd eaten three of those Triazolam-laced chocolates. None of it made any sense, but as you know, I chocked it up to a weird reaction to the drug and the fact that Stan had been more gone than home lately."

With a long sigh, I gazed around the group. "You all noticed the differences, too. He cooked. He cleaned and did laundry. He adored Nellie—my new kitty. He sprinted on the beach until he was a sweat-ball. And you assumed he was the same old Stan."

They sipped wine, glanced sheepishly at each other, and eye shrugged.

"That was only the beginning of the craziness. Stan's truck was broken into, and George kept storming over to our house, demanding that Stan go crabbing with him and bring the "bait." As you know, he finally did. George was so angry and aggressive that I followed them and kept watch with my binoculars. I saw this giant gorilla guy rough up George, and some crazy things went on out in the bay. We didn't know what it all meant until later."

I paused to gather my thoughts and skip past the young man tailing me and the check Phil had dropped into Colton's lap, then noticed my wineglass was empty. I held it out to Laura, and she filled it. After a sustaining sip and a shared look with Phil that I hoped assured him his secret was safe, I plodded on.

"In the meantime, I learned that Stan was living a secret life. He'd been fired from his job, and he and Denise were going at it on my deck and probably anywhere else they found a hidey-hole." A painful jab somewhere near my heart halted me. My eyes locked with Harley's. "I also learned that Stan had a girlfriend.

"Memory or no memory, I was ready to throttle the guy," I muttered, staring at Colton. "He escaped to the beach to run off my tongue-lashing."

"But you said he's not Stan," Laura argued.

"He's not, but I didn't know that at that time. I was as in the dark as all of you . . . and thoroughly confused," I explained, wondering how Colton could sit there so calmly with that touch of a smile softening his features when everyone but me was dissecting every square inch of him.

I gazed out the window at a shadowy couple making their way through the beach grass toward the beach while I rehashed the timeline. "That night someone broke into my garage and trashed it. The security alarm went off when they tried to get into the house. It was becoming clear that someone was looking for something. The next day, Colton and I searched the garage and house but found nothing unusual." Except for the bag of money, of course, but I'd been ordered to keep quiet about that for now. "As you know, George showed up on our deck that night, too—beaten and stabbed. The sheriff was back to question us."

"Word is he died," Javier added, a sad look in his eyes. "I wasn't a fan of the guy, but I didn't wish him dead . . . and what an awful way to go. I suppose we should support Denise through this, though, for her part, I'm picturing more a celebration than a wake."

Denise is going to need more than support and none of it from me, I almost snapped. But we'd soon get to that. No one nodded or seconded Javier's motion, so I braced myself and moved on. "Midst break-ins and George's pummeling, I finally realized that the man I'd been living with since my birthday wasn't Stan."

"So you slept with him," Laura chirped, her rosy lips pursed in disgust.

Stunned into silence, I stared at her, tongue-tied, my cheeks burning.

"Polly confronted me, and I confessed," Colton told them, neither admitting to, nor denying, Laura's allegation. "My name's

Colton. As I said, Stan was my younger brother. I work for the Secret Service. A couple of weeks ago, Stan contacted me. He said he was involved in something, and the only way out of it was to disappear for a while. I knew there was an undercover investigation going on in this area that had to do with drug trafficking, so of course, my first thought was that Stan had gotten himself tangled up in that."

I glanced around the room at the bugged eyes, the gaping jaws. Colton had certainly captured their attention.

"The night of Polly's birthday, Stan was supposed to meet me on the beach, right out there." He nodded toward Laura's picture windows, and everyone turned to the hazy ginger glow stretching across the sky.

Images of the many things I'd experienced on the area's beaches during the past few days flitted through my mind. I wondered if I'd ever see them as a safe haven again. I hoped so.

"Stan didn't show up," Colton continued, a catch to his voice. "I came up to his house and found him on the deck—dead." He paused and appeared to struggle with his emotions. It seemed that the death of his brother had finally hit him. I'd known Stan for a few brief, tumultuous years. Colton had been his older brother for thirty-nine.

"I figured my best bet for uncovering who'd murdered Stan and what he'd been involved in was to take his place. We'd always looked enough alike to pass for twins, so it was worth a try. I consulted with my superiors, and it was agreed that I'd become Stan. A team was brought in to take care of his body and process the scene. It was the middle of the night. Polly slept through the whole thing.

"All was going as planned until they drove off. I'd already eaten one of those sedative-laced chocolates, but I was so hungry that I ate a couple more. The next thing I knew it was morning, and the sheriff was shaking me. I was pretty much out of it for a couple of days. The memory loss thing evolved, and I went with it, which made the charade a whole lot easier for me."

He smiled and shook his head. "You all gawked at me like I was some weird creature who'd crawled out of the sea, but you didn't ever question who I was—except for Polly. And once she figured it out, she had to keep it quiet because of the undercover investigation. Not even the sheriff could know."

Which brought to mind Sheriff Bronson. He had Stan's murderer behind bars in his jail. Maybe George's, too. The feds might've been invasive and secretive, but they'd also helped to clean up his county.

Surely, he wouldn't hold onto his grudge.

Colton's voice hacked into my thoughts. "To cut to the chase here, let's just say that Polly's life has been pure hell lately, and she's had to endure it without much support. Besides all the other things we've discussed, she's been stalked, threatened, and attacked. Some of it she can talk about, and some she can't. The shortened version is that it soon became clear that Stan and George were involved in the drug trafficking, and Stan had died in possession of something that someone wanted badly. We suspect George's death had something to do with that.

"Yesterday morning Polly found a packet of heroin hidden in her office. That's why the sheriff was back. Thanks to Polly, we had a pretty clear picture of how the drugs were being passed and how the drugs were entering the country. This afternoon we made the arrests." He skewered Laura with a significant look. "Thus, the use of George's boat and the fresh crab you're eating."

And what an afternoon it had been. Around eleven, Colton had driven off with George's boat in tow, along with a package of raw chicken and a white plastic bundle, and I'd struggled with the overpowering urge to follow him. Progress on Frank's book wasn't in my cards. Instead, I paced and fidgeted, then finally scrubbed and scoured the kitchen and bathrooms, checking my cell phone every few minutes.

At three o'clock, Colton's tired voice reached across the sound waves, and I sank to the floor in relief. All had gone as planned, he'd assured me. He'd dropped the traps and returned to the marina. The packaged bundle had been lifted from his traps not long after that by a couple of boaters, who'd transported it upriver to a house. They were arrested, along with several other people who were in the building and a couple of men in a second boat.

Colton's contemplative gaze focused on Laura. "Thanks to you, we nailed the guy in charge—at least, in this area."

Laura fidgeted, her blonde curls bouncing. Worry creased her forehead when she glanced at me, then Harley. "Me?" she muttered.

"Uh-huh. It was something you mentioned to Polly . . . about Louis Eastman."

"OMG! Louis Eastman is involved in a drug ring?" she gasped.

"Not just involved; he was smuggling drugs into the country in antiques. With the evidence we collected at his home and business, it'll be a long time before he sells another old thing."

Laura's sparkling eyes flashed to me. "Good—karma and all of that, you know."

I couldn't agree more. Louis Eastman was a bully and a predator. He deserved to be locked away in a prison cell.

"Seems Eastman got word there were DEA agents in the area," Colton explained. "He'd been transporting the drugs in antiques, but he was afraid DEA might catch on and trace them back to him. That's where George came in. He golfed with Eastman and, at times, helped him transport the loaded antiques. He suggested some of the heroin might be trafficked through his crab traps, for a fee, of course. George needed the money. He pulled Stan into the scheme."

"So Eastman killed Stan?" Phil asked in his hushed voice.

They were the first words he'd spoken since I'd arrived. Clearly, he'd relaxed with the revealing of Colton's true identity. His muscles were no longer bunched as if he were set to spring from the room, and the network of lines on his face had loosened.

"No," I told him. "Denise killed Stan."

"Denise!" It was a choral gasp. Wide eyes gleamed in the lamplight. Jaws hung. Harley looked lost.

"Yes, and thank God Polly was there to save my life when Denise tried to drown me last night," Colton avowed.

Confusion muddled those stunned looks. "Why did she try to drown *you*," Javier asked.

"She thought he was Stan," I explained. "To get her to go away yesterday, I implied that Stan might be getting his memory back. Denise was afraid he'd remember that she'd tried to kill him, so she decided to get rid of him for good.

"Somehow, Denise got a key to Stan's truck. She used that to get into the truck at the Whale's Spout last night. She hid there until Colton was on the highway. Then she put a gun to his head and told him to drive to the beach access at Siletz Bay, just past Mo's. You know how treacherous the ocean there gets at high tide."

Colton made a scolding noise. "Fortunately for me, Polly doesn't take orders well. She promised she wouldn't tail me, but she did."

"I agreed to stay away from Newport today. Nothing was mentioned about last night," I asserted.

He studied me, then smiled. "Whatever the case, Denise had me up to my waist in some killer currents. Polly pulled me out when I went under and walloped Denise with a piece of driftwood a couple of times, hard enough that Denise dropped the gun and landed on the sand. She's in the county jail."

"Oh, Polly girl, you *have* been through hell," Javier lamented. "I'm sorry I wasn't there for you. If I'd only known, I would've—well I'm not sure what I would've done, but it would've been good. Maybe a massage at Saunia's or some of my double chocolate brownies that you go loopy over."

Laura stepped over to fill my wineglass, her eyes riddled with guilt. *I'm sorry,* she lipped.

I held up a hand to halt their self-reproach. "Hey, you have nothing to feel bad about. You didn't know what was going on, and my lips were sealed. Besides, it's over, and I made it through the whole ordeal in one piece. I know you've all wished Stan was out of my life. Well, now he is. It'll be difficult for me to get used to the fact that he's gone, but I know you'll be there to help me deal. I appreciate that."

"Why'd she kill him," Harley asked. All eyes turned to him. Harley was new to the group and out of the loop. To the rest of us, it was a silly question.

"Stan and Denise had a thing going on," Laura informed him. "Remember when you told me Stan had a young, blonde girlfriend on the side. Evidently, Denise must've made that discovery, too, huh?" she asked, turning to me.

"Yep," I confirmed. "And she didn't take it well. When she confronted Stan, he blew her off. He should've done it when he was sober. She grabbed a pillow off my bed—I was right there on that bed, sleeping off one of those chocolates—and held it over his face until he was dead."

I thought about Amber and the many broken promises Stan had made to her and decided it best to leave her name out of this. She'd been punished enough for her indiscretions. Hopefully, she'd learned a valuable lesson. I certainly had.

"Yikes. That's gruesome," Javier muttered. "I'm glad I never crossed dear Denise."

"Everything started with those doctored truffles," Laura reminded us. "Who left them there?"

Unable to tell another lie, I shrugged.

"You left out something," Phil asserted, drawing our attention. His black eyes had an odd sheen to them. His brawny hands shook. I braced myself, my heart going out to him.

"Polly failed to mention that Stan was blackmailing me," he said, his soft voice trembling. "I appreciate her silence, but I'm tired of living my life in constant fear that someone's going to discover my secret. It is what it is, and I need to accept that and move on. If someone doesn't want to be my friend or buy my art because of who I once was, so be it."

"What are you talking about, Phil?" Laura probed

Javier patted Phil's shoulder, his eyes brimming with concern. "Phil has a shady past."

"Don't we all?" Harley blurted.

What in the heck did that mean? My eyes grazed Harley, then Laura. Except for the facts that he despised adulterers, he rode a honkin' big, flashy bike, and he made dynamite fudge, what did I know about Laura's man friend? Nothing.

"Well, mine's shadier than most," Phil confessed. "I paid for my sins in a prison cell, but they still cling to me like wet seaweed. If I stop hiding them, maybe they'll stop tormenting me."

"You are the most loving, thoughtful, talented man I know. None of us are going to judge you by what you did in another life," Laura assured him.

"That's right," I confirmed. "And you're also a very brave man. We're here for you, Phil"

And I knew that, come what may, my friends would be there for me, too. I gazed around the group at their concerned faces, and my eyes paused on Colton. All those warm, sunny feelings faded. I had one more major hurdle to leap before this whole ordeal was over.

〰️ ☼ 〰️

Stan's canvas duffel bag sat by my front door, a glaring reminder of the loved ones trekking in, then out of my life: Mom, David—my first husband, Dad, Sara, and now Colton. Every time I passed by, my eyes were drawn to it, and another painful glob of sadness settled inside me. I stared at it now, wondering if Stan would end up on my "loved ones" list or not. For now, he was an empty, floating blob.

"Let him float," I murmured. I hadn't drummed up the desire to deal with him yet. Maybe I never would.

It was Colton's meager possessions that were packed inside that bag. It was Colton who was leaving. Something twisted inside me. Tears stung my eyes. I swallowed hard and walked away.

Colton is leaving. Period, I told myself.

I'd asked him to take anything of Stan's he wanted. Evidently, he didn't want much.

My eyes landed on a furry black patch in my comfy chair—Nellie. She was on her side, legs stretched out straight. I picked her up and dropped into the chair, cradling her in my lap and stroking her silky fur. "He'd take you in a heartbeat," I cooed. "But I need you here with me."

I snuffled and braced against an onslaught of tears. "We'll miss him, but we'll get through this together. After all, like your namesake, we're both strong women, huh?" My answer was a loud, contented purr.

"I'll miss you, too," a husky male voice murmured from behind me.

I froze and struggled to pull myself together, then plastered what I hoped passed as a smile onto my face before I rose to my feet and faced him. "You're ready to take off then?" I mumbled to have something to say.

He nodded and reached for Nellie. She clung to his shirt and climbed up to lick his clean-shaven chin. "You take care of Polly, hear me?" he murmured. "Keep her out of trouble." His eyes locked on mine with that last sentence, dark and intense.

I pressed on my heart to still it and the sick feeling swirling inside me. "With you and your brother out of my life, there'll be no trouble to get into," I assured him.

And that was as it should be. *Colton is your late husband's brother, your late husband who has been deceased for less than two weeks,* I reminded myself for the umpteenth time. *Circumstance brought you and Colton together; that's all.*

With an eye shrug, that searing look retreated. "You sure you don't want his ashes?" he asked.

"No. You'll know what to do with them." Heck, I hadn't even known Stan. How would I know what he'd want done with his remains?

Colton breathed deeply, tugged Nellie loose, gave her a final pet, and handed her to me before he stepped to the door and picked up his bag. "I spend much of my time under the radar," he told me, as if he were lecturing a group of students on a field trip. "I'll try to check in on you, though."

We both knew he wouldn't. I nodded. "That'd be nice."

With that, he opened the door and walked out of my life. Nellie and I watched him disappear into the darkness in his black SUV, already missing him. "Why didn't he just stab me in my heart and put me out of this misery?" I muttered.

Then I spotted Laura across the street, hose in hand, watering the pink geraniums in her driveway. "Irish coffee on the back porch," she yelled. "Come on over, and we'll talk about it."

"Be right there," I told her. I might not have a man in my life, but I had something far better—friends and family.

Nellie meowed softly, and my eyes dropped to meet hers. "You're right," I told her. "As much as I wanted to, I didn't leap from one disaster into another. I deserve super kudos for that."

And an Irish coffee.

CHAPTER 18

"Hurry, Mom. We're gonna be late," Sara's exasperated voice screamed down the hallway.

"I'm coming," I yelled back as I tugged on a too high-heeled, strappy sandal that I'd probably fall off of before the night was over.

As I headed out my bedroom door, I paused to stroke Nellie's silky pelt. She raised two sleepy eyelids and meowed lazily. Stretched out on my king-size bed, she was a languorous, two-foot-long swathe of black fur. "Be back soon," I told her, "after a night of revelry with Sara and my friends."

Since my fortieth birthday had been such a bust, they'd insisted that my forty-first demanded a celebration fit for a queen—me being the queen. I'd spent the day at Saunia's Spassage with Laura and Sara. Newly revived—scrubbed, coiffed, and polished—I was ready for a night on the town, or at least, dinner and a nice chat.

As I teetered down the hall, my mind flashed back a year, to the disastrous night when I'd waited for Stan to arrive home. Unsettling tingles whispered inside me. I tossed them aside. My days of coping with Stan's shenanigans were gone. I'd moved on.

"Wow! You look great," Sara gasped. "Everyone will think you're my sister."

"I feel great," I told her, "except for these darn shoes. How'd I let you talk me into them?"

She rolled her eyes. "They're perfect for that dress."

"You don't think it's too snug?" I asked, tugging the bodice up and the skirt down. Still, I felt like my breasts and thighs were more out than in.

"I'm your daughter. Do you think I'd let you embarrass me?"

I studied her blonde bob, hazel eyes, and perky features, then smiled. "Of course, you wouldn't." Sara had yet to conquer the art of subtlety. If I looked like a hussy, she'd tell me. Besides, compared to her little black dress, mine was a mu-mu.

She'd graduated from Oregon State in June and was home for a couple of months before she returned to Corvallis to begin work on a graduate degree. I treasured the time we spent together—running on the beach or talking with our toes digging deep into the hot sand, exploring quaint little shops and eateries, sitting on the deck sipping a glass of chilled wine and chattering drivel. We'd even tackled a couple of long hikes and spent several lazy afternoons at the neighborhood pool with Javier and Rosa, Phil's seven-year-old niece who was spending time with her uncle while her mother pulled her life together.

I'd cry when Sara headed off to school, but she'd be back.

"Your carriage awaits," she chirped, dangling my car keys from an index finger.

"Does that mean you're the designated driver?" I asked, always the mother.

She huffed. "Yes, Mom."

We made our way past the laundry room, where I punched the security alarm, and into the garage. I slithered into the passenger seat, and Sara manned the controls. As we backed out of the garage, my eyes landed on Stan's old beat-up Chevy. Memories tugged at my heart. It was the one remaining thing I had of Stan's. But every time I convinced myself it was time to get rid of it, Colton's fervent features flashed before me. I'd seen the look in those eyes when he'd caressed that hunk of rusty metal—infatuation. Maybe he'd return some day to claim it. Probably not.

In the meantime, I received an email or text from him every couple of months or so: *Just got home. Busy. Heading out on an assignment.* I swore he copied the previous message and pasted it into the current one, but who was I to complain. My replies were equally as generic.

Something kept me from telling him how I really felt—pride? Maybe fear? It didn't matter. If he stayed away long enough, the gnawing pain and longing would eventually fade. I hoped.

I yanked myself from futile fantasies to wave at Ben, my new next-door-neighbor. He was polishing his black Lexus, a ritual he performed religiously every single evening. After the creditors had ransacked the place, Madge and her estate sale gang had arrived at George and Denise's house in February to sell off everything that wasn't nailed down. Ben and his wife, both newly retired, had moved in several weeks later.

Denise had confessed to killing Stan. She'd be strutting her stuff in prison for a good long time.

As for George, since no one else confessed to breaking into Stan's truck and my garage, word on the street was that he must've done it, desperate to find the stash of heroin Stan had hidden.

The two goons finally admitted they might've gotten a little carried away when they were roughing up George. I'd seen him; it was more than a little. Whatever the case, they were taking up space in the pen, too, along with Louis Eastman and a slew of other lowlifes involved in Louis' drug scheme.

I'd come to the conclusion that Stan had lucked out. No way would those inmates have put up with his crap. He'd have been beaten to a pulp daily. The feds still had his bag of money, which was fine with me. I doubted they'd ever figure out where it all had come from.

As my dad used to say, "That's all done and gone." I'd come a long way since that night Stan had lain in his cedar recliner, cold and lifeless. Looking back now, I couldn't fathom why I'd panicked at the prospect of being alone. Living alone was a breeze. I could do whatever I wanted, whenever I wanted to do it. And if I didn't want to, I could do that, too.

Did I get lonely? Yes, but then I'd call Sara or hunt up a friend or head to the beach and chat with a total stranger.

The truth was: I enjoyed my own company—go figure.

I sighed contentedly and turned to Sara. She pulled onto the Coast Highway, heading south. "So where are we going?"

She laughed. "It's a surprise."

"Can I order fresh seafood?"

"Yes, and champagne—as much as you want."

"Wow. I really am the queen."

"Yes, you are. And you deserve it," she agreed. "Not only is it your birthday, but you can finally wash your hands of that book. You won't have to deal with that snarly Brad ever again."

"The best birthday gift ever—except for yours, of course," I told her.

And it was. Frank Ellis' family history had dragged on into four-hundred-plus pages of text, photos, diagrams, and charts. Organizing the thing had been a feat similar to working a five-thousand-piece jigsaw puzzle, and Bradley Ellis had challenged Frank and me with each piece we connected, until I was seriously considering hiring Marta to doctor up a batch of chocolates for him.

I'd reclaimed the box of original documents from Frank to search for stashed drugs and cull some family treasures for the tome. Every person in Frank's lineage, every pet, every family accomplishment and event was in that book, even the true version of his grandfather's birth.

He'd surprised me with that one. Out of the blue, he'd phoned to say he'd consulted with his attorney, who claimed Frank's genetic links were irrelevant. He, his father, and his grandfather had inherited the family lumber business fair and square. The only things that could take it away from Frank were failure to pay his taxes and bills or death. Brad had thrown a mind-dazzling tizzy fit, but Frank had stood his ground. I had to hand it to him; for an old guy, Frank still had more than his share of spunk.

I didn't want to brag, but as family recordings go, the book wasn't all that bad. Yes, it had its snooze moments, but Frank's family had actually led lives interesting enough to spice up most of the pages. If nothing else, it should point more clients in my direction. In the meantime, I'd gleaned from my vast experience and knowledge and was now penning—actually typing—my own mystery novel.

As for Brad and Marta's foolhardy scheme? Well, that was the one secret I still held onto. I couldn't help but wonder how it all would've played out if Marta hadn't left those sedative-laced chocolates at my front door.

Would Stan now be in prison, or sunbathing on some tropic island beach with Amber? Would George be Stan's cellmate? And Denise, would she have expressed her anger in a less deadly manner than murder?

Chances are, I wouldn't have met Colton. And for sure, I wouldn't still be married to Stan. Tammy Wynette might stand by her good-timing man through thick and thin, but I would've ditched mine. For me, cheating, blackmail, and drug-running were deal-breakers.

Yes, Marta's doctored truffles had instigated the whole mixed-up mess. Ironically, she's the one who'd emerged from it unscathed.

But enough about my fortieth birthday. This was my forty-first, and it promised to make up for last year's fiasco. I drew a deep breath and melted into my seat. "It's really sweet of you all to do this for me," I murmured.

And it was. With Phil's activities in the art world and Rosa to entertain, he and Javier led busy lives. Laura was up to her curly locks in wedding plans. She and Harley would tie the knot in early September on the beach behind her house. Following the nuptials, a fifties-era reception would be held at Harley's log house, overlooking the Pacific. The debate was still raging as to whose house they'd live in.

Sara's lips curled into a smirky grin. "Of course, it is," she chided. Then she glanced at me and added, "Hey, nothing can make up for the nightmare you went through last year. Maybe this will help." Her eyes returned to the road, but I kept mine on her. How had she known the path my meandering thoughts had taken? Was she, like Millie, a bit psychic?

She signaled and turned off the highway, which pulled my mind from eerie notions. "Yikes! Are we dining at Harriot's?" I yelped, ecstatic. Harriot's was the most expensive dining adventure in the area. I'd only dreamed of sliding their epicurean creations into my mouth. The building perched on a cliff, high above the water. The local buzz was that if you were seated favorably, you could dine and gaze straight down into the churning Pacific Ocean.

"Yes, Mom. We all know you've always wanted to eat here, so we decided why not?"

She braked in front of the grey stone building that stretched along the sea cliff like a monstrous lazy lizard. Red geraniums overflowed from white window boxes, and a discreet white sign with black and gold lettering claimed this place really was Harriot's. The exterior had ambiance galore. I couldn't wait to get inside.

"Thank you," I murmured, suddenly choked up.

"You're welcome. Now get out of here before a valet shows up, or I'll make you tackle the trek from the parking lot in those heels. I'll park the car and be right behind you."

My eyes dropped to Sara's feet. Her shoes sported heels that could pass for skewers.

"I'm used to walking in them; you're not. Now go get our table. The reservation's under *Morton*."

"Yes, maam," I muttered, wiggling out of my seat. I tugged up and down on my frock, struggling to cover as much as possible, then stepped toward the front door.

Miraculously, it opened. "Good evening," a man with a detached stare and a classy black suit declared.

"Yes, it is," I agreed. "I believe I have a reservation."

"And your name?"

"It should be under *Morton*."

"*Ahhh*, yes," he hissed, interest flashing in eyes that roved down, then up. "The birthday girl. Hannah will seat you."

"Thank you," I muttered, glad to distance myself from the guy as I stepped further into the room. The lobby sparkled as if a cleaning crew swept through every five minutes—dark hardwood floors splashed with an expensive-looking carpet, heavy wooden furniture, and fresh bouquets of colorful summer blossoms.

A young woman, presumably Hannah, in a tasteful black dress, hair pulled tightly into a perfect French knot, appeared. "Morton," the man cooed.

She smiled. "*Ah*, your other party is here. Follow me, please."

So I wasn't the first to arrive. Good. Sitting alone at a large table was always an uncomfortable experience—everyone gawking at you and all. I followed in her footsteps, awestruck by the ocean view out the trailing wall of windows that stretched from the ceiling nearly to the floor. Walking along beside it, I felt as if I were on a winding path floating over the Pacific itself.

I suppose that's why I was so dumbfounded when I glanced forward, and there was Colton sitting right there in front of me, smiling his special smile, his dark eyes sparkling like twinkling Christmas lights. Only the table he sat at—the one covered with pink roses, a box of what looked like chocolates, and a bottle of iced champagne—was perfect for two, not seven.

I froze, quivering on my spiky heels, because my legs, arms, and most of the rest of my body trembled, too. Hummingbirds flitted blissfully inside me, and, horror of horrors, tears tickled my cheeks—probably black ones due to the numerous layers of mascara the makeup lady had caked onto my eyelashes.

With a throat that refused to work, I swallowed at the burning blockage, then swiped at my splotched face before I stepped to the table, grabbed my hemline in a death grip, and sat.

Colton looked worried. "You're crying," he said, pulling a handkerchief from his slacks pocket to hand to me.

I patted my cheeks with it and ran a finger under each eye to catch the drip, then sniffed. No dark marks spotted the cloth. Maybe I didn't look like a raccoon. "I didn't think you'd come back," I confessed, my voice hoarse with emotion.

He reached out and took my hand in his, stroking the top of it with his thumb. "We both needed time."

I nodded.

"Was it enough time for you to work through everything you needed to?"

I nodded again. "You?"

"Uh-huh. I missed you . . . and Nellie. I missed being with you everyday. I missed sleeping next to you in that enormous bed and sharing the cooking and meals with you."

"Me, too—with you, I mean. And I really missed talking with you." I snuffled and felt my lips curve into a smile. "But what I missed most was tailing you. There hasn't been anyone in my life worth stalking since you left."

He laughed and stood. "Come here," he murmured, tugging me up next to him.

His arms dropped to my waist to pull me even closer. My arms reached up to caress his neck. Our eyes locked, and though shivers rushed through me, I swore I was steaming.

Then his lips were on mine—really on mine—and mine were on his. It was like we had a year to make up for in one kiss. A hungry need consumed me, and if I hadn't heard Sara's frantic voice barking, "Good lord, Mom. Now I *am* embarrassed," in the distance, I probably would've ripped Colton's very nice looking suit and tie off of him right there in that dining room.

Evidently, we both got the message, because he pulled back, too. I glanced sheepishly around, and there they all stood beside a much larger table, gaping—Laura, Harley, Javier, Phil, Rosa, and Sara. "Happy Birthday!" they chirped as one.

"Thank you," I murmured, trying to ignore nosey stares from other diners. Colton wrapped an arm around my shoulder and walked me closer to them, so we weren't the evening's entertainment. "You got me the perfect gift. How did you know?" I asked them.

Laura rolled her eyes and shook her head. "FYI, Pol. As much as you've tried to hide it, you've moped around like a lovesick mourning dove since Colton left. What a downer. None of us could stand to see you so miserable. Lucky for us, Colton contacted me and asked me to set this up."

I turned to him. "You did?"

He smiled. "Yep, as soon as I knew things were going to work out."

"Work out?" I asked.

"It seems Sheriff Bronson is a forgiving man. He had an opening for a detective. I applied and got the job."

I held my breath, afraid I'd misunderstood. "You'll live here . . . with me?"

"If you're okay with that?"

Okay? I was ecstatic. "Thrilled," I assured him.

"Well then, it's set."

Yes, it was. Perfectly set.

Mystery novels by Suzanne Grant

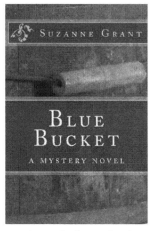

Tracking down a killer is not a part of Kit O'Maley's life plan. She's content with her safe, uncomplicated existence until it's blown to bits by an unexpected invitation. Soon Kit is saddled with a historic home, an antique shop, snoopy neighbors who seem to have their own agendas, and a pack of money-hungry kinfolk who aren't feeling that family love. And everywhere she turns, she's confronted by whispers from the past, a cache of gold nuggets—Oregon's lost Blue Bucket. To top it off, Kit must uncover a murderer before she becomes the next victim.

A mysterious letter brings Lizzy Stewart back to her childhood home, one that was written twenty-five years ago. It's a call for help from a close childhood friend. All these years she's believed he took his own life, but the letter tells a different story. Lizzy packs up the secrets she's clung to far too long and returns to her grandparents' ramshackle farm. As she pulls together the remnants of her tattered life and tries to solve the puzzle of John's death, she's plagued by unsettling threats. And by Sam Craig. Sam has his own problems. From the moment Lizzy arrives, he's hounded by the realization that he's not privy to the frayed web of life-altering secrets and lies lurking about. There are strange goings-on around the Stewart farm, and Sam is determined to get to the bottom of them. If he doesn't, Lizzy just might end up dead.

Made in the USA
San Bernardino, CA
07 July 2016